OUT OF TIME

Out of Time, Book Five

C.B. Lewis

A NineStar Press Publication

Published by NineStar Press
P.O. Box 91792,
Albuquerque, New Mexico, 87199 USA.
www.ninestarpress.com

Out of Time

Printed in the USA
First Edition
January, 2020

Print ISBN: 978-1-951880-30-9

Also available in eBook, ISBN: 978-1-951880-25-5

Warning: This book contains sexually explicit content, which may only be suitable for mature readers, and some scenes depicting panic attacks.

To Beth, who was there when I created this world and cheered all the way from the first draft of the first book.

Chapter One

The house was unnaturally quiet.

It looked the same as usual: portraits of a family—mother and baby, father and toddler—on the walls, a scatter of Lego and jigsaw puzzles on the floor, a forgotten coat slung over the bannister at the top of the stairs.

The man walked onwards towards the staircase.

It was too quiet.

All he had to do was call out and break the silence, but he couldn't.

Run and hide.

That was what his dad had told him. He had done what he was told.

The front door was cracked open, a thin slice of pale morning light cutting across the patterned tiles on the hall floor. It stretched on towards the lab, which was impossible. The sun was too high for it to stretch so far.

Something wasn't right.

The stairs creaked underfoot as he crept down. The tiles in the hall were cold. His clothes were soaked. He didn't remember why. They were wet, and he was cold, and it was all too quiet.

He saw—did he?—the body. A sheet. A shoe on a foot from under it. He saw it. A glimpse. He walked closer, and the sheet was still there. He reached out and grabbed the sheet to see the face of the one who did it.

There was nothing there. No one. The sheet fell from his numb fingers, vanishing before it hit the floor, and he walked onwards.

The door was open, no longer secret. They had cleaned the bloodstains, but he'd heard them talking quietly when they thought he couldn't hear, and the handprints were back, smeared on the wall. Whose? He didn't know.

Light shone up from the basement. The walls were white where they weren't red. It wasn't silent down there. The electric crackle of power hummed around him as he made his way down. It should all have been bigger. When he was there the first time, it all seemed so much bigger. He remembered the crackle, too, and knew what it meant.

Their secret, something no one had ever known.

He crossed the floor of the laboratory, ignoring the computers and the information all over them. The sound was coming from the next room, and he knew what he was going to see.

The temporal gate connected, blazing with light. The man standing before it, barely more than a silhouette.

"We're running out of time."

The voice was familiar, but it was wrong too, not the voice he remembered. Too many years without. Too many years of his memories being worn away. He couldn't remember it now, not exactly, not the intonation, not the lilt or the accent.

He tried to speak, but his throat was closing up. He reached out towards his father, trying to catch him before he did what he always did. His fingers passed through his father's shoulder as if it was nothing more than a shadow; then his father stepped through the gate. The world blazed white, dazzling him.

"No!" He ran towards the gate only to collide with a solid wall. Wall on all sides. Enclosed. Trapped. He was somewhere safe. Safe and closed and dark and alone until Dad came for him. The door was sealed and there was no way out, and in the dark he screamed—

Ben Sanders jolted, sitting bolt upright, panting. Iron bands squeezed his chest. He twisted frantically towards the glowing nightlight on the stool beside his bed. Staring at it, he counted down from thirty until his heartbeat evened out, and he could breathe again. He always kept the lighting low throughout the studio in case the nightlight failed. A shaft of white cracked through the ajar bathroom door. Not dark. Never dark.

His sheets clung to him, soaked with sweat. He pushed them aside and got out of the bed on unsteady legs. It took more effort than he liked to make it to the bathroom. He sank to the floor to sit by the toilet. The porcelain was cold as he propped his elbow on the seat, his fingers sinking into his sweat-matted hair.

Every night, it was getting worse. He knew why. How could he not? With every day that went by, he took another step closer to the day that would ruin his life. Time, time, time. That was what it came down to.

His stomach clenched, and he vomited, acid burning in his throat.

Any day now.

He got up and filled a glass of water at the sink. His reflection seemed more like someone half-dead, pale, with deep shadows beneath his eyes. He needed to rest, but not now. Not with his heart still pounding and the faint echo of his father's voice lingering in his ears.

There was still so much to do.

Chapter Two

"And this is all I will say of the abomination." Enoch pressed one hand to his chest and bowed his head. "Farewell, and God be with ye."

There were several seconds of silence.

"Cut!"

Enoch raised his head, grinning. "It were all right, then?"

"Was," Mack Robertson corrected for the fifteenth time in as many days. He glanced up from his folio, returning Enoch's grin. "And yeah. Brilliant. I've never heard anyone get so angry with a spork before."

Enoch snorted. "Neither fork, nor spoon, and twice as useless." He scrambled off his couch and hurried over to Mack's side. "They liked it?"

Janos Nagy returned from the sink and handed Enoch a cup of water. "They *always* like it." Despite being some thirty years older than both Mack and Enoch, he took as much pleasure in the streams as either of them.

"Not all of them." Enoch sat on the arm of Mack's chair, trying to read some of the comments.

"I'll get them all in a file for you," Mack said. "The live ones as well."

Enoch squeezed his shoulder gratefully. Though he'd been given the best tutors money could hire, he still did poorly with his letters. They became worse when there were a lot of them moving too fast for him to keep up.

Only a few years earlier, he had scarce been able to read at all. He'd had some schooling as a child, but his letters were so poor they thought him thickheaded. He cared naught when he worked the land, but then his life had been turned about when he'd walked through a shining gateway into another time.

Once, he had been a man of the 1750s, working hard to earn a scrap and doing what he had to. Now, thanks to the gateway, he had a grand home in one of the towering buildings of the Temporal Research Institute, dyslexia to confuse his letters, and something called a live-stream where thousands of people about the world would listen to what he had to say about strange things from modern life.

"I would that they would let me do another stream from those…" He knocked his knuckles on the chair, trying to recall the word. "The soup-markets?"

"Supermarket," Janos said, sitting on the empty couch. He was a solemn man, but his mouth twitched. "You know why they say no."

Enoch frowned at him, shaking his head. "The chicken was monstrous! Did you not see the size on it? I swear I might fit my whole head up its arse!"

"Oh, we know." Mack's eyes were dancing. "Everyone in a three-mile radius heard you yelling about it." He closed the screens. "Anyway, we can't go again. We're banned. Officially."

"Banned?" Enoch glanced between the two men.

"Banished," Mack said gravely. "Forbidden."

"For the chicken?"

Janos leaned forward, propping his forearms on his knees. One arm was false, the other real, but both seemed to work as well as the other. "They say your fans have been causing trouble." His smile was there for true. "Some of them have been putting chickens on their heads."

Enoch was both flattered and confused. "Why?"

Mack sniggered. "Because you said it. People listen."

It greatly puzzled Enoch. It was true he was the first man from history to walk in modern times, and people thought him a strange marvel. It was strange to be in a world where people wanted to know his thoughts. They listened to him, and on their account, he found himself well paid and admired.

Sometimes, scholars came to speak to him, but they wanted to know about dull things, like crops and farming traditions. Waving a ten-pound chicken over his head and crying rage about it in a vast shop was much more fun.

It amazed him to learn people would pay money for him to talk and so much money too! He had more than fifty thousand a year, only for talking. No labour, no harvest, no hunting. For only his words, they thought him worth as much as his former master.

"About a chicken's arse?"

Janos bit down on a smirk, and Mack laughed. "People like stupid shit." Mack twisted his chair and elbowed Enoch on the hip. "They're calling it 'Noching' when they go and find something you've done and copy it for a video."

Sometimes, Mack made it easy to play the fool with him. "This one," Enoch said, keeping his face solemn as the grave, "should be called Noch's Cocks."

To his delight, Janos chuckled.

Enoch stared at Mack instead, wide-eyed and puzzled. "Is something amiss?"

Mack's face twisted up. He wanted to laugh, but Enoch knew Mack was never certain when Enoch was speaking in jest or seriousness. "I...I'm not sure it would be a good idea," he finally said, his voice tight.

Jesu, it was too easy. "Why not?" Enoch widened his eyes. "The words sound akin to one another, and a cock is only a male chicken."

Janos had his fist pressed to his mouth, muffling laughter. He scarce seemed to notice Mack glowering at him.

"Noooo," Mack eventually said when it was clear Janos would be no help to him. "No. It—there's another meaning..."

Enoch fought a smile. "Aye, and they would not be putting the chickens on their head, I think."

"Ha!" Janos exclaimed, clapping his hands together. "Again! Dieter owes me another twenty."

"Owes..." Mack narrowed his dark eyes to slits. "Shit, Enoch! Not again! I thought—" He groaned, dropping his head back against the couch. "One of these days, you're not going to catch me out."

"Shame on you," Enoch sighed. "I know cocks well, upon my head or otherwise." Janos made a choked sound. Some found him a hard man to amuse, but Enoch had never found it so. Enoch pantomimed putting a chicken against the front of his trews. "The security people would like it even less, I think."

Both men burst out laughing, and Mack elbowed him in the thigh. "You're a dick."

"Cock," Enoch corrected. "Best we dunt give them the idea, eh?"

"I'll say! The chicken-hats are causing enough problems."

Janos raised a finger. "Ah, but he was a farmhand. There are many stories of things lonely farmhands do..."

Enoch had to fight a laugh. So many of the people in the TRI went carefully about him, as if he might break apart if they jested about him. Janos was never like that. He had teased Enoch since the first months after he came through the gate. "I was but a virtuous labourer. I never saw a chicken, and no man can say otherwise."

Mack rubbed at his brow with his knuckles. "Well, this conversation has taken a weird turn."

"You began it," Enoch said cheerfully.

"No!" Mack waved a finger at him. "I'm not taking the blame for you bringing up cocks!"

Enoch pressed his hand to his chest. "I have few enough skills, but bringing up cocks is one of them."

Janos, it seemed, took his meaning where Mack did not. "No one from the world outside would believe the garbage you speak," he said as he rose from the couch. "All this show of chaste little farmhand bullshit..."

Enoch smiled up at him. Janos was a man who favoured men and was married to one. Enoch had never told Janos of his own tastes, but sometimes, when a man was himself before friends, like called out to like. "Best no one tells them, then."

"One day," Mack said, "you're going to say something in the streams, and everyone's going to know what a gutter-minded troll you are."

"I live for the day," Janos said as he walked towards the door. "I'll laugh at the expressions on their faces." He saluted them both. "You know where I can be found if you need anything."

Enoch waved him out, then scratched at his cheek with a fingertip. "You say these people have made videos?" he said to Mack. "Would you be able to gather me some of them? I would see how well they did."

"I'll make a compilation," Mack agreed, getting up. "There were a few messages from Diaval too."

Enoch couldn't keep from smiling. Diaval was one of the people who had watched his videos from the first day and always made time to speak his thoughts on them. "He's been quiet of late."

"I noticed," said Mack. "Last couple of videos didn't even get a peep out of him."

"I should tell him he was missed."

Mack screwed up his face. "You shouldn't encourage your groupies."

"I don't encourage," Enoch protested.

"Mm-hm. Sending private messages and saying you missed him can be considered encouraging."

Enoch snorted. "You're blethering again. He only likes my videos."

"Encouraging," Mack said, amused. He checked the time. "Now, though, I should get back to my department." He gave Enoch his folio bud. "I'll send over all the comments and videos as soon as I'm done this afternoon."

Enoch watched him go.

Mack was always happy to help out with the streams. He said it was because he liked working with media, but Enoch knew Mack found it more interesting than his own work in the historical department of the TRI. There were others who could help, but Mack was useful and always pleased to come.

It was easier with Mack being close to the same age as him. They had offered older, wiser people, but Enoch said he liked to see how someone of his own age and manner lived. Mack let him see such things.

Sometimes, Enoch was tempted to see how far his requests could go.

The TRI wanted to keep him happy. He knew they blamed themselves for his life going awry.

A man called Ben Sanders, once a TRI worker, was the reason Enoch was living out his days in a future more than three hundred years beyond his own. The TRI had been responsible for the man, so they felt they were responsible for Enoch.

It wasn't a bad life.

The TRI had offered to make him a home and a life outside the TRI, but he'd chosen to stay. There were plenty of reasons, not least because his letters were bad, and he scarce knew enough of the world to live alone. Having Mack's company was another good reason.

Anyway, he had enough to keep him well busy.

He opened the folio bud and pulled up a screen to see the messages from Diaval. No matter how often he used it, the shining screen in front of his face felt like some kind of magic.

The text hung in the middle of the screen, and he touched the tiny triangle below it. At once, a melodic voice spoke the words. Enoch had never learned who the owner of the voice was, but it saved him struggling to read the letters.

Sporks? Really? Definitely not as interesting as your chicken.

Enoch made a face at the screen. "They forbade me another chicken." The text appeared on the screen, and he waited.

I'm not surprised. I thought security was going to catch you.

Enoch pulled his feet up on the seat and propped his arms on his knees, trying to squash a grin. "I am quick as a rabbit." He rested his chin on his arms. "Might I tell you something?"

Always.

Enoch gazed at the letters. "They keep telling me not to speak with you again. Or any of those who speak of my stream." He made a disgusted sound, then paused to admire the blur of letters that spelled it. "M says I'm..." He tried to remember the phrase. "Encouraging my groupies."

To protect the TRI, he could not use the full names of their staff members when talking to people online. Some people, they'd told him, didn't enjoy the attention as much as he did.

Well, there are some weirdos out there.

Enoch snickered. "Aye. And you among them."

You know what I mean.

Enoch smiled crookedly. In the twelve and six months since he'd begun the streams, a lot of the TRI people had said not to trust strangers on the end of a line. Sometimes, they'd said, the person was not who they claimed. It was easy enough to stop their fretting when he reminded them of Ben Sanders. They'd known him, and Ben Sanders still managed to do more damage to them than nameless folk on the end of a line.

It was on account of where Enoch had come from, he knew. They thought him from a simple time, when folk were innocent and foolish and could not understand deception. They yet saw him so—a soft-headed farmer's lad from times gone by. It was simpler to allow them to believe such things.

Is M your tech man?

"He likes the daft things I do as much as you," Enoch confirmed. "Someone in the market had a camera on him and all. Folk like to show everyone what they saw."

I saw that. I think they called it two crazy guys and a chicken.

Enoch couldn't help laughing. "If I am to be remembered for anything, I pray it's for the chicken." Across the room, the main door chimed. Enoch frowned. "I must away. Be well."

You too.

Enoch closed the link then wandered across to open the door.

Sabine Hausmann smiled. A small lady compared to most others in the TRI, scarce a handspan taller than him, fair, and blue-eyed, she was the master of the TRI. "Another successful stream, I see."

"It's all well." He pulled the door wider. "What will you?"

She crossed the threshold and waited until he closed the door. "I've received a message from Mr. O'Donohue. He asked you and Danny to head to the taskforce headquarters at noon tomorrow."

Enoch blinked at her. "Aye? Did he say why?"

"Only that you might want to be there. I wanted to tell you in person and to see if you wanted me to arrange a pod."

"Aye. I think I must go." He scratched his chin. "They would only ask me if it were important..."

Sabine agreed. "Lysander wouldn't say what's going on, but it's been weeks since you were last updated, so maybe they have news?"

If they had news, the world would turn again.

The task force was hunting for Ben Sanders, their rogue agent, led by Lysander O'Donohue, the man who had been master of the TRI before Sabine. They'd been seeking Sanders since his escape nearly three years earlier, and Enoch had a small part in it. They all knew Ben was to blame for Enoch's place in the modern world, and they all thought it right and proper Enoch should have a part in catching him.

They'd once said that if Ben were found, they might find a way to return Enoch whence he came.

The matter was he didn't want to return. His friends might think him mad, but he liked this new world for the monstrous chickens and the sporks and all the strange things. He had too many reasons to want to stay.

Enoch returned to his couch, sinking to sit. "Do you think they have found him?"

"I couldn't tell you," Sabine said. "It could just be some new development."

"Tomorrow." Enoch drew his feet onto the couch and propped his arms on his knees. "Aye. Let them know I'll come. I'd like to know what news there is."

Chapter Three

It was good weather to be inside a coffee shop, holding a mug of hot coffee in chilly fingers. It had some kind of fancy name, all frothy and surprisingly sweet. Ben eased his way between the tall tables to one of the couches by the window, settling against the cushioned seat.

From there, he could keep an eye on anyone coming or going into the building opposite.

Through the sheeting rain, it would've matched all the other buildings on the block, if not for the black-and-white checks discreetly placed on the marquee. The giant worn letters above the door declaring 'Police' were about as subtle.

It wasn't technically a functioning police station anymore.

According to all of his information, it belonged to the local police force, although part of it was currently let out to a private task force led by Lysander O'Donohue, the former head of the TRI. A dozen officers, and Mariam Ashraf and Jacob Ofori—both formerly of the TRI—made up his support.

Ben added some sugar to his frothy coffee, stirring it as he watched out of the window. He knew he shouldn't keep on returning, but he couldn't help himself. It was a lonely business, being on the run, but it made him feel a little better to see the people he'd considered friends when he worked with the TRI.

He missed the TRI too. For so many years, it was his home.

Ben's father had been the creative force behind it all, something Ben had desperately tried to hold on to. His father built the first temporal gates and started the organisation. Some people thought it was in the name of scientific research, but it was much more personal. His wife had been lost somewhere in the past, and he spent years developing the means to find her.

He'd failed.

Ben turned his cup between his palms, trying to push away those thoughts.

Outside, there were more pods on the road than usual. No one wanted to walk anywhere. Ben couldn't blame them. The rain wasn't heavy, but it hadn't stopped for hours. The glory of the Mersey basin, bouncing off umbrellas and pavements and unfortunate people.

Every time a pod slowed outside the building, Ben leaned closer to the glass, and almost every time, he retreated with a sigh. He'd almost finished his second coffee when a familiar figure clambered out of one. Small and as round as ever, her face paler than usual against the dark cloth of her hijab. She flicked up an umbrella and bustled towards the police station: Mariam Ashraf.

Ben stared through the glass, half willing her to turn, to glance his way. It was one thing to abandon your friends, but something else to leave behind the woman who had chosen to be your mother.

Twenty-four years earlier, when Ben was tiny, thieves had come to steal his dad's technology. Ben had fled to hide in the safe room. His dad...well, his dad tried to escape through the illicit temporal gate he had in his basement.

It hadn't ended well.

Mariam Ashraf had become his dad's successor in the TRI. It was also when Jacob Ofori figured out time travel was real, proving himself one of the top detectives in the region. He'd dragged the TRI kicking and screaming into the public sphere.

None of it had mattered to Ben when he was a scared kid. All he remembered was Mariam hugging him through his childhood nightmares, soothing him, comforting him, and filling the void where his parents should have been. Her sons had adopted him as a very pale brother, sharing their toys, their rooms, their jokes. They'd even celebrated Christmas for him alongside Ramadan.

It had all fallen away almost ten years ago when Mariam had shut down the search for his father. He'd reacted badly, said things he shouldn't have, and gone off and screwed up everything. There was no way back, and no amount of apologies could undo what he had done.

She vanished into the building to join the other people who were hunting him.

Ben sighed. It was stupid to keep coming. Seeing friendly faces from a distance was worse than being alone. He picked up a spoon and stirred the foam on his coffee. It didn't help, and every time he came, it was like another step closer to surrender.

The door was opened, letting in a brief gust of wind.

"You need not come with me."

Ben's stomach twisted at the familiar voice.

A quick glance at his reflection in the window told him the camo-patch was holding. An unfamiliar face gazed at him, his features digitally masked. The grey contact lenses and his cropped and dyed hair were window dressing.

He turned away from the window and opened a screen from his Leaf. It shimmered into place in front of his face, translucent enough for him to see through but enough to distort his appearance.

Two men had entered. Ben couldn't help staring at the smaller of the two, one of the reasons he was on the run: Enoch Baker, the famous accidental time traveller.

Not so accidental to those who knew the truth. Almost three years earlier, Ben had been responsible for Enoch's arrival through a mess of misdirection and time gates. It was one of the many reasons the task force was searching for him for...help with their inquiries.

Sometimes, he wondered what Enoch's life would have been like without his intervention. He'd seen the medical assessment when Enoch was first brought in to the TRI, his body telling the story of a hard life and the promise of an inevitably early death.

This world was better for him by far.

At least that was what Ben told himself repeatedly. It was pointless to think of it, but sometimes, it helped assuage the guilt of turning the man's world upside down as he had.

Ben pulled his legs up to sit cross-legged on the couch, watching the two men. It had been a while since he'd seen either of them.

Enoch's companion laughed. Danny Ferguson. Burly and cheerful as ever, he had some grey showing in his sandy beard, but otherwise looked exactly the same. Three years ago, his coding genius had forced Ben to go on the run after the brilliant asshole uncovered his plans.

"Come on. You expect me to miss out on fresh coffee?"

Enoch pushed his hood off, his hair a rumpled mess, his sideburns fluffier than they appeared on the streams. "I would bring you some if you wanted. I can buy drinks well enough my own self."

"I don't doubt it," Danny replied, wandering to the counter behind him. "But you only have two hands, and Lysander'd think the world was ending if I didn't show up with our favourite drinks and some kind of cake."

They looked well, but no surprise there. The TRI took care of its people, especially significant and useful people. Ben hid a smile as Enoch carefully enunciated his drink of choice to the barista. Extra syrup, extra sugar, extra coffee. All the things he would never have encountered in his own time.

"You'll have no teeth left if you keep drinking that shit." Danny snorted in amusement.

Enoch grinned at him. "Then I'll have them made. I'm a rich man now. A rich man can carry his teeth at his belt."

Danny made a face as he bent to examine the cakes on display. "You're so weird." He leaned over the counter, placed his own order, and glanced about. "I'm amazed your fan club doesn't know about this place. You'd think we'd be mobbed."

"Mr. O'Donohue said it's best we keep the task force secret. I dunt speak of it on the streams and none have found it yet." Enoch waved in the direction of the window and the police building beyond it, and Ben hastily ducked his head, rubbing at his earlobe distractedly as he pretended to read from his Leaf. "Best we keep this place secret."

"Yeah..." Danny sounded puzzled.

Ben risked a glance through the screen. Enoch was examining the cakes, but Danny was eyeing him. Ben's heart pounded, and it only got worse when Danny wandered over to him.

"'Scuse me."

Ben's throat was unbearably tight. "Yes?" His voice was hoarse enough to be unrecognisable.

"Is that a Leaf 7?"

Ben blinked as if he'd been walloped across the head, reeling in confusion. "What?"

Danny motioned to the screen. "This. Is it a Leaf 7? I've been thinking about getting one, and I was wondering how they handled."

"Yes," Ben said, relieved. He tried to shift his accent to something unlike his own. "It's not bad. Some teething problems, but nothing you can't work around. Isn't that always the way?"

Danny made a face. "Aye. You'd think they'd've tested it properly before unleashing it, but money, eh?"

Ben smiled crookedly. "Money, indeed."

Danny opened his mouth to say something but was interrupted by Enoch calling his name.

"Your drinks!" Enoch was waving to a growing row of cups on the counter.

"Duty calls," Danny grumbled good-naturedly. "Thanks for the heads-up. I might see about getting one."

"No problem."

He ducked his head over the screen as they gathered up their orders and headed for the exit. As they passed near his seat, he overheard their conversation.

"...sometimes see him when I come for my drink."

"Look at you," Danny chuckled. "You've gone and become a regular."

Enoch made a haughty face. "It's nearby to the station is all. I like it's—"

The door closed behind him, cutting off his words. Ben slanted a glance through the window, watching as they crossed the street. His pulse was still racing. No surprise, since he'd gone out of his way to make himself inconspicuous. He tugged his earlobe again, frowning.

Of all the people to come into the café and approach him, it had to be Danny, didn't it?

Even if it was a coincidence, it made his palms sweat and his stomach churn.

He'd been pushing his luck for far too long already. All it would take was one cock-up and they'd be onto him, something he couldn't allow to happen, not after everything he'd done.

He abandoned his half-finished drink and pulled on his jacket, then headed out into the streets, losing himself in the lunchtime crowd as fast as he could.

Chapter Four

The station was always busy.

Enoch had been dazed the first time he visited the offices. There were desks and people in every space. Words were dancing along the walls, pictures and information everywhere. It was grand and a lot to take in all at once.

Now, it was like a second home for him.

"Right on time." Lysander O'Donohue came out of his smaller office, smiling. "I'm glad you could make it."

Enoch smiled back. Lysander was a good man, even if he could put the fear of God into everyone in the room with a flash of his dark eyes. Though smaller than Danny and Jacob Ofori, something in him made him seem much more powerful than either of them. Still, he had only ever been kind to Enoch. He also always dressed up fine, like a proper gentleman, though his hair was far longer than any man Enoch had ever known, oft braided or twisted about fancy sticks to hold upon his head.

"We went for drinks and that." Enoch held up his cup. "Danny said..." He turned and frowned. Danny was already at one of the desks, bent over it. The lass who sat at it leaned aside, all agog at him. He must've shoved her by to get to her machine.

"Danny?" O'Donohue sounded puzzled.

Danny held up a finger. "Wait."

O'Donohue glanced at Enoch. "Did he mention anything on the way in? Did anything happen?"

"He spoke to a man in the coffee shop about a Leaf." Enoch said, befuddled. Danny always was a strange one, watching everything and listening to everything and talking and laughing a bit too loud. "Mayhap he's trying to find a one to buy?"

"Do we have local CCTV access?" Danny demanded suddenly. "Anything facing out onto the street?"

"What are we checking for?" Jacob Ofori was there and all, at his own desk. O'Donohue had his hand on the reins, but Jacob was the one who led the team. He had once been a police chief, afore he joined the TRI, and though old enough to step away, he remained to see they finished what they had begun.

"Ben."

"Ben?" At least four of them said it, Enoch among them.

"At the coffee shop across the street."

If the room was busy before, it was as if someone had touched a flame to kindling; everyone moving and talking fast and loud, and Enoch, like a feather caught in the wind, turning this way and that.

They'd been chasing Ben for more than two and a half years. They'd never come close to catching him, and now, Danny had seen him? Enoch's heart thundered on his ribs.

"But Ben weren't there," he said to anyone who would listen. "I never saw him."

"He was," Danny said, bent over the desk. "You wouldn't recognise him. He had a digital mask or something on. A disguise."

Enoch leaned against another desk, shaken. Danny, always paying heed to everything about him, seeing something no one noticed. "He was hiding there?"

Lysander touched Danny's shoulder. "Are you sure?"

Danny spun, sharp-like. "It was him. You can cover a piano with a cloth but it's still a piano. He was watching us as well." His face twisted in a frown. "Unless it was a coincidence, and I don't believe in those."

"But Ben's right clever," Enoch protested. "He kept hidden for this long. Why would he come to a place by us? He's not so daft."

"Not daft," Mariam said, coming over by Enoch. "If he was there, it was for a reason."

Enoch swallowed hard. His cup was shaking in his hands, and Mariam took it off him and set it aside.

"You should sit," she said, holding his arm. "I know this must be a shock."

"Aye, ma'am." He sank onto the nearest seat, watching Danny working on the machine. "I dint think we'd catch him. Not right by us."

"I don't think any of us expected this."

"Got a feed from the street," Jacob called out. "Danny, give me your eyes."

Danny ran to Jacob's side and leaned over his shoulder. "Check the five minutes since we left..." He watched close, then jabbed the screen. "There. Him."

Enoch watched Jacob as he leaned forward to study the screen and the face. "Is it?" he asked, crunching his hands up in fists. "Is it him?"

"I'm not sure," Jacob admitted. "If it is, he's got a good disguise." He beckoned Mariam over to join him. "You knew him better than anyone here."

Enoch sat away from them all like a pudding as they spoke quietly to each another. His hands shook, no matter how hard he squeezed them shut. If they found Ben and everything he took, his life would be turned about all over again.

"He sat exactly like Ben did," Danny said. "The same posture, the same tics, the same expressions even with his face masked." He glanced at Lysander, and Enoch could guess why. It was easier for a man to be believed by his lover. "Lysander, I swear it was him. We need eyes on him now."

Nothing was said for moments, like the air before a storm. Jacob and Lysander gazed the one at the other, then Lysander gave a wee jerk of his chin.

"Danny's been right too many times to ignore this," he said. "This guy, he left on foot, right? Get his face out into facial recognition. See if we can pick him up on any other cameras in the last ten minutes and get a direction."

Jacob started calling out orders to the other people in the team. They all moved to their machines, everything busy again. Enoch wedged his hands between his knees, squeezing until they ached. He would be of no use to anyone. Better to sit quiet until he knew what was amiss.

Mariam came and sat by him. She was a kind lady, very stern and always sad. She'd been a mother to Ben when Ben's own parents were lost. For that alone, Enoch always treated her as best he could. No need to make things worse for her.

"You don't need to worry," she said. "You couldn't have known."

He swallowed hard around the lump in his throat. "Changing his face is like some strange magic."

"Ben always did love his technology." She patted his shoulder. "I bet I wouldn't have spotted him either."

Enoch doubted it. If Danny, who had known Ben but a few months, could see him, then the woman who had raised him would have known him. He stared at his pressed hands. His chest ached as if waiting for the chance to breathe again.

Footsteps came by.

"Enoch," Jacob crouched in front of him. A big man, dark-skinned and dark-eyed, it would be easy for him to make any man afeard of him, but he never did. He was especially gentle to Enoch and always had been. "Danny said you'd crossed paths with this man before."

Enoch glanced to Danny, but Danny was busy at a machine. "I dunt know. I—he— Was it the fellow he asked about the Leaf?"

Jacob opened up the image of the man leaving the coffee bar on his own Leaf. "This is the man."

Before he fled the TRI, Ben had sandy hair and pale skin. The man in the image was olive-skinned with dark hair.

"He's the wrong colours to be Ben."

Jacob glanced at the screen. "That doesn't matter. What I need to know is whether you met him? Spoke to him?"

Enoch licked his lip. "Aye."

Jacob glanced to Mariam. "Can you give us a minute?"

Mariam rose. "Do you want me to see if I can pinpoint his Leaf? I might be able to track his signal and get us a location."

"If you can." Jacob sat in her seat and waited until she was out of earshot. "If Danny is right about this being Ben, then he's been at the café before. Did you see him there many times?"

Enoch stared at the picture. "Many." He could remember the first time clear enough. "He knocked my drink from the counter. He bought me another in penance." He knuckled at his nose. "I thanked him. Sat with him. Next time I went there, he were there too."

Jacob's face was all tight lines. "Do you remember when he first came?"

Enoch chewed his lip. "Close upon two years, I think. Do you think he wanted to find out what we were doing here?"

"It's possible." Jacob's face gave away none of his thoughts. "Did he tell you his name?"

"Angelo." Enoch tried to smile. "It's a daft name. He said he were from foreign parts."

Jacob made a note of it. "What did you talk about with him?"

Enoch pressed his hands hard about his knees. "Nothing of here. Only of my lessons and the coffee I liked and the cake." He squeezed his knees until they ached. "I know this place is to be kept secret. I dint say anything of it. It were—"

Jacob held up a hand. "I never said you said anything. If he wasn't asking leading questions, he didn't want information."

"You dunt think he wanted to know of here?"

"I don't know yet. If it turns out to be some random person, I'm sorry we put your friend under suspicion."

Enoch drew his hands out from betwixt his knees. "You have a job to do. I cannit fault—"

"Jacob!"

Jacob was on his feet and across the room in four steps. "What do you have for me, Anton?"

Anton, one of the police officers, spread out a dozen screens. "We've got him. Trail is solid, and he's on the move, heading towards the city centre. If I didn't know better, I'd say he's trying to hide out in plain sight in the crowds." He glanced over. "I can get a tail on him from central. He's only two minutes away from them on foot."

"Do it," Jacob ordered. "We need to keep eyes on this guy and see where he goes."

"You're not going to stop him?" Lysander sounded surprised. Enoch darted a peek at him and saw the moment Lysander understood. "He's got the tech…"

"And we need to find it, so no one else accidentally stumbles on it." Jacob braced his hands on Anton's chair. "If we get him pinned down, that's when we take him."

"And if it int him?" Enoch asked, getting up.

"Then we start again," Lysander said, "but Danny's rarely wrong about things like this."

Enoch fidgeted with the bud of his Leaf. It hung on a string from his neck. For want of anything better to do with his hands, wiser to toy with it than twist his fingers 'til breaking point. Mariam was doing the same, spinning her Leaf bud on the beaded bracelet at her wrist, speckles of light rolling up her dress.

Enoch moved closer to stand by her. "You and all?" he murmured, pointing to her bud.

She smiled unsteadily. "I can't believe we might actually have him."

Enoch returned his eyes to the screen. "Aye." He closed his hand on his bud, praying nothing went wrong.

Chapter Five

The proximity alarm shrilled less than fifteen minutes after Ben got to his lab, distracting him from his current work on a gate timer.

It wasn't unusual, a few times a week at least. Sometimes, a truck rolling by was enough to trigger the alarm, and given his location, that happened a lot. His facilities were scattered in the more industrial parts of the city and the refurbished factories near the docklands, places where people could come and go at all hours, and high-power usage wasn't suspicious.

This particular hideout was in a warehouse that had once been a factory. Former owners had been more than happy to leave the equipment in some of the larger rooms when Ben took the whole lot off their hands, no questions asked. It was amazing how agreeable people could be when you handed them a hell of a lot of money.

Even though he owned the whole place, he barely used any of it. Most of it he'd filled with massive shipping crates. If something seemed like a storage facility, people didn't ask questions.

All of his real work went on in a basement, far away from any windows.

Compared to the rest of the building, it was low ceilinged and dark. Wires and cables connected in from the walls to an array of computers. The glow from the projected screens and the single strip light along the ceiling illuminated a thick metallic doorframe: a temporal gate.

Ben leaned against the frame, waiting, but when the proximity alarm didn't shut down, he left the timer propped against the gate's chassis, linked by a thick cord of twisted cables, and headed for his security station. The room was unfurnished apart from his workbench, his gate, and the security installations he'd put in place.

Ben opened out the screens to the security feed and scanned the dozens of images. There were the standard security cameras, provided by the previous owners, but as a precaution, he'd added a dozen of his own, giving himself eyes on all sides of the building.

Two screens were flashing where the proximity violation had occurred.

There was no truck.

Ben frowned.

"What's wrong with you?" he murmured, touching the console and skimming back a few seconds.

The alarm wailed again, but another screen had just lit up.

"What...?"

In all his time in this location, the machines had never malfunctioned. His Leaf vibrated in his pocket, and his heart skipped a beat—an incoming message, but no one was meant to know how to contact him. He tapped the Leaf, trying to calm himself. "Speak."

The automated speaker uttered a single word.

"Run."

Bands closed tight around his ribs, and he saw it. Them. Multiple shadows on the ground, people scattering along the external walls, staying in the blind spots of the visible cameras.

"Shit..." he breathed, searching every other camera. All exits covered. All doors blocked.

They must have followed him all the way from the city. Maybe they'd tagged something off about his pod or...

Danny.

Bloody Danny!

He must have made Ben and called in the cavalry.

Ben wrenched the camo-patch off, shoved it in his pocket. That face was compromised. He'd need to load another one, change the settings, and figure out how in the hell Danny had made him in less than two minutes. Not a priority right now, though. The enemy was already at the gate, and if he didn't make it out, no amount of camo-patches would help him.

He whirled and ran across the room. The timer gaped open, wires trailing out, and nerves had him shivering so much he could barely reattach the connections to get the gate up and running again.

Another alarm started to wail, higher than the others. The doors. They were coming for the doors.

He glanced over at the screens that showed all the doors. A large group, uniformed, with heavy-duty battering rams. Fuck. The doors were reinforced, but if they couldn't get through them, they'd find another way in. The police were stubborn like that.

Blood surged wildly through him as he pulled up the cables, sweat trickling down his forehead.

The alarm on the side door screamed. Weakest of the lot, he remembered, hissing as a loose wire sliced across his thumb. He'd been meaning to get it up to spec but never had time, and now, they were slamming against the metal of the door. The pounding echoed through the empty halls and corridors, and, Jesus, with any luck, he had maybe five minutes until they got in.

"Shit, shit, shit..." he whispered frantically.

The timer locked in place. He pulled out his Leaf, opened out a screen, and swiped through the programmes and code until he found what he needed. Jesus Christ, he had to be desperate.

A deafening crash echoed in the distance as one of the doors gave way.

Ben raced across the room to the computers.

The hard drives fitted into his satchel, but anything else was too big, and if the police got it, it'd be enough to stand as evidence against him. He rattled in a series of keys and held his breath, releasing it as the computers started wiping themselves.

Shouts—voices echoed off metal and high roofs.

Ben staggered to his feet and ran towards the gate, his Leaf clutched tightly in his hand.

"Stop where you are!"

Ben froze, an arm's length from the gate.

He knew that voice.

The shouts and the battering at the door must have been misdirection, while their leader infiltrated the place silently and found his way to Ben's hiding place. Decades off the force yet Jacob Ofori was still the best police officer Ben had ever encountered. Professional, too. It would be easier to slip away from Lysander than Jacob.

"Hi, Jacob."

"That's all you have to say to me?"

Ben glanced over his shoulder. Jacob must've pulled some pretty significant strings to be allowed a firearm again, and it was levelled at Ben. It wasn't steady. Maybe nerves. Maybe age. Something at least...

Ben managed a brittle smile as he turned to face him. "I'm guessing sorry won't cut it?"

Tight lines scored Jacob's expression. "I need you to raise your hands."

Ben licked his lip nervously, lifting his arms above his head. His Leaf vibrated against his palm, the code at work, but with the reboot, it was taking its sweet time. Christ only knew where he'd end up. "You know why I did it," he said, shifting his weight.

"I know." Jacob motioned with the gun. "Drop what you're holding."

Ben stared at him, the vibrating pulses closer together.

"Ben..." Jacob's voice was almost a plea. "Drop it."

Three...

Two...

One...

Ben pressed his eyes shut as the gate flared to life behind him. Jacob swore, dazzled by the brilliant light.

"I'm sorry!" Ben shouted and threw himself backwards through the gate.

Chapter Six

"We lost him."

Like a thunderclap, everybody in the room giving out a breath.

"What do you mean 'lost him'?" Lysander's voice was short, each word clipped up. "You said you had him closed in on all sides."

Jacob was quiet for a moment. "He had a gate."

"A gate?" Enoch breathed, hands clutched to his fluttering breast. "For time moving and that?"

"Yes. He used it. Escaped."

Enoch's stomach twisted all in knots as Lysander leaned against the edge of a desk. Mariam turned away, her face grey as ash. She— It would be good to comfort her, but he could think of no words. Helpless, he reached out and squeezed her hand. It was quivering as much as his own.

"Fuck!" Danny shoved himself away from his desk.

Enoch pressed his fist to his middle. They'd made an oath to catch Ben on his account, but a man couldn't be caught if he went to another time. None of them had thought on him using a gate to flee. "He's gone, then?" His voice trembled. "If he went into time, he's gone?"

It seemed they were thinking the same. If Ben went through a gate without any way to return, he was lost, and if he was lost...

"The gate has a timer," Jacob said. "It may be that he's set it up to recover him when we're not paying attention."

"No," Lysander said. "He's not that stupid. If he knows we have the gate, he knows we'll be waiting for him if he came back."

"What, then?" Mariam sounded afeard. "Do you think he'd be desperate enough to do that? After everything he's done?" Her hand shivered in Enoch's. "I lost his father that way, I *can't*..."

"He'll be all right," Enoch said, praying it was true. "You said yourself, he allus knows what he's about."

It couldn't be that Ben Sanders was gone. The man had a skill for planning, clever and careful and always thinking ahead. Two years had gone by before he had made a mistake. If he was lost, then the last two and more years had all been for naught. Enoch's work on the task force would mean nothing.

He squeezed Mariam's fingers. She wrapped her other hand around his, warm and soft.

"Wait…" Danny said, frowning. "Wait, how many battery cores did he take when he legged it?"

"Eh?" Enoch squinted at him in confusion, but Lysander seemed to take his meaning.

"He has one core left. He could have another gate."

"Knowing Ben, that sounds about right." Jacob sounded relieved, as did Lysander. As much as they were angered with Ben, Enoch knew they yet cared for him. None of them wanted to see him lost even if they would see him imprisoned. "He's a sneaky little bastard. He would have planned ahead."

"I dunt understand," Enoch said. "How will another gate help if they dunt know where he went?"

"They?" Danny asked, puzzled.

Enoch waved a hand. "Them that would open it for him, to let him return."

"He might have sent his destination on to his partner," Mariam said.

Enoch pointed at her. "Aye. That." Even before the creation of the task force, they thought Ben had someone to help him. They had searched as much as they might, but never found him. "Best we try to find them aga—"

"He doesn't need someone to open them," Danny said. "Even if he has a partner, it doesn't matter. He used timers before. I bet he's made them again." He walked in a circle and turned suddenly. "Jacob, the timer on the gate—is it fully functional?"

There was a long silence.

"I'm not sure. Half the cables are disconnected."

"Is that like them that opened the gates for me?" Enoch asked.

"Exactly." Lysander rubbed his small beard. "Jacob, see if you can find anything he's left in the building that gives us answers."

"From what I've seen so far, it's not likely," Jacob said. "He's wiped anything on the computers, and there wasn't much here to speak of anyway."

"All the same." Lysander touched a control on his desk, bringing up a fresh screen. "I'll call Sabine to send a team to deal with the gate, and we'll start digging into the building and whether there are any others bought or hired under the same name or company."

"I don't think Ben would be that careless," Danny said. "He's been two steps ahead of us all the time."

Enoch cleared his throat. "Yet daft enough to come over by, more than one time." If Ben hadn't come to the coffee bar, then Danny would never have seen him and sent Jacob chasing after him. "Like as not, he didn't think we would find his place."

"How *did* he know we'd found him?" Anton asked.

"Our boy took precautions," Jacob said. He sounded right proud. "You wouldn't believe the security array he had here. I'm amazed we got so close to catching him."

"Sounds like he took your lessons seriously," Mariam murmured. She wasn't so grey, but still pale. Enoch patted her hand, wishing he could offer some assurance to her.

"Aye," Danny said with a heavy sigh. "Let's hope it's not *too* well, eh?" He glanced to Lysander. "Do you want us to hang about, or will we be in the way?"

Lysander gazed at nothing for a minute. "You should go. This is all we'll be focussing on now." He turned to Enoch. "I'm sorry to bring you in all this way only to send you home again."

Enoch drew on a smile as best he could. "You dint know it would happen." He reached for the fastenings of his coat, but his hands yet betrayed him. "Is there a pod?"

Mariam touched his arm. "Danny can go on his own." She exchanged a glance with Lysander. It was heavy with meaning, but Enoch could not understand it. Her smile returned for Enoch. "I think we should get a cup of tea over the road, don't you?"

Enoch blinked dumbly at her. "Cup of tea?"

She put her arm around his shoulders, warm and soft as his own mam once was. "We've both had a bit of a shock today. I know I could use one, and I'd appreciate the company."

"Aye." He dropped the fastening of his coat. It would make no mind now. "Tea. Tea is good."

In minutes, she had him across the road, sat in a quiet nook, a pot of tea and two cups in front of him. He watched as she poured, only nodding for sugar and milk, then reaching out to take the cup. His hands were steadier. Not much, but enough to cradle the cup betwixt his palms. The china was warm, driving off the chill that had gone right to his bones.

"Far too much excitement for one day." Mariam was pouring her own tea. It splashed against the inside of her cup, but he could not bring himself to look up. He took a sip and shivered. "He'll be back. Don't worry. He'll be back, and we'll find him."

Enoch met her eyes. "You dunt know that."

She set down the pot with a thump on the table. "I know Ben." She sounded certain. "He's spent more than ten years trying to find his father. Do you think he would put himself in a situation where that would be impossible?" Certainty was writ all over her face. "He would never give that up."

Enoch took a mouthful of tea, so hot it near burned his mouth. He hissed, catching a breath. "If he had no other choice, mayhap he would."

She raised her thin grey eyebrows at him. "You've seen what he's like and what he's done in the past. Do you really believe that?"

Enoch stared at her. No. Ben Sanders was many things, but God's bones, he was a stubborn and determined bugger who had made a right mess of his own life as well as Enoch's. Finding his father was his life's work, and he had given up everything he had for it. He would not lay by his tools lightly.

Given the choice of failing or surrender, he would surrender afore risking failure.

"No," Enoch agreed. "He would sooner cut his hand off." The knot in his chest loosened. He laughed weakly. "Jesu, but it was a fright."

"It was," she agreed. "Ben's very good at those."

Enoch sank into his seat, hugging his tea to him. Mariam had to be right. Of all of the people in the task force, she knew Ben the best, in good humours and bad. Ben would come by again and the task force would chase him, and all would be as it ever was.

"I thought we were done. The task force," he said, lest she wonder why he had been so afeard. "If we were done with it, I dunt know what I would do. I know I can be of use there."

Her expression was as soft as his mam's had ever been. "You don't have to worry about anything if that happens. We'll take care of you. Even if there isn't a task force." She considered her tea. "I'm only sorry we haven't been able to find you a way home."

Enoch reached for one of the biscuits on the plate. "You dunt need to be sorry."

She seemed surprised. "Even if you're never going to be able to go home?"

Enoch took a bite of the biscuit, thinking afore he spoke. It was difficult to explain it all. "I did," he finally said. He broke a piece of chocolate off the biscuit and nibbled on it. "When I first come through, it was...different. Loud and big and bright. I was angry and afeard of it all, but now..." He waved a hand, scattering crumbs about. "This is better. I am never too cold nor too hot. I'm never beat. I'm never hungry or thirsty, and if I am, I only need to say so and there is food and drink."

Her brow rumpled as if she could not believe it. "But don't you miss your friends? Your family? Won't they wonder what happened to you?"

There spoke the mother who had lost the boy who was all but her son.

Enoch supped his tea. There was no harm in telling some of his secrets, if it comforted her. "I was—my family was all but gone. I had few enough friends." He frowned. He had not thought on it for a long while and for good reason. "There were those who thought ill of me and let their tongues wag. My name was...not well-liked by those with authority."

That surprised her. "You kept that quiet."

He almost laughed. "Aye. In this place, the new folk with authority dint know. I thought it best to have them like me." He broke the biscuit into two. "And they dunt bring me up afore the Priest here when I take drink and profane and pay court where I should not."

She chuckled. "I can see why you might like it."

"I like it here," he confessed. "I dint think I would, but I do."

"I'm glad." She sighed softly. "Don't get me wrong, I'm still furious Ben put you in this situation to begin with and didn't at least leave us a way to send you home, but I'm glad it's worked out well for you."

Enoch folded his arms on the table. "Can I tell you something in secret?"

Mariam leaned closer. "If you like."

Enoch glanced about and confided, "I think he believed he did right by me."

Mariam gawped at him. "My guess is he didn't plan that far ahead. He didn't really have time, did he?"

Enoch shrugged. "You said he might have left a way to put me by. He knew of my life and the hurts I had. I think he wanted to spare me further pains."

"He didn't have the right to choose!" Mariam said, spots of red showing on her brown cheeks. "It was your *life*. No man has the right to control another's life."

Enoch flinched from the anger in her voice. It was meant for Ben, but with all that had happened, it felt that he had some part in it as well.

She saw his flinch and held up her hands. "Sorry. I'm sorry." She pushed up her glasses and rubbed at her eyes. "I just thought— He was such a good boy." She lowered her hands and, for a moment, seemed older and much wearier. "I thought I understood why he did what he did, but some of it..." She sighed. "Never mind."

"He was your lad," Enoch said quietly.

"Was?" She met his eyes sadly. "No. No matter what happens or what he's done, he's still my boy." She took an unsteady breath and rubbed her eyes again. "And when I get my hands on him, he's going to hear about it for all the worry and upset he's caused."

Enoch grinned crookedly. Mariam was a slight, plump woman, but those were the ones who were most fearsome when crossed. "Now that is a show I would well like to see."

She smiled across the table, her lined face creasing up. "I think I can arrange that."

Chapter Seven

Darkness surrounded Ben as he fell.

He hit the ground hard, sprawled on his back. His teeth clacked together, his mouth filling up with blood, and he rolled onto his side, spluttering. He'd tripped over something when he'd emerged through the gate. A rock, maybe, or a root?

Christ, it was cold! The smell of rain was on the air, and the ground squished damply under him as he struggled to get up. Nature too. The wind whispered through trees he couldn't see yet, his eyes adjusting after the brilliance of the gate.

Grass surrounded him, brushing his hands as he stood up, too long and thick to be a garden. That would have been an awkward place to arrive anyway.

He squinted to his right where the horizon was growing gradually brighter.

Sunrise.

Well, that was something.

He was, at least temporarily, safe and intact—even if he had a wet arse, a burst lip, and no bloody clue where he'd ended up. Or when.

Safe.

Ha.

They'd seen him use an illegal gate. If he hadn't been in a hell of a lot of trouble before, he definitely was now. Somewhere in the maybe distant future, there were a lot of people who were going to line up to give him a good kicking for being an idiot. A few of them still cared about him. Jacob did. He'd hesitated.

And if Jacob had found him, the task force was probably listening in, which meant not just Jacob but everyone else as well.

"Shit," Ben whispered under his breath.

All the people he gave a damn about, under one roof, watching him screw up again.

It wouldn't help, not thinking about them all, and the arms that had held and comforted him when he cried.

First things first, he had to survive the day. As he waited for the sun to get high enough for him to get his bearings, he stamped his feet, swinging his arms to try to keep himself even a little warm.

Deep blue became lighter, skimmed with frothy pink clouds. Gradually, gold started riming the edges of the shapeless shadowy trees surrounding him. Not too close, he noticed. He spun, checking again, his pulse quickening. He was in the middle of a clearing. And in almost a perfect circle around him...

"Oh my God..." he breathed.

The circle of standing stones.

Ben pressed his fist to his bloodied lip, staring as the light crept higher.

He *knew* this place.

Decades ago, he'd held his dad's hand and walked through a gate for the first time. Back then, the stones seemed so big, towering over him. Now, they barely even reached his shoulder, but they were the same.

No, not quite.

They were older.

As if he were dreaming, he faced north and walked forward, stepping out from between the stones. It was as if he were reliving the day; if he glanced around, he would see his dad standing in front of the open gateway, smiling.

In front of him, stood a vast oak tree, taller than he remembered. Much taller. Maybe centuries?

If he was right, if this was the place he thought...

Close to his eye level, he found it: two large letters carved into the bark.

Ben reached out, his fingers trembling, to trace them. TS + BS. Their letters. He'd stood here by his dad's side and watched as their mark was put on the tree.

"So we'll know we've been here," his dad had said, brushed away curls of wood.

Ben hadn't understood what he meant then, but now it made sense.

The letters weren't as cleanly cut as they had been. Some of the bark had grown inwards, distorting them, but they were there and visible. None of the moss curling up the sides of the trunk had covered them.

There were some marks circling them as well, uneven chips knocked out in a ragged ring.

"Of course," he whispered.

When his parents had started developing the temporal gates, they'd chosen a nearby location as an anchor point as they tried to focus the temporal calibration. The circle of stubby standing stones was less than two miles from their house. His dad had made wry notes in his records suggesting it wouldn't raise questions if gates flickered in and out of existence there. Any accidental witnesses in the past wouldn't be surprised by anything happening on a fairy knoll.

God only knew how many gates they'd opened there before they were able to get the coding and the settings right.

Ben's own gate had been built based on his dad's original design and settings. The only difference was the power source. Rebooting and activating it in the middle of repairs wasn't a great idea, but it explained why he'd ended up there. The time was harder to pinpoint, but he knew where he was, if not when.

He had a bigger problem as well...

He scanned the clearing before cautiously opening out his Leaf. Unsurprisingly, there was no signal, but he could at least check whether the last bit of information had transferred before he stepped through the gate.

He clenched his hands to steady them. If he'd cocked up his programming, he was fucked. Unless the TRI managed to crack his security protocols, restore his wiped drives, and somehow log his coordinates, everything depended on his own work and the semi-repaired gate.

Screeds of data rolled up the projected screen; he stared at it wildly and released an explosive breath when he spotted the data he needed. Even if he didn't know where he was, his temporal coordinates had been logged through the software and dispatched to the various comms he'd left scattered at his half-dozen bases of operation.

Technically, hopefully, if everything was working as planned, it would just be a matter of waiting. With any luck, it'd be exactly twenty-four hours.

He shut his Leaf down. Slipping the bud into his pocket, he closed his eyes and took a steadying breath.

Right.

Twenty-four hours in the past.

There were rules he needed to abide by. Even before the TRI was doing its thing, his dad had told him time and again history was history. It couldn't be meddled with or changed. He'd cocked up once before, but at least this time, there would be no drunken mistakes.

The nearest village was at least six miles away, based on his dad's vintage maps, with a scattering of small houses about, but none too close. Most people avoided the circle in the middle of the woods. Uncanny happenings, the urban legends said. He laughed weakly. Uncanny happenings. Like random people appearing out of glowing doorways with small puzzled children and leaving strange marks on trees.

He stared up at the mark on the tree, and the mirth dissolved into a half-choked sob.

"They probably thought you were some kind of evil fairy," he said, his eyes burning. "Saw you with me in tow and ran off to protect their own kids." He reached up to trace the letters. He'd forgotten them. Somehow, he'd forgotten.

No one else knew about it.

Oh, they knew about his dad using the gates, but none of them had asked Ben. They knew he'd learned about the gates, but they never thought he'd been through one. None of them had believed his dad would be so reckless as to take his child into the past. But what was the alternative? Leaving him behind, on his own?

His father had done that once, and Ben knew it wasn't by choice.

If only his dad hadn't chosen to try to save his tech. If only he'd come with Ben to the safe room. If only the thief hadn't chased him into the lab. If only, if only, if only...

Ben scrubbed at his face with both hands.

Getting worked up couldn't help.

"Okay..." he said, taking a deep breath, "Twenty-four hours."

The best thing would be to stay within easy reach of the stones. It would be the sensible thing to do while he waited for pickup, but that only worked if a man could get by on thin air alone. Especially when said man had barely escaped a police cordon and an armed confrontation with an old friend and his adrenaline high was only starting to ebb.

Christ, he was thirsty.

Running about like a mad thing would do that.

If he remembered right, there was a stream nearby. He dug out his Leaf again and opened up the files. Among them, there were a dozen maps of the area from his dad's records. Nearby. Ha! Almost two miles off, as the crow flies.

Water was the priority. He had some snacks in his satchel at least, a protein bar and some biscuits, but he needed water. Twenty-four hours wasn't long, and as soon as he got home, he'd be able to stuff his face.

It would be better not to think beyond those twenty-four hours until he had to.

Ben glanced around the clearing with a grimace.

Nature had never been his strong point. Machines, engines, computers were easy. Forests weren't. Not when they squelched under his feet and long greenish ropes trailed across the ground and snagged his ankles. Then there were the roots, which made perfectly level ground into a tripping hazard.

There wasn't even a path. Or maybe there was, but a secret one only non-city people could see.

He reduced his Leaf projection, flicking on the compass function. The Leaf blinked off. Ben stared at the bud in dismay.

"No...no, no, no..." He reset it, holding his breath as the screen projected up again. It was the map, but it was frozen. It wouldn't resize or let him open the compass to do anything more than switch it off and on another three times in the hopes it might help.

He glanced about, examining his surroundings. East was where the sun came up. North was the carved tree. All fine, except when he had to go wandering off through uneven ground with no visible pointers. He crouched, opened up the satchel, and rooted through it.

No magnets, which was a problem. Not like he had any need for them. Metal, though.

He chewed his lip, picking through the fragments of computer and cables he had.

In his brief spell attending a normal school, he remembered a particular lesson involving metal and wires and a bowl of water. Everyone else in the class had been awed as the sliver of metal spun to point north. Even if it seemed boring compared to his dad's gates, he'd paid attention.

Thank God, he thought, as he sat at the foot of one of the standing stones and started breaking open bits of his tech to get to the battery and the wires. The pieces were so small and fiddly—especially with only basic tools—his fingers were bleeding as he worked. In lieu of water, he tugged a loose thread from his shirt and suspended the magnetised sliver of metal from a small stick, watching it spin to point towards the tree.

Conveniently, it was the bloodied tip that pointed north.

It took a good fifteen minutes and the sun was creeping higher as he got to his feet. A quick glance confirmed he hadn't left any pieces of modern tech scattered about. He opened up his map again, turning to face the right direction, and started walking.

By the time he heard running water, he was about ready to kick something. His trousers were sodden to the knee and filthy from all the times he'd tripped and landed in the dirt. Scratches covered his arms from pushing through the sodding spiky bush things. He'd stood in something disgusting, and it was leaking into his shoe. The sun was high as well, and despite being in the north of bleeding England, sweat was pouring off him.

It was closer, and he stumbled on towards a break in the trees. God, he'd never been so glad to see water, and he staggered towards the stream winding its way through the glade.

The water was cool and so clear he could see every pebble through the ripples. He fell to his knees and stuck his face into the water, gulping mouthful after mouthful. It was so cold his teeth ached. He set aside his bud and compass to plunge his hands into the flow, scooping up handfuls and splashing it on his face, scrubbing off blood and dirt.

He was rinsing the back of his neck, letting trickles run under his collar, when he heard the crack of a twig underfoot.

Ben's heart stopped as he looked up.

He wasn't alone.

Chapter Eight

"What about another food-tasting video?"

Enoch lifted his chin from his folded arms. "Hm?"

Mack sat on the other side of the table, and a number of screens floated between them, covered with videos and data. "I was skimming through your streams for the last few weeks, and you haven't done a taste-test one for almost two months."

"Oh." Enoch frowned. "Well enough."

Mack started blethering again, but Enoch found he had no wish to listen. His mind was on the task force and the gate they had found. He'd had word from Lysander that they had people working on the gate to seek where Ben might be found.

It could not be so difficult.

From all he understood, any temporal gate should hold a record of the places and times the gate had visited. The gate was new, so by rights, there should only be a few places, yet it seemed Ben had thought beyond that, and it was no longer so simple.

He lowered his chin to rest on his folded arms on the table again.

It would do none of them any good if they could not find Ben. No matter how much historical information Enoch could give to the TRI, the task force was more important. He had to be there. Nowhere else had need of him.

Mack reached over the table to prod his elbow. "You okay?"

Enoch twisted up his face. "There are troubles at the task force," he murmured. "I were only thinking on that." He sat up again and drew on a happier face. "It's no matter. You said something about food?"

Mack smiled bright. "I was thinking we could try you on Mexican food."

Enoch had learned well enough to be wary of Mack's suggestions. "Is it mouth-warming like Indian food?"

"Some of it, sort of."

Enoch gazed at him. Mack was happy to offer things for him to try, curious how Enoch would find them. For him, Enoch was all but from another world. He thought it funny how curry made Enoch's eyes so wet he almost seemed to weep.

"I have a thought," Enoch said.

Mack seemed wary as a feart cat. "Oh?"

"I'll have food made from my time, and you can test taste it."

Mack opened and shut him mouth. "Uh. I don't—it's not—I—"

Enoch bit down on a smirk. Oh, so not as funny if he were the one trying things, eh? "What's the harm? People would know what I et back in the day. I cannit be the one to taste it, for I know what it's like. You gave me curry. I can give you calf brain."

Mack went grey, and Enoch gave a great guffaw for the first time in hours.

"You're still a cock!" Mack grumbled, spinning a pen across the table to Enoch.

"Your face!" Enoch chuckled, clapping his hands. "I would I had a camera."

"You're not really going to get me eating brains?"

"I wouldn't share such a feast with the likes of you," Enoch sniffed, dignified as a Lord. "It were only for those as could afford it. My meat was none so fancy. I had to fetch it myself."

Mack narrowed his eyes, suspicious-like. "Fetch it yourself? You mean...catch it?"

It would do no harm for them to know. "I got a leathering on account of taking some rabbits."

Mack's eyes were round as plates. "Shit, Enoch! You were a poacher?"

Enoch wrinkled his nose. "I were *hungry*. You take what food you might find. What's the harm when there are none as would miss it?"

Mack seemed surprised. "And all this time, I thought you were just a humble farm hand." He put his head to one side. "You got beaten for the rabbits?"

"Mm." Enoch grimaced. "It were meant to be a lesson to keep me from being a sinful man."

Mack hissed through his teeth. "That's awful."

It had been. He had screamed like a babe until he had no breath left. Blood and pain, and the minister's lass tending his wounds for him under her father's careful eye. Not careful enough, mind. A small pleasure after a world of pain.

"There's many had worse and done worse." He shrugged. "I healed, by and by."

"Did it work?" Mack asked.

Enoch cocked his head. "Did what work?"

"The lesson?"

Enoch scratched at his cheek. "I had a fine pheasant for supper three weeks after."

Mack burst out in a great peal of laughter. "You thieving bugger."

"It weren't so big as your monstrous chickens, but it were a fair size." Enoch could scarce hide a grin. "I had them as would pay me well enough to fetch them some game from the forests as well." The minister's lass, for one. On her father's askance and all.

"Even though you got beaten for it?"

Enoch pulled one foot up onto his seat and propped his arm atop his knee. "It were only the once." He grinned wider. "I were never caught again after, and them that asked for meat weren't like to tell the master."

Mack whistled between his teeth. "So I should add sneaky thief and poacher into your list of known skills?"

"There's a list of that?" The TRI were good at lists—lists of health, lists of food, lists of medicine, lists of all sorts.

"Probably." Mack made a face. "Do they know any of this?"

Enoch paused. There were things it was best they didn't know, leastways because they might think ill of him. "I were afeard they would not be so kind to a confessed thief," he admitted. "Like as not, it would make no mind to them, but when I first come here..."

"You didn't know if they'd hurt you," Mack finished for him. "I don't blame you, with a life like that."

"It were all right," Enoch said. Sometimes, it had been. Sometimes, there was pain and it was hard, but it was his life as he'd known it. "I had those I called friend, we had the inn, we laughed and drank." He met Mack's eyes. "Do you think it strange I miss that? The laughter and the drinks?"

"Everyone wants to have a good time with their friends." Mack was quiet for a minute and then leaned forward, bracing his arms on the table. "Look, I know you're restricted with where you can go and what you can do, since you're all famous, but d'you want to come out with me and Orla at the weekend? We're going to a dance bar near ours."

Enoch could not help but be grateful. Mack was always the same, giving of his time and company. A good lad and the kind a man would want as a friend. And not only offering his company, but his woman's as well. "You need not take me out of pity."

"Pity?" Mack rolled his eyes. "I want you to meet Orla so she'll believe me when I tell her you're a bit of a shit."

The first time Mack—and Janos—had said such a thing, Enoch had been outraged, but with time, he'd learned it was meant with affection.

"Like speaks to like," he said, widening his eyes. He grinned again when Mack gave a shout of mirth.

"That! Exactly that!" Mack said, jabbing a finger at him. "I want her to hear you say stuff like that so she'll believe me."

Enoch chewed on his thumbnail. He didn't like the city much. Everything was busy and noisy and loud with more people than he liked. Then again, it *was* Mack. It would be different to see him when he didn't hold his tongue for the sake of the TRI. A brew or two in him and he might tell all manner of tales. A man could learn much from a drink-loosed tongue.

"It would be the three of us alone?"

Mack scratched his chin in thought. "If you like, I can see if one of Orla's friends would come to be your partner for the night."

Enoch's mouth fell open. "My...partner?"

Mack nodded happily. "Significant other? Like a date? When you get to know someone and see if you want to...you know...get together with them."

Enoch pressed his knuckles to his mouth, unsure how best to react. "Fornication, you mean?"

"I didn't say that exactly!" Mack's face went red as blood. "I—I meant as a friend. Not more than that, unless you want it to be. If you don't want to see anyone or you know...*you know*..." When Enoch raised his eyebrows, Mack sheepishly said, "Fornicate..."

Mack meant well even if he had no idea what he spoke of. "If I wished to find someone to fornicate with, I could do it myself. I have no need of some poor lass or lad being pushed at me because they know your woman."

Mack blinked stupidly at him. "Lad or lass?"

Enoch could scarce stifle his chortle. "You think I'd choose between them?"

Mack gaped at him. "You're bi?"

"By what?"

Mack waved a hand impatiently. "Bisexual?"

Enoch cocked his head. "Is that an offence to me?"

"No, no, no!" Mack seemed all wound up like he did when Enoch played him the fool, but for once, Enoch was as confused as Mack. "I mean—that is—if you were to...lie with someone, you wouldn't mind if they were a woman or a man?"

"Oh!" Enoch beamed at him. "Aye! I'm a sometime sodomite." He frowned and scratched the end of his nose. "Not much of late, but I like a hard yard as much as a fine pair of teats."

"Holy shit!"

Enoch eyed him, amused. Poor Mack saw the world so simply; it was a shame how easy it was to turn him about. "I thought you were the modern one of us. Do you not know Mr. Ofori and Mr. O'Donohue and Mr. Ferguson are all sodomites? There are many, all wed and that."

"I—it—but—" Mack spluttered. "But you're from *history*. I thought you'd be...I don't know...weird about it. Wasn't—didn't—I didn't think you could be gay then without getting in trouble!"

Enoch curled his lips wickedly. "You remember my beating, aye? It's only a matter if you get caught."

Mack stared at him, then sagged, bemused. "I guess," he agreed. "And you never got caught?"

Enoch ducked his head. "Never for that."

Mack chuckled. "I'm learning a lot about you today."

Enoch could not keep from smiling. "You only needed to ask."

"I'll remember next time." Mack got to his feet. "So, Mr. Poacher, thief and sexually adventurous rogue, do you want to come out with me and Orla?" He raised his hands before Enoch could speak. "No fornicator friends unless you ask for them."

Enoch considered him and nodded. "I'd be happy to."

Mack's face lit up. "I'll plan something for the weekend, then. I have a couple of days off."

Enoch watched him go. The weekend. Another two days away.

He sighed. Would they could have gone for a brew this same night. It would have been distraction enough from the gate and the task force. It was better to drink in company instead of mulling over a brew at home, but there was no choice in the matter.

Enoch went to his pantry. Even after years, it amazed him to open it and see it full with food he could eat when he pleased. It would never run empty either. He had fretted in the beginning, hoarding it lest they take it from him. For as long as he could remember, there were times where he had gone hungry.

Janos had come and spoken to him about it without making Enoch feel like a fool. He explained that in this time, there was plenty, and if Enoch ever needed anything, he had but to ask. It took some months for him to truly believe it. Once, he even asked for the finest steak he could think on. It was delivered within hours.

Now, he could take a small steel vessel, sealed top and bottom, and open it for a beer clearer and far better than any he might have had in the past. There was even a small ring to allow him to open a neat hole in the canister. Life in the modern world was so much easier.

He wandered across the broad room to the couch. It amused him that he lived in a set of rooms the size of his old inn. He supped his ale and reached for the bud of his Leaf to open a screen up. Bright icons lit up along the edges. He thumbed one open, then another.

There were the videos Mack had gathered and a set of messages taken from his streams. Enoch lay on the couch and watched the videos first. They were enough to draw his mind from dark thoughts, and he laughed aloud when one brave man tried to balance three chickens atop his head.

When they were done, he turned his attention to the comments. Much the same as usual—mirth and suggestions for his next stream. None needed a reply. He scrolled to his more personal messages, but there was naught to see. No Diaval to entertain. That made his mood sink even lower.

Enoch sighed and tossed the bud aside. They would tell him if they knew anything. He knew that to be true. If something was amiss, they always told him. He drank the rest of his ale, then rose and went for another. They would tell him, and until they did, he would distract himself with the comfort of the drink.

Chapter Nine

Ben's day had gone from bad to weird.

It turned out his dad's maps weren't 100 per cent right. There was a small stone house not even half a mile from the stream, half-hidden by undergrowth, a thick layer of moss covering the roof.

The occupant was an elderly lady who seemed to embrace the witch aesthetic of the place, dressed all in dark colours with a shock of grey hair.

Ben knew this because he was sitting inside the smoke-stained cottage, smiling uncomfortably as the woman fussed and poured him a cup of some kind of herbal tea. God, he hoped it was herbal and not some kind of magic mushroom infusion.

"You have made a right mess of yourself, have you not?" she said, catching his chin in her hand and clucking as she examined his bruised face and split lip.

Ben forced himself to stay still. The rules had to be maintained. Act as a local would. Blend in. Don't make a fuss. The last time—the first time—he'd travelled solo, he'd forgotten that rule, and it changed everything.

Agreeing to a cup of tea probably wouldn't do any damage.

When he'd crossed paths with the woman at the stream, she'd insisted he come to her home so she could patch his wounds. It seemed easier not to argue when his shirt was caked with blood and his only other option was running away.

"I had a fall," he said.

"Hm." She released his chin. "Yarrow, I think." She shuffled off across the dirt floor to a makeshift shelf stacked with small bottles.

I swear—Ben held his cup of...whatever tightly—*if she brings out a cauldron, I'm running. Sod the rules.*

She returned a moment later with two bottles and a handful of surprisingly clean cloth. "Now bide still," she said, tipping a few drops from each bottle onto the cloth, which she pressed to his lip.

Ben stifled a curse, the burn on his skin making his eyes water. "Wh-what is that?"

Up close, her face was a mass of lines, and she grinned at him, showing a lot more teeth than he'd expect in a wood-lurking not-witch.

"A physik." A second dab and she stepped away, satisfied. "None'll look twice now."

The burn was fading, replaced with a soothing tingle. Ben cautiously touched his lip. It was swollen, but it hurt less than it had. "Thank you," he said, surprised. "I—you didn't have to do that."

The woman chuckled, settling herself on the other small chair opposite him. "Those wandering these paths come to me for help," she said, adjusting her heavy skirts. "One wandering wounded and lost but asks for naught? I would help them."

Ben turned his clay cup in his hand. "I wasn't lost."

"Hm." She propped her arms on the arms of the chair. "Divining your path with cords and sticks and you were not lost?"

Ben's stomach twisted. She must have seen him enter the clearing with his compass, which meant she might have seen his Leaf and the glowing image of the map. If she had...

She watched with her dark, glinting eyes. Now he studied her, he wondered if she was as old as he'd first thought. Despite the lines on her face, something in her expression and her eyes suggested someone a lot younger than she looked.

"You've come a long way, I think," she said, folding her bony hands in her lap. "You're far from home."

Ben took a mouthful of the hot, herbal tea to hide his discomfort. It was bitter, but soothing too. "I only stopped at the stream for some water. I should be on my way soon."

"Have a long way to go, do you?"

He didn't know why, but he didn't lie. "Only a couple of miles east."

She raised feathery eyebrows. "Indeed?" She chuckled again. "A few miles east...best you keep that to yourself if you meet another on the road. They might think you a creature from the circle." She nodded to his shirt. "Your dress and speech are strange enough for such a beast."

He took another careful sip of the tea. "You don't seem afraid of me, if I am..."

There was something darker in her expression. "I've seen many a strange thing, boy." She leaned forward, studying him intently. "I think this is not your first time in these woods."

Ben almost choked on his tea. "Wh-what?"

She stared at him intently. "You know where you are and where you should be. Mayhap you are not so lost as I first thought."

Of course, he thought wryly, he had to run into the weird cryptic not-witch in the incredibly creepy woods. Naturally. Last time, he'd crashed an unexpected witch trial, this time, tea from an actual potential witch. Sort of.

He drained the cup as quickly as he could, coughing when the dregs hit his throat. "Thank you for your hospitality." He held out the cup to her. "I think I should go."

She got up at once and stepped closer to him, staring at him. He wanted to retreat, but the chair was pressing against the back of his legs and running sideways for the door was probably about equal amounts rude and stupid. It was daft how a woman almost a head shorter than him could be so effortlessly intimidating.

"The rains will come," she said. "Best not go at once."

"I really should," Ben demurred, wondering how far up the scale of inconsiderate arsehole he would be if he knocked over an old lady and fled. "I'm expected."

She smiled again, her face wrinkling like old leather. "Well enough. Will you pay your fee?"

Ben glanced at the cup in his hand, then at her. All he had were his protein bars and that wasn't really something you could give a weird old witch woman. "I—what fee?"

"Your name."

Well, that wasn't creepy at *all*.

"Why do you want my name?"

She chuckled. "You have little else to give. Slake an old woman's curiosity."

If it meant he could leave, it was simple enough. "Ben. My name is Ben."

"Ben." She whispered it like a prayer, plucked the cup from him, and turned away. "Ben." She rolled the cup in her hands. "Yes. Very well, Ben. You have a road to travel." She waved one hand towards the door. "Off with you, before the rains come."

Ben picked up his satchel from the floor and hesitated. "Thank you, ma'am. You've been very generous."

She set the cup on one of the rickety shelves. "Little enough." She waved again. "Off."

He slipped out of the door, gulping a breath of the fresher air. It was cooler as well, and the scent of rain hung on the air. He glanced over his shoulder into the house. The old woman hadn't moved, standing in the middle of the room.

Maybe it would be considered rude in the context of the time. It wasn't something his dad had spent many lessons on, but there was only so much weird tea and cryptic bullshit he could take, especially when he needed to be at the stones and waiting for his return gate.

Ben turned and headed in the direction of the stream, pulling the pieces of his compass out of his satchel to remagnetise it.

It was easier to retrace his steps, the compass dangling from one hand and his map hovering over the other. The forest was unpleasant, but it wasn't as intimidating. He'd managed it once. He could do it again.

Halfway there, the promised rain started to fall. Light at first, it rapidly got heavier. He huddled under the broadest trees, close to the trunks, and any time there was a lull, he ran for the next clump of thick trees. His trousers, which had almost been dry, were sodden again. The rest of him wasn't much better.

No matter how creepy and weird the old woman had been, it was almost tempting to go and beg shelter for a few hours.

Not a real option. He needed to be near the stones.

By the time he reached the clearing, the rain had eased off, which only left the problem of finding some kind of shelter for the night. It was possible. He'd watched enough adventure films with Mariam and her family with people building whole tree houses with nothing more than a penknife and some string.

He swiped a hand over his face and peered about. Mostly, all he could see were bushes and trees and the stones. The trees were nothing like Hollywood's, all rough and mossy bark and wiry prickly branches that trailed almost as low as the ground.

The film industry had a lot to answer for.

Ben swore under his breath, squinting about.

Movement between the trees caught his eye, and his heart jumped. He stared at the spot and slid one hand into his satchel to pull out a screwdriver. He had no idea what he planned to do with it, but in a creepy forest, it felt better to be armed than not.

Nothing moved.

Or at least nothing moved again.

Several minutes later, he relaxed his grip on the screwdriver. Probably nothing more than a deer or a rabbit or...something else living in the woods.

A second priority, then. Fire. Something to keep whatever was out there well away from him.

First things first, though. Somewhere dry—or at least not too wet— to set up a shelter. The spreading branches of the trees seemed like the best place. It took a few attempts and a lot of spiky leaves in his hair and down his neck before he found somewhere dry enough to consider sitting.

The wind was up as well and probably would only get worse through the night, so he dragged some loose and fallen branches from other trees to prop over the small hollow as a windbreak. Not perfect, but better than sitting in a draught. His hands were scratched and bleeding by the time he sat and devoured his protein bar.

No more nature, ever again, he vowed to himself. Stupid trees and bushes and spiky bits.

The vow was only solidified when he tried to start a fire and the bloody wood wouldn't catch, until it did and started giving off thick, unpleasant smoke, choking him. Too wet, he realised as—half-blinded— he stamped the smouldering sticks into the dirt.

He managed eventually, though it was well after nightfall when the flames took hold. Not well and not much, but it was better than sitting in the open air, and he huddled over the fire, warming his hands. *First thing I'm doing when I get home is showering for as long as humanly possible without dissolving. And updating my tetanus shot.*

The fire burned out during the night.

Ben woke, shivering, in the darkness, propped against the trunk of the tree. Screeches and hoots and rustling that definitely weren't the wind disturbed the quiet. Nature was terrifying, and he clung onto his screwdriver again, in case.

He was sitting there, stiff and cold and aching when his multitool beeped.

With numb fingers, he pressed the button. Five minutes until the gate might open...

His legs almost folded under him as he tried to get up. It took a few attempts, and when he staggered out from his shelter, he didn't even care about getting more scratched up by the low branches. He tilted the light of his multitool towards the stone circle, stumbling onwards into the middle of the ring.

The beam skimmed over the grass, illuminating the faint scorch mark where the gate had opened the day before.

"Please..." he whispered, retreating to a safe distance. "Please open..."

The countdown was blinking.

Ben felt sick with trepidation. If the gate didn't open, if he didn't get back today, then he had no clue what he would do. Technically, the TRI had his gate, so maybe they would find him if his plans failed, but if they didn't either, he was screwed. Sitting in a damp, dirty shelter was okay for one night, but if it wasn't...

A sound made him whip around.

A twig cracking, like something had stepped on it beyond the edge of the circle. For it to crack like that, whatever stood on it had to be pretty big, and he swept the light out, searching for the source. No movement, no animals. Nothing.

He scanned the circle, breathing hard. Jesus, if the gate didn't open and there was something out there, stalking him...

The countdown beeped again, and he slammed his eyes closed. The electric crackle of the gate opening behind him was like music to his ears and even through his eyelids, the brightness of the gate glowed. He turned, raising an arm to shield his eyes, and ran towards the light.

Long, whippy grass gave way to metal under his feet, his boots clattering. He opened his eyes, staggering forward with relief. His secondary lab. His backup gate. The scent of metal and the hum of power and not a bloody tree in sight.

He closed his eyes and breathed deeply. Home. He was home.

Behind him, the gate powered down, and then a sound that shouldn't have been there: heavy, panting breaths.

There'd been nothing in the circle. There'd been no one there.

He turned, groping for his screwdriver again, and froze.

The old woman from the forest leaned heavily against the frame of the gate. Her face ash-pale, she stared around wild-eyed.

The screwdriver fell from Ben's grip. Clattered. Rolled.

What are you doing here? He wanted to scream. *Why did you follow me? What do you want?*

He wanted to, but he couldn't. Mouth dry, pulse like thunder drowning out every sound.

"Sweet Jesus..." The woman's eyes found his, and she stared at him, shocked, and took one hesitant step away from the doorframe before she swayed. Ben dropped his bag and dived forward to catch her before she hit the floor.

She lay there, light as a child in his arms and insensate.

Ben stared up at the gate.

Not again. *Not again.*

Chapter Ten

The corner was dark and quiet.

Enoch wondered if it made him a coward to seek out the table almost hidden in the shadow at the back of the inn. His head was thumping from the music in the dance hall and even now, he could swear there were lights flashing afore his eyes. He pressed both palms to them, taking a breath.

It was a foolish thing, to agree to go to such a place. Too many people with too much light and music. It was all too much.

Yet he had gone knowing that.

Better than sitting alone with only his thoughts for company.

Too much to worry on with the task force and TRI and all that came with them.

He lowered his hands, drew out his bud, and opened the last messages he had received. From Lysander to tell him there was no news. From Jacob to ask more questions about his masked friend. From Danny asking the same. From DCI Temple, the leader of the police people in the task force, seeking a summary.

There was no place for good humour, it seemed.

Even Diaval was sharper than usual.

Enoch had sent him a message or two, urging him to send suggestions for the next stream, since he always took such pleasure in them. When Diaval eventually replied, it was but one line: Busy. Will be in touch soon.

That, on top of all else, was like a blow.

He touched the triangle and played the message again.

"Friend of yours?" Orla slipped into one of the chairs at his table. She had a tall glass in her hands, full of a colourful drink. She was a rare woman, her hair all blue spirals about her shoulders. Her dress was small and her boots high. Enoch could only wonder what his mam would think of such clothing.

"One of them that watches my streams," Enoch said, closing the bud. "I have nothing to speak of on my next one."

She supped some of her drink through a long paper straw, a thoughtful look on her face. "I'm sure there's something." She grinned suddenly. "You could try cocktails."

"Cock...tails?" That sounded wrong. "Off a bird?"

She laughed, holding up the glass. "It's what we call the mixed drinks." She leaned closer and murmured, "I heard about Noch's Cocks from His Shyness." She waved towards Mack, who was at the bar. "He gets so bashful about that kind of thing. I'd pay good money to see his expression when you ask him for Sex on the Beach."

Despite himself he laughed. "There's such a drink?"

"Mm." She took another sip from her straw. "Ask him. I dare you."

"Mayhap for the stream," he said, thinking it would be best to check such a thing lest he make a fool of himself. He raised his eyes as Mack returned from the bar with two glasses in his hands. He seemed worried.

"Is this place better?"

Enoch accepted one of the glasses of ale gratefully. "Aye, much better." He glanced about the inn. It was quieter by far than the dancing hall, with much less people. "Your pardon. I dint mean to change your night."

"It's all right," Orla said, waving her free hand. "It was too loud for me as well. At least we can talk here."

She was only being kind, he knew. He had watched her dancing with Mack, both of them laughing and moving to the music throbbing like a pulse. They went well together, both of a height, neither as tall as some or small as some. In their shining clothes with their colourful hair, they belonged. They liked the loudness as well, but they saw Enoch didn't and had brought him elsewhere.

The inn was close to the old dock district. There were all manner of new warehouses about, but the inn itself was small and old-fashioned. It had cushioned seats at a number of tables and wooden walls with paintings and tools hung upon them. Everyone else—and there were but a half dozen—was grey-haired and wrinkled. It was not an inn made for dancing or loudness.

Mack slid into the seat by Orla. "We invited you as well. It'd be rude to leave you sitting on your own by the dance floor all night."

Enoch raised his glass to them. "To talking, then?"

Mack and Orla clattered their glasses together.

They talked of little things at first—Orla of her job in computer engineering, Mack about their plans to find a new flat when they saved enough money, Enoch about ideas for the next streams. It was like a different life, talking with friends of everyday things.

And yet, as much as Enoch hoped it would distract him, the task force and the absent Ben kept coming to mind. After another pint, then another, he knew too well he wasn't acting right proper. A man with a brew ought to have laughed and jested, but he felt strange and sad.

"You okay?" Orla asked when he set by his glass half-drunk. "You don't seem too happy."

He laughed, shaky. "I dint think a brew or two would make it so." He pushed his fingers through his hair. "It's all much these days. My work, the taskforce. It's all...nothing is as it should be, and I cannit do anything to help it."

To his surprise, Mack raised his glass again. "To feeling useless."

"Mack..." Orla murmured.

"You're not useless," Enoch agreed. "You help with the streams and the TRI and—"

"And I'll never be more than a desk jockey." Mack put down his glass hard enough beer slopped over the rim.

Enoch put his head to one side. "A what?"

"Mack, you don't—"

Mack waved his woman's words away. "I *do.*" He stared across the table at Enoch. His eyes were too shiny and his face red. "When they brought me into the TRI, d'you know what I thought? I thought they'd picked me because I knew so much history, so I'd be able to blend in and go back in time and see everything."

Enoch winced. Many people who came through the TRI wanted that. Many who joined the TRI did so, hoping for it. Mack had never spoken of such things, even if Enoch had guessed that reading and researching day in and out bored him. "And you cannit?"

Mack squeezed his right eye shut, and when he opened it, it was glowing. A machine replacement for an eye that had never worked, Enoch knew. Modern technology would never be allowed in the past.

"This thing," Mack said, bitter. "This thing stops me."

"And it doesn't get any less creepy when you turn it into a light show," Orla said, making a face.

Mack pressed his eye shut again to dim it. "I don't see why I should be penalised because I have a visual aid." He snatched his ale and drank a mouthful. "I don't know why they— What's wrong with—" He gave a great breath and drained the rest of his glass.

Orla sighed and smoothed his silver-struck dark hair. "You know why." She sounded like she'd heard Mack's grievances many a time. He leaned into her, and she pressed her brow to his. "If they could let you, they would."

"It's not all good, being there," Enoch offered. "Leastways, you don't have to catch your monstrous chickens here."

They both smiled, but only a little.

"See?" Orla said fondly. "No chicken hunting."

"Or when someone is hunted as a witch," Enoch added. "That's no good at all."

Both of them stared at him. "You hunted witches?" Mack said, his eyebrows rising high.

Enoch blinked at them. Oh. Right. Aye. No speaking of the witch trials, lest more questions were asked. There were few enough trials, and if they put together what they knew of him, they might find the lies and send him whence he came. It seemed the drink had done more than making him forlorn. "No?"

"But you said witch-hunting," Orla said. "Did you see them?"

Enoch shook his head. "Heard of them." He took a hasty drink to give himself a moment to think. If they believed him a hunter, they would think ill of him, but if they went seeking for the trials, it would be another kind of trouble. "They come through my town."

Orla shuddered. "Even thinking about people being burned at the stake..."

"Faggots and fire," Enoch remembered. "With luck, they would strangle you first."

"Your idea of luck isn't like mine." Mack's face twisted up and he raised a hand. "I thought you were from some time in the 1700s. The history books said most of the witch trials ended earlier."

"Fut..." Enoch muttered under his breath. Mack always knew too much. "There are always those who would try and bring back the old ways. Hunt as they might, like as not they never found a witch."

"Fuckers!" Mack declared. "S'rude to barbecue a lady!"

Orla snickered along with Enoch. "I think," she said as she pried Mack's drink out of his hand, "that's a sign someone's had a bit too much."

"You've had a bit too much." Mack groped for his drink. "I wasn't finished that. I'm not wasting it…"

Enoch was relieved. If Mack was drunk enough, he wouldn't think on anything they'd said. He might even forget anything was mentioned of witch trials and the like. "You should let him finish his brew. Best not to waste it."

"See?" Mack said smugly to Orla, his eyes half-closed. "Enoch agrees with me." He groped into his pocket with his free hand. "I want a picture."

Orla groaned. "Now? At the end of the night? With my face half melted off?"

Mack pressed a kiss to her pink-painted cheek. "Still beautiful."

Orla's face went warm and soft. "Oh, *fine.*" She beckoned to Enoch. "Come over here. Time to make your groupies jealous."

Enoch sprawled over them as Mack held out his bud. "We'll be gone afore any of them can find us?"

"'Course!" Mack tapped the bud. "Unless they live next door or something." He kissed the top of Enoch's head. "An' if they come, we'll fight them off."

Orla squeezed Enoch's shoulder as she helped him sit up. "He's not wrong."

Mack pulled up the image in front of them. Enoch stared at it. It was still strange to see himself like that, all tousle-headed and wide-eyed.

"I'm smiling like a madman," he complained.

"That's how you always smile," Mack said. He moved his fingers across the letter board too fast for Enoch to follow. "And away it goes! Off into the world."

Orla nudged his drink towards him. "And now, you're going to finish your drink, and we're going to see Enoch to his hotel."

"And have another brew there?" Enoch suggested.

"Yes!" Mack crowed.

"No."

Mack turned his eyes to her, wide and pleading. "Yes?"

"If you can walk in a straight line from here to the pod."

Within the half hour, they were in the pod, the horseless and driverless carriage without wheels favoured by all people now. Mack sulked in his corner. He had reeled his way to the pod, his last drink denied him. In truth, Enoch was relieved. Company was well and good, but he seldom stayed awake so long after dark.

"Will you be heading to the TRI in the morning?" Orla asked when they came to a stop outside his hotel.

Enoch nodded. "It would be too much excitement to stay out longer. I'm not one who does well in cities. The compound is better. Quiet. Less people."

"Boring," Mack said gloomily. "All closed up with nowhere to go."

Orla took Enoch's hand and squeezed it. Her nails were all bright colours. "Ignore the drunk baby in the corner. You can go wherever you feel comfortable going." She smiled at him, and he could see some of the reasons why Mack loved her well. "Actually, if you're free on Wednesday, do you fancy a trip to the beach with us? Mack and I managed to coordinate a day off so we can take advantage of the good weather."

Enoch drew up, surprised. "You would have me come?"

"You seem like the kind of person who needs a bit more fun in your life." She leaned closer. "And if we're lucky, we'll get to see some very cute people wearing very little clothing."

"Perv," Mack grumbled from the corner, but he struggled to mask his grin.

Enoch laughed. "You make it sound inviting," he agreed. "If weather permits, I would be happy to join you." He bowed over her hand and kissed it. It made her laugh and in turn made him smile as he got out the pod. "Safe travels and rest well."

"You too."

He stepped away and watched their pod draw away, then turned and went into his hotel.

It was a grand and expensive place. Better, Sabine said, for his privacy. They feared his admirers might try to reach him, and a hotel with a secured door made them feel better. It was big and bright, like a lord's house only shinier.

His room was high up on the fifteenth floor. An elevator—a gleaming box of gold and mirrors—carried him all the way there. Such a strange thing, but better than many hundreds of stairs after too much ale.

The halls were all quiet as he walked to his room, fumbling with the card that served as a key. It chirped as he slipped it into the lock and the wee light turned green, so he let himself in.

He meandered into the bathroom to take a piss and was washing off his hands when there was a click in the room outside, like a door shutting, but he had shut the door. The lights all went out at once and all. Mayhap it was the technology playing silly buggers, but he had lived too long to be unwary.

Enoch took a step out of the bathroom, stomach all knots, then another.

"Is someone there?"

He reached for the lights, but a hand caught his wrist and another hand closed over his mouth, stifling his cry.

"Don't scream." A breath in his ear.

Enoch froze, heart thundering. He knew the voice.

It was Ben Sanders.

Chapter Eleven

The lights were on again. Once Enoch had closed the curtains, Ben raised the lights. They didn't need someone from the opposite block peeking in. It had been risky enough walking into the hotel, praying their security cameras weren't good enough to pick up on his camo-patch.

"What in God's name are you doing here?" Enoch's voice shook. He was still by the window, away from Ben and the door. Ben didn't blame him.

"Enoch—"

"You were in the past," Enoch snarled. "They said you jumped, that you were gone, that they would not find you, and now, you come here?"

Ben moved a step closer to him. "They knew I'd be back."

"No." Enoch stormed towards him. "They *hoped*, but they could not *know*." He struck Ben hard in the chest. "How *dare* you come!" His face was twisted in anger. "I need only call, and they'll come for you."

"Enoch—"

"I could bring them down on you!" Enoch's voice broke. "You would deserve it!"

Ben stared at him, stricken. "I didn't— E..."

By the half-light, Enoch's eyes were too bright, and his face crumpled. "I thought you were *gone*," he snarled, but there was more than anger in his words. "You went and done something stupid *again* and left me here on my own!"

If Enoch had punched him, it would have hurt less.

"I'm sorry," he said quietly. "Fuck, I'm sorry. I shouldn't have done that."

Enoch bared his teeth at him. "You knew where I was, you shit!" He beat his fist against Ben's chest. "You *knew* who I was with! You saw me walk into the building with them and you did this and you *knew* they would see me."

Ben's stomach dropped like a rock. In the panic of his flight, he hadn't even thought. "And you thought I was gone..." He caught Enoch's hand in his, holding it tightly. "I'm sorry. I didn't think. I didn't even remember..."

"Aye, your watchword." Enoch wrenched himself away, taking gulping breaths.

Ben reached out to him, but shit, he was right. Forgotten rules of time travel—lost in a haze of drink—and a forgotten multitool were the very reasons Enoch was in the wrong time.

"How am I to keep your secrets," Enoch's voice was flat, "if you will show them my true face like that?" He shuddered. "You, of all people, know what it is to be left helpless, not knowing what has happened."

Ben's stomach clenched. He remembered being closed alone in the dark, his world ripped away, and the terror it brought. "Shit..." He reached out, almost sighing in relief when Enoch grudgingly took his hand. "I really scared you, didn't I?"

Enoch stared up at him. His face was waxen and stiff, but his eyes gave him away. Ben could remember seeing the expression on his face only once before, with the rope at his neck and the pyre at his feet. "Dunt do it again."

"Shit," Ben whispered. "Shit." He pulled Enoch into his arms. "I'm sorry. I'm so sorry."

Enoch clung onto him, his fingers sinking into his ribs. "You shit."

"I deserve that." Ben nuzzled Enoch's hair. "I'm back now. I'm back and I'm here."

Enoch drew away enough to gaze up at him, and then he reached up, caught the back of Ben's head, and pulled Ben's mouth to meet his. Ben wanted to argue they didn't have time, there was so much going on, but Jesus Christ, they had come so close to losing each other and everything they'd worked towards.

Ben wasn't sure which of them opened their mouth first, but Enoch's tongue darted against his, and he stifled a groan. Nimble hands were on his body, pulling his shirt from his belt. Enoch spread his hands up Ben's back and dragged them down.

"Off?" Ben suggested hoarsely.

Enoch stepped away enough but didn't wait for Ben to pull at his shirt. He wrenched Ben's jacket off his shoulders, over his arms, and pulled it tight, pinioning Ben's arms behind him. Ben's pulse fluttered as Enoch leaned up, baring his teeth. "You owe me something."

"Sorry isn't enough?" Ben hissed as Enoch twisted his hand in his jacket, pulling it hard against his arms. Pleasant pain shot through Ben's arms, and he caught his breath as those teeth were pressed to his throat.

"What do you think?"

Ben laughed breathlessly at the ceiling. God, he'd missed this. Everyone in his life had treated him as if he would shatter like glass until he met Enoch. "No?"

The press of Enoch's teeth, tight enough to leave bruises, made it more difficult to breathe, and hell, the giddiness only made things feel much better. Ben could almost swear he felt every pulse of blood through his body, and he arched his neck against Enoch's mouth.

Months, years since he'd felt those hands and that mouth with no fear of someone walking in on them. Last time, it had been on the floor of a bathroom in the TRI, Lysander talking into his earpiece with no idea he had interrupted anything. Hands and mouth and cock and everything.

When Enoch drew away, Ben swayed where he stood, his fingers twitching, and his legs unsteady under him. Enoch must've felt it too because he tore Ben's jacket from his arms, let it fall, and caught him under the elbows, drawing him into the dimly lit room.

"I shouldn't stay..." he heard himself murmur.

"No." Enoch drew him around, and his legs knocked against the end of the bed. His shirt was gone, and a hot mouth was on his chest, tongue and teeth and catching one nipple and pulling sharp enough to make him grab at Enoch's hair. The lick was soothing after the bite. Enoch's breath was warm on the damp skin. "No more talking, Master Ben."

Ben shivered in anticipation. He knew that tone. He tugged Enoch's hair, dragging Enoch's mouth up to his. Enoch rose on his toes, tongue plunging between Ben's lips, stealing what breath he had left. He worked fast on Ben's trousers, shoving them down and wrapping callused, rough fingers on Ben's throbbing cock.

Ben fumbled for Enoch's shirt, pulling at it, but Enoch caught his wrist.

"Not yet," he warned, raising his head. He stroked Ben's cock slowly, tightening then easing his grip. "I'm not yet happy with you."

"I kn—"

Enoch moved his hand from Ben's wrist to his mouth. "I telt you no more talking," Enoch growled, and Ben's breath hitched. Rough fingers ran along his lips, and Ben couldn't help but suck on them, a wordless offer and invitation.

He could tell Enoch understood from the way his grip froze on Ben's cock.

"You would, eh?" Enoch slowly started thrusting two fingers into Ben's mouth, then matched the strokes on Ben's cock. Ben groaned softly against Enoch's fingers, imagining Enoch's mouth on him or his mouth on Enoch.

Enoch drew his fingers free, trailing strings of saliva along Ben's cheek as Enoch kissed him again.

"On your back," Enoch murmured. "Trews off."

Ben nodded, but his hands were all over the place. Want and need and everything else. He made a small, angry sound, struggling to shake himself free and heard Enoch's mischievous chuckle a second before Enoch yanked his trousers to his ankles.

"Not so hard, eh?" The words were punctuated by a brief and startling suck on Ben's cock that made Ben swear out loud. Enoch rose in front of him and even by the faint light, Ben could see the smug smirk. "I telt you," Enoch repeated, spreading his palm on Ben's chest, "no more talking."

He shoved hard, and Ben's knees caught the edge of the bed. He fell, landing sprawled on the mattress, his feet tangled in his trousers. Enoch pressed his foot on the tangle of cloth, holding him there, even as Ben pushed himself up on his elbows.

"On your back," Enoch said quietly. "Do I have to tell you again?"

Ben darted his tongue along his lower lip. God, he'd forgotten how much Enoch liked to push. And he'd even managed to forget how much he liked to be pushed. Two years, almost three, since they'd been this close, alone. Too many things to think about, too much in his life, but not now.

He lay at once, spreading his arms obediently.

"And close your eyes."

Ben almost groaned, but obeyed, even with the rustle of clothing being removed, falling heavy on the floor. The bed shifted under him, right side, close, but not close enough to touch, though Enoch's heat was so damn close. Christ, the bastard was trailing a hand maybe half an inch from his body, so near the warmth and the movement to raise goosebumps across his skin, could tell, as if the son of bitch hadn't done it a dozen times before and kept him right on the edge just because he could and he liked it.

Enoch squeezed lightly on Ben's throat. "You scared me," he murmured. Ben remembered enough to keep quiet, but he could nod. Enoch tightened his fingers. "You knew where I was when you done it. You knew who was with me."

Ben pressed his neck towards Enoch's palm, offering penance.

Enoch leaned over him and kissed him on the mouth. "I cannit keep fooling them." His words brushed against Ben's lips. "Not if you do such things." A little more pressure was enough to make Ben gasp for air. "You'll be more careful."

Ben nodded, drawing thin quivering breaths.

"Good." The mattress shifted and the pressure on his neck eased as Enoch moved behind his head. Ben gulped in breaths of air until fingers cupped his chin. "Open."

Ben laughed breathlessly, tilted his head, and parted his lips. Enoch's favourite from every angle, he thought, darting out his tongue as the tip of Enoch's cock brushed against his lips. Salty precum coated his tongue as he swirled it over the head a split second before Enoch thrust into Ben's mouth.

He closed his mouth around him. Enoch was small all over, but Christ, he was vigorous. He slid a hand under Ben's neck, squeezing as he rocked his hips. Ben swallowed greedily, licking, raking lightly with his teeth, all and anything he could think of as Enoch fucked his mouth.

No words. Not a sound except his breathing and his hand and the heat of him against Ben's tongue. Ben wanted to reach for him, pull him closer, but Enoch was right. He owed him something for the shit he'd put him through, and if it meant going without so Enoch could get off, so be it. Even if every thrust and the salt on his tongue and the huffed breaths and the grip on his neck was making his own cock throb demandingly for someone's touch.

Ben curled his fingers into the covers, angling his head even further, sucking and licking at Enoch until Enoch squeezed his neck painfully hard. His hips pounded against Ben's swollen lips, his cock pulsing against Ben's tongue, and Ben swallowed again, greedily, as Enoch came with a sharp gasp.

The grip on Ben's neck loosened, and Enoch braced his other hand on Ben's chest.

"Sweet Jesus..." He took a deep breath. "Fut..."

Ben said nothing, licking lazily as if he could milk every last drop of cum out of his lover. Enoch was kneading at his chest, and Ben had to curl his fingers into the covers more tightly and force his eyes shut to keep from disappointing him.

Enoch didn't draw away. Instead, he leaned forward to let Ben continue to suck and lick at him. Ben had to fight a grin. Always the same, wasn't he? A mouth on his knob, limp or hard, and Enoch loved every second of it. If it was limp, it didn't usually stay that way for long.

"You're doing as you're telt," Enoch murmured.

Ben hummed then sucked him again, fluttering his tongue across the tip. He hissed aloud when Enoch pinched and tugged both his nipples sharply enough to send a shockwave through him. If his mouth hadn't been occupied, Ben knew he'd have sworn.

Enoch laughed hoarsely. "I almost had you there, eh?" He spread one hand and slid it right down Ben's chest to his belly. He was so close to touching now, and Ben almost forgot to keep his mouth working. "My good lad."

Ben hesitated, then stroked Enoch's thigh. When Enoch didn't rebuff him, he moved the other, running his palm over Enoch's arse. To his surprise and relief, that wasn't rebuffed either. Enoch even made things easier, leaning over him, bracing his arm by Ben's hip.

"Make it good for me," Enoch murmured, his face so close his breath was a warm ripple on Ben's skin. The pulse went straight to Ben's already-hard cock, and he groaned again as he slid his fingers up, tracing the crease of Enoch's arse.

He'd barely grazed a fingertip closer when Enoch closed his mouth on Ben's aching prick. Ben grabbed at his thigh, squeezing, and felt more than heard Enoch's chuckle. Jesus Christ, he'd forgotten what a distracting tease Enoch could be. Well, two could play at that game...

No lube in reach, a persistent demanding little bugger on top though...

He pulled one hand away and tilted his head away from Enoch long enough to suck and slather two fingers with saliva. If he kept his fingers in his mouth a few seconds too long, echoing the way his hips were rocking against Enoch's mouth, that was his problem.

"Forgetting something?" Enoch's mouth wasn't where it was meant to be.

Blindly, Ben opened his mouth, seeking out Enoch's prick again. He almost laughed aloud as it slid across his cheeks and lips. Bobbing for dicks. Always fun. As he lipped at Enoch's cock, he trailed a path with the edge of his hand, then slid his two moistened fingers along the crease of Enoch's arse and pressed against his opening.

Enoch shuddered as Ben fingered him, his mouth closing on Ben's erection again, his breathing unsteady. Ben wasn't surprised. It wasn't Enoch's favourite, but when he wanted it, he knew Ben could do it right, and all Ben had to do was curl his fingers and skim across his prostate and Enoch's whole body twitched.

It was hard to focus on it, on stroking right, on not pressing too hard or too far or making Enoch tense up when there was a mouth on his cock, sucking and licking like the best lollipop in all the land. And a cock in his face as well to be sucked and licked too, still half-soft, nowhere near hard, but Enoch liked, and if Enoch liked, Enoch was getting.

Ben wrapped his other arm over Enoch's thigh, hugging it as he tried to ignore the need to hump against Enoch's hot mouth and try try try to keep his fingers stroking right and his mouth closing and swallowing and licking and tasting.

Wasn't working, not when Enoch was sucking him deep and pumping against his face and writhing against his fingers, and Ben's world was dark and narrowed to the heat of Enoch, the taste, the feel, and Christ, his mouth! His mouth and his warmth and he couldn't stop himself moving, pushing up, demanding, begging, thrusting against Enoch's waiting mouth, stroking so deep and shuddering hard when he came.

Enoch jerked his head away, laughing and spluttering. "Jesus, Ben!"

Ben dropped his head back, Enoch's cock swinging back and forth across his lips. "Fuck..." he groaned and, out of sheer vindictiveness, stroked his fingers inside Enoch the way he'd planned all along and burst out in breathless laughter when Enoch gave a strangled moan and headbutted him on the thigh.

Chapter Twelve

Ben was still asleep when the door chimed.

Enoch had been watching him, wondering at the new lines scored by his eyes. Close upon three years alone had been hard on him. It was true Enoch had seen him at least once a month, but in the coffee bar, he always wore his mask. It hid so much of him.

The clothes too. They covered the way the weight had fallen from his lover. There were bones showing where they should not have been. His arms, folded beneath his head on the pillow, were too thin.

The moment the door chimed, Ben was up and out of the bed, reaching for his clothes.

"Wait," Enoch said, sitting up in the sheets.

Ben was wrenching on his trousers. "I shouldn't have stayed—"

"Ben, it's food."

There was a long silence.

Ben peered at him. "What?"

Enoch propped his arms upon his knees. "You got thin. I would have you eat something before I see you on your way." The door chimed again, so he rose and picked up his underthings. "Stay out of sight, lest I'm mistaken."

He knew he needn't check to be sure Ben was hiding as he opened the door.

There was no one there but a cart. Enoch touched the glowing button beside the hatch, which slid open. The tray inside was stacked with all manner of hot breakfast foods. Enoch carried it into the room and set it on the table close by the window.

"I didn't know they made food this late," Ben murmured. He stood on the far side of the bed, his shirt clutched in his hand.

"In this manner of place?" Enoch grinned at him. "I would wager I could ask them for anything, and it would be done without question."

Ben set by his shirt. "I need to go after."

"Best be gone afore dawn." He carried a couple of plates to the bed. "Here."

"In the bed?"

Enoch widened his eyes to seem as saintly as he might. "I am from times gone by. Should I know better?"

Ben's tense face broke into a smile. "You're still an idiot," he said as he pushed his trousers off and then climbed into the bed.

"And you the fool that saved my life," Enoch said happily. He set his plate aside, then went to pour a cup of hot sweet tea for each of them. By the time he returned to the bed, Ben was already halfway through a bacon sandwich. "Hungry, eh?"

Ben shifted his food into his cheek so he might put out his tongue.

Enoch snickered as he climbed onto the bed and offered one of the cups. "I *am* wise sometimes."

"Yeah, oh wise chicken-hat man." Ben snorted, taking the cup. "I saw what your groupies are up to."

"It pleases them." He paused, waiting until Ben had taken a bite of his sandwich. "I telt Mack they should call it Noch's Cocks."

Ben choked, mirth smothered by coughing. He set aside his cup to thump himself on the chest, his eyes streaming with tears. "Oh, you arse!"

Enoch unfolded his leg to knock his calf against Ben's knee. "He dint know how to tell me what it meant. I swear he went red as a berry."

Ben shuddered with amusement as he wiped his eyes. "I bet. Poor Mack. He never was the brightest candle on the cake." He sniffed and cleared his throat, then took a sup of his tea. "I saw you were out with him."

"As you're here, I guessed you got my message about it."

Ben blinked foolishly at him. "Eh?"

"What eh? You dint get the message I sent?"

"My Leaf picked up a proximity notification from the picture Mack took at the bar." Ben flushed, guilty. "I got to the bar maybe two minutes before you left. Followed you in a pod and skimmed the hotel registry onto my Leaf to find your room."

Enoch gazed at him fondly. "You made it a lot more work for yourself."

Ben had the grace to be contrite. "I've been—it's been weird." He took another bite of his sandwich and asked, "Do you have anything new about him? Mack?"

"He's as he seems," he admitted with a sigh. "I know you think he has some part in what happened to your pa, but he never speaks of any such thing, not even when in his cups."

Ben's brow creased. "Shit."

Enoch reached out to pat Ben's knee. "He and his woman will take me out again soon. It might yet happen."

Ben sighed and covered Enoch's hand with his own, squeezing Enoch's fingers. "I'm sorry I put you in this position. I was so sure he knew...God, I don't even know what. I thought if—when—"

"You speak as if you made me go," Enoch murmured, putting his plate aside. "You only asked. I might have said no."

Ben raised his eyes to Enoch's. "You're stuck in the TRI, though. You—I put you in a cage on a wild guess. You must hate—"

Enoch moved to his knees and leaned closer to take Ben's face between his hands. "If I chose to leave, I could and I would," he said as gently as he could. Ben had lost so much already and was so afeard to lose more. "It might seem a cage, but I'm no prisoner." He kissed Ben firmly. He tasted of tea and ketchup, and Enoch licked bacon grease from his lip. "Would I keep you by me if I hated you?"

Ben's smile was frail and false. "Sorry."

Enoch kissed it away, cradling Ben's head. "My poor little cock..."

That earned him a brief chuckle.

Enoch sank to sit on his heels, stroking his thumb along Ben's cheek. "If you think we are done with him, you need only ask, and I can make myself free."

Ben closed his eyes, tilting his head into Enoch's touch. He covered Enoch's hand with his own. "God, I'd like that." He breathed out a warm gust on Enoch's bare wrist. "But right now, he's the only link we have."

Enoch drew Ben's head down and pressing their brows together. "If it'll bring you peace, I will stay as long as you need me to. It's little enough payment for you saving my life."

Ben jerked his head tightly. "I—it's—I have to know."

Enoch stroked the nape of Ben's neck, offering what comfort he could. "It pains me you're alone in all of this."

There was something in the way Ben froze, a rabbit in a trap. "Ah."

Enoch sat back again, frowning. "You have someone else minding you?"

"Not...exactly." Ben picked up his cup of tea and turned it in his hands. "You—do you remember how we met?"

Enoch rolled his eyes. "Some daft bugger in his cups roaming through a gate he should not have." A thought came upon him, recalling why he had been so worried. "You just went for another walk in times gone by."

Ben shifted awkwardly, staring into his cup.

"You brung someone else back and all?"

"Not brought!" Ben exclaimed, indignant. "I didn't do a thing. The mad old bat followed me. I think she thought I was a fairy or spirit or something."

Enoch kept his peace for three ticks of the clock, then gave a great shout of laughter. "Jesu! The TRI do so many missions with none coming after them, and you cannit even keep your eyes open to notice an old woman walking behind you?"

"Enoch, this is serious!"

Enoch rocked forward, slapping his hands on his knees. "Aye, indeed. And you dint just put her where she come from?"

Ben grimaced. "She wouldn't go. I opened the gate, told her to bugger off, but she wouldn't. I tried spiking her tea and tossing her through, but she told me it smelled like cat's water and poured it out to make her own."

"God have mercy..." Enoch pressed his fist to his mouth to stifle the mirth. "Never take food given by the Gentry."

Ben gaped at him. "What?"

"Old wives tales." Enoch cocked his head. Ben's mood and wariness made a good deal more sense. Best not to let him brood too deeply on it. He always took such things to heart. "A pity you are so terrible a time traveller. You brung one person from the past. That could be an accident, but two?" He clicked his tongue and sighed mournfully. "Best you stop doing it."

Ben knocked his leg against Enoch's knee. "It's not funny."

Enoch waved a hand from side to side between them. "Mayhap. Did you dress as a devil and throw your wee fireballs and steal this baggage from under the nose of them that would kill her for being a witch?"

Ben could not help but smile at that. "No. That's just you."

Enoch patted his thigh. "That's all right then. Not so funny, but all right."

"But I'm pretty sure this woman's an actual witch."

Sometimes, his precious Ben made matters too simple. "You must have called her to you with your sinful temptations." Enoch playacted horror. "You are the Diaval after all."

Ben dunked his fingers in his tea and flicked it in Enoch's face. "Shut up."

Enoch grinned and patted Ben's thigh. "So, Master Lucifer, what will you do with your witch?"

Ben held the cup threateningly over Enoch's head. "Don't make me use this…"

Enoch considered him, then the cup, then the bed that would not be his to clean and flung himself at Ben. Lukewarm tea spilled all over them, and Ben made a sound of dismay as he landed upon the remains of his forgotten food.

"My sandwich!"

Enoch sat astride him, beaming. "You should have et it faster."

Ben swatted his leg. "I don't know why I like you."

All it took was a roll of Enoch's hips, and Ben's eyes closed up and he groaned.

"That?" Enoch said, all innocence.

Ben cracked his eyes open to slits. "I'm meant to be leaving."

Enoch made a distracted sound. He'd seen many interesting—and at first shocking—streams since last he saw Ben. There were things in them he'd wanted to try for months. He rocked his hips again, pressing his hands to Ben's chest as he moved.

"Enoch…"

"Your debt int paid yet." Ben was growing hard against him, and that in turn was making his cock harden in his shorts. Skin to skin would be better, but if he moved, he might let Ben escape too soon, and he was having none of that.

Ben slid his hands up Enoch's thighs, which were framing his hips. "I don't think I'm meant to feel sexy with a bacon sandwich stuck to my ribs," he said with a rueful chuckle.

"Yet here you are," Enoch countered, raising himself enough to draw Ben's cock up beneath him. He stroked it a couple of times, then lowered himself to grind his hips against Ben's again. "If you must fuss, I'll lick the bacon and sauce from you after."

Ben made a hoarse sound, and his grip tightened. "You ass."

Enoch tossed his head, rocking hard against him. "That I'd lick you? I would and every inch at that." A pleasant shiver passed through him as Ben grabbed at his hips, both of them rubbing against each other. "I've heard tell"—Enoch kept his eyes on Ben's—"of chocolate and cream and all other foods that might be played with."

"Yeah?" Ben's face was flushed, his grip tight.

"Mm." Enoch pressed his hands on Ben's chest and leaned over him. "I watched streams of them. All manner of interesting things." He grazed his lips over Ben's, not quite touching. "I'd tie your hands so you could not stop me, then lick honey from every inch of you."

"Fuck, Enoch!" Ben slid one hand up Enoch's back and pulled him down. Their mouths crashed together, and Ben's tongue slid between his lips, thrusting as wantonly as Ben's hips were.

It took no trouble at all for him to pinch one of Ben's nipples between his fingers, making Ben hiss into the kiss, making his hips jolt, pushing his cock hard against Enoch's. Ben was careless, shameless and demanding and Jesu, Enoch's cock was throbbing with want of him.

"Fuck..." Ben breathed, pressing his head against the covers. "Fuck..."

Enoch's heart was beating fast, and he pushed himself up over Ben, hands on his shoulders. "Look to me," he commanded as strong as he could. When Ben's eyes stayed closed, Enoch caught his throat. "Ben, look to me."

Ben's eyes flew open and his lips parted. He pushed his throat to Enoch's hand, one of his own hands still at Enoch's hip, the other raking over Enoch's back, catching on scars, making Enoch draw sharp breaths betwixt his teeth.

"You'll look at me," Enoch breathed and started moving his hips. Not just rocking. No, like in those streams, moving in a grinding circle, cock to cock, even with the shorts between them, his eyes on Ben's. He moved one hand, pushed his shorts lower enough to bring skin to skin. Ben's fingers dug hard into his back, and his cock was leaking already.

"When this is done," Enoch breathed, moving his hips in tighter circles. "I'll have you abed for so many days, you'll be spent." Ben nodded, breathing hard. "I'll have my hands on you, my mouth, all I will, and you'll take it and you'll demand it and, Christ, I'll give you all you wish..."

Both Ben's hands were on his arse, both of them rubbing against each other urgently, slick with sweat and cum. Enoch caught both their cocks in his hand, stroking them against the other, watching Ben's face as Ben's breathing hitched again and his hips jerked hard and cum spattered over his own skin.

The pleasure on his face, the heat of his cum and the throb of his cock was enough to let Enoch follow, his own cock pulsing in his hand. He sagged forward, one hand to Ben's chest, sated, his cum pooling with Ben's on the rising and falling hollow of Ben's belly.

"Fuck me," Ben breathed out. "Did someone let you watch porn?"

Enoch ducked his head, fighting a laugh. "Only a little. You could tell?"

"New moves," Ben said, patting his arse.

Enoch leaned in to kiss him again. "And you liked it well enough?"

Ben combed his fingers through Enoch's hair. "I wouldn't say no to more."

Enoch darted his tongue out to lick Ben's lower lip, tasting the salt of his sweat. "One day soon," he promised. He pushed himself up, sliding down Ben's body. "Now, though, I have a promise to keep you." He dabbed his tongue at the hollow of Ben's throat. "A licking, I think..."

"Enoch!" Ben caught his hair.

Enoch stared at him, wide-eyed. "To get you clean, naught more."

"Bullshit."

"Maybe." Enoch tugged himself free then lowered his head further and dragged his tongue through the cum on Ben's belly. Ben caught his hair again and dragged him up. "You dunt want to be cleansed?"

Ben sat to meet him. "I don't want you to start something we know we can't finish," he said, pulling Enoch closer to kiss him again. It took no effort at all to have him flat on his back again, chest to chest, their bodies sliding against each other.

For once, Ben rolled him over and pinned him in place with his own body.

"I can't stay."

Enoch hooked one leg about his hips, holding him there for but a moment, and drew Ben's mouth to his again. "Allow me this," he murmured against Ben's lips. "Before we have to part again."

Ben raised himself on the hand pressing into the covers by Enoch's head. "Are you trying to guilt-sex me?"

Enoch only widened his eyes, then broke, laughing. "Aye, maybe a little." He reached between them and swept his fingers across Ben's belly, then examined them. "You know I like the taste of us."

"Because you're a kinky sod." Ben pushed Enoch's thigh from his hip and knelt between Enoch's splayed legs. "Three licks and you're done."

Enoch sat, grinning. "Then I best make them count." He shifted to his knees then took Ben's hips between his hands and lowered his head.

The first lick dragged from the top of Ben's cock all the way to his navel and swirled there. Ben caught his hair, not restraining this time, but guiding. The second lick went back and forth, side to side, gathering every smear Enoch could find.

The third, in darting dabs, journeyed from navel to flick over nipple, to trace over collarbone, to tease earlobe, and finally to smooth along Ben's lower lip. Ben stifled a groan into Enoch's mouth, sucking greedily on his tongue, tasting their cum fresh from Enoch's lips.

Enoch nibbled Ben's lip and sucked it gently before drawing away. "Enough?"

Ben stroked his thumb along Enoch's jaw. "For now, it'll have to be." He climbed off the bed and reached behind him to brush the remains of his ruined breakfast from his skin.

Enoch sprawled out on the bed and watched as Ben dressed and put himself in order. He wanted to demand Ben stay or that he could go with him, but he had a job to do. Until Ben knew what had come to pass with his father, it would torment him. Enoch would do anything to help him find peace, even if it meant parting the ways for a time.

"We can't do the coffee shop anymore," Ben said quietly as he fastened his jacket. "They'll be watching for me there."

"We can find a new place." Enoch smiled suddenly. "That inn by the docks. It's close by you, int it? You said you had a prox...proxity?"

"Proximity alert." Ben ran his fingers through his short hair, smoothing it. "I have one of my warehouses near there."

Enoch sat up in the sheets. "I'll tell them at the TRI I like it there. That I'd go for a brew once in a while." He wanted to smile, but it was hard when he had to hide his heart and his self so much. "I miss you."

Ben stooped over the bed and kissed him again. It was gentler this time. "I miss you too." He knocked his brow against Enoch's. "We'll arrange something. You can send me a message."

Enoch nodded, sitting back, knowing if he stayed close, he'd catch Ben's wrist again and never let him go. "You'd best be off. You have a witch to take care of."

"Yeah." Ben tried to smile, but it was as forced as Enoch's own.

He drew a small patch from his pocket and placed it against his temple. His features seemed to shift. The skin was darkening. The mask settled into an unfamiliar face, so flawless Enoch would never have recognised him.

"Take care of yourself, okay?"

Enoch could only nod. He held himself up until Ben was out and closed the door, then sagged upon the covers, pressing the heels of his hands to his eyes. One day, it would be done with and they could live as normal people would, but until then...

Until then, he had work to do.

Chapter Thirteen

The woman was standing at one of the uncovered windows when Ben got out of the pod at the warehouse serving as his latest base. She was barely visible in the hazy morning light and retreated as soon as she saw him.

Ben sighed and headed into the side alleys leading to the concealed rear door.

It had been reckless and selfish to leave her alone, but with everything that had happened, he'd needed to see Enoch. Any other thought had gone out the window. He needed to know he hadn't screwed up and that they were okay.

He couldn't decide if he was more relieved or disappointed she hadn't smashed a window and made her escape. No. Not escape. She wasn't a prisoner. He'd told her he would send her home, and she'd refused. That wasn't his fault. Yes, it was his fault she'd ended up there in the first place, but he couldn't undo it if she wouldn't let him.

It didn't help she was as wary as a scared cat, as if she expected him to pick her up and drag her to the gate. He'd considered it once or twice, but in the couple of days since he'd returned, she'd never let him get close enough.

He should have opened the gate when she had fainted. Opened it and rolled her straight through into the circle and let her think it was all a dream.

Only he hadn't. He'd been shitting himself because he had some mad old bag from the past in the present, and he could imagine all the extra trouble he'd be in because of it. By the time he realised he could put her back, she was conscious and staring at him.

He slipped in through the coded door and the second level of security. Once the door was closed, he shut down his camo-patch and headed across the factory floor and up the stairs to his temporary home.

Once, it had probably been the boss's office. Now, it was an open plan with a camp bed and a couch and windows thickly covered with paper. A small kitchen area in the next room over might have been a staff canteen once, but Ben rarely used it. There were enough places to eat nearby. Still, the cupboards had enough food to keep his unexpected guest from starving.

She waited for him there, holding two cups—well, one mug and one chipped tin cup he usually kept his spare screws in—in her bony hands. Ben stopped at the top of the stairs, gazing across the floor at her.

"I made tea, I think, with the magic jug." She held out one of the cups. "I found strange bags of leaf. It smelled of tea."

Ben approached her carefully. "You didn't need to do that."

Her wrinkles shifted as she smiled nervously. "I wished to. For your favour."

Ben gestured towards the next room. "Will you sit with me?"

To his surprise, she agreed.

They sat in awkward silence for several minutes at either end of the couch. For want of anything better to do, Ben sipped the tea. It was a little stronger than he liked, but with enough sugar and milk to taste. She must have watched him making his own to realise those things he liked to add.

She was watching him, carefully.

"It's good." God, that sounded lame. "The tea. Thank you."

She gave him another cautious smile. "I'm glad."

He stared into his cup. There were so many things he wanted to ask and to say. For someone from the past, the world probably seemed completely alien now. It had to be terrifying.

He could remember how badly Enoch took the change at first. He'd railed against Ben, furious and afraid. It took him several days to recall the rope Ben had cut from his neck, saving him from the lynch mob bent on killing him. It took Ben a lot longer to forgive himself.

If only he hadn't screwed up his first solo jump.

He'd messed up Enoch's life so badly. Saved it too, but if he hadn't cocked up, he'd never have needed to save it in the first place.

This time it was different, though.

The woman had followed him. She had chosen to come and to stay, despite not knowing where or when she was.

"Don't you want to go home?" Ben finally asked.

Her dark eyes were fixed on his face. "I have known of the world within the circle for all of my life. Do you think I would not want to see all it has to show me?"

He couldn't help smiling sadly. "There were stories of the circle?"

"Lights and people coming and going," she confirmed. "Never in my lifetime, not until now." She tilted her head, watching him. "You look sad, child."

Child.

It was a long time since anyone had called him that.

"You're far from your home." He knew what that was like. "Don't you have friends? Family? People who will be worrying about you?"

She laughed then, a surprisingly hearty sound. "I'm old, my boy. I live far from all people, and those coming by me only come when they seek some physik or wisdom. I have lived my life in their service. Best I take the time I have left for myself." Her smile softened. "A great adventure for my aged days."

He studied her. "You're a bit mad, aren't you?"

She grinned suddenly. "When you are of an age as I am, they call it eccentric." She sipped her tea and asked, "And what of you? No friends nor family hereabouts?" She waved one hand about the room. "This is much space for very little."

Ben shrugged. "It's a long story."

"We have the time."

"Why do you want to know?"

She shrugged. "To know the manner of man who is my host." There was a glint of humour in her eyes. "Mayhap, you'll put the fear of God into me so much I will beg to go home."

Ben made a face at her. "Well, we both know that's not true."

She turned her cup, warming her hands. "What harm can be done for telling me? Who am I to tell? Who will know but me?"

It was true, and for once, he wanted to be honest from the word go. There were too many deceptions and lies already. He had no reason to tell her anything, but God, he wanted to tell someone, explain himself, have more than one other person understand the reason behind his madness and exactly what he was trying to do.

Enoch was the only other person who knew everything, and he was out of reach again.

Years ago, Enoch had pried the whole mess out of him. Ben couldn't remember exactly how. There'd been fighting, he knew that much. It was still in the early days when Enoch refused an alternative home in his own timeline and Ben was terrified of being caught. Voices had been raised, emotions had run high and...

Well, Ben was damned sure the old woman wasn't about to try to fuck the answer out of him.

He remembered lying in Enoch's embrace after, spent emotionally and physically, his face wet with tears and all the anger and frustration drained out, leaving only grief in its place. That was when Enoch had sighed and kissed him and called him a stupid bugger who needed someone to take care of him.

And yet...

And yet, he wanted—needed—to tell her something.

"My dad—father—did something stupid before I was born," he finally said. "He invented time travel, the gates that brought you here. Things went wrong, and here we are."

"Only a small part of the story, I'd wager."

He looked at her. "Why do you need to know more?"

She tilted her head, reminding him of a small, dark-eyed bird. "As I said—to know the manner of man who is my host. Man, you seem to be, but with those from the circle, that may not be true. Some manner of beast? That I don't yet know."

Ben took a scalding mouthful of tea. She didn't have anyone she could tell. There was no reason for her not to know. She wouldn't understand half of it anyway. Maybe it would be enough to show her how much trouble he could be and convince her it would be in her best interests to leave.

"All right." He put the cup on the floor. "I'll tell you, but it's a long and complicated story."

She turned on the couch, facing him, and for the first time, he felt the weight of her full attention, like a child in front of a teacher. "Give me your words, then."

Where to start?

Now? With this place and time? On the run, hiding from friends and loved ones? Or earlier, before he committed those crimes, when he first started the long and desperate search for his father so many years ago? Or maybe it was best to simply start at the beginning, with a father and a son and a secret door.

He pulled his feet up onto the couch, pressed his hands to his crossed ankles, and stared at his knuckles as they whitened.

"I told you my dad made the time gates." God, he wanted his voice to be steady. Neutral. It wouldn't help to let her see how much it got to him. "It all started from then, when he— My mum got lost through a gate, and he tried to find her..."

And so he talked until his mouth was dry and his eyes were wet. His voice broke remembering the day that had changed everything. He almost choked on his dad's last words to him, the frantic warning to hide as strangers rattled at the door.

It took all his effort to speak about the sealed safe room and the dark that had filled his nightmares for decades. Jacob had opened the secret door for him then and made a promise to find the strangers who had stolen his dad and his dad's machines. He'd done it too. He'd found them, but everything they took that day was never seen again. Especially not Dad.

It should have been an end to it, but then there was his dad's will when he turned eighteen, and those letters from the past had given him fresh hope. Then there was Qasim, his friend, who had proved his wild theories could be true.

It was all so much: the TRI's two years failed search, his disappointment, his withdrawal, and the fact that he knew they were wrong. Misery, frustration, a heavy night of drinking, and an illegally constructed time gate led him to Enoch, and Christ, what a shitstorm that had turned into.

"Did you return to this TRI?"

Ben nodded, staring at his hands on his ankles. He would have bruises if he didn't loosen his grip, but he couldn't let go of them. Always the way, ever since the safe room when he couldn't see or hear anything, after the power died.

"I'd hit a wall," he said quietly. "I couldn't find any more information, and I..." He exhaled unsteadily. "It's awful, but I almost gave up. I went back because I—it—I needed to do something to remember him, if I couldn't find him. It was his. The TRI. So I thought I'd go and make it better, but..." He shrugged. "Then I found more breadcrumbs and a new trail and I screwed up everything to chase it."

The woman laid her bony hands over his. He flinched in surprise.

"You've suffered much." She shook her grey head gravely.

"I'm a criminal," he pointed out. "I'm on the run from the law. That's the manner of man your host is. I've betrayed my friends. I'm hunted by the people who took me in and cared for me. I have more enemies than you can know."

"And you're alone in it."

He gazed at her hands curled over his. "I'm doing what I have to do."

She turned over his hands in hers and studied his palms as if she could read them. When her eyes returned to his, her expression was set. "Then I will aid you until your task is done, and only then will I return through the circle."

Ben blinked stupidly at her. "Why?"

She grinned at him again. No one so old should have been able to look so impish. "If I am to have an adventure in my ageing days, how better than this? A master criminal, treason, a lost father? A grand adventure indeed."

Ben couldn't help laughing. "You really *are* a bit mad, aren't you?"

She made a noncommittal sound. "My life is...quiet. There is little for me to do, save help those who knock at my door. A lifetime of quiet might allow for a little noise once in a while."

Ben envied her. His whole life had been a constant state of noise. "It won't be easy," he warned, motioning towards the window. "It's a big world out there. If it's too much, you don't need to go out. Enoch—my friend—hates the city. It's too much for him. I don't want you to be overwhelmed."

She gazed at him. "I've passed through the circle. Where else would I be but a magical realm of strange and wondrous things?"

That was a fair point, if she really believed the fairy-ring, magic-stone-circle bollocks. Even if she didn't, she still didn't want to go back. If she thought she could handle the modern world, who was he to contradict her? Enoch had managed the change so well no one even questioned the fact now.

"All right," he agreed, wondering whether she might be as mad as him. He studied her. "What do I call you?"

She hesitated. "Ada."

"That's not your name, is it?"

She flashed a strange smile at him. "I would be mad indeed if I gave my name to the Gentry."

The Gentry again, as Enoch had said. Lords and ladies and fairy tales.

"Fair enough." He held out a hand to her. "Then I'm pleased to make your acquaintance, Ada."

She laid her fingers in his, light as a bird. "And you, Master Ben."

Chapter Fourteen

The weather held true on Wednesday.

In part, Enoch thought Orla would forget her invitation. They had all been well-warmed by alcohol at the bar. But when Mack came to his door on Tuesday, it seemed the plans were all well in hand. They would meet him at the main parking bay of the compound, come the morning, and sweep him off on an adventure.

As he waited for them to arrive, he considered his bag. He took everything out of it and laid it on the table again. He had packed and repacked it thrice already, as if it would assure him he had not forgotten anything.

He wanted to go to the sea anyway, but he could not deny there were other reasons too. He had a job to do. Seeing Ben had reminded him of it, especially with Ben so drawn and thin. He had been left alone for too long. He needed information only Enoch could get, and if that meant being even closer to Mack, then Enoch would do it without question.

And yet, the guilt gnawed at his belly.

When it had all begun, he only meant to gather knowledge from Mack, but Mack was a hard man to dislike, ready with laughter and generous to a fault. Enoch had not meant to befriend him, and yet...

Enoch sighed, running a hand over his face again.

Thinking himself in circles would help no one, least of all himself. Better to act now and think of everything else later. He would go to the sea with his friends, and if his friends happened to speak of things that could help his other friend, then all to the good. If not, then...

Then, God have mercy, he didn't know what they would do.

His bud chirped to let him know there was a message.

"We're ten minutes away," Mack's voice rang out. "See you there."

"Fut!"

The parking bay was a good fifteen minutes from the main compound by means of a small train, and he still had to cross the grounds to get to it. He shoved everything into his bag, pushed his feet into his running shoes, and fled for the door.

Mack was leaning against a pod, grinning as Enoch finally puffed into the parking bay. "Slept in?"

Enoch held up his bulging bag. "Making sure I had all things."

"If you've missed anything, I'm pretty sure we can cover you," Orla said, leaning out of the door, eyes dancing. Enoch would scarce have recognised the painted woman from the club in the woman before him. Her hair was shorter, though still bright colours, and there was only a little paint at her eyes and on her lips. "Come on. I don't want to miss any more sun."

The ride was pleasant enough, all but flying through the countryside. It went by faster over hands of cards and music. Enoch could not help but smile. For them, it all seemed natural to fly above the ground, holding cards formed of light, while music echoed about them. Like Ben, they were born of this time and wore it well.

"There!" Orla said suddenly, waving a hand. "We're almost there!"

Enoch swung about, all but pressing his nose to the glass of the pod window as it came about the curve of the narrow road. A field spread before them, but beyond it stretched the sun-spotted dark blue of the sea neath a sky with scarce a cloud. He gave a shout of delight, rising up on his knees on the seat.

"Excited?" Orla said with a laugh.

"It is some time since I have seen the sea," he admitted, sitting away from the window.

"It was probably a bit of a trek in your day," Mack said, "wasn't it?"

Enoch nodded. "If the weather held fair, much of a day to get there on foot. Less if you had the luck to seek passage on one of the boats upon the river." He remembered the first time he had ever seen the water, more than three centuries after his birth. It had scared him at first, but Ben had made it seem less fearsome, splashing about like an excited pup and bringing him handfuls of shells and crabs and shining pebbles. "T'was far bigger than I imagined."

"I bet." Orla peered out. "We're lucky. This place is always pretty quiet. Most people can't be bothered with the effort to get to it."

"Aye." Enoch gave a mournful sigh. "More than two hours of travel. How dire and exhausting..."

They both laughed as the pod came to a stop in a small fence-lined square close to the grassy dunes. The ground was powdered with crushed stone and there were lines marked on it with spaces for many more pods. Aside from them, there were but two others.

"The only downside of this place is the lack of ice cream," Mack informed Enoch as they walked along the small path winding from the parking square to the sands. "But at least we can bring our own."

"We feast like kings," Enoch said happily, hauling along his bag and a folded blanket for them to sit on. Mack and Orla were weighted down with a freeze box and several large bags between them.

Firm stone and gravel gave way to softer ground, and Enoch found himself grinning like a fool as the dunes parted afore them and he could see the water. It seemed more blue than the first time he saw it with Ben, though it was whipped up with white and foaming upon the beach as it had then. He could not help himself and dashed forward with a whoop, kicking up spouts of soft sand against his bare calves as he ran.

A good distance from the water, he dropped the bag and blanket on the sand and kept running, hopping from one foot to the other as he pulled his shoes off. A dozen steps later, his feet sank into the wet sand, and he careened on until he sank knee-deep in the cool curling waves.

He saw Orla standing further up the beach and laughing. She set her bags by the blanket and drew out a plastic disc. With a flick of her wrist, she sent it spinning through the air towards him, and he lunged to catch it before it landed in the water.

A lifetime ago, he could stun a rabbit with a stone from twenty paces, but the disc seemed to have a mind of its own. It turned in the air and rolled away across the sand more than once, caught by a breath of wind. It took four tries before he made it spin back towards her, and even then, it landed short.

Orla ran to pick it up. "Not bad."

He made a face at her. "I need no false comfort."

She tossed it to him again. "Hardly false. First time I played, it took me a dozen tries to make it go anywhere."

He turned it over in his hands. "Why does it have curves on the edge? Do you also use it as a platter?"

She burst out laughing. "I s'pose you could." She dove to catch it afore it hit the sand. "As for the curves..." She frowned, studying it as she got up. "I never thought to ask. Probably physics. Some kind of science anyway."

"Ah." Enoch shuddered dramatically. "Witchcraft."

Orla giggled, throwing the disc again. "If a frisbee is bad, God knows what they'd make of pods and freezer boxes and buds in your time."

Enoch could well remember angry, fearful hands and cudgels and a rope about his neck. "I dunt think they would like it." He glanced towards Mack who had spread out the blanket on the sand and was pulling out boxes and bottles from the freezer box. "Does Mack catch also?"

Orla sighed fondly. "He tries, but right now, I think he's trying to give us a hint he's hungry." She started towards him.

Enoch ran after her, sand clinging to his legs. "You spoke of ice cream." He dropped to kneel on the edge of the blanket. "What manner of ice cream?"

"I remember your ice cream episode," Mack said and pulled a packet out of the freezer box with a flourish. Enoch made a hungry sound at the sight of the ice cream bar he had so favoured—caramel inside with something called praline wrapped in ice cream and nut-crusted chocolate.

"You'd make me have a cold brain and a fat belly again," he protested, even as he tore open the wrapper and bit into it.

"I don't make you do anything," Mack said as virtuous as a saint.

"And it's only a snack," Orla added, taking her own with a smile.

Enoch nodded keenly, his mouth full of sweetness. Somehow, with the sun on his head and the scent of the sea, the ice cream tasted even better. The next time, he and Ben...no. No. It would do no good to turn his thoughts that way when the future was so uncertain.

"We should do a stream," he said suddenly as he licked the chocolate from his fingers. Mayhap Ben could not join them, but the streams gave him joy, and he always liked best to see Enoch enjoying all the pleasures of modern times. "They like it when I am in the world."

Mack winced. "I don't think that's the best idea."

"Why not?" Enoch frowned, puzzled. "Have we not been in markets and inns? Why not the seaside?"

Mack scratched at his jaw, smudging chocolate on his cheek. "It's just— I don't think..." He turned wide eyes on Orla beseechingly.

"What he's trying to say, in his I'm-a-giant-wimp way," Orla said, rolling her eyes towards the sky, "is your fans are a bit...excitable." She took out her bud, opened up a screen, and touched some letters. Dozens of pictures appeared.

Enoch leaned forward, staring at them. "Is that..."

"The pub we were in on Saturday." There were many people in the pictures. Some were wearing clothes from Enoch's era. Others were striking daft poses. Every picture was marked with the same word: Noching. "We're just lucky the landlady appreciates the extra customers we brought her way."

"And they go everywhere they know I have been?" Enoch glanced along the pale stretch of beach. Christ, if he showed this place, they would swarm like flies on muck. "Mayhap it would be best not to share this, then."

"Yeah," Mack said apologetically. "Sorry. I mean, we could try and do it without giving away any landmarks, but there aren't many places nearby with sand like this, and they'd probably figure it out."

Enoch gazed at the scatter of pictures again, a gloomy thought descending on him. "And that inn?" He had liked it, and it was close enough to Ben they might have met there, but now, that seemed impossible. "I suppose I can no longer go there?"

"Unless you want to be mobbed." Mack gave him an apologetic smile. "I'll find you some others. It's not like there's a shortage of old-fashioned bars in the city."

"That would be well," he said gratefully. "Now, though, I will enjoy my seaside." He pointed towards the water. "Is it safe to swim here?"

"As long as you don't go out too far." Mack pointed out to a rocky crest running from the beach out into the sea. "No farther than the end of the outcrop. The currents can get a bit tricky beyond it."

"Not so far, then." Enoch got up and caught the ends of his shirt and drew it off.

Orla and Mack both caught their breaths, and Enoch frowned in puzzlement. True, he was half-clad, but he was no fine-formed man, too soft in some places and too thin in others, his legs too short for his body on account of broken bones in his younger days. He glanced about the beach, uncertain. There were others half-clad too, so that was not the trouble.

Yet Mack was gaping at him. Orla, though, was staring hard at a spot on her shorts, rubbing at it with her thumb.

Enoch closed his hands about his shirt uneasily. "What's the matter?"

"What's the—" Mack's face twisted in dismay. "Enoch! Your back! What the fuck happened?"

"My..."

Enoch groaned in understanding. In the TRI, his clothes kept his stripes covered. "I telt you I was beat."

"Beat..." Mack echoed, horrified. "I thought you meant beaten up. I didn't—isn't—you were flogged?"

"Aye." Enoch shrugged. "It were only a dozen stripes. The master was merciful on account that I were but fourteen."

Orla made a small sound, pressing her hand to her mouth. Mack had gone grey.

Enoch twisted up his shirt, uncomfortable. "Would it be best for you if I cover them?"

"No!" Orla said quickly. She forced a smile, but it fooled no one. "It's—it's fine. Don't worry. It was just...a bit of a shock. That's all. I've—we've never seen anything like that before. Not in person, I mean. In films and things, but..." She trailed off helplessly.

"Yeah." Mack nodded. "Don't worry. We're just—it's on us. Don't worry."

Enoch glanced about the beach again. There were other people there as well. None close by, but there might be more soon. "Better to cover them, I think," he said, pulling the shirt on. "I—your pardon. I'll go and swim."

Even as he started down the beach, he heard Orla whisper, "Holy shit...Mack..."

Christ, it should not have grieved him so, but the shock and pity and horror on their faces was not something he wished to see. His eyes burned with anger that such damned foolish things could turn the mood of a day so fast. Blinking hard, he kicked at the sand in useless rage. "Fut!"

A swim in the cold sea would help. He swam out as far as he dared, then in again thrice. It was far better than the strong-smelling clear blue water of the TRI bathing pool. True, seaweed caught upon his legs, and more than once, he knocked his foot against unseen rocks, but it smelled as it was meant to and the salt was on his tongue and in his eyes.

By the time he stumbled out of the waves, his legs were shaking. More people were scattered on the sands, but Mack and Orla were not far from the waterline, tossing the plastic disc between them. When Mack noticed Enoch, he spun it towards him.

"Show me what you've got, then!" Mack called, though his voice was tight to breaking.

Enoch forced a smile. He turned the disc in his hand and threw it back. It seemed to catch on the breeze and bounced away, rolling off along the sands. Orla burst out laughing as Mack gave chase and Enoch managed to laugh.

It grew easier with practise, he noticed—both smiling and throwing—and by the time they were flush-faced and hungry, his damp clothes were almost dry against his skin.

"You could use some sun cream," Orla said as Mack made a start laying out a picnic lunch for them.

Enoch sat cross-legged on the blanket. "For what?"

She dug about in her bag and drew out a bottle. "To keep your skin from burning." She held out the bottle to him. "Here."

He eyed it doubtfully. "I drink it?"

From her amused expression, he guessed not.

"No." She flicked the lid open and poured some into her palm. It was smooth as milk and twice as thick. "You put it on your skin, and it acts like a barrier to stop the sun from cooking you. Here." She knelt forward and after dipping two fingers into the cream, drew a strip across each of his cheeks and his forehead. "You'll just need to rub it in to make sure it covers everywhere."

He lifted both hands to his cheeks and hesitated. "Into the hair and all?"

She considered the sideburns he had grown in defiance of so many clean-shaven people about him. Better than being thought young and childish, he combed them out each day so they jutted proudly from his cheeks. "To the edge of them would be enough, I guess."

He rubbed the cream in readily then peered at his fingers in surprise. It almost seemed to have disappeared. "Good?"

She tapped the end of his nose with one creamy finger. "Perfect." She offered the bottle. "You should probably put some on your arms and legs as well. You're not *quite* as hairy there." She hesitated for just too long before saying, "And no one'll mind if you want to put it on your—"

"Arms and legs are good," Mack said firmly. "You don't need to if you don't want to."

Enoch sighed, pouring a little of the cream into his palms. "It's an old wound," he said quietly as he rubbed the cream into his arms, making the hair stick in all directions. "You need not fuss so."

Mack and Orla shared an uncomfortable glance. "Yeah," Mack said. "Sorry. I mean— Christ, I'm useless at this."

"Would you fuss so over Janos's arm?" Enoch pointed out. "Or if someone saw your eye?"

"Point." Mack pushed a plastic plate stacked with sandwiches towards him. "Please accept my humble offering and apology."

Enoch peered at the sandwiches. "What kind of sandwich?"

"Brawn," Orla said quickly. "Mack said you liked it, so I dug out some recipes."

One side of his mouth curled up. "Aye. I do." He wiped a hand on his shorts and picked up a sandwich. "I'll accept your apology and your offering and all."

Mack seemed relieved and pleased. "But if it's disgusting, it's not on me."

"Hey!" Orla smacked him on the knee.

He flashed a smile at her. "Love you."

Enoch snickered as Orla tried her best to glower.

"You're lucky you're cute," she said, rolling her eyes as she opened a bottle of fizzing juice.

Mack beamed at her. "I know." He reached into his bag. "And I remembered your beer." He pulled out a can and held it out to Enoch. "If you fancy a drink."

Enoch took it, recalling the last drink they had shared. He remembered Orla's idea for a stream and made his face as innocent as an angel. "I think," he said as gravely as he could, "I would like something else." Mayhap it was a cruel trick to wait until Orla took a drink from her bottle afore he asked, "Can we have sex on the beach?"

At once, Mack was red-faced, and Orla spouted her drink all over herself.

Enoch grinned at both of them as they sputtered indignation at him. All was well again.

Chapter Fifteen

Ben checked his reflection for the sixth time since he'd gotten in the pod.

The new calibration for the camo-patch seemed to be holding. This time around, he'd loaded the face of a nondescript snub-nosed and freckled white man. Blue contact lenses made his eyes different, and he'd elected to go with a cap instead of dyeing his hair again. Luckily, it was part of the uniform.

Maybe it was bloody stupid to do the delivery himself, but after everything that had happened, he wanted a chance to see the place he'd called home for most of his childhood. He'd taken precautions as well, in case they went chasing him through the delivery company and the paperwork. It was easy enough to poke about in their computers and leave a false trail.

He straightened the cap, then took a deep breath and pushed the control to open the door.

The moment his feet touched the pavement, he faltered, legs unsteady under him. The street was so familiar and yet somehow it seemed so much smaller than he remembered.

It hadn't changed much, the quiet road flanked by two rows of brick-terraced houses with their French windows and immaculate little gardens. No one dared to have a messy garden. Ben remembered the neighbourhood flying squad of tutting old ladies who would glower at people until their gardens didn't lower the tone of the street. Heaven help you if you kicked a ball into someone's hydrangeas.

His destination was the house he'd parked in front of.

He forced himself to move forward. It was also bloody stupid to freeze up at the sight of the place. It was just a building. No one was going to be there, and he only had to deliver a gift.

The front gate was new. Wrought iron and a bit fancier than the old one. Recently repainted too, fresh and shiny. It still squealed when he pushed it open, and he winced. If the new curtain twitchers were anything like the previous generation, the sound would be like a dog whistle.

Technically, he was counting on their eyes. They would report the deliveryman was in a uniform. No one would ever know it was him.

He hurried up the flagstone path to the front door, the beribboned bundle hugged to his chest. It was daft how safe the street always was. No one would dare touch something left on a doorstep. Didn't need any security cameras back in the day, not when old Mrs Khatib was on watch.

He crouched and set the boxed vase in the little nook between the doorstep and the edge of the French windows. It would be sheltered from the wind there, and the edges of the box were high enough to protect the flowers. He hesitated, tucked the small envelope inside the box as well, and scrambled to his feet.

Halfway to the gate, he froze when a painfully familiar voice spoke behind him.

"You don't need me to sign, do you?"

Christ, he should have vaulted the wall and bolted down the street.

But it was Aunt M.

He pivoted as if on casters, trying to think, but the same thought was rattling through his brain on a loop: she wasn't meant to be in. Enoch had kept him up-to-date with her babysitting schedule, and she wasn't meant to be in. She was meant to be out, taking care of Faraz's kids like she did every Monday.

"Sorry?"

Mariam stood in the open doorway and stooped to pick up the boxed bouquet of flowers. "Last time one of your lot came, I had to sign for my parcel."

"Och, no." He groaned inwardly. A Scottish accent? How the fuck was putting on a dodgy Scottish accent going to help? "Ah wuz telled ye wouldnae be in, and I could leave it by the stair."

"Normally, yes, but my son's on holiday." She reached into the bouquet and pulled out the card, and Ben's heart drummed harder as she opened it. A flash of surprise and relief skimmed across her face as she read his apology for scaring her, but then her brow furrowed and her dark eyes returned to him, scrutinising him. He knew that calculating expression on her face, adding up numbers that didn't make sense, and with Aunt M, it didn't pay to underestimate her. "You were told I'd be out?"

"Aye, madam." He took a step towards the gate. "But here you are, and all delivered safe." He jerked his thumb to his pod. "I'll be off then."

She was watching him. He darted a glance at the card as she snapped it shut again between finger and thumb.

"Who told you?"

He could barely hear her over the blood rushing in his ears. "Madam?"

"Who," she repeated, stepping off the front step, "told you I wouldn't be here?"

Thank fuck for a brain that was good at thinking in emergencies. "The depot, madam. The notification on the delivery manifest. It didnae have any name for the customer." He forced himself to look bewildered. "Is something wrong with them? I can return them if you'd like."

She gave him a cool stare he had seen a thousand times before, more often than not when he'd forgotten about clearing the table because he got caught up working on a new circuit and tried to blame someone else. "No. They're fine. Unexpected."

It took him a second to realise his forced smile had collapsed. "A surprise, then?" He took another small step away. "If you're satisfied..."

"They remembered my favourites." She gazed at him, and he felt like he'd been stripped bare, his camo-patch ripped away. "I only ever got flowers from them when they really felt like they'd made a mess of things."

"Aye?" The gate was cold against his groping fingers. "Sounds like he wanted to say sorry for something, eh?"

"He." She echoed. "You're not very good at this, are you?"

He fumbled with the latch. It was stuck, and he didn't dare turn his back on her. "Madam?"

"No customer name, you said, but now it's a 'he.'" She took a step closer. "No signing when I know it's company policy to ask for a signature. The accent you forgot you were doing." She gazed up at him. "You don't need to keep running, Ben."

His stomach dropped like a rock.

Sod the gate.

He vaulted the wall and was in his pod in ten seconds.

As it shuttled away, he stared out through the windscreen.

Mariam had her arm raised, and the bud at her wrist glowed.

Fuck!

He gulped a breath, pressing his hands to his face. Right. Image on record. His pod. Had he changed the licence panel? Yes. Right. Good. That was something.

Yeah, he'd put the colours of the company on the pod, but that didn't mean anything when you had a technical genius with an image of your make and model of vehicle and a whole police task force with the equipment to track and trace you at a moment's notice.

Which meant it could be backtracked. Which meant the current safe house would be identified, and everything there could be compromised.

He touched the bud on his shirt, pulse racing.

"Good day?" Ada appeared on a glowing screen in front of him. She'd put on some of the modern clothes he'd bought for her—a dark scoop-neck shirt and patterned cardigan—and with her hair brushed and braided, she almost seemed like a modern woman.

Ben tried to keep his voice steady. "We have a problem. You've been downstairs? Where I keep all my machines?"

She flushed as if he'd caught her doing something she shouldn't. "Yes, but—"

"No time. There's a trolley there. It has a dozen crates on it. Do you think you can move it?" She nodded, opening her mouth to speak, but he cut over her again. "Get it to the main big doors for me. We need to clear out of the warehouse."

"I am to take the cart out into the city?"

"I'm going to send a pickup team to get you," he explained as quickly as he could. "They'll have a pod—a vehicle like the ones you see from the windows. They'll pack everything up, and I'll need you to go with them in the pod. They'll know where to take it all. I need you to be ready as soon as possible, and when they come, you press the big green button by the door to let them in."

"What of everything else? All of your machines in the basement?"

Shit. The gate.

Mariam would have notified the task force about his location.

They'd probably be tracking through old footage, and if he didn't get a pickup team to Ada soon, he would lose everything else he had left as well. There was no time to explain how to safely dismantle a temporal gate to someone who had only just been introduced to the concept of electricity.

"Leave it. Just get the crates ready for the pickup team."

Ada seemed even more worried. "How am I to know these people come from you?"

"They'll be in red and black, and I'll tell them to ask for Mrs. Sanders."

She smiled then. "Mrs. Sanders. Well enough." She hesitated. "The new place I am going, will you be there when we come?"

He shook his head. "There's a small red case on my work desk and a bunch of keys with a red tag. Those keys'll get you through the gate and the main door of the new building, and I'll be there as soon as I can." He hoped he sounded calmer than he felt. "You'll be fine."

As soon as he closed the call, he turned his attention to finding a pickup firm. Thank Christ there were so many private hires flying under the radar and more than happy to take immediate payment with no questions asked.

Next issue was his own pod, which was far too noticeable. No chance of keeping it, not when they were tracking it. He hit the controls, turning it in the direction of the nearest surveillance blackout zone, then set to work on the main drive.

By the time the pod slowed, he'd shed his courier uniform, recalibrated his camo-patch, and had removed or wiped the bulk of the pod's memory drive, leaving just enough for it to trundle on to a random field in the backside of nowhere without any further coordinates.

The door had barely cracked open when he leapt out of the pod, racing away from the proximity sensor so the door would close faster. He watched as it picked up speed again and headed out into the streets. Only when it was out of sight did he sag against the nearest wall and let out a slow, exhausted sigh.

They could—and probably would—find it soon. Jacob's people were smart. They would backtrack and figure out where he'd made a run for it. Foot was the best option. Public transport would have to wait until he hit a busier area. He turned into a side street and hurried on.

Half an hour and several blocks later, after an emergency stop in a café as a police pod sped by, he finally made it onto one of the bus pods. There was something safe about being lost in a crowd, shielded by the bodies and faces of dozens of strangers.

For a few minutes at least, he could breathe and think beyond escape.

Enoch was going to kill him.

It was sloppy to almost get caught once because of sentimentality. Doing it twice in less than a fortnight was downright embarrassing.

He couldn't help laughing, relief and panic colliding somewhere in the middle. He touched his bud, surprised his hands were trembling. "Idiot," he muttered, popping open a small screen.

Had a thought for your next stream, he typed rapidly. *Public transport. I had an outing with the family today and I'm heading home on a bus now and thought of you. No credit necessary.*

He could picture Enoch's expression when he got the message. Sometimes Ben couldn't help admiring just how discreet Enoch could be, but then again, Enoch *had* managed to get to his midtwenties without getting himself arrested or locked up in the past, which was quite a feat given some of the bullshit he'd pulled off in his lifetime.

At least, he'd managed until a drunken idiot had wandered into his life, cried on his shoulder, and wandered out again and screwed everything up for both of them.

There was no reply by the time Ben got off the bus, and he wasn't surprised. There was only so much a man could say when his words were monitored, but Ben had a sneaking suspicion he would get an earful the next time he and Enoch saw each other.

Until then, he had a new safe house to set up and another rogue time traveller to wrangle.

She was waiting for him when he arrived and, in her world, waiting apparently meant swinging an iron bar at his head when he slipped in through the door and into the derelict hall.

"Shit!" He blocked it with his arm and swore again. "Ada! What the hell?!"

Ada's mouth dropped open. "It's you!" She dropped the bar. "Jesu! I thought it was some stranger, come to capture me!"

Ben rubbed his arm, wincing. "Yes, it's me." He deactivated his camo-patch, then rolled up his sleeve. There was a dark red stripe across his forearm. It'd be black and blue by evening. "Ow."

She had her hands pressed to her mouth but lowered them to reach out for his arm. "I'm sorry." She turned his arm over, examining it and gently pressing with her bony fingers. "Unbroken, I think." She gave him a wary, awkward smile. "Your pardon. There were so many people coming and going nearby I was afraid someone might come for me, and you came in with a different face again."

He had to smile. "Yeah. I know that feeling." He drew his arm back, flexing his fingers to make sure everything was working. "Did everything get delivered all right?"

She nodded, relieved. "I had them put your boxes in the room in the cellar where no curious eyes might spy them." She pointed towards the stairs leading up to the second level of the building. Once, it had been a shop but upstairs had been the stock and staff rooms. "Are we to stay up there? There is a place to cook and a couch there."

"Yeah. It's almost like an actual house."

"And we are safe here?"

"Well..." He held up his arm. "Apart from dangerous women attacking me with iron rods..."

She made a face at him. "Such insolence and I might do it again."

Ben raised both hands in surrender. The tension and panic were evaporating, and he swayed, suddenly exhausted. "Mercy, please. That's the last thing I need after the morning I've had."

"I'll make something for you to eat, then. I brought what little food we had." She bustled away up the stairs, leaving him alone.

He crossed the dusty floor, boards creaking underfoot. The half-light from the tall covered windows was enough to let him find the stairs, and he made his way into the basement. The crates were stacked there, and he ran his hand across one of them.

There were enough parts for one more gate, and there was no chance he'd be able to get more. Not now. It was too late. And it was all his own stupid fault as well.

Two gates, stable, complete and fully functional, lost because he was a sentimental idiot. Two battery cores too! He would have to resort to electricity to power it. A power surge like that would give away their location. Only once chance left and no other options.

He knocked his fist against the lid of the crate.

No more risks, he vowed. No matter what. They had to finish what he had started.

Chapter Sixteen

"You're sure?" Enoch widened his eyes, leaning closer to the screen. Mayhap it was too much, but better too surprised than too little. "He's back?"

Lysander's relief was writ on his face. "We're sure of it."

Every day since Ben had fled through the temporal gate, the task force had been sure to call Enoch with an update. That he knew Ben was back four days afore they did was neither here nor there. It did beg one question, though.

"How?" Enoch feigned puzzlement. He well remembered Diaval's message of buses and family. Family, to Ben, meant one person: Mariam. "Did someone see him?"

Lysander's mouth tightened to a thin line. "He made contact."

Enoch groaned inwardly. It was a foolish action, but it said much of Ben's character. Even though the task force were hunting him, he had no wish for them to be distressed as Enoch had been. They cared for him, and he knew it. Of course, he would offer them some assurance he'd made it back alive and well and in his right time again.

"Is that not a great risk for him?"

"I don't think he could help himself." Lysander sounded weary. "He always does the thing he shouldn't."

Enoch nodded. "Like the coffee house."

And like the town square three centuries ago and the secret gates and the hotel and all the things Ben should not have done but did because his foolish heart was far too big. They all thought him careless, but the trouble was he cared too much.

"Exactly." Lysander ran a hand over his face. "Things are kind of hectic here. It might be easier for you to stay put for a few days until we get things sorted out."

That was no surprise. If Ben had made contact, then they had a new link to him, and they would need to follow where it led. Nowhere, Enoch was certain, for Ben was very skilled at setting out a wild goose chase, but they would go after it in case he made a mistake.

"I have enough to entertain me," he assured Lysander. "I have a new inn to visit soon. I even went to the sea with Mack and Orla."

Lysander seemed pleased. Like so many in the TRI and task force, he liked to hear Enoch was doing well. "How was it?"

Enoch scratched his sideburn thoughtfully. "Wet."

It made Lysander laugh, which was rare enough. "That's what I've heard." He glanced away for a moment. "If there's any news, we'll keep you updated. Try to keep out of mischief."

"What mischief could I do?" He clasped a hand to his chest in feigned horror.

Lysander chuckled as he reached out, and the screen went blank.

Enoch sprawled on his couch, tugging at his sideburn with a sigh. What mischief indeed, when he had been abed but a few days earlier with the very man Lysander was hunting. It was a bugger of a thing to lie to a man such as Lysander, someone so decent and honourable, but Ben needed Enoch's help far more than Lysander did.

One day, it will all be done, and there will be no need for lying to anyone anymore.

Enoch tipped himself sideways upon the couch and rolled to his back to stare up at the ceiling.

A promise had been made years ago, bound in salt. A debt, he'd told himself then. A life for a life. Aid for aid. It was nothing so foolish as love. He'd been so sure of it then, but Jesu, what a fool he was proving to be after all.

God above, he wanted to return to the hotel and spend a lazy day finding his way about Ben's body all over again. He had forgotten how much pleasure he could take in it, which was madness itself. How could he forget such a thing?

"Fut..." he murmured, dropping his arm over his face.

His mind was already returning to the hotel room, and all too soon, his other hand strayed neath his trews to take a hold of his cock. It was daft how easily even the thought of Ben could rouse him. That night in the hotel had been a feast given to a half-starved man. Five and twenty months of hasty, secret touches in the toilet of the coffee house was nothing compared to it.

Ben was always so good and all, always willing to do as he was telt, and Enoch could scarce believe anyone would do so for him.

Next time, he thought, tightening his hand and stroking himself, he'd have Ben kneel. He'd see him looking up as he—

The door chimed, making him damned near leap from his skin. He yelped as he lost his balance and fell from the couch with a crash. "Shit!"

There was a silence outside the door, and a moment later Sabine said carefully, "Enoch? You okay?"

Enoch groaned, yanking his hand from his trews and trying to put himself in a more respectable order. "A moment," he called, struggling to his feet. His cock was not so shy, poking up against his trews. A moment would not be long enough.

He glanced about him, then hurried over to the dining table and sat behind it, opening his bud up before him. "Come in!"

She peeped her head around the door. "I'm not disturbing you, am I?"

Enoch made a show of shutting the screens afore him and tried his utmost to ignore the ache beneath the table. "No," he lied. "I only was drowsing at my work. You startled me."

She winced, aggrieved. "Sorry." To his dismay, she pulled out the chair opposite him and sat. "I thought I'd better bring this to you as soon as possible."

"This" was a small object, which she slid over to him. Enoch drew it towards himself and stared. It was silvery and round as a penny with a tiny jewel-like button upon it. Something like a bud, mayhap? And not his, which meant...Jesu! Ben and his feeble memory again!

The only small mercy was that the pangs beneath the table were easing, replaced instead with a knot of dread in his middle.

He raised his eyes to Sabine.

"I know it's not yours." She smiled a little, but that did naught to calm him. "But since it was in the room where you were staying, the cleaning crew assumed it was, so I can only guess you had some company."

Enoch felt his face grow hot, and he closed his hand on the small device. All she needed to do was seek the security cameras in the halls and show it to Danny. He would recognise Ben at once, masked or not; Enoch had no doubt of that.

"I—it were—" He darted his tongue on his lip. "I had—"

"It's all right," she said gently. "I'm not about to air your private business."

Enoch sighed gratefully, his pulse thrumming. "I dunt— I mean, this—it's—I never—"

Sabine reached over the table to catch his hand. "Enoch, I'm not judging you." She squeezed his fingers. "There's no shame in it. I only wanted to make sure you knew it's just between us. You don't need to be afraid of gossip."

The relief was like cool water on a hot day.

He nodded again. "Thank you, Miss Sabine."

She squeezed his hand again.

As soon as she left the room, Enoch all but fell into his seat, his legs like jelly, the edge of the medallion pressing against his fingers. Next time Ben crossed his path, there had best be naught in his pockets.

He turned the medallion over in his palm.

The first one had all but cost him his life had been shattered and burned on the pyre that would have been his. Such a small thing and now, again, giving away the secret of Ben's presence.

He took it through to his room and closed it up in one of his drawers. He was already thinking on how he might warn Ben of his mistake as he walked through into the main room.

"All right?"

"Zooth!" Enoch whipped around like a startled hare.

Mack held up his hands. "Sorry! Sorry! I thought you were expecting us!"

"You look as if you have seen a ghost," Janos agreed, frowning. "You are all right?"

"Aye. Aye." Enoch pressed his hand to his breast, unsteady. "You might have rung or knocked afore!" He shook his head. "Sweet Jesu...what are you doing here?"

Mack held up his Leaf. "It's stream day."

Enoch stared at them. It had gone from his mind with all that was happening. Why else would they both come, but for that? "Fut..."

"You had forgotten?" Janos's frown deepened. "Is something wrong?"

Enoch pushed his fingers through his hair. Merciful Christ, there was too much going on. "Only a poor night's sleep," he lied. "Do we have something to speak of?" Mack and Janos exchanged a glance, and he knew they had nothing. "No matter. I can think of something."

"The club?" Mack suggested. "You've never talked about one of those before."

It was easy to talk of, though Enoch hoped his dislike of the place would not give Mack cause to regret taking him. Too loud, he'd said, and like a crowd of people all but rutting and well in their cups. In a world so loud and strange, the dance club was even louder and stranger.

"That bad, eh?" Mack tucked his Leaf into his breast pocket.

Enoch pulled one foot up on the couch. "Too much of all the things I dunt like. People and darkness and loudness and that."

"It is difficult to talk to people in such places," Janos agreed. "Better to find a bar with tables."

"That list I sent you—were any of them any good?" Mack asked hopefully.

Enoch took pity on him. "There's one down by the canal walk that seems quiet enough."

"Armstrongs? The one with the very small windows and an anchor upon the door?"

Enoch and Mack both gaped at Janos, surprised.

"Aye," Enoch said. "You know it?"

A fond, soft expression crossed Janos's face. "It is the first place Dieter took me to in the city when we went out for the first time. They had good whisky and comfortable chairs. It has changed owner since then, but the atmosphere is still comfortable."

Mack snickered. "You sound like such an old man when you talk like that. Do you need a footstool and your pipe?"

Janos smiled wryly. "It becomes more tempting with each year. I need a fireplace and a blanket for my shoulders also."

Enoch could picture him huddled before a fire, gold-and-silver hair all silver. "A fine way to spend a winter." He glanced about his clean and bright room with its hidden heating pipes and pale lights. "Much as I like this, I cannit help but miss a fire, by and by."

"Better to not light one," Janos advised. "They do not like it."

Enoch grinned. "Have you tried?"

Janos was silent for a moment, then rose from his chair. "I have work I must do." He pointed a stern finger at Enoch. "Remember—no fire."

Enoch watched him go, laughing. "I think he has set a fire where he should not have," he said to Mack, who was yet sitting on his usual seat. "What say you?"

"Yeah. Probably." Mack shifted, eyes darting from Enoch to the table and back again, as if he wanted to say something. Normally, when they finished, he would sit and relax, but now, he perched on the edge of his seat, his hands twisting and turning over in front of him.

Enoch watched him for a moment. "Is aught amiss?"

Mack flushed to his ears and twisted at his hands. "Sort of. Maybe." He cleared his throat, his voice stronger. "If I tell you, you can't tell anyone."

Enoch's skin prickled all over. For two and more years, he had been waiting for Mack to tell him all, to find if he knew the folk who had harmed Ben's father. Best not to seem too keen, else Mack might fall silent.

"Aye," he said as light as he could. "I keep much to myself. I can keep your secret and all."

Mack licked his lips anxiously. Enoch had seen him in many moods, but never nervous. "I might be leaving the TRI. I've been offered a job."

Enoch's blood turned to ice, but he only tilted his head and raised his eyebrows. "You said you had been looking afore…"

The flush drained from Mack's face. "Yeah. I—it—" He tightened his hands together until his knuckles were white as bone. "They say the fact I work for the TRI is as good as a free pass into this job. Better paid. Closer to the city."

Something about that was wrong.

"But there's none as know that you work for the TRI," Enoch said, befuddled. It was one of the main rules they bided by. None outside knew names, save for the high-up staff, lest they were taken advantage of.

Mack chewed his lower lip. "They guessed I do."

"How?"

Mack met his eyes and pointed a finger towards him. For a moment, Enoch didn't understand, and then he remembered the picture that had sent his fans running to a quiet pub and the video turning them on the chickens in supermarkets. Mack had been visible in both of them.

"Oh." Enoch tightened his arm on his upraised knee. "And on account of it, they come for you? What manner of job is it?"

"Historical stuff," Mack said, though there was something in his tone that made Enoch frown again. "Just…sorting through things. Data. You know. The usual."

"So, same as here?"

Mack didn't meet Enoch's eyes when he said, "Near enough."

He was too guarded and nervous. If a man had a chance for better work, there was no reason to be so secret. There was something more in the job than what he was saying. It was too strange for him to keep it secret, if it was naught more than he did already.

"Have you telt anybody else?"

Mack shook his head. "There—it—they've given me a condition."

"A condition?"

Mack darted his tongue along his pale lips. "They want to meet you. For me to get this job, they want to meet you. Confirmation I'm affiliated with the TRI."

Enoch sank on the couch, staring at him. "Me?"

Mack flushed. "I didn't want to ask," he said all in a rush. "I told them to stuff it, but it's a good job, and I figured it wouldn't hurt to ask, but if you don't want to do it, you don't need to…"

Enoch stared at him as he blethered on and on, but his mind was miles away. If Mack left the TRI, then Enoch's voluntary captivity had been for naught. Ben's only connection to his father would walk away, and they would be none the wiser.

All he had to do was say no, and Mack would remain. He would be unhappy, but as much as he liked Mack, Enoch knew whose happiness would always come first.

"I dunt think that's a good idea," he said.

Mack flinched as one stricken. "It's—you don't need to do anything. Just a cuppa with them. Prove I know you."

Enoch had to turn his face away. It was too hard to see Mack's disappointment. "I cannit be a lucky charm for you." He studied his clenched hands, his thoughts tumbling upon themselves. There was no reason to demand proof of a man. That could only mean one thing. "It sounds like they only offer the job so they might meet me."

Mack shifted on his seat. "It's not—"

"It *is*." Enoch forced himself to meet Mack's eyes. "Would they have come to you had you not been seen with me?"

Mack flushed angrily. "They *chose* to come to me. Not everything is about you, Enoch."

Enoch wished it was not so. But why else would they offer so much money to a lad who had skills any historian might have? "I think this time, it is."

Mack had his hands clenched on his knees. "This could be my future," he said, his voice tight as a drum. "All I'm asking is one favour."

"If they wanted to give you a future," Enoch replied quietly, "they would offer it with no chains and no ties. You dunt need to prove anything to them."

"It's one meeting!"

It was, but it would mean throwing away all of Ben's sacrifices—and his own—for so many years.

"I'm sorry," Enoch murmured. "I cannit."

Mack was quiet for a long time. "Right. Thanks."

He got up, stiff-like, to go to the door and stopped there, like he had something else to say. Instead, he shook his head and went out, face like a storm cloud.

Enoch ran a hand over his face. God above, he had but a handful of close friends in the TRI, and now, he had driven one off. Mack wanted out of the TRI, and Enoch had closed the door to keep him in.

Enoch leaned back on the couch and stared at the ceiling. "Fut."

Chapter Seventeen

"How does it work?"

Ben glanced towards the doorway of the small kitchenette. He was throwing together lunch and had left Ada unsupervised, which apparently meant giving her free rein to go through his stuff. She wandered through the doorway holding the box containing his camo-patch.

"It's a digital projection, like the screens of a Leaf," he explained.

She examined it thoughtfully, turning it over. "A mask made of light?"

Technology fascinated her.

He'd dug out an old Leaf for her a few days after her arrival and showed her how to use it. She had exclaimed in delight at the projected images, spinning them with her fingers. Fortunately for both of them, she could read, and Ben wasn't sure if it made him lazy or cowardly when he left her alone with a search engine to answer all her questions.

Sometimes in the night, he woke to see a pale glow rising over the back of the couch where she slept. He couldn't blame her for her curiosity. If he had ended up a new world, he would have wanted to discover everything he could as well.

She peered in at the camo-patch. "It's scarcely anything, is it?"

Ben smiled crookedly as he flipped the omelette over with a spatula. "Scarcely anything, but very controversial. They were banned for private use a few years ago."

"And yet you have one." She chuckled. "Wicked boy." The lid of the box snapped shut. "You will use it when you go out on the morrow?"

"Hiding in plain sight," he confirmed. "I have a lot of different faces I can use." She hummed, and he glanced over at her. "What is it?"

"I have a means to make you invisible to those who hunt you." She tapped the box. "More than this alone."

Witch, he thought. "Oh?" he inquired.

Wrinkles deepened around Ada's eyes when she smiled. "They are seeking one man. You need not be one man." He opened his mouth to comment, but she held up a finger. "You say this can give you many faces, yes?"

"Dozens," Ben agreed, frowning. "Why?"

"They hunt a young man, alone, suspicious. They would not take note of an elderly man and woman, would they?" She made a vaguely mystic gesture with her fingers. "Misdirect them. Become invisible by being two instead of one."

It was reckless to consider taking her out, especially on a trip to see Enoch.

He snorted and dished up the omelette. She said no more about it, but as he returned to his research that afternoon, he couldn't help thinking she was right.

Twenty-four hours later, she sat by his side in the pod when he set out to meet Enoch.

She was distracted by the world outside, staring as it flew by, which meant he could fiddle with his tie unnoticed. He had a feeling he looked ridiculous. The clothes reminded him of his father's, but the grey wig and walking stick picked up the previous afternoon gave him an Einstein-meets-Poirot vibe. He glanced at his reflection in the pod window. Definitely unrecognisable.

God, Enoch was going to piss himself laughing.

"This is all Manchester?" Ada's voice drew his attention.

"Part of it," he confirmed, glancing out of the window. They were coming in towards the canal where the bar was. It was within walking distance of Ben's old hiding place as well, which made him grateful for Ada's presence as a second mask. If the task force was still on the hunt, it was definitely much safer to travel in a pair.

She breathed out slowly, dazed. "It is far bigger than I remember."

The stone circle and her old home were only a few miles from the city, so it wasn't surprising she must have seen it in the past. "Did you go there often?"

She gazed through the glass. "When I was young. I was wed there."

Ben blinked, startled. "You were married?"

"Mm." Her fingers were pressing to the edge of the window, the tips white. "Not for many years. We had a home in the city for a time, but the work was difficult, and we could not find a place to our liking, and all too soon he was gone." She turned to him, but her smile was more brittle than usual. "And so, I ended where you found me."

"I'm sorry."

"It was not your doing, lamb," she said gently, glancing out. "It has become bigger, though. I would not have known it."

"We could try to find the church where you were married, if you like," he offered. "See what it's like now."

She patted him on the hand. "It is a kind thought, my boy, but best not."

Ben could understand the sentiment. It would probably bring back too many memories. He leaned towards the window. "Here we are."

The pub—Armstrongs—was one of the rare preserved old inns and probably seemed more familiar to Ada than the rest of the city. Ben offered her his arm and leaned deliberately on his new walking stick as they made their way inside.

There was every chance they were in the wrong place. The coffee shop meetings had been simple. Enoch just needed to send a message saying he was 'off out,' and Ben would know where to find him. This time, Enoch had tried to send a completely unnecessary coded message.

It was lucky the pub's name could be broken down into a noun and an adjective. At least, if he'd interpreted Enoch's words right—something about strengthening limbs by hoisting many a good pint by the waterway.

Leather-seated booths lined the walls, with small round tables and age-stained wooden chairs. Compared to the shining, polished architecture framing it, it felt like stepping back in time. The pub was almost empty as well, only a few people sitting here and there.

Ben glanced around the bar, relief flooding him when he saw Enoch peering around the edge of the booth in the corner, ducking away like a badger in its hole. Ada was suddenly irrelevant, and Ben reminded himself to buy drinks before making his way towards the table.

Enoch had a screen projected in front of him and peered up warily. There wasn't even a glimpse of recognition, and Ben couldn't resist the impulse to be a complete bugger for once.

"Pardon me, young man," he croaked, "may we join you?"

Enoch stared at him, then burst out laughing. "Jesu! Look at you!"

Ben made a face as he set their drinks on the table. "You weren't meant to recognise me so quickly."

Enoch chuckled as he scrambled to his feet. "I'd know your eyes anywhere." He froze when Ada moved to Ben's side, wary. "And who would this be?"

Ben motioned for him to keep his voice low, for fear of drawing attention. "This would be the woman I told you about last time I saw you."

Instantly, Enoch's attention was completely focussed on her, studying her. "You came through his doorway and all?"

Ada inclined her head. "As yourself." She boldly held out a hand towards him. "Ada. Of 1837."

Enoch grinned and grasped her hand. "Enoch, of 1756."

Ben almost buried his face in his own hand. "And this," he said low, "isn't something we should be talking about out loud in public." He pulled one of the chairs out for Ada then sat beside her. "I was going to tell you I'd be bringing company..." He trailed off, not sure how to explain that he half expected Ada to panic and stay indoors.

"He told me of his predicament," Ada said, taking one of the drinks from the table. "That he is hunted as a rogue." She offered a smile to Ben, which he couldn't help returning. "I thought it might send them hunting elsewhere, if there were two instead of one."

Enoch seemed impressed. "Like as not, they'd never give you a glance." He beamed, all innocence, before he slid one knee between Ben's. "As much as I'd like to have you to myself, I'll share you this once."

Ben closed his thighs on Enoch's. "Very gracious."

The table was small, and Enoch slid close to it, folding his arms on the top. To anyone else, it looked like he was leaning in for an intimate conversation, and Ben wanted to give him a kick when the thigh between his pushed a little closer to his groin.

"How do you find this time, Ada?" Enoch inquired. No one would believe he was trying to grind his leg against Ben's knob. "I dislike the loudness of it all. The brightness."

"Much the same," she agreed, then jumped when Ben's grip on Enoch's thigh gave way, and Ben's knee cracked against the bottom of the table. "Are you well?"

Ben glowered across the table at Enoch, who blinked at him innocently and withdrew his leg. "A cramp, that's all."

"A terrible thing," Enoch lamented, picking up his beer and sipping at it as if he wasn't a complete and wonderful pervert.

Ben's ears were burning, and he wondered how much of the blush was showing through the digital mesh of his camo-patch.

"Likewise, terrible..." Enoch reached into his pocket and withdrew a familiar device, which he laid on the table. A small business button. "Have you not learned to keep your machines safe?"

Ben picked it up, bemused. "Why did you bring it back?"

Enoch seemed equally puzzled. "Is it not yours?"

"I left it *for* you." Ben had a horrible sinking feeling at Enoch's expression. "Oh. Shit. I didn't tell you, did I? I meant to give it to you, and it wasn't in my pocket when I checked, and I couldn't remember..."

"Fut..." Enoch shook his head. "The cleaning people found it. They brung it to Sabine. She thought I had taken a lover who left it behind."

Well, they weren't wrong. Thank God Ben hadn't decided to put some kind of sentimental bollocks on the welcome message. "Have you switched it on?"

Enoch picked it up and turned it over. It was one of the most basic comm devices, little more than a business card for certain professions, discreetly decorated as a medallion. Enoch pressed the small gem, and a screen opened, barely the size of Ben's palm.

"Hello." Ben found it strange hearing his own words in an automated voice. "If you want to call on me again, leave me a message where and when. If suitable, you will receive a confirmation."

"A calling device?" Ada said doubtfully. "You said this place he lives has all manner of machines. Would they not suspect such a device?"

Ben could see the light come on for Enoch.

"A machine which only allows me to send a message out? A time and a place?" A grin lit Enoch's face. "So we might meet without codes and playing with words?" He hesitated, then flicked the machine off and on again, listening to the message. His eyes went wide, and he stared at Ben. "You bugger! This is a whore's tool!"

Ben winced. "Not...exactly!" He held up his hands defensively. "That's what people might think, but it's just for us."

"Sabine had it!" Enoch sputtered indignantly. "She said the security folk permitted it!" He pressed his face into his palm. "Jesu! They will think I paid for favours!"

Both of them became aware of a muffled sound and turned to see Ada stifling laughter in her hand, her cheeks flushed. "Is it common to speak of such things so publicly?" she inquired once she had calmed down, her dark eyes glinting.

Ben made a face. "With this one? Very."

Enoch matched his face-pulling. "Aye, from the man who would have me visiting a nunnery." His expression sobered. "I do have some news for you, mind."

Of course. Enoch was practical. Most of their meetings were both business and pleasure. "Task force related?"

Enoch glanced at Ada. "How much does she know?"

"Most of it," Ben admitted. "I left out some of the specifics, but the task force and what we're doing..."

"Mack?"

Ben straightened. "This is about Mack?" Thank God. Years, he'd been waiting to find out what was going on and why the TRI had hired someone so unskilled but with some inexplicable link to Ben's father's disappearance. "Do you know—"

"Someone has a job for him. He plans to leave the TRI."

It felt like all the air had left the room. Ben's hand trembled around his glass. He stared at it, setting it down undrunk. "Leave the TRI?" Enoch's expression was grim. "But he—we don't know what he—if they had him there for a reason..."

"This is a bad thing?" Ada murmured. "Why so bad?"

"He's the only link we have to the people who attacked my father," Ben said blankly. "If he leaves the TRI, I have no way to keep track of him. He won't lead me to the one who started all of this." He glanced at Enoch, who had been living in the gilded cage for years for him. "Everything you've done..."

"I tried to keep him where he is," Enoch said quickly. "I might have angered him by doing so, but we can't have him running loose."

"The TRI would keep tabs on him." All the sound in the room, even his own voice, echoed as if through a tunnel, coming from a long way away. "It— I wanted to be the one to find him. I wanted to..." He trailed off helplessly, unable to say the words.

Stop them? Convince them not to do what they were going to do? Even if meant breaking more of the laws the TRI upheld? Even if it would change his whole life to that point, sacrifice who he had become to have his father back?

Logically, it was impossible. It had to be impossible. He knew his own history. If anything had changed in the past—anything for the better—he would not be where he was. Which meant either he hadn't reached the point where the change happened in the present to alter the past, or he had failed, and Jesus, he didn't want to fail.

Enoch caught his hand.

"I telt you I'd do all I could to help you find the one that did this," he said, his eyes fixed on Ben's. "I telt you. I'm not stopping now."

Ben turned his hand to clasp Enoch's fingers. He wanted to thank him for all he'd done, but his words had dried up so all he could do was hold onto Enoch. He jolted when another hand—Ada—touched his arm.

"You say your friend here works with them."

"Yeah."

"I'm his eyes in their halls." Enoch was still holding Ben's hand, running his thumb along Ben's knuckles. "Anything they tell me, I bring for him, but there's plenty they keep from me. They speak of people without names."

"I think they know who's behind it all," Ben said. "They don't want me to know in case I do something I shouldn't."

Enoch laughed. "Mind who you are sitting with. You gave them reason enough to doubt you," he said gently, and Ben flinched at his words. Enoch squeezed his fingers again. "And yet you showed your face to them again."

Ben stared at their linked hands. "Mariam," he murmured. "I wanted to let her know at least."

"I know." Enoch's smile was warm and reassuring. "I dint come here to reproach you for caring."

God, Ben wished he'd left Ada at the warehouse. There was no appropriate way to slip off into the bathroom with Enoch. More than anything, he wanted to kiss the man, bury his face in his shoulder and breathe him in, and remember there was someone who stood by him, no matter how crazy and desperate he sounded.

All of them jumped when a Leaf chimed. Enoch withdrew his hand and groped in his breast pocket for his bud. When he opened the screen, a tiny image of Jacob Ofori was visible at the top of the text. "Speak."

"Sorry to interrupt you on your day off," the automated voice said. "Come by the office if you have the time."

Enoch stared at it, then at Ben. The task force only ever called Enoch in if there was a development in the case. "They know you're back."

Ben tried to steady himself, blood rushing dizzyingly, and he searched his memories. Yes, he'd been out to grab some pieces for his disguise, but he'd taken every precaution. The old warehouse had no connection to the new safe house. "We didn't leave any trail. I burned everything that could have given us away."

"Best I go and see what they've found then." Enoch snapped away his screen and slipped the bud away into his pocket. "You should get somewhere safe." He got up, picking up his jacket from the seat beside him. "I'll send word when I know what's amiss."

Ben caught his wrist. "Be careful."

Enoch gazed at him with a fond smile. "I dunt think I am the one who should do that, do you?" For a split second, Ben thought he might lean in for a kiss, but instead, he only moved his hand to press Ben's wrist. "Stay out of any more trouble, aye?"

Ben's mouth was dry, but he nodded. "I'll see you soon."

Enoch stepped behind him, then paused and offered his hand to Ada. "It was a pleasure to meet you, madam."

Ada smiled up at him. "And you, Master Baker."

Enoch shot a furtive glance at Ben, then leaned closer and said in a stage whisper, "Be sure to keep an eye on our lad, eh? I would not be best pleased if he found himself in trouble."

Ada chuckled, covering Enoch's hand with her own. "I shall do my utmost."

Satisfied, Enoch headed for the door. Ben turned in his chair to watch him go. Enoch was halfway to the door when it opened, and a man entered. He was older, thin, and grey-haired, and didn't even hesitate before walking straight up to Enoch.

"Mr. Baker, isn't it?"

Chapter Eighteen

Enoch stared at the man.

He had a good memory for faces, but he'd met so many folk with his work at the TRI. Any older folk were like as not to be from some fine school. The younger ones who came were the ones who saw his streams.

This man was older than most, and Enoch was sure he'd remember someone with a face like a skinny, plucked-bald chicken. He had to have at least seventy years. No face tucks either. He had saggy flaps of skin under his bony chin and all, like he'd had more meat on his bones and lost it all too quick.

"Have we met afore?" Enoch asked.

The man smiled and held out his hand. "Not in person, no."

Habit—proper etiquette and that—made Enoch take the man's hand and shake it, even if his belly was twisting in knots. He heard the scrape of the chair behind him and knew Ben was likely watching and worried. Enoch tucked his free hand behind him as if he meant to bow like a gentleman. He gestured as much as he could, praying Ben would take his meaning, stay still, and not give himself away.

"You've seen the streams, then?"

The man chuckled, releasing Enoch's hand. "One or two, but I've heard a lot about you. You could say I'm...a friend of a friend."

The knots were twisting tighter. The man had come to this place and walked up to him as if he'd expected him, and now talked about friends of friends. Someone had learned he would be there and had spread the word, and if one man knew...

"Begging your pardon, sir." He drew himself up as tall as he might, though he barely stood eye-to-mouth with the fellow. "I have a place to get to. Best be off if I'm to be on time."

The man smiled warmly, but it scarce reached his eyes. "Of course." He stepped aside. "Pass my regards onto our mutual friend."

Enoch hurried on, but the minute he was in his pod, he turned the words over. 'Mutual friend.' Someone he knew who knew where he'd be.

He sank in the seat as the pod moved off, trying to think. There were a few people that knew he was off out for the day, but there was none who knew where. He'd made sure of it. Save for Ben…

But Ben would never tell a soul.

Enoch ran his hand over his mouth.

Even if someone knew, no one at the TRI was allowed to say anything of him to friends or anyone else. There were contracts and all that in place. A body could get in all manner of trouble for speaking about him.

He glanced out the window. The pod was moving faster, the edge of the docklands falling away behind him. If someone knew to find him there, then mayhap it was best not to go anymore. He could ask…

Enoch stared at the glass.

Two people knew of the places he might be, but only one person had asked him to meet someone on their behalf.

No.

Enoch pressed his knuckles to his lips. He had known Mack for two years now. He never seemed the kind of man to sell out a friend's trust for his own benefit. He was a good lad, kind and well meaning.

But he wanted the new job. All he needed to do was have Enoch meet…

"Fut…" Enoch breathed.

The lying prick.

Enoch groped in his pocket for his Leaf. Mayhap they had news, but Jesu, his heart was in his throat. He clenched his fingers to fists, opened up the call panel, and tapped a name.

Jacob Ofori's face appeared on the screen. "Enoch! Good to see you."

"This matter you called about," Enoch said. His voice sounded too high, too sharp, even in his own ears. "Is it of import?"

Jacob was puzzled for a moment. "Oh. No. It can wait if you're not able to get in."

Nothing too urgent. No hunt. No chase. They would tell him if it were so. "I'll not be in," he said. "I'm feeling not well."

Jacob eyed him. "You okay?"

"No." Enoch's throat was tight. "I would go home. Your pardon."

He cut off the call before Jacob could ask any more questions, then touched the pod's navigation. It only had a few settings for the places he went. He touched 'home,' then lay against the seat and stared ahead of him.

Being angry would do no one any good, but Christ's blood! What manner of man would betray the trust of a friend so? What manner of man forgot to honour his friend's wishes? And for a job? For nothing more than a job?

Enoch pressed his hands to the seat under him.

The anger had him quivering. It was not for Ben's sake, though that should have angered him too. But no. This anger, this grief, was for a friendship now broken. God above, he had so little he could say yay or nay to in his life, and Mack had ignored his choice anyway.

"Devil-poxed bastard!" It helped little to scream and profane, but Enoch felt better for it. "Thrice-frigged son of a sow! Filthy, snake-tongued Judas!"

His throat was sore and raw by the time the pod left the city limits, and he sat in silence for the rest of the journey, nursing his rage.

It was close upon an hour before he reached the TRI buildings, and when he did, people stepped away at the sight of him. The anger must be showing on his face. None approached, nor asked him what the matter was. Good. None to get in the way.

He went to the lift and touched the button for the historical team. As the lift rose, he turned over his hands. His nails—short as they were—had scratched flakes out of his palms. They were bleeding.

The lift slowed. The doors chimed. They opened.

Enoch walked along the corridor towards the research suites. The doors were wide open, and he could hear them talking and laughing. The laughter trailed off when he came into the room, some puzzled, some smiling in welcome.

One face went grey as ash.

"Enoch..." Mack rose from his work base. "How're things?"

His expression said everything. He was the 'mutual friend.'

Enoch stared at him as he walked towards him. He had no words, but Christ, he was angrier than he had been in his life. For playing the innocent. For the betrayal.

Mack edged around the base, trying to keep it between them. "Are you okay?"

Okay.

"You telt him." His voice sounded so calm. It surprised him.

Mack darted his tongue along his lips, his eyes flicking about. "What?"

"You," Enoch repeated, circling the base. "You telt him. You telt him where to find me."

Someone nearby swore, and someone else drew a sharp breath.

Mack went pale as wax. "Enoch, don't—"

Two quick steps and Enoch struck him hard across the face. "You shite." He grabbed Mack by the collar and wrenched him down, so they were eye to eye. People called out, grabbing at his arms, but he shoved them off. "I telt you no, and you done it anyway!"

"It w—"

Enoch jerked his arm free from a restraining hand and struck Mack again. "De'il take you, you treacherous wagtail." He pushed him hard. Mack caught himself on his own feet and fell on his arse on the floor, staring up, afeared.

"Enoch..." There was a hand on his arm again. He turned to see one of the historians—Anya?—staring at him nervously. "Please, calm down."

Enoch stared at her, then pointed at Mack, who had scrambled up on his feet. "The bastard telt some stranger where I might be found."

"You didn't—"

"No!" Enoch stormed after him. "No! I telt you no in trust! You said you were a friend to me!"

"I am!" Mack protested.

"Enoch!" Another set of hands, thrown off just as quick.

"Friends dunt betray friends!" Enoch snarled, lunging forward and catching Mack by the collar again. "Not for work!"

"Enoch!" Sabine's voice. "Stop this."

Enoch went still as stone. Mack had his hands up between them, as if to push Enoch away. He was quivering and pale as a scared maid. Neither of them moved.

"Clear the room," Sabine said, voice hard.

Her heels tapped closer as the rest of the people fled for the door, but Enoch kept his eyes on Mack, glaring at him. Best to keep his anger, instead of turning to face her.

"What the hell is going on?" When Enoch didn't turn, she snapped, "Enoch. Now."

"This one thought to use me to gain himself a new job," Enoch spat.

Sabine drew a breath. "How?"

"They wanted to meet with me afore they gave him a place." Enoch twisted his fingers in Mack's collar, snarling at him. "I telt him no. I'm no prize cow to be shown."

"I asked!" Mack burst out all a sudden. "I've done so much for you! Kept you company! Did your streams! All you had to do was one favour! That's what *friends* do!"

Enoch stared at him. "I said no," he repeated, his voice cracked with rage. "Does that mean nothing? Do you not think I want some little part of my life no other can control? Where I am more than a strange man from history to be eyed and poked and prodded?" He shoved Mack away from him. "When a man says no, that dunt give you leave to do as you please anyway!"

Mack was pale. "It was one favour."

"A favour is given! You took it. It weren't given!"

"Enoch." Sabine stepped between them, putting her hand to his chest. "It's all right. We'll deal with this"

He stepped back. His hands were trembling at his sides and his thoughts whirling. It was only right Mack be punished for breaking the rules of the TRI. It was Sabine's right to choose the punishment, but Jesu, Enoch knew it would do naught to stifle his own anger and shock.

"What will you?" he asked, his voice hoarse. "What will you with him?"

"If he's done what you say," Sabine murmured, "that's a decision for the Board."

Behind her, Mack went from white to grey. God's blood, Enoch thought numbly, the Board would dismiss him. Mayhap even jail him. Had Enoch not come in shouting like a fool, the Board would have no reason to spare Mack a second thought.

Enoch touched his hand to his mouth, his stomach curdling. Ben's chance to find the link to his father might be gone.

Sabine took a step closer to Enoch and touched his arm. "Go and get some fresh air, all right? Maybe a walk? You don't need to worry about this."

Christ, he wished it was so simple. One of his only friends using him as so many wished to do. His own anger pushing that friend to the door. If Mack left the TRI, then it was all for naught, and Ben's last wish was impossible. Better to say stop breathing, for it would be easier to do that than keep from worrying.

It must have showed on his face, for she squeezed his arm. "Is there someone I can get for you?"

With one of his few true friends hiding behind her and too much rushing through his mind, it was better to be away from everyone for a while. "I'll—a walk. I think I will walk." He met Mack's eyes over Sabine's shoulder and could almost believe Mack felt guilty for what he had done.

He had to turn away, clenching his fists.

The rest of the historians were in the hall, fluttering about like nervous birds. As soon as he came out the door, they cleared a path for him the length of the hall. One or two stepped forward as if they might say something, but they stepped back just as quick when he glowered at them.

The lift was empty, and he leaned against the wall all the way down, head to the glass. A walk. A walk to clear his head. It would be easier when he could think and find out what Sabine was going to do and...

Then, he would have to tell Ben and see what could be done.

Chapter Nineteen

"Do you know this man?"

Ben shook his head, gazing out of the pod window at the man as he walked towards the main doors of a towering office building. "I've never seen him before."

Their pod was motionless in a parking bay. It would raise questions if they didn't get out or get back on the road. Ben knew they should be on their way, but his eyes were fixed on the man who had crossed paths with Enoch in the pub.

"Your friend said we should return to safety."

"He did."

"Then why follow this one?"

Ben wasn't sure himself. He'd been close enough to hear the stranger's words. There wasn't anything threatening in them, but the TRI was careful with Enoch's privacy. They had been since the minute he'd arrived. The 'friend of a friend' comment felt wrong. No one in the TRI would tell a stranger where to find him. Ben had remained at the pub until the man left, only minutes after Enoch did, but he had taken the chance to capture an image of the man on his Leaf.

"Enoch's meant to be anonymous when he's out in the world," Ben replied, leaning closer to the window to watch as the man ascending up the outside of the building in one of the glass-walled lifts. "I don't trust anyone who says they know someone who knows him."

Ada touched his arm. "Do you think him a threat?"

Ben drew back as the man vanished into the building. "I don't know, but if I can find out who he is or where he comes from, I can let Enoch know to keep his eyes open for him."

"We could go in. Seek him ourselves."

It was tempting, but they needed to be more cautious. "We can't risk going in there. That kind of business always has the highest quality of technology. It would see straight through my camo-patch." He touched the controls of the pod, sweeping them into the street. "I'll run a search on social media, see if any of their algorithms can pick him up through facial recognition, but if that doesn't work, it'll be the old-fashioned way."

Ada gazed through the rear window of the pod. "He went into the twelfth level of the building. Have you the means to find him there?"

Ben thumbed open his Leaf. "It might be possible. You're sure it was twelve?"

"It seemed so. The glass box rose to that level." She studied his screen. "Perhaps he is the master of the building? Perhaps the level means nothing?"

"The sign outside suggested there were a lot of businesses based there." He opened up the directory of the building. "We just have to narrow down which one he came from and whether he's based there at all."

Ada glanced again at the towering building. "Ah. So simple." She tapped her fingertips on her knee. "Do we need to return to the house at once? Can we not take some air?"

Ben sighed. It wasn't fair to keep her closed up all the time, as much as he'd prefer to be where all his tech was. "Okay. Yes." He rubbed at his brow. "There's a walk by the canal a few minutes in the other direction. We can stop there for a little while."

By the time they drew up at the canal walkway, Ben's social media search had turned up nothing. Either the man had no online presence or had managed to avoid having his picture uploaded on any of the major sites. Ben swore under his breath and began the sift through every company on the twelfth floor of the building.

Some of the business link sites provided names of their managing executives and some of their employees, but few of them had any pictures. The best he could do was start whittling down the names he could find, even if it meant a lot more work and time.

"This seems like much work for very little gain," Ada murmured as he flicked open another three screens in front of him.

He flashed a glare at her. "No offence, but Enoch is my friend, and if someone is bothering him, I want to know who it is. The TRI can't protect him all the time."

She was quiet for a moment. "Is it so important to you?"

"What do you think?" he snapped. Ada didn't recoil, but he saw the way she clenched her hands in her lap. He ran a hand over his face. "Sorry. I'm sorry. Yes. Enoch—he's important to me. I can't do much for him, but at least I can do this."

Ada frowned, the lines creasing up her face. She glanced out of the window, then pushed the control to slide the door open. "I'll leave you to your work for a time. Would an hour be enough for you?"

He wondered if he should feel guilty about leaving her alone in the city. "You don't mind if I don't walk with you?"

She gazed out over the canal. "It seems a safe place to walk. There are many people with small dogs and children. I only need a means to find my way to you, if I become lost."

Ben removed the smaller bud from his lapel. It was a useful little device but lacked the memory or capacity for the searches he wanted to do. He fanned out a map on a screen the size of her hand. "You're the small red dot." He tapped the screen and added a pin. "That's where I am. You just need to follow the red dot. I can use my Leaf to track you as well if you get disorientated."

She smiled. "Like your string and sticks." She ducked out of the pod and into the bright daylight. "An hour, then."

It was probably a stupid mistake to let her go roaming, but Enoch had to be his priority. Ada couldn't really do any harm, and he had much more important things to do than babysit another historical figure, especially when the one he actually cared about needed his help. And if she did end up in the care of the TRI, she would have more freedom and support than he could offer, even if it did mean he'd be on his own again.

Ben closed his eyes, drawing a breath. There was work he had to do.

He was still working on the numerous staff members when a notification came in, a message from Enoch.

Ben popped it open at once, his pulse racing.

I am very sad today. It seems I am to lose my tech man.

"Shit…" Ben breathed. He darted his fingers over the keys. *I'm sorry. What happened?*

He had a big mouth.

Ben groaned inwardly. The confidentiality clauses of the TRI were ironclad. He glanced at the rest of his screens and understood exactly which matters Mack must have spoken about. The 'mutual friend.' Someone who had helped Enoch pick out the pub for his meeting.

Which begged one question…

Well, it's lucky someone reported him. You don't want someone like that around.

Enoch didn't reply at once. *It was my doing.*

Ben stared blankly at the screen. That went against everything Enoch had said in the pub, the promise he'd made to keep Mack at the TRI until they found out the link between him and the people who had attacked Ben's father.

He lied to me. I was angry.

Ben sank in the seat.

Enoch had been angry, and because of that, Mack would face the consequences of crossing the TRI and breaking their strict confidentiality clauses. If the TRI dismissed him, then they snatched away the only clue Ben had. Some nameless man in a pub wasn't any good to them if Mack and his leads were off the table.

"Shit…" he said again.

He knew he should reply to Enoch, reassure him somehow, but the words were gone, and he was so damned tired. He stared at the screens of information that might hold the identity of the man they were searching for, but how could they be sure the man was even relevant at all? Maybe he was no one, nothing more than a messenger, expendable once he had served his purpose.

Ben closed all the screens and pressed the heels of his hands against his eyes.

It was too much to pin his hope on a random stranger. He'd already put an unfair amount of responsibility on Enoch's shoulders. Enoch had given up his freedom to try to help him, and he'd done as much as he could.

"Shit…" he whispered into his wrists.

There were—things. He had things he needed to do. Names. The names needed to be sifted. He needed to find it. Him. The stranger. The only link they had left. He couldn't go to Mack. They—the TRI—the task force—someone would be watching. Someone was always watching.

"Shit, shit, shit." The pod felt too small and closed in, smothering and suffocatingly hot. He shoved the door open and scrambled out.

Fresh air washed over him. Cool. Bright sunlight.

He sagged against the pod, gulping breaths, his eyes closed against the light.

Calm and quiet. Needed a moment. Needed to gather himself up again.

He made his way to a bench a dozen paces away. He sat, legs drawn up cross-legged on the seat, and stared at the canal. The sun shimmered on the surface. A small rowing boat slid by. There were people. Children.

Laughter. No gates or closed rooms or dead parents he would never be able to find.

Ben bowed his head, squeezing his eyes shut. Christ, he was useless. Falling apart wouldn't help. He wrapped his hands over his ankles, squeezing until it hurt, and counted back from ten to try to steady his breathing again. It didn't work as well as usual, and his face was wet, but he couldn't—wouldn't—loosen his hands to wipe his cheeks. People would notice. People didn't need to notice. Not when he had his camo-patch in place, and it would draw attention.

A few minutes—or maybe more?—later, a rustle of cloth beside him made him startle.

"'Tis I," Ada said quietly.

Ben subsided on the bench and opened his eyes. "Sorry," he said, forcing a quick smile. "I was miles away."

She studied him and gently brushed her knuckles up his cheek, drying the remains of the tears. He flinched in surprise, and she drew away at once. "You are distressed?"

"Tired," he admitted. "Frustrated. It's— I've been working so hard for this, and it's all falling apart."

Her mouth twisted in a sympathetic grimace. "You know of this man. The one we saw."

He sighed heavily. "I don't even know if he's involved. Even if he is, I don't know who he is or if he has anything to do with the building he went into."

"He does."

"You can't know that."

Ada dipped her hand into her pocket and withdrew a small rectangle card. An old-fashioned business card. "I know." She held the card out to him. "These are his people. I could not find his name for you, but I found his people."

Ben stared at her, then at the card. "What—? How?"

She spread her hands. "You spoke of the old-fashioned way, using your machines and the like. I thought upon my manner of old-fashioned way." She jerked her head in the direction of the buildings. "I have my feet and I walked. I have my mouth and I asked."

Ben's pulse was thundering. Christ, she might have gotten in trouble, gotten arrested, anything. She could even have ended up locked up as a mad old woman. "But—it could have been dangerous! You—you're not exactly used to this world."

"Fear not." She patted him on the knee with her free hand. "I spoke as you and yours do. I have watched your movers and seen how women speak now. They gave me a small brooch to grant me leave to visit my grandson upon the twelfth level." Her eyes widened in feigned innocence, and in a convincingly frail and bewildered voice, she said, "I cannot recall his name, but I know I was to meet him on the twelfth level. He said to meet him there."

Ben realised his mouth was open, gaping like an idiot. "You...tricked them?"

"I thought it wiser than showing the picture about, as if the man we seek has a bounty upon his head." She gestured at herself with a rueful chuckle. "I am no sheriff to chase after thieves and vagabonds." She returned her gaze to his with a smile. "Will you have it?"

She was still holding the card, and he reached out to take it.

"You didn't need to do this."

Ada smiled and patted his knee again. "I know, but 'tis done."

Ben's vision blurred, his eyes wet, but for a completely different reason. He wrapped his fingers around the card. "Thank you."

Chapter Twenty

"You look like shit."

Enoch peered up at Janos through half-closed eyes. Why Janos had come, he did not know, nor did he care, not when there was a man beating his head with a hammer. "I had—" He pressed one hand on the doorframe to stop it from moving. "I had a brew or two."

Janos peered over his head into Enoch's home. He winced as if pained, and Enoch had no need to turn to know why. The bottles and cans were still cast about on the floor. Enoch had woken up among them when Janos had buzzed at the door. "Ah."

Enoch held up a finger. He had risen too fast, and his stomach was only now minding all he had put into it the night before. "Your pard—" He cut himself off and closed a hand over his mouth. He took a step and swayed, clutching at the wall, as the bile rose.

All at once, two broad arms looped about his middle and hefted him off the floor.

Janos had him to the bathroom and beside the toilet with scarce a moment to spare.

Christ above, he felt like hell. He bowed over the cool white seat, groaning between every fresh twist from his belly. Everything inside him was trying to come out, and when he retched his last, he rested his chin on the rim, moaning as if he might die.

"Here." Janos lowered a glass of water into his line of sight. "This will help."

"Will you not just drown me instead?" Enoch moaned plaintively. "It would be a kindness."

Janos gave him a stern glare like a father to a son. "Drink your water. I will make you some toast."

"Nooooo..." Enoch dropped his head to the toilet seat.

Janos silently held the glass close to his hand until Enoch took it, then walked out towards the kitchen.

Enoch lifted his head and sipped the water carefully. Janos was right. It was better to undo the worst of it than lie on the bathroom floor and whine. No matter how cold and pleasant the floor would feel.

It was a foolish thing to drink all he had in his fridge. He drank little enough, lest he say the wrong thing to the wrong person, but now...now, he had done that. He had taken all their careful plans and smashed them to dust.

And so, one drink became two and more.

He was already well into his cups when Ben—Diaval—finally replied to Enoch's last message to say he had found himself a new friend just that afternoon and maybe Enoch could do the same. It was a bad message to hear when he had a bottle in his hand and the fear he had ruined all things between them.

He had beer. He had bottles of clear spirits with strange names. He drank more and more and swore at the walls and the floor and at the thrice-damned buggery of it all. It was dark when he fell from the couch, landing on bottles and cans, and slept where he lay.

Now, there was a pain in his head, a burning in his throat, and a big Hungarian man singing loudly in the kitchen.

Enoch pressed his hand to his head and rose on quaking legs. Best to keep to his role until he could speak to Ben again and understand what they were to do. He padded through to the kitchen and sat on one of the high-backed chairs beside the small table. There were two pieces of toasted bread with butter on a plate and two small white pills beside it.

"You need to eat something first, then you take the pills," Janos said as he made a pot of coffee. "You must have something in your stomach, or it will be worse."

Enoch winced and picked up a piece of toast. The last thing he wanted to do was eat. "Why dint they make something to help right off?" he complained, then nibbled along the edge of the crust.

"Because they want to teach us a lesson," Janos said, chuckling. He brought the coffee over, carrying two cups in one hand and the pot in the other. "Will you tell me why you drank so much? I don't think this is normal for you."

Enoch chewed the toast, staring at his plate. "Mack." It was the start of the reason, and Enoch knew everyone in the TRI would know of it. It was like a village sometimes with stories and gossip passing about. "You heard what happened?"

Janos grimaced sympathetically. "I heard about it." He sipped his coffee and waited as if Enoch might tell him more. Enoch stared forlornly at his toast, chewing and swallowing as much as he could. Janos finally said, "Mack is why I am here."

Enoch paused, mouth full. "Mm?"

"You have heard he will be dismissed?" Enoch nodded slowly. "And that he spoke to a man who is not from the TRI?" Another nod. "The task force would like to know about this man."

Enoch wished his head was clearer. Janos was no part of the task force, but he knew what they wanted. Someone from the task force had spoken to him. Enoch could not be sure why. It would make more sense if his head was not pounding like a regimental drum. He set down the toast and picked up the tablets. "Do they know who it is?"

"This is why they want to talk to you," Janos said. "If someone outside of the TRI has found our staff, we need to know who they are. We need to keep our staff safe." He smiled crookedly. "I think you can wait until your head is not so bad."

It took scarce fifteen minutes before the tablets did their magic. As soon as the ache in his head and the knot in his belly were gone, Enoch made some more toast and had a second cup of coffee, praying it might wake his mind enough to make sense of what was going on.

"Why did they send you to me?" he inquired through a mouthful of toast and honey. "If the task force ask for me, Sabine is the one who comes."

Janos took a sip from his cup. "You acted unexpectedly yesterday. Sabine said you tried to attack Mack."

Enoch winced in understanding. "You are bigger than she."

"And better to sit on you, if you try and run out and do something foolish," Janos said gravely, but his eyes were glinting. "She knows I would not be afraid to carry you under my arm like a goose to be plucked."

"She thought I would do something? To Mack?"

"That, we didn't know," Janos replied. "She didn't think you would take him by the throat, but you did. I didn't think you would drink every bottle you had in your refrigerator, but you did. It is a day of many new and strange things." He set down his cup and reached for the coffee pot again. "She is very busy also. She needs to deal with Mack formally. There will be meetings."

He offered to pour another cup for Enoch, who shook his head.

"I thought it were decided," he said. "Int he being dismissed? I got a message from Sabine to say so."

"Dismissed, yes," Janos confirmed, "but they need to decide if it counts as leaking TRI information when it is not about the TRI." He waved with his machine-hand towards Enoch. "*You* are not TRI information, but they need to decide how much you fall under the confidentiality clause."

Enoch put by the last of his toast, his taste for food gone. "That—he—I dunt care about the confiddle-el-ility bollocks. It weren't the TRI he telt them about. It were me."

"I know." Janos set down his cup. "People are fuckers sometimes."

Enoch blinked at him in surprise. Janos never profaned in front of him. "You can swear? In the English?"

Janos laughed aloud. "You have met my husband, yes? If I did not know my swearing before I met him, then I know it all now." His expression turned serious. "But it is right. Sometimes, people you like will be fuckers, and you cannot change them. You can only know there are people who are not fuckers."

"Fucker," Enoch echoed. Saying it made him feel better. "Aye. He is one of them, right enough." It would do no man any good to sit and think on how the word felt on his tongue. Best to make use of what he knew, and do what little he could before Ben was done with him and all. He pushed his plate by. "Will you come to the task force with me? I would find somewhere else for a brew once I am done."

Janos raised his eyebrows. "After the night you had?"

Enoch made a face. "The ale I keep here is like cat piss. I would find something *good.*"

Janos chuckled. "I'll arrange it." He got up from the table. "Get dressed. I will clean up here, and we can go."

The journey into the city went quick enough as Enoch dozed through much of it. The hangover was gone, but he had stayed up into the small hours, drowning his sorrows. It was a sad truth to realise your lover had no more use for you. He chose to close his eyes and think of anything else and was woken by Janos shaking his shoulder.

As Enoch climbed out of the pod, he glanced over to the coffee bar across the road. For the first time in months, he had no reason to go for coffee. They had talked and laughed there, when none had known of Ben's disguise. Now, it was impossible he would come back.

"Are you all right?" Janos asked suddenly from beside him.

Enoch forced a smile. "All's well." He turned towards the task force offices and made his way up the stairs. To his surprise, it was as noisy and busy as the day they had lost Ben through the time gate. People were talking and moving and talking again. No one even noticed him enter at first. "What's amiss?"

Jacob spun about. He had been standing over one of the officers working on a computer. "Good. You're here." He strode over and caught Enoch by the shoulder, steering him through the bustle of people to Lysander's office. "Ly, he's here."

Lysander glanced up. He had screens up in front of them, but he moved his hand and shut them at once. Enoch only saw a glimpse of a face, not enough to recognise it.

"Enoch." Lysander motioned to the chair opposite him. "Sit down."

Enoch did so. Lysander's tone was shorter than usual. No smiles or please and thank yous. That meant something was very amiss. His heart skipped a beat. Mayhap they had found Ben's trail, as he feared. Zooth, Enoch wished he had asked to go for his usual coffee. It seemed a time to be aware and alert.

"Has something happened?" he asked, glancing between Jacob and Lysander. "It all seems a rush here today."

Jacob sat in the seat by him. "We have some things we're working on, but we need to talk to you about the man you ran into yesterday."

"Janos said it would be so. On account of him knowing TRI matters?"

"Exactly." Lysander rested his arms on his desk and folded his hands. "Sabine said when you went to confront Mack, you knew he had arranged the encounter?"

Enoch hesitated, then explained, "He had word about new work, and they wanted to meet with me afore they gave him any job."

"Did he say what the job was?" Jacob asked.

"Not much." Enoch rubbed his nose thoughtfully with his knuckle. "Much like he has now, he said. Studying history and data and that."

"Did Mack say why they wanted to see you?"

Enoch eyed Lysander curiously. He was a calm man all the time, but there was something off. His hands were clenching together until the knuckles were white. If something was amiss, it was something serious. "He said he needed to prove where he worked."

"Validation," Jacob murmured.

"Eh?" Enoch glanced up at him.

"We think this man wasn't convinced about Mack's involvement with the TRI. The only evidence was the fact that Mack was seen out with you on two occasions." Jacob sighed. "It's a very roundabout way to get the proof he wanted."

"Why would he want Mack?" Enoch asked. "Are there not many who know..." He trailed off, feeling like an idiot. "He wants him for what he knows of the TRI. He has no wish to use Mack for his learning."

Jacob and Lysander exchanged a glance.

"That's what we're afraid of," Lysander said. "Did this man say anything to you?"

Enoch tried to recall. His mind had been in a dozen directions in that moment with Ben behind him and a stranger before him. "Only that he was a friend of a friend. He bid me pass on his greetings to our 'mutual friend.'"

Another glance passed between Jacob and Lysander.

"You're sure that's all?"

"I dint want to talk to a man that had come hunting me. I telt him I was going, and he let me be. He only telt me we had a shared friend. I dint think on it until I was in the pod, and then..." He paused, a thought coming to him. He had left the inn early and only now remembered why. "You called me in. Afore I saw the fellow, you called me in from my day out. I never asked why."

If Enoch had not watched Jacob carefully for the years he had known him, he would not have recognised the tight twitch at Jacob's mouth. He was troubled.

"We wanted you to review some footage," he said after a moment. "Nothing that can't wait."

Nothing that can't wait. That was a fine manner of a lie. Jacob would never call him in unless it was something of great importance. The footage was like as not about Ben, and there was too much excitement in the office for it to be aught but him. And yet, they were sitting and speaking of the stranger?

Enoch tried to hide his puzzlement. Why did the task force—only created to find Ben—need to know so much about the man?

"Do you think he knows Master Ben? The man I saw?" he asked, watching them carefully.

"No." Jacob spoke too quick, too certain.

"We're not sure," Lysander said only a moment later.

Enoch rubbed his knuckle with his thumb, glancing betwixt them. He'd never seen them both uneasy. One or the other, aye, but never both. This man was right important if he'd rattled them so. "But there's something between him and Ben, aye?"

Lysander narrowed his eyes like a cat. "What makes you think that?"

Enoch knew he'd touched on something there. He shrugged, trying to playact the puzzled fool. "Everything done hereabout is to find Ben Sanders, int it? The task force, I mean? That's who you're seeking. Why are you keeping an eye on this fellow, if it int anything to do with Ben?"

Jacob and Lysander shared a look that said Enoch was asking too many of the right questions.

"As far as we know," Jacob said finally, with the care of a man with something to hide, "this man has had no contact with Ben. We're pretty sure Mack was his only point of interest, and you were just collateral. We just want to be sure."

It gave no sign of why they were so interested in him. They were dancing about the truth so carefully Enoch knew he would get no answer from them. But leastways, he knew one thing: they had not yet found Ben's trail.

"Ah." He hummed as if it made sense. "I'm seeing plots where there are none."

It was scarce visible, but he saw the way they both relaxed.

Even if they weren't saying so, he knew there was something amiss. They were too worried about the stranger for it to be naught. That was something Ben would want to know about. After all, no one else had shifted the gaze of the task force from Ben himself afore.

"Do you think he'll come by me again?" he asked. "Should I be mindful?"

Jacob shook his head at once. "If he let you walk away so easily, I don't think he had any interest in anyone but Mack."

Enoch cocked his head. "Though I know of the TRI as well?"

For a moment, Lysander almost smiled. "Do you know how the gates work?"

In truth, after seeing Ben build some of them up from wires and bolts and metal, he likely knew more about them than Jacob or Lysander put together, but he waved a hand as if it were a jape. "Only how to walk through one."

Jacob patted his shoulder with a wry smile. "I think you'll be safe."

Enoch wanted to breathe out in relief—another day, another secret kept. "Long may it stay so."

Chapter Twenty-One

On any other day, Ben didn't mind missing out on the great outdoors. He always preferred to be indoors, working on his machines when he could. Once upon a time, when he was a kid, Mariam had resorted to bribery to make sure he got at least an hour of fresh air a day. It was a win-win situation—an attempt at good health and the most up-to-date and high-end tech for him to play with.

Now, he was sitting in front of a dozen screens, hands resting on his ankles, and wishing like hell he could be by the canal with Ada.

"Do you see him yet?" she murmured, earpiece in one ear, camera with microphone in a pretty brooch on her blouse, another camera in the clasp pinning up her long silver hair.

He searched the screens. "Not yet."

Ada continued to walk, stepping by children and politely greeting adults. "You're sure he'll come?"

Ben nodded distractedly, scanning the faces of the people walking by and chewing on his thumbnail.

Enoch's message with a time and a place had come unexpectedly. Maybe he only wanted to meet to discuss what to do next or maybe it was something more serious. There weren't any hints in messages he sent to Diaval, which made Ben think it was the former.

If they could find him. The trouble with picking a pleasant walkway in the middle of the city. It was always going to be busy on a sunny day. A crowd could be useful, but they could also get in the way.

"Wait!"

Ada came to an immediate stop. From the pantomime on his screen, she'd paused to fish a handkerchief out of her bag. "Where?"

"Other side of the canal." Ben scaled up the footage. "Find an empty bench. Sit down. He's seen you, so he'll find you."

It was easier said than done with the throngs of people, but she managed it. Ten minutes later, Ben heard the wonderfully familiar voice through her mike. "Would you mind if I sit?"

Ada sounded like she was smiling. "You're welcome to it."

Ben could hear the ruffle of fabric and the satisfied sigh as Enoch sat. For a few seconds, neither of them spoke.

"He int here?" Enoch sounded disappointed.

"With all that has happened in the past few days, he thought discretion was wise." Ada tilted her brooch on her blouse, and Enoch's face swam into view. At least his jaw, cheek, and ear were visible. "He gave me a small device. He can hear us both when we speak."

Enoch glanced at her with a wan smile. "Aye, he does that. All his wee machines and the like." He sighed again. "Is he...displeased with me? Is that why he int here?"

Ben wanted to kick himself. "Tell him no! Tell him it's nothing to do with that!" he blurted out. "With Mariam and the café and everything, I thought it was better to keep at a distance in case we push our luck, and we only have one gate and one chance left to..."

Mercifully, Ada managed to reduce his embarrassing word-vomit to a more reasonable, "He feared your run of ill fortune might continue and that you might be caught together. He would keep you both from trouble."

Enoch snorted, but Ben recognised the relief in the sound. "Then he is too late."

"Idiot," Ben murmured fondly. "Ada, can you give him the second earpiece?" He waited until he saw Enoch casually scratch at his hair to slip the earpiece in. "You're talking out your arse again."

Enoch laughed, but it sounded forced. "Says you."

Ben wished he could have been there in person to reassure him. "I just think we need to be careful. We didn't think anyone would notice us at the coffee shop, but they did, and you remember what happened there. After what happened at the pub, I don't want to risk that again."

Enoch's mouth was a grim line. "Right enough." Out of line of sight, he opened up something with a rustle of paper. "I missed lunch, wandering about like a lost lamb," he informed them before taking a bite from a sausage roll. "Ben, you're missing a fine length of sausage."

Ben couldn't help the bubble of happiness welling up in him. Same old Enoch. "You can owe me one."

Ada chuckled, and Enoch forced a smile. He chewed the mess of sausage and pastry and swallowed before saying, "I'll not forget it." He offered Ada a bite of the roll, but she waved it away. "I was by at the task force the other day. You dunt need to worry so. They dunt know where you are."

"Yet," Ben murmured.

"Can you not take some good news when it is given?" Enoch grumbled, exasperated.

"Old habits," Ben admitted ruefully. "We've come too close too many times in the past few weeks."

Enoch made a sound of assent. "D'you know aught else about the fellow in the inn?"

The day after Mack's dismissal, Enoch had sent a single-lined message to the Diaval account: *I have no liking for strangers.* Why he'd brought the man up, Ben didn't know, but it couldn't be a coincidence that both he and Enoch were suspicious.

"I found the name of the company he works within," Ada said quickly. "Ben is seeking out his name, but thus far, there has been little enough. He is very careful about where he puts his face or his name."

"Fut..." Enoch muttered, his mouth full of food.

"What are you thinking?" Ben asked.

Enoch washed down his food with a drink from a bottle. "This man has stolen the attention of the task force from you."

That made Ben frown. "This guy? Did they say why?"

Enoch wiped his mouth. "Only that it was to do with Mack." He dusted the crumbs off his shirt. "But it was enough to get Jacob and Lysander all het up."

Enough to draw the attention of the task force *and* bother Jacob and Ly?

"They're the ones who hunt you?" Ada inquired.

"They're the leaders," Ben confirmed, unfolding from his chair and pacing in a circle.

Something was off about it. The man was a nonentity, private and cautious. The company they'd linked to him was some kind of trade and shipping business. Not exactly historical research, unless it was a private interest for their mysterious stranger.

"I asked if they thought the fellow knew you," Enoch said, "Jacob said no."

"Strange, then," Ada said thoughtfully, "that they put aside their quarry to pay attention to someone of no importance."

"Fut!" Enoch swore suddenly. "Christ's blood! That's it!"

Ben blinked. "What?" Ada echoed him.

"No importance...but what if he *is*?" Enoch ran a hand over his mouth. "Aye...aye, it would make a manner of sense." He was staring ahead of him. "Jesu, if that's so..."

He stayed silent for so long Ada reached out and touched his arm. Enoch flung up a hand, fingers twitching. His eyes were darting about, and Ben recognised his expression.

"Let him be," he said quickly. "Ada, leave him. Let him think."

Ada jolted as if he'd yanked her on a string. "Is he all right?" she asked in an undertone.

Ben watched his lover intently. "If I know that cunning little brain of his, God, yes."

"They're after the bigger prize," Enoch finally said. "They're after you, aye, but you're not the first-time thief they've had dealings with. There was another, far worse, that came afore. Who else would they put you aside for?" He peeped at her brooch and into the camera. "Who else but someone worse?"

The world seemed to shudder to a stop. "Him? It's him?"

"Jacob said this man wanted Mack for what he knows of the TRI," Enoch said, his words coming in a rush. "What if he believes Mack can use your father's machines? If that is all that has stopped him until now, no small wonder Jacob and Lysander are afeared."

"But..." Ben felt as if he'd slammed into a wall, his brain whirling. "But they said they caught the person responsible. Years ago, I mean. They know who he is. Why didn't they keep an eye on him to stop him interfering with people from the TRI...?" He stared at Enoch's face on the screen and remembered their last encounter in the pub. "Fuck..."

"Ben?" Ada prompted, sounding confused.

"Why did Jacob want you at the task force the other day?" Ben demanded sharply. "When he called you and asked you to come in?"

Enoch shrugged. "He said it could wait, but I dunt—"

"He wanted you out of the pub." Ben's ribs heaved with every unsteady breath. "They'd never call you in on your day off if it wasn't something major. They saw this guy coming towards a pub and must have pegged you were there and tried to extract you."

"For fear he would meet me..." Enoch finished for him. "They *do* have eyes on this bugger, then?"

Ben stared blindly at the screen. After everything he'd done and all the shit he'd dug himself into, they'd found the man. Even if the TRI and the police and the task force were trying to keep his identity under wraps, they knew where he based his operations. They had a face. Christ, they might actually be able to figure it all out!

He was brought back to himself by Ada saying his name. She sounded worried.

"What?"

"Are you well? You went quiet?"

"Yeah." His voice broke, and he laughed unsteadily. "Yes. I'm fine. I—we shouldn't get our hopes up. It might not be him."

Enoch voiced his thought for him, "But 'tis better than anything we have found thus far."

"This will take caution," Ada said thoughtfully. "This task force sounds like it has the means to put eyes and ears anywhere."

"What of the man?" Enoch inquired. "Do you think you will be able to find his name?"

"It would be impossible to hide him forever," Ada said.

"Everyone leaves a mark somewhere," Ben agreed. "There has to be some way to identify him and see who he is or who he might be working for."

"Would you have me find out what the task force knows?" Enoch asked quickly. "They know I have an interest in finding you, but since this man came to me, they know I have reason to seek him too."

Ben chewed his lip. He'd seen Jacob and Lysander under pressure before. Something about a threat made them more alert and more suspicious. He remembered when his own plans had been rapidly unravelling and Jacob and Lysander came so close to catching him.

He'd only escaped by frantic planning, timing, and throwing Enoch—voluntarily—at them as a distraction. The fact that it had accidentally triggered a borderline breakdown in Lysander was something he'd never expected. Lysander always seemed so together it came as a shock to know the man had limits. He'd hated himself for taking advantage of Lysander's recovery to make his break for it, but at the time, he'd seen no other choice.

"I don't think that's a good idea," he finally said. "You said they were worried about this man. If we're right and they've already got eyes on him, it means they'll be paying even more attention than usual. You don't want them turning their attention to you." He saw the set of Enoch's jaw and added quickly, "I'm serious, Enoch. You know how good they are. We don't need to give them an excuse to suspect you."

"And if you have no means to find out who this man is?" Enoch said stubbornly. "I have the means."

"As long as you've been there, you've had the means, and we were never able to dig up what they were hiding," Ben snapped. "Do you really think they're going to cock up now something is happening with him?"

Enoch scowled, turning away, and Ben subsided in his chair, pressing his knuckles to his mouth. God, he shouldn't have yelled, but it was all too close. He didn't know what else he could say, but Ada—and the camera—moved a little closer to Enoch.

"It's too great a danger," she added to Ben's argument. "You heard what our lad says. These men will be on their guard more than ever. He fears for you. Pray give him no further cause to fear."

Enoch glanced at her unhappily, then away. "I would see you again soon," he said, rising and refastening his coat. He wasn't looking at Ada, and his words were definitely not for her.

"Enoch..." Ben began haltingly.

Enoch feigned scratching his ear and then dropped his earpiece into Ada's lap. He gave her a shallow bow, his voice clipped as he said, "God bless, madam."

"Shit..." Ben whispered. Shit, shit, shit. As if Enoch needed anything else to feel guilty about. He already blamed himself for what happened with Mack. Yelling at him about the lack of progress they'd made was just adding fuel to the fire.

Ada turned on the bench to watch him go. "Do you think he might do something foolish?"

Ben took a deep breath. He had dug his fingers into his ankles again, painful to the point of bruising, and he had to prise them away. Enoch hated sitting and waiting. He hated not doing *something*. "Don't know." He pressed the heels of his hands against his eyes and wished it wasn't a lie.

Of course Enoch would do something foolish. The scars all over his back screamed how reckless he could be. If he considered something a fair and right plan of action, he would take it and damn the consequences. That was why he'd ended up in the TRI: Ben needed someone he trusted to help him there, so Enoch launched himself in without question.

God, he was going to do something stupid, and if Ly or Jacob or Danny or any of them figured it out and realised he'd fooled them all—

"Ben," Ada murmured. "He's a clever lad. He mayn't get caught."

Ben's breathing hitched again. He didn't know when he'd started gasping for air, but his chest had tightened unbearably. "Fuck…" he whispered. "Fuck."

"I'll come home." Ada was on the move.

The room was darker. Even the screens weren't so bright. *Stupid.* He dug his fingers into his chest. Barely even felt it, his breaths too small and short. The chair was too high, dizzyingly high, so he slid down. Cool, stable, even floor. He sagged against the side of the desk and tried to remember how to breathe.

Somewhere, a long way away, he heard footsteps. It felt like too much effort to open his eyes when a hand touched his.

"Enoch…?"

"Only me," Ada said, her voice tense. "Jesu, Ben…" She brushed his brow, her palm so warm he almost flinched. Ah. Yes. The cold sweats came after a panic attack. He forced his eyes open, and she was as pale as he probably was. "You—are you well?"

He managed a nod, his head aching and his whole body wrung out. "Sorry. Worrying myself sick."

She stroked his brow, worry creased her face. "He will be fine," she murmured. "You need not fear for him. If anything happens, we steal him away and bring him here and none shall harm him."

He laughed unsteadily. "Three rogue time travellers on the run. Great plan." He struggled to get up, swaying, his head spinning. Ada had one hand under his arm, her grip surprisingly strong for someone so old. "I can't let him get in more trouble. Not on my behalf."

She smiled, the light from a dozen screens casting a thousand more lines in her wrinkled face. "Then we work faster than he does and find that which he would seek before he even sets foot in their domain."

"We?" he echoed. "This won't be easy."

She grinned at him, eyes gleaming. "I like a challenge."

Chapter Twenty-Two

Enoch was not best pleased.

For two days, he had been kept from the task force. It had happened in the past, but it had never rubbed him the wrong way afore. They were busy, he knew. No doubt they were still hunting Ben, but there was the stranger too.

He wished to Christ he could know what was happening. He felt stuck like a lamb in a ditch, pacing about and bleating uselessly at any who would listen.

It was made worse because Ben and Ada could do something, but he had to keep careful and quiet. Ben could do his magic with his machines to find information that none would think to look at, and all the while, Enoch could do nothing but try to keep his temper.

It had grown difficult after Mack's betrayal, but at least it gave him an excuse for storming about and snapping like a lord when anyone asked him the matter. Janos made sure to keep him company when he could. But to know how close they were to ending it all and that Enoch was of no use weighed heavy on him.

"Does it help?" Janos asked, late in the second afternoon as they walked about the grounds.

"Your pardon?"

"Getting angry with everyone around you?"

Enoch scuffed his boot in the grass. "No." He sighed. "I would that it did." He glanced up at Janos. "I hate to do nothing when I know this stranger is about, and Mack is—" Jesu, he had no notion what Mack was now. "They haven't telt me what has happened, but I know something is going on because they keep me away."

Janos patted him on the shoulder. "Communication is not an easy thing when you are very busy. Give them some time, and they will call on you."

Time, one of the few things Enoch had enough of.

"Aye," he agreed gloomily. He scratched at his jaw. "Would you have a drink afore you leave for the night?"

Janos smiled. "If I am promised better company."

Enoch smiled back wryly. "I dunt think I can make any oath, but I'll try my best."

By the time Janos left him, Enoch felt a little better.

Mayhap it was the several cans of ale or mayhap it was Janos being a good friend to him.

They had played a few hands of cards and talked over their drinks. It was harvest time in the world beyond the TRI, Janos had mentioned. Enoch was all too pleased to miss it and the chaff in his hair and his ears and his arsecrack, which made Janos laugh. A laugh shared felt like a trouble halved.

Still, after Janos was gone, Enoch opened up his Leaf lest there be any news from Ben, but there was only one message from an unknown sender. He frowned, opening it and touching the small arrow on the screen.

"Enoch, it's Orla," the automated voice read. "I know things have gone to hell, and you probably don't want anything to do with me anymore, but if you do, please can I talk to you? Please. I need your help. I don't know who else to ask."

Enoch stared blankly at the screen, remembering brawn sandwiches and colourful hair and a bright smile.

They had only met a handful of times. For her to call to him, she had to be truly desperate. Mayhap she wanted to speak to him on Mack's behalf to make his excuses. He played the message again. It would be simple to say no, to draw a line in the earth marking the end of it all.

"Why?" He replied.

It seemed like a long time before another message arrived. "I'm worried about Mack. I know he screwed up, but I need your help. I think he might do something stupid."

It was too much to be asked to help the one who had betrayed his trust. He closed the screen and lay on his side on the couch, staring at the back. There was a thread loose there. He watched it stir with every breath he gave out.

He had no reason to help Mack, not when Mack had used him. He had no reason to care. Mack didn't listen to him anyway. What use could he be to a man who had ignored everything he had asked? None. He would be no use to Mack or Orla, just as he was no use to Ben.

And yet he knew he would never stop trying.

He rolled over with a groan and snatched his bud from the table to open his Leaf screen again. "Can you meet me on the morrow?" he asked, watching the text appear on the screen.

"Yes. Thank you. Where and when?"

The inn where he had crossed paths with the stranger was the only choice. Mack knew of it, so it scarcely mattered if he found out Enoch was going there again. Better than finding a new place to meet and being forced to leave it behind because his former friends knew of it.

At noon the next day, he drew up outside in his pod. It was lashing with rain outside and he sat for some time, gathering himself to go in.

The windows were too small to allow him to see who was there. He wondered if it was foolish to hope Mack might be there. It was daft to think it when their friendship had ended so hard. He had no notion if he might get angry again, or if he might strike Mack on the arm for being a fool, then take a drink with him and make things better between them.

When he finally ran in from the pod, his coat above his head to keep off the rain, his heart sank when he saw all his worries had been for naught. Mack was nowhere to be seen, but Orla sat alone at a table with a glass half-drunk before her.

She started to rise when she saw him at the door. Enoch stared at her. She had aged some ten years in only a few weeks, pale, and her eyes were rimmed with red as if she had been weeping for a long while and had only recently stopped. Even the smile was not the same.

He walked towards her as one in a dream and, without thought, offered her his hand. Orla's eyes grew shiny again, and she reached over the table for his hand. Her grip was tight, almost to the point of pain.

"So bad?" he asked quietly.

She nodded mutely. The clock on the wall ticked, and they stared at each other until she took a breath and drew away, rubbing at her eyes. "Sorry. God, I'm sorry." She tried another smile, but it was false and unsteady. "D'you want a drink or something?"

There had been enough of that already. Better to keep a clear head. "Not now." He sat opposite her. She wrapped her hands around the glass, staring at them. "What's the matter?"

Orla darted out her tongue to wet her lips. "Mack's been offered this new job."

"Aye." Enoch folded his hands on the tabletop, then unfolded them again. "He spoke about it."

"He's still—even after everything that's happened, he thinks he can take it."

Enoch stared at her. "Does he truly think the TRI are done with him? He has broken their laws!"

"I know," Orla said unhappily. "They let him come home, but they've slapped him with all kinds of waivers and nondisclosures and blocked his dismissal until charges are laid." She shook her head slowly. "He's so damned stubborn. I can't get him to see what a mess he's in."

"And you called on me?" Enoch scratched at his jaw. "He's the one wanting this job. I dunt think I could stop him."

"I need to know I'm not being paranoid." She met his eyes. "I don't like it. Any of it. The way they approached him. The demands they made of him to prove his position. It doesn't feel *right*."

"I telt him that," he said. "I telt him they weren't after him; they were after anyone that might be in the TRI."

Orla took a sharp breath. "You think so too?"

"If they wanted him so bad, they dint need to see me," Enoch replied. "They dunt care about him. Everybody thinks it too. They only went to him on account of knowing of his place in the TRI, not on account of him having any skills."

Orla pressed her fist to her mouth, closing her eyes. "God damn it," she finally breathed. "I've tried to make him see it, but they've offered him enough to make him put on blinkers."

"He said he could be doing research," Enoch said, confused. "Just as he is—" Orla's face told him that was wrong. "What did they offer him?"

She turned her glass between fingertip and thumb. "Do you remember how upset he got when we went out?"

"Aye. About being a...desk jockey?"

"Because he always wanted to time travel..."

Enoch sighed. "Aye. Many coming to the TRI wish to do so."

"And he's been sitting in there for years, watching and not being able to do a thing." Orla wet her lower lip. "That's what they've offered him— a chance to do what he's always wanted."

Enoch sank lower in his seat. If Mack was to be a time traveller, it meant the man from the inn had a gate for him to use. No more question, then. It should have been a joy to know they were right, but something was tugging at Enoch's attention, and he tugged at his sideburn, trying to see what he was missing.

The tick of the clock seemed to get louder, and the world seemed to have slowed, as if caught in a tar pit.

There were many small pieces they knew, but all scattered about: Mack and the part he might play in the loss of Ben's father; the man from the inn; now, time gates needing someone to use them; thieves who came from...

"Oh Jesu!" It was as if someone had struck him with a rock.

"Enoch?" Orla was staring at him, worried.

At least two time travellers had gone after Ben's father those twenty-odd years ago. Many of the details had been kept from Ben, but he could remember whispers in the days following his father's disappearance. One of the time travellers—a man—had died in their home. Blood on the walls. A body on the floor.

Enoch's stomach turned. Christ above, the future—and the past—was taking a terrible shape.

If they had the gate as they promised, if they allowed Mack to use it, and if he was the man who went to Tom Sanders' house, then...

God's blood, Jacob had been the police officer in charge when Tom Sanders went missing. He saw the body then. He had to know! He had brought Mack in to the TRI as well, though Ben had no notion why he had done it. Jacob *knew*. Why else bring Mack into the TRI if not to keep him under their eye?

"You must stop him," he said wildly. "He mustn't go."

"I know, but—"

"No but. We must stop him."

"I know," Orla said, her voice sharper. She pushed her glass aside, leaning in over the table. "How the hell am I meant to persuade him when he's spent so many years wanting this and has the chance right in front of him? He doesn't even care if he ends up in jail!"

Enoch shoved his fingers through his hair. True enough. "The TRI—"

"Won't let him, and you know it." She sounded as distressed as Enoch felt. "If we could break contact between him and whoever this man is..." She propped both elbows on the table, her face in her hands. "Christ, if he could just do it *once* and get it out of his system, I'd be happy for him, but not like this. Not with someone as shady as this guy. I don't even know his *name* or anything about him, and the TRI are pissed about him too, which doesn't sound good to me."

Enoch pressed his knuckles to his lips, trying to think. "The TRI dunt like it when people steal their technology. The police will keep eyes on those who claim to have it."

Orla stared at him. "Shit. That's why this is such a big deal?"

Had he gathered his scattered wits, Enoch might've been more alarmed about spilling the task force's secrets, but all he could picture was Mack laid out, bloody and dead. Mayhap it wasn't him. Mayhap it was some other. But mayhap it was, and if they could find no way to stop him...

"D'you truly think one jump would satisfy him?" he demanded. "A single chance?"

Orla blinked at him as if confused by his change in tone. "What?"

"Mack. If a way could be found, would one jump be enough?"

She sounded bewildered. "I don't—I think so? Maybe?"

The world seemed to go dim as Enoch stared at her. Mayhap it wasn't Mack in the Sanders house, but why take the chance?

"I can speak to people," he said carefully. "See if there is aught that can be done."

"But you said the TRI—"

He glanced about, holding up a hand to quiet her. "I have friends." He kept his voice low. "We might be able to arrange matters. It would not be...official."

"That—it can't be possible."

Common sense was catching up to Enoch, but the idea was there now. If he could keep Mack from being harmed, if it might save Ben from the grief of losing his father, then it would be well worth it. Only...

Only, the task force had eyes on Mack, and, if Enoch was right, they wanted to find the stranger's cache of stolen technology. They would follow him, and if Enoch took Mack to Ben, they would find Ben and all would be lost.

"I need a drink," he said, rising.

In the time it took him to go from chair to bar and back again, he knew it was impossible. It would take guile the likes of which Mack scarce possessed. Enoch sank into his chair, staring into his glass, then took a mouthful of the golden spirit within.

Orla gazed at him, resigned. "You were just being kind, weren't you? A kind lie to try and make this mess easier to deal with."

"If I could help him, I would," Enoch said quietly. "He's a friend to me, even if he has become a shit of late."

She smiled sadly. "Yeah." Her eyes were too bright, and she rubbed at them with her fingertips, smudging the makeup on her lashes. "Sorry. I— This isn't your responsibility. I just—I needed to talk to someone else about it all. Someone who knew."

Enoch tilted his half-full glass towards her. "A trouble shared is a burden eased." He hesitated, considering his drink. For him, a trouble shared was always shared with Ben. Ben would know what to do. He always had plans upon plans, and if anyone could find the means to reach Mack, he could. "I can ask my friends, but I can make no promises. If it can be done, I'll send you a message that I'll come over by."

"That's not going to be easy," she said. "Not when he's already on edge."

Try years, Enoch wanted to say. Try a lifetime.

"Give me three days. If it's not in hand by then…"

"Three days," she agreed. "Do you want me to tell Mack?"

Enoch nodded at once. Anything to keep Mack from running off and doing something foolish right away. "Best you do. Tell him I will do my utmost to fix matters for him."

Orla reached across the table and grasped his hand. *Thank you.*

Chapter Twenty-Three

Ben's head was throbbing.

"I'm only saying it might be done!" On the other end of an earpiece, Enoch sounded as agitated as Ben felt, only in a whisper instead of a shout. "Mayhap we're wrong about the part he plays, but can we, in good conscience, allow him to walk to his death?"

No, Ben wanted to say. Of course not.

But his mouth was dust-dry because, for the first time, the mad jumble of information was starting to make sense. *Of course* Jacob would want to save the life of a naive and reckless child. *Of course* the TRI would monitor the people who had time jumped before. But the fact that they'd sat Ben down to train a boy knowing he would one day die at the hands of Ben's father...

Jesus Christ.

"Ben?" Ada murmured. "Are you well, lamb?"

He glanced up at the screens. Ada was wearing a digi-lens for the first time, which meant he got to see exactly how anxious Enoch was. Far too anxious for someone sitting in a quiet café on a sunny afternoon.

"Try not to look like you're shitting bricks, E," he suggested hoarsely. "It'll make people suspicious."

Enoch's mouth twitched in a tight smile. "And if that's what I'm doing?"

Ben ran a hand over his jaw, short hair rasping against his fingers. God, he couldn't remember the last time he'd shaved. Too busy trying to find their elusive enemy. He'd even tried hacking into the police records again, but Jacob and his merry band had always been careful there. They must have seen him coming—or maybe he'd gotten sloppy—because yet another safe house was burned.

Everyone knew they were running out of time.

No one was taking any chances anymore.

"I can't meet him," he said abruptly. "Mack. I can't meet him. If we're right and they know everything that's coming, they'll have eyes on him. I don't think they'll let him out of their sight for a second."

Enoch subsided in his chair, propping his elbow on the arm and knocking his fist against his tightly pressed lips. "Can we not— S'blood, we cannot let him die! He's my *friend*."

"I know," Ben whispered, sinking forward, head in his hands. He could remember being in this situation before. He'd dug up Enoch's name in the old church records out of curiosity and had been horrified when Enoch's death was recorded a handful of days after Ben had left his time. He remembered desperately riffling through papers and trying to find out why a healthy—and admittedly troublemaking—young man had suddenly dropped dead.

Of course, he was an idiot, and he'd gone running in to save the day, changing history and breaking more laws than he could count in one fell swoop.

This time was different, though. Mack wasn't condemned. Not yet.

"You have your magic gates," Ada said suddenly. "Can you not make use of them?"

"It's not that simple," Ben replied. "First off, I'd need to get him before he can use them—"

"No, no." Ada's eyes dropped to her hand. She sketched on the table with her fingertip. "Can you not open a gate to a place where he is and allow him to walk through it? As you did at the stone circle? You open the gate to yesterday, he comes through to you, and then you open another doorway to set him into the past?" She traced the journey with each of her forefingers. "Would that not work? Then once his time in the past is done, you can put him where you found him, and none but us would be the wiser."

"No," Enoch replied before Ben could. "He would be twice in the same time." He rubbed his chest, and Ben wished he could reach out and grasp his hand, remembering the horrifying moment when Enoch had crossed his own timeline for a few seconds and almost died. They had both known the risks and expected it, but it was terrifying when it happened. "Even for a moment, it might well kill him."

"Truly?" Ada sounded shocked. "The gates are so dangerous?"

"Only if there's an overlap," Ben said. "If it was instantaneous, it would have been okay, but we have to take the risk into consideration."

"But surely 'might' is far better than the certainty of death?"

"The gate isn't an option," Ben admitted unhappily. He rubbed at his forehead with the heel of his hand, focussing anywhere but Enoch's shocked face. "We don't have the resources anymore. I lost both my battery cores when they almost caught up with us. Without them, we're using a wired gate. The second we use it, there'll be a power spike, and they'll be able to pinpoint where we are. They'll be able to find us. I can't open a gate for him, not without getting all of us caught."

"You mean you would let him die." Enoch's voice was flat with anger, his dark eyes narrowed.

"No!" Ben exhaled noisily. "God, no, but we need—this— I don't know how we could do it— Even if we did, they'd find us before we could get him back. We need to be careful."

"I doubt you would know the word if it struck you across the face," Ada said ruefully, which got her a faint smile from both Ben and Enoch. She glanced around the café. "If you will give me a moment, I have pressing matters to attend to."

Ben flicked the connection to Enoch's earpiece off for a second. "Do you mind if I put you on silent for a minute? I'd like a private word with Enoch."

Ada laughed. "As long as you grant me the same privacy as I tend my business. I would not want an audience."

It took him a second to realise what she meant, and he winced. "Oh! Right! Yes! I'll blanket your signal for a few minutes." He touched his consoles and the screens went black, then he switched his attention to Enoch. "You there?"

"Aye."

"It's just us for now," Ben said quickly. "Ada wanted radio silence while she peed."

He heard Enoch's muffled snort. "You have no wish to listen to an old wife pissing? I hear tell of them that like it. Golden showers, they call it."

Ben made a face. "Porn again?"

"Mm. I thought it might have gold coins or the like." There was a pause and a crunch of a biscuit. "It very much did not."

Ben almost smiled. "No, It wouldn't." He scratched at his jaw again, considering the more significant problem at hand. "You know I want to help Mack, don't you? I mean, what I was saying before..." He trailed off helplessly.

"I know." Enoch sighed. "It's just— I never thought it would be his doing. Part of it, aye, but I hate to think he caused all of your misery."

"And he has no idea." Ben pinched the bridge of his nose, then rubbed at his eyes. They were burning again. Too much screen time, he tried to tell himself. Nothing more. "If we could tell him, maybe it would be enough to stop him."

"Would you believe it? If some criminal came and told you so?"

He was right. "No," Ben admitted, pushing his fingers through his mussed hair. "He'd probably think we're nuts." He laughed hoarsely, wishing to God his chest didn't feel tight. "Hey, Mack. Remember how your death was the reason the TRI was forced to go public. How about that? You only want to do it because you know it exists, and you only know it exists because you already did it." His voice broke, and he drew a sharp breath. "Fuck. I'm so sick of fucking time travel."

"But we are almost done," Enoch murmured. "When it's all done with, we can burn those gates to ash."

Ben would happily light the flame. The gates had taken so much of his life already. He couldn't—wouldn't—let them take any more. "Yes," he breathed. "God, yes."

"Still," Enoch said, "at least one good thing has come of it."

"Oh?"

"Aye." There was a small, thoughtful pause. "You had the fortune of having my cock in your mouth."

Ben choked on a laugh and ran his hand over his mouth again. "Yeah, there's that." He took a deep breath and released it. "What are we going to do?"

Enoch exhaled noisily. "Would that I knew. This is—it's all shite and no mistake." He crunched on a biscuit. "Can I ask you something?"

Ben folded his arms on the workbench, resting his chin on them. "Mm?"

"If we—if it—if he listens to us, what will happen?"

"How do you mean?"

"If he *is* the thief that died then, what happens if he int there to thieve and die?" Enoch sounded preoccupied. "Int that changing the past? Will it change things? If your da int dead and you have no reason to go seeking for him?"

Ben stared blindly at the blank screens. Time had been buggered with once before. The only person who remembered history as it had been was the man who had witnessed the moment everything had changed. No one else remembered.

For so long, Ben hadn't even dared to imagine the possibilities. At best, he had hoped to open a gate and bring his father home, but to imagine he could stop it all from happening was something he hadn't even considered.

If they were right about Mack, if they stopped him from going on the fatal jump, then everything would change. Ben's stomach twisted into a knot. His dad would be alive, and his life would be infinitely more normal, but...

But without his dad's disappearance and everything that came after, so much would change. It was like dominoes falling, knocking one after the other. He would have his father, his home, no need for all the lies and subterfuge and everything else.

No need to go on the run.

No illegal jumps.

No Enoch.

"Shit."

Enoch was speaking, but Ben couldn't hear a word. He could only see the choice before him: his father and Mack's survival or everything between him and Enoch. A life that had been stolen or a life he had made for himself. One kind of security and happiness over another. Jesus. But it wasn't even a choice at all. It couldn't even be a choice at all, not when a life—lives—hung in the balance.

"Oi!"

Ben jolted. "What? What?"

"Ada's on her way," Enoch said sharply. "We'll talk later, eh?"

Ben couldn't speak, numb. He touched the console in front of him to reconnect her feed. The screens filled with the sight of Enoch again as the woman walked towards him. He was smiling, but forcing it. Ada must have noticed it too.

"Is something amiss?"

"Only the difficulty in finding a way to Mack," Enoch said with an almost convincing laugh. "It's daft. I swore I would never give a fig for the man after all he did, and now, he is all I think of."

"If I can be of any use, you need only ask."

Ben kneaded at his temples. "I don't know how he'd take that—some random old lady coming up to him."

"A random old man already has his ear," Enoch pointed out. "Mayhap Ada could pretend to speak on the man's behalf?"

"Maybe," Ben murmured. Maybe. Maybe, maybe, maybe.

They were talking again, but Ben couldn't focus on the words. Jesus, he'd missed out on what might be his last chance to see Enoch in person. If they acted—and they would have to soon—then everything could change, and they'd never see or know about each other again.

His hands were shaking as he opened up another screen and searched the area nearby. They were a safe distance from the latest safe house, but not too far. If they were careful, if they timed it right, then...

"Enoch, give Ada the contact details for Orla," he said, cutting over their words. "I've got somewhere I need you to go."

"And I?" Ada asked.

"No. You stay put. I'll send you a message once we've sorted out some details. Have a cup of tea. A cake. Anything you fancy." Ben rubbed at his palm with his thumb. "Enoch, keep the earpiece."

Enoch frowned, confused. "Where am I to go?"

Ben scanned the map in front of him. "There's an office building four blocks to the south. Head in that direction. I'll give you more instructions once you get there." He shoved his chair out. "Whatever you do, don't lose the earpiece."

As Enoch walked away on the screens, Ben grabbed his coat and his camo-patch and headed for the door.

Chapter Twenty-Four

Enoch was worried as he hurried along another street, following yet another instruction.

Ben sounded fraught, which was never a good thing, but worse than that were the silences that had come before. Enoch had seen it in years gone by, when Ben sank too deep into his own thoughts and the rest of the world seemed cut off from him.

If something they had spoken of had upset Ben enough to fall silent, Enoch was unsure if he wanted to know what it was.

He paused on the junction of four wide roads. He was all but in the centre of the city, towering glass and metal buildings on all sides. A few older buildings nestled between them, but they were few and far between. Mercifully, it was not as busy as it could have been. There was plenty of traffic on the road, but not too many people. He tilted his bud up at the sign on the nearest wall. An automated voice announced the street name.

"Here," Enoch murmured, glancing about.

"There's a hotel with a purple sign with white writing on that street. It has two plant pots, one on either side of the main doors."

Enoch spun, scanning the buildings. After a moment, he saw it. "Aye."

"Go there. Room 423 on level four."

He tried to walk as if he were calm and smooth as fresh snow, but his mind was awhirl, and his walk turned into a run as he neared the doors. He scarce stopped to ask for directions to the right room. There were a pair of lifts, and he ran into the first. Jesu, he thought as he shifted from foot to foot. He must seem half-mad, running in straight across the lobby with nary a greeting.

It felt like an age before the door opened onto a long hallway lined with doors and opening off into other halls. Enoch held up his bud, searching for guidance, but he barely even needed it beyond the first turn. A door was open close to the end, and a barefoot man leaned in the doorway as if it were natural. When he smiled in relief and welcome,

Enoch knew he would have recognised Ben anywhere, masked or unmasked.

"Found you," Enoch said once he was in arm's reach.

Ben didn't speak at once, opening the door wider, and both of them hurried into the room.

A more fretful man might have asked what was amiss, but Enoch knew Ben well enough to know he would be thinking himself in knots. Better to divert him from the knots and calm him to give him time to think.

Of course, best way to do that was to crowd him up against the nearest wall, kiss him open-mouthed, and press one palm to his covered prick.

Ben made a small, urgent sound and sank his fingers into Enoch's hair, lips parting and tongue darting against Enoch's. Enoch drew away long enough to search the half-familiar face, then reached up and turned off the mask.

"Better," he declared before reclaiming Ben's mouth and working his hand down the front of Ben's trews. Too loose, he thought, even as skin brushed warm skin. Ben's fingers tightened, and his breath hitched, and for a moment, Enoch wondered if he might make his usual protest. But Ben only tilted his head and bared his throat. It was an invitation too welcome to ignore, and Enoch closed his lips about Ben's throat, squeezing slow with his teeth as he wrapped his hand about Ben's hardening cock.

Ben was breathing short and fast, pressed to the wall, each gasp dragged betwixt clenched teeth, his fingers curling and pulling at Enoch's hair. "Fuck..."

He was coming harder in Enoch's hand, slicker with every stroke of Enoch's fingers. When he yanked twice on Enoch's hair, Enoch withdrew his teeth at once, letting Ben gulp in breaths, his head knocking against the wall. The faint red ring on his throat made Enoch's own cock twitch, and he leaned close to drag his tongue across it. Ben shuddered pleasantly and pushed his cock against Enoch's waiting palm.

Always so wanton, his Ben...

Enoch glanced about the room. It might have been any room, basic and clean, though the bed was well high enough to give him some interesting ideas. He wrapped his free hand around Ben's belt. "There's a bed wasting," he murmured, pulling Ben forward with both hands.

There was a flash of hunger in Ben's eyes, and his tongue darted out to wet his lips. "Will you do as you're telt?"

"Always."

Enoch laughed hoarsely. God above, it was true as well. Defy his kin, his employer, his country's very laws, but oh, he could be such a good lad for them that earned it. "Good." He drew his hands from Ben's trews. "Now, close your eyes."

Ben nodded, eyes falling closed, his hands hanging—twitching—by his sides.

Enoch watched him for a moment, then undid Ben's belt, drew it loose from the loops that held it, and let the trews fall. The belt buckle rattled as he tossed it onto the bed. Later, he knew, there would be a use for it. He made short work of Ben's shirt, touching every part of the skin he bared and letting his hand linger on the smoothness of Ben's back. Ben was pale as milk and so thin now. With every shivering breath he took, Enoch could count his ribs through his taut skin.

"Next time, I'll bring a pudding to fatten you up," he murmured, running his fingertips up from Ben's arse to his nape. So close, he saw the way Ben's body tensed and he knew there were matters unspoken, matters that had no place here and now, not until Ben was no longer coiled in knots.

"Enoch..."

"Later." He spread his hand between Ben's shoulders and pressed, gentle enough, but Ben swayed forward obediently. "Bend. Rest your arms on the bed."

It was low enough that Ben needed to bend his knees, pressing his forearms to the covers. He would have stayed there too, as long as Enoch wished it, motionless, and trembling with want, cock hard against his belly. Jesu, he could make himself so fair without even knowing it.

The belt buckle rattled again as Enoch wrapped his fingers around the long strip of leather. Old leather too. Softer, with a curve to it that felt pleasant against his palm. He saw the gooseflesh rise across Ben's skin, saw the way his ribs heaved as the belt rustled across the bed covers.

"You're being uncommon quiet." Enoch ran the edge of the belt along Ben's side, watching him shiver again.

"Took my breath," Ben rasped, his fingers hooking into the covers.

Enoch reached under his body and caught his cock again. "Not as much as that." He ran the tip of the belt up the back of Ben's thigh and squeezed with his hand as Ben's body jolted against him like a skittish colt. Enoch stepped a mite closer, the front of his own trews rubbing against Ben's bared arse. "Would you have me?"

There was something in the catch in Ben's voice, too sharp and shaking when he gasped out, "Fuck, yes."

Enoch set the belt down by Ben's hip and shed his overcoat. His shirt followed, pulled over his head, but he only loosened his trews enough to free his cock. He stepped close, rubbing his self against Ben's arse, one hand settling on Ben's hip.

Ben tried to push against him, and Enoch smothered a fond chuckle. Always in such a hurry, his Ben. Such a modern man, rushing about like a mad thing, even when it came to a sound buggering.

"Not yet," Enoch murmured. He fished in his pocket and closed his fingers on the small tube he had picked up on his way. They would laugh about it later, he knew, the fact that he would always come with some tube or bottle. Just in case. A man never knew his luck after all.

He popped the lid open with his thumb, then squeezed some of the colourful fluid onto his other hand, spreading it along his fingers with his thumb until it turned from cold to warm.

"No daft fruit flavour this time?" Ben's voice was muffled against his forearm.

Enoch made a face at him, slipping his hand between their bodies, his fingers sliding along the crease of Ben's arse. "You'd fuss about the colour if you could see it." He eased one finger into Ben's arse, watching the tension ripple through Ben's body. A while since they'd done this, right enough. Enoch leaned forward and kissed Ben's shoulder. "D'you like having green fingers in your arse, then?" he murmured.

Ben caught his breath as Enoch slowly moved his finger, adding another and pressing them both a little deeper. "I'm not a fucking garden."

Enoch smirked and nipped at Ben's shoulder with his teeth. "I would say otherwise," he said, sliding his other hand beneath Ben's body and catching him by the prick. "A fine trunk and some ripe fruit."

All the tautness in Ben's shoulders vanished like morning dew as he half gasped, half laughed, shifting his hips into and against Enoch's hands. "Hardly a garden," he breathed, curling his fingers into the covers beneath him. "A tree..."

"Mm." Enoch teasingly squeezed his bollocks. "A plum tree."

Ben's pressed his cheek into his forearm, groaning. "Shut up."

"Is that your wish?" Enoch stroked his fingers 'gainst both arse and prick, his heart drumming with every small shudder that ran through Ben's body and every little sound he made. Ben's eyes were closed, squeezed tight, and there was colour high in his face, half-hidden in his arms.

"No," Ben breathed out. His toes were pushing against the floor, the muscles in his thighs twitching.

Enoch stilled his hands, leaning down to breathe close to Ben's ear. "Tell me then," he murmured, voice thickening with want. "Tell me what you would have me do."

Ben arched his shoulders up, his fingers fisting into the bedding. "Fuck, Enoch!" His body jolted when Enoch curled his fingertips, stroking him again, squeezing with his other hand. "Please!" He shivered when Enoch withdrew his hands and flinched when Enoch covered one of his tightly balled fists. God above, he was wound taut as a spring. A buggering would scarce be enough.

"More, I think," Enoch murmured. He slid his fingers—slickened by Ben—against Ben's knuckles, till those clenched fingers loosed, and they were holding to each other. "Ask me."

Ben pressed his cheek to the bedding, his eye cracking open a sliver. "Make—make it quiet."

Enoch kissed his shoulder again, Ben's lips just out of reach. "Aye." He squeezed Ben's hand again, then withdrew his fingers. "I'll see it done." He reached up and brushed his thumb over Ben's eyelid. "Eyes closed, Master Ben. I'll no tell you again."

Ben closed his eyes obediently and gave out a shuddering breath. He curled his fingers into the covers as Enoch caught the belt, the buckle tinking quietly across the bedding as he pulled it closer.

Enoch darted his tongue along his lip as he drew the belt up, watching Ben tremble all over as the soft leather brushed against his ribs and the cool metal trailed up his spine. Ben was breathing faster, ribs rising and falling, and his head jerked as the long strip of leather slithered over his shoulder, skimming his throat.

"Easy, love," Enoch murmured. "I have you." He reached between Ben's neck and the bedding, pausing a moment to play his fingertips the length of Ben's throat. Ben swallowed hard, and his breath was a warm, frantic gust. "Easy..."

Enoch caught the end of the belt and drew it up and close with both hands. The ruddy leather rested smooth against Ben's pale throat, and Ben pushed against it.

"Ah, ah," Enoch loosed his grip. "No, Master Ben. My rein, not yours."

"'Kay." Ben nodded, his cheeks flushed.

Enoch shifted the two ends of the belt to one hand, tight enough to bind, loose enough to let Ben breathe. With his green-fingered hand free once more, he stroked his cock and slowly drew the belt tighter against Ben's throat. Ben parted his lips, his breaths smaller and urgent. His eyes were yet closed, his whole body quivering with need, even as the colour darkened in his face.

Enoch loosed his hold, just a little. "Good," he breathed as he took Ben by the hip again. Ben's thighs, taut as iron, twitched with the effort of holding himself still. God above, he'd scarce moved an inch without leave. Scarce a finger's breadth. That mute obedience was all out of want for him and the thought made Enoch's cock ache. He stroked himself against Ben's arse, stifling a laugh.

"Mm?" Ben's voice was muffled.

"Not just green fingers in your garden," Enoch said with a mischievous pat to Ben's arse.

Ben gave a small, hoarse chuff of laughter that turned into a low groan as Enoch sank his cock into him. It would be easy to fuck him hard and have it done, but Ben wanted quiet, and that was what he would get.

The world seemed a long way off as Enoch twisted his hand into the belt and drew it tighter as he started to move. Ben's body was hot and tight around him, the air full of short, sharp breaths and the creak of the bed, and God above, going slow was a trial. Christ have mercy...

Ben clutched at the covers again, pushing against him now. Enoch squeezed his hip, trying to keep his mind all on Ben, though his blood throbbed through him, in his cock and everywhere between. He moved again, seeking out the place that made Ben come apart, and caught his own breath at the choked and wanton cries escaping Ben.

"Good..." Enoch repeated, watching the red in Ben's face, the darkening flush, knowing to release just enough, pull tight again, watch the catch of air, feel Ben's body tense and tighten, and Christ, his hips were jerking hard, scarce meeting Enoch's thrusts.

"Fu—" Ben crushed his face to the bed, his legs shuddering.

Close, but not enough.

Enoch pulled the belt tighter and moved harder. Ben choked, tossing his head, the belt biting into his pale skin. Enoch's own breath was coming harder, and Jesu, Ben was gasping, wrenching at the covers, eyes tight shut, and lips parted and skin darkening, trusting Enoch to know, to watch, to keep him from going too far.

"Good, Master Ben," Enoch panted, grinding against him even as Ben's feet slid and skittered on the floor and his hands tore at the covers. "Good..."

He felt more than saw when Ben spent himself, a spasm tearing through Ben's body, his legs giving way and his breath little more than whistling gasp. Enoch dropped the belt at once and caught Ben's other hip, holding him up, keeping him from falling from the bed as Ben sagged, limp and quiet, face dark and lips frothing with every whispered breath.

Enoch drew himself free, still hard, but that scarce mattered. With effort, he managed to hoist Ben fully onto the bed and climbed up beside him.

"I have you," he whispered, though he knew Ben would not hear. "I have you."

Chapter Twenty-Five

Everything felt nicely muffled. A pale blur somewhere...up. Warmth. Hands...?

Ben blinked slowly.

The pale blur came into focus—a round frosted lampshade on the ceiling. He watched it as everything started drawing together. A hand in his hair. Another hand pressed to his chest.

Ben tilted his head. Enoch. Sitting by him, stroking his hair. He didn't even say anything, but then—Ben remembered a time that seemed like ages ago—Enoch had been asked for quiet, and now, he was giving it in spades. Enoch sat back as Ben pushed himself up on his elbows, then struggled to sit, the world spinning at the edges.

Enoch reached over to the bedside table and returned with a glass of water, which he offered to Ben. It was icy cold. God, it ached to swallow it. Ben gingerly touched the tender skin of his throat. There would be bruises, but sometimes, it was worth it.

"Thank you," he said, startled by how hoarse his voice was.

Enoch reached up to catch a handful of his hair and pulled his head down to kiss him. "You asked," he said with a crooked smile. "T'was the least I could do." He ran his hand to the nape of Ben's neck, sending a prickle of goosebumps rising across Ben's skin. Always the way, the combination of pleasant blankness and tingling all over. "I feared I may have held too long."

Ben shook his head slowly. "No. No, I'm fine." He groped for Enoch's other hand and squeezed it.

Enoch shifted onto his knees, wrapped his arm around Ben's shoulders, and pressed his forehead to Ben's brow. It felt...good. Safe. Just sitting like that, quiet. Enoch's breath warmed Ben's shoulder, and Ben gazed sidelong at him as fragments of thoughts started piecing together.

They were scattered again when he noticed something. Enoch had not only lost his trousers, but...

"Jesus Christ..."

Enoch followed his line of sight. "Looks like I have the pox or some strange plague," he said, giving his iridescent green cock a poke before flashing an impish grin at Ben. "You'll be the same colour on the inside."

Ben couldn't help laughing. "At least I'll know what's happening when I take a shit." He took another sip from the glass of water. Condensation was forming under his fingers, trickling down and dripping on his bare legs. He dragged his thumb up the glass to catch a drop.

"Ben." Enoch's hand curled over the nape of his neck. "You bade me come here." His voice was quieter than usual, serious. "It wasn't for the buggery alone, was it?"

Ben closed his eyes, wishing Enoch had waited another few minutes before asking. It wasn't fair to bring such a good moment back to reality. It wasn't fair to ask about the end of the world as they knew it.

The mattress shifted as Enoch moved even closer. He slid his arm to Ben's waist, his rough fingers spreading across Ben's ribs. "Tell me," he murmured against Ben's bare shoulder. "If it's so terrible, better you share the burden."

Ben turned his glass between his hands. It took effort to hold them steady. "You asked me what'll happen if we stop Mack." Enoch's chin knocked against Ben's shoulder. "If we save my dad—if we stop him running through that gate—" He turned the glass clockwise ninety degrees, then forty-five anticlockwise. "You know why I started using the gates myself."

"To find your pa."

Ben turned the glass again, staring at it. "If I never lost him in the first place," he said quietly, "then I'll never need to use the gates to try to find him."

The arm around him tensed, fingers digging into his side. "And if you never go back," Enoch said slowly, "you'll never...we'll never..." Enoch hissed a sharp pained breath. "Christ wept."

Ben slowly nodded.

The timeline would change. There would be no chance or reason for their paths to cross. There would be no lies or deception or secret meetings and carefully structured plans or urgent, passionate fucking. There would be no them. Just two strangers in different eras who would never know or care that the other existed.

"And we'll neither of us know?" Enoch's voice was unsteady. "Of any of this? We'll forget everything?"

Ben inhaled slowly, then steadied himself to speak. "It'll never have happened. You can't remember something that didn't happen."

It wasn't meant to go like this. He'd always imagined finding his dad after everything. It had never even crossed his mind that he might be able to stop it. That seemed too much like chance, but now, it was the choice sitting in front of him.

After all the shit he'd gone through, after everything he'd lost, the universe still managed to find a way to fuck him over one more time.

Enoch tightened his hold on Ben, hot breaths hissing against Ben's skin. "Right..." he said finally. "Right..." He rubbed his chin against Ben's shoulder. "Then we had best make the most of the time left."

Ben's eyes were stinging, and he stared at the wall. "Easy as that?"

"Easy?" Enoch laughed. It sounded oddly hollow. "God's bones, d'you think this is easy? D'you think any of this has been easy?" He lifted his free hand to Ben's throat and ran his finger gently along the line left by the belt. "I never had one who gave his self to me as you have." He shook his head. "I never had one I would keep by me."

Ben pressed his eyes shut. "Don't say shit like that," he whispered.

Enoch's lips were at his shoulder, then teeth, hot breath hissing between them. "Then don't call this *easy*, Master Ben." His fingers dug into Ben's side. "I *know* you. I have seen every step you have taken, every part of this journey of yours. You think I would see you give up every part of that for my sake? You think I would see you lose your father all over again? And live knowing every moment you saw my face, you would remember I am the reason he is still gone?"

"Fuck you." Ben's voice broke, and his eyes were burning. He wanted to scream and hurl the glass at the wall and tear the room apart. He wanted to do everything and yet, couldn't find the strength to do anything. "Fuck you."

Enoch rose on his knees beside him and pulled Ben closer. The glass slid from Ben's fingers, spilling, but he didn't care. He twisted on the bed, clinging to Enoch, fingers sinking into Enoch's back, his face buried in the curve of Enoch's shoulder.

"I know." Enoch's lips brushed his forehead, ruffling his hair. His arms tightened around Ben, one hand fisting in Ben's hair. "Christ, love, I know." He twisted his fingers, pulling Ben's head up, kissing Ben as if it was the last chance they would get. Hell, maybe it was.

Ben was the one to break the kiss, breathing hard. There were words that needed to be said. Admissions. Confessions. All the useless sentimental shit that wouldn't make a bit of difference. "Enoch, I—"

Enoch bared his teeth, tightening his grip on Ben's hair. "Don't say shit like that," he echoed Ben's own words. His eyes were as bright and wet as Ben's.

Ben nodded as much as Enoch's grip would allow. "No more shit," he agreed hoarsely. He reached between their bodies and caught Enoch's bright green prick. "This?"

Despite everything, Enoch managed to grin. "Have you known me to refuse your attentions afore, Master Ben?" He tugged at Ben's hair once more and untangled his fingers. "On your back, aye?"

"You're such a pushy bastard," Ben complained, even though it sounded more forced than he would have liked. He reclined on his elbows, gazing up at Enoch, whose smile seemed as forced as Ben's own.

"Would you have me meek?" Enoch swung one leg over Ben's body to straddle his belly and pressed both hands to Ben's shoulders, pushing him down. "I'd wager you would grow tired of me within a day."

Ben wrapped one arm around Enoch, spreading his palm on the ridged scars that covered every inch of it. "I don't think you would know how to be meek if they tried to beat it into you."

Enoch rocked his hips, grinding himself against Ben's belly. "Oh, they tried..." His eyes were fixed on Ben's face, and he hissed approvingly when Ben reached between them and caught Enoch's cock again.

"If I end up green all over..." Ben began.

"Oh, hush." Enoch sank his fingers into the covers on either side of Ben's head, crushing his mouth to Ben's, darting his tongue against Ben's. Ben tightened his grip on Enoch's cock, dragging his nails the length of Enoch's spine.

It was the work of a few minutes to get Enoch hard, and he panted rapidly against Ben's lips, grinding himself between hand and belly. Ben nuzzled his way along Enoch's cheek, relieved when Enoch buried his face in Ben's shoulder. That way he wouldn't see Ben's eyes. That way, he might not notice his expression.

God, it should have been good if it was going to be their last time, but it was beating against his mind like a gong: The last time. Could be the last time. Might be the last time. And Enoch was willing to stand aside for Ben, for his happiness, for his sake.

"Fuck me…" Enoch groaned, covering Ben's fingers with one of his hands, moving their linked hands harder and faster. His breath hitched, the spatter of cum hot on Ben's belly, and Enoch sagged forward, his body damp with sweat. Ben closed his eyes, trying to breathe evenly and not think. He tightened his arm around Enoch and tried to concentrate everything on the warm sated breaths on his throat.

For a long time, they lay there.

Enoch tilted his head enough to let his lips brush Ben's throat. "I'm not a fool," he murmured.

"Mm?"

"I know that was for me alone." He sighed quietly. "I was all but atop you, Ben. Did you think I'd not notice you took no pleasure in it?" He looked at Ben's face. "The quiet didn't last, did it?"

Ben turned away from him, but he was drawn back to Enoch's dark eyes, solemn as the grave. "I'm sorry."

Enoch kissed him, cupping his cheek. "No more of your daft talk."

"But we—"

Enoch kissed him again. "I said, no more of your daft talk." He braced a hand on Ben's shoulder, sitting up over him, and Ben watched as he traced patterns in the cum smeared on his belly. "What would you have me do?"

Ben blinked, confused. "Now?"

Enoch met his eyes. "The TRI. They will give me leave to go if I wish it. We know what is to come. If you want me by your side until the end, I can make it so."

Ben's breath caught as if the air had been squeezed out of his lungs. They could spend whatever was left of this timeline together and do it all together and when—if—they had to go their separate ways forever, then at least they'd see their plans through to the bitter end. Yes. It would only be fair. It would only be right.

"Please."

Enoch's smile brightened his face. "Aye?"

Ben pushed himself up on one elbow and reached up with his other hand to draw Enoch over him. "Yes. We've been in this together. Let's finish it together."

Chapter Twenty-Six

Rain was beating against the windows as Enoch paced about the room.

He had spent the journey to the TRI lost in thought. For almost three years, he had lived in their halls. He had spoken often of how strange and uncomfortable he found the world beyond the compound walls. To ask for freedom now would lead to questions.

They would not refuse him, that much he was sure of. Many of them had asked him time and again if he would not be happier living outside the walls and fences of their facility. They seemed to think him a prisoner of his own making. They had offered a home somewhere quiet and finances to help.

No, they would not refuse him.

As soon as he reached his room, he sent a message to Sabine asking her for a moment of her time. There was no reply, but as master of the TRI, she was like as not busy with her duties. He sat and waited for a time, but his mind was whirling, and he rose and walked the length and breadth of his rooms, trying to calm himself.

The sooner he could leave, the better. He'd done everything Ben had asked him to do there. He'd found all that Ben needed to know. Now, it all lay in Ben's brilliant mind—the means to save Mack and, in doing so, save his own father and his own ruined life. He would find a way. He always did, even if his ways were strange and wild sometimes.

Enoch retreated to his couch and sank down.

They had so little time left. Only yesterday, he had spoken to Orla. Today, Ben. Tomorrow...

Christ, he should have fled with Ben. He could not be sure when— if—he would be allowed to leave. To be certain, he should have run. The task force had never found Ben. Now, they would be thinking all about his enemy instead. Sweet Jesu, he could have stayed with him instead of wasting hours and mayhap days by returning to the TRI.

Enoch propped his elbows upon his knees and pressed his face into his hands, trying not to think on it all. He had done everything he could.

He had found all Ben needed to know. Until he could be by Ben's side, there was nothing else he could do.

The chime of the door made him jump, and he scrambled up, mastering his expression. It would do no good to make Sabine worry about him. If she worried, then she might try to keep him at the TRI to be sure he was well. He even drew on a smile, no matter how false, as he opened the door.

His thoughts came to a standstill as he found himself nose to chest with someone who was very clearly not Sabine. He raised his eyes.

"I heard you were home from the city again," Janos said cheerfully, holding up two beer bottles in his real hand. "Since you will not be making a stream today, I thought beer would help."

Enoch was too confounded to keep the other man from wandering into the apartment. When the world was falling apart, this one part remained so steady and solid in front of him. And God above, Janos was right. It would have been the day for a stream. With Mack gone, he had no notion what to do.

He stared at his hand on the door handle. None of it mattered anyway. And yet, some part of him wanted to turn back the clock and to have his friends laughing with him as he talked some manner of nonsense. He glanced over at Janos. At least one was here.

Janos rattled through the drawer in the kitchen, then turned, breaking open the lid of the bottle of beer. "I think you need this." He held it out. "Sit. You're pale as a ghost."

Enoch took the bottle in hand—warm, he noticed and almost smiled. Once, Mack had plied him with a chilled beer. He could not recall whether Mack or Janos had laughed more at his outrage. It was only luck that Mack had not thought to make a live stream of the tirade.

"Thank you."

Janos made a dismissive gesture as he slouched onto the couch. For a man of such long limbs, he folded like cloth. "A beer, nothing more." He took a mouthful from his own bottle. "Is it raining in the city?"

Enoch shrugged as he sat on the edge of one of the chairs, supping his own beer. Truth be told, he had scarcely noticed anything from the moment he left Ben's side at the hotel. "It seems the way here."

For several minutes, neither of them spoke as they drank. Often, it was the way with Janos. Sometimes there were words and laughter. Sometimes silence was enough.

"I want to leave the TRI." Enoch almost flinched as he spoke. The words had been sitting on the tip of his tongue, waiting for someone to tell. It was meant to be Sabine, but Jesu, he needed to tell someone, and Janos... He could trust Janos at least. The man had been his guide and his friend even before Mack.

Janos had been partway to raising his bottle to his lips. He lowered it. "Yes?"

Enoch hesitated. "Yes." He squeezed the bottle between his white-tipped fingers, the brown glass casting golden hues on his pale skin. He remembered Ben, the water dripping between his fingers. "I—it—" The words caught in his throat, the excuses and the half-truths. No. No lies. Janos had earned more than that. "I'm tired."

"I am not surprised. You have not stopped for all the time I have known you."

Enoch pressed his thumbs to the bottle, the tips whitening. Janos had no notion of how right he was. "I don't know what I am to do." He turned the bottle, the glass warmed by his skin. "I want to be of use, but I have no purpose here. I—my streams. I think I am done with them."

There was a clink of glass on wood, and he peered up from his bottle to see Janos setting his drink on the table.

"You don't need to have a purpose." Janos studied him, a furrow between his eyebrows. "It is all right to take some time to understand yourself and where you wish to go." He tilted his head. "You have told the management about this? Sabine? Anyone?"

"I am waiting for her to come over by."

"They will provide for you." Janos sounded so sure that it eased a little of the dread resting in Enoch's belly.

It was strange to be so fearful after years of hiding right in front of them. Mayhap because he *was* so close to returning to Ben's side that he dreaded capture. To be so close and to have that chance taken from him, not least when they had so little time left...

"How long—" he began and hastily stopped himself. It would look ill if he pressed for answers. He had stayed with them happily for so long. Best not to seem too keen to flee. He waved a hand dismissively. "Ne'er mind." He released a short breath. "Your pardon. I'm in poor enough spirits today."

Janos waved away his apology. "A man has good days and bad. What kind of friend stays only for the good?"

Enoch tried to smile. "Aye, true enough." He took another sup from his bottle, a small token of Janos's friendship. It would be hard to leave that behind. Or worse, knowing he would forget it altogether when the timeline changed. "T'will be strange to be in another place."

"Perhaps I can make things easier for you?"

Enoch glanced to Janos. "Aye?"

Janos smiled. "My husband and I have a house outside of the city. It might be easier for you to stay there for a while. You could take some time and choose your path there. It would let you see life outside of the walls, but without facing it all alone."

Enoch ducked his head. Jesu, what had he done to deserve a kindness like that? "I would hate to be a burden."

Janos laughed. "You are not a difficult house guest, I think." A wave of his hand took in the tidy apartment. "You take care of your place." He leaned forward, propping his forearm on his knee. "You have met my husband, yes?"

They had met a score of times, but one thing stood out. "He...likes to talk."

"And write on a dozen different notebooks and leave all things about him and cups on every table." Janos gave a heavy sigh. "I tell him and I tell him to make things tidy, but he gets distracted or he distracts me, and the cups stay where they are."

Enoch smiled weakly, remembering another person with a knack for leaving things behind where they fell. "I think, in a pair, there must always be one who knows where all things are and one who would lose their own arse if they were not bound to it."

Janos chuckled. "So, so. The world would be dull enough if we all were the same." He picked up his bottle again. "If you want to stay with us when you leave this place, I know he would be happy to welcome you too. It might be easier instead of having some stranger from the TRI keep you company in a new place."

That gave Enoch pause. "Why would I have a stranger with me?"

Janos grimaced as if he had said too much. "They did not tell you?"

The knot tightened in Enoch's belly. "Tell me what?"

"If you leave the TRI, they would not be able to leave you unsupported until they were sure you could manage alone." Janos eyed him. "You're sure they did not tell you this?"

Enoch wracked his memory but could not recall. Mayhap they had some time ago, but then, he hadn't listened. He had no need to leave then, and now, when he wanted to, he would be shackled to a gaoler and kept from Ben all over again? Jesu, he should never have returned.

He put down his bottle, thirst gone.

"I am to have a warden? Like a prisoner?"

Janos sighed. "No, no. I'm telling you badly." He ran a hand over his face. "This— You would have a companion. Someone to help you settle in a new home in case there is anything that you can't do or understand."

"And if I don't want a companion?" Enoch shook his head. "I wish to leave to be away from the TRI, not to take one of them with me."

Janos held up his hand. "I know, but there are things in this time that may cause you problems. They only want to make everything simple for you. It wouldn't last for long times."

Enoch watched his plans vanish like smoke. Leaving or staying would make no difference if he was yet under the TRI's protection. If they gave him someone new, someone who would guard him as if he were the innocent fool he played, then there would be no means to join Ben. It would be another cage, only smaller.

Janos was right. It would be simple to accept the invitation to stay with him and his husband. Of all the people in the TRI, Janos knew Enoch best. He knew well enough what Enoch was able to do or not. He would not trail after him to keep him from harm.

Enoch chewed his lip, lost in thought. If they only had a little time left, then he might even be able to slip away from Janos's home for long enough to see Ben and his mission to the end. Some lie about a seaside visit alone, mayhap. Beyond that, it scarce mattered.

"If they will allow it," he finally said, glancing across the table at Janos, "I think I would like to come to your home." He tried to smile, though it felt forced. "Better to be with a friend than a stranger."

Janos smiled warmly. "I'll talk to Sabine for you. It will make it easier, so you don't need to explain everything again."

Enoch touched Ben's pendant on its chain at his neck. If Janos was speaking for him, then it would be done sooner, and even that was not soon enough. "Thank you."

Chapter Twenty-Seven

"Are you all right?" Ada asked quietly.

Ben glanced out of the pod window into the darkened street. There was a junction a little way down the street that turned into a long cul-de-sac lined with terraced houses. It was late enough that a lot of the windows were already dark, upstairs and down. "I wish there was another way we could do this."

After Enoch left him in the hotel, he'd retreated to his latest safe house with Ada and spent hours turning over idea after idea. It was much harder than usual. He kept opening his bud, checking, waiting for messages that didn't come. A time, a place, anything that was a clue about when Enoch would join them.

With that pounding against his mind, trying to find a logical, sensible, safe way to get at Mack felt like catching water in a sieve.

The task force was the big problem. Ben knew they weren't just after him. They were after the person who had pushed the first domino in the cascade that ruined his childhood. They would be watching Mack. There was no way to approach him personally or snatch him from under their noses without a lot more resources. The gates were out of the question. Enoch had made that absolutely clear.

In the end, it was Enoch's hopeless suggestion that won out.

Ada reached across the space between them and squeezed his forearm. "I will be as quick as can be. You need not worry."

He wanted to lie and say he wasn't worried, but it felt like everything was balanced on a knife-edge. If this didn't work, then there wouldn't be another chance to stop Mack from going through the gate. "You know where the rendezvous point is?"

Ada touched her brooch that had a bud imbedded in it. "I have my guide." She leaned closer with a waft of camomile and honey. "I can do this for you. Have no fear."

They were only words, but they helped. "I know." He took a breath and blew it out. "Okay. Okay. You know which door to go to?" Ada pointed it out. "He probably won't listen, but make sure you tell him everything I told you."

"And his woman is sure to be there?"

Ben nodded. "I don't think she'd leave him alone, not when she thinks he might run off and do something stupid."

Ada checked her reflection in the window. Ben had to admit she had a knack for blending in. Her current disguise was a respectable dowager with a fitted suit and woollen overcoat. She had modelled her hair on some ageing film star, a complicated array of curls pinned and twisted like rolling waves. No one would ever suspect her of being a mad hedge-witch from the 1800s.

"Very well," she said, giving him a quick smile. "To battle, then."

As the door slid open, Ben leaned away from the pale-yellow spill of the streetlight. "I'll see you at the rendezvous."

Ada strode off down the street, coat swirling. Ben waited for a few seconds, then touched the pod controls.

It felt strange to be leaving her to handle things on her own, but if the task force was keeping as close a watch on Mack as Ben suspected, they might consider any strangers a potential threat. It was safer for Ada to go in solo, leaving behind any comms with a direct link to Ben. That way, if they did pick her up, there would be no ties to him, and they'd have no reason to hold onto her.

If everything went smoothly, they'd be in the safe house in an hour, maybe two.

There was no reason it wouldn't. At best, she'd follow his script and be done in half an hour. At the very worst, the task force would pick her up, and she'd used the legal jargon and false paperwork and address to get out of their custody since there was nothing to charge her with.

Of course, it didn't do much to settle Ben's nerves.

As the pod shuttled towards the rendezvous, he checked his bud again, but there was no message incoming from Enoch. He turned the screen off with a dejected sigh and settled against the door to watch the world whip by in strips of light and dark.

The rendezvous was on the edge of the city centre, almost three miles from Mack Robertson's house. It was as close to a dead zone as they were going to get with only a couple of surveillance cameras, one of which he knew was definitely broken. A taxi pod to a residential precinct was phase one, then she only needed to walk half a mile, and he could pick her up without anyone being the wiser.

Ben slid the pod into the side street. A wedge of shadow cast by the corner of the building provided some additional cover. He touched the controls, powering down the engines and dimming the interior lights, then sat in the half-light to wait.

Time felt like it was crawling by. Five minutes, then ten.

Ben picked at his nails, watching the glowing digits on the screen in front of him.

How long would it take? Would the task force even have people in the house? If they were trying to keep eyes on him, it would be a sensible precaution. And if they had someone in the house, then Ada was compromised, and if she told them anything, then they might be the ones to walk around the corner instead of her and—

He winced at a crack and a sharp pain in his hand. A bit of a nail had cracked off to the quick, and his fingers were red. He stuck the bleeding fingertip on his mouth and closed his eyes, trying to calm himself.

It was all right. They would be all right. Enoch would join them soon, and they would finish everything, and everything would return to the way it should have been.

Without Enoch...

He took a shuddering breath. Dad or Enoch. It was one or the other. There was no way around it, not unless he waited and let Mack go off and get himself killed. If he did that, Enoch would never forgive him. God, as if he could forgive himself. Twenty-odd years of guilt about hiding and doing nothing while his dad was attacked was bad enough. Someone dying as a direct result of him doing nothing was even worse.

He'd tried to think of some way to get a message to himself, something hidden in his dad's papers, some hint of where he should go and when to find Enoch, but it would never work. Once the timeline shifted, the message—and the version of Ben who wrote it—would never have existed to begin with.

Half an hour and no sign.

Ben scrolled through the screens on his Leaf. No message from Enoch either. Maybe it was too much to get his hopes up and think the TRI would just let Enoch walk out the door without supervision, especially with everything that had been going on. He chewed at his broken nail, staring at screen after screen.

It would have been easier if he'd given Ada some kind of beacon so he could at least keep track of her. But then that would defeat the whole purpose of disconnecting her from him. He grimaced at the taste of fresh blood on his tongue.

Another half an hour. No message. No Ada. Nothing.

He was tempted to get out of the pod and do a circuit of the block. He needed to be doing something, and it felt too much like four walls closing in on him and no way out and no way of knowing if anyone would come and find him again. It was enough to make his throat burn with acid, and he scrambled out of the pod, gulping in the chilly night air.

He leaned against the pod, the coolness of the metal seeping through his clothes. It was late enough to be quiet on the roads and so dark no one would really be able to see him. He was still standing there, face turned up to the sky when he heard the tap of boots on the pavement.

"Forgive me," Ada said as he turned. She was approaching from the nearby underpass, moving through pools of pale yellow from the streetlights. "I'm late."

Ben managed a quick smile. "You're back. That's the important thing." He motioned for her to join him, clambering into the pod. As soon as the door had closed behind her and the pod shuttled off into the streets, he searched her face. "How did it go? Did you see him? Speak to him?"

"It went as you expected. He would not listen to reason."

"Thought as much." He ran a hand over his face. "Did you talk to her?"

Ada nodded. "She can make no promises, but if she cannot stop him, she says she will send word where they can be found. I gave her your beacon to summon us." She reached over and caught Ben's hand, her fingers ice-cold. "There's more. The reason I was late."

Ben's stomach dropped. "Did you—was there trouble?"

"Not trouble," Ada replied, but her brow was furrowed, and her lips pursed. "A...concern, perhaps." She opened up the screens of his Leaf and skimmed through them. It never failed to amaze him how quickly she had learned to use them. She turned one of the files towards him, a picture. "This man."

"Anton?" Ben stared at the screen. Anton was one of Jacob's people and had been drafted into the task force from the police force. Ben had shown his files on all the task force staff to Ada as a precaution in case anyone tried to follow her.

"When I left Mack's home, he approached me on the main street. He told me he was of the police and he sought witnesses to an incident that had happened nearby."

"Bullshit. He probably wanted to see who was visiting Mack."

Ada gave him a reproachful look for the profanity. "I thought much alike. A man who I know to be working for the task force would not be carrying out the duties of a constable. I told him I saw nothing and could not help him."

"Of course you didn't. I bet there wasn't even an incident."

"So," Ada agreed. "But he asked for my name and call number, lest they need to confirm there was nothing to be seen where I stood."

"Bull—" Ben cut himself off. "That's a load of bollocks. But of course, it's suspicious if you refuse..."

"Mm. I gave him the name and number you gave me." She shut the image. "Had you not shown me his face before, I might have thought nothing of it."

Ben rubbed his jaw. The task force was definitely getting edgy if they had officers watching all the comings and goings at Mack's house and making identification spot-checks on everyone who went near it. Whatever they were expecting, it seemed like it was going to happen soon.

"We need to get to the safe house," he said. "I don't think we're nearly ready enough."

Chapter Twenty-Eight

A day had come and gone, yet Enoch had not seen Sabine. She had sent a message saying she would come by once everything was arranged, but time was wasting that could be better spent elsewhere.

He ought to have run, but if he had, no doubt they would seek him out to be sure he had not come to harm. And so, he waited.

Enoch tried to comfort himself. He would have been happy enough to wait, if not for the world falling apart around him. Every minute seemed a lifetime. No matter how many times he glanced to the clock, it scarce seemed to change.

He stared blindly at the pile of letters in front of him. All the machinery in the world and yet people wrote to him on a piece of paper to thank him for his streams. Sometimes, they asked for him to send his name writ on a page. Sometimes, they asked for pictures, which seemed a kind of madness, paying them for their gratitude with his name on paper.

Too often, he delayed and forgot, but it was something to do and easier than sitting and staring at the walls. It was growing more and more tempting to send a message to Ben and to run. Anything but this sitting and waiting and doing nothing to be of use to anyone.

He sighed, dropping the letter he was holding and falling back against the couch.

He was still slouched in that attitude when his door chimed. Enoch's spirits leapt, and he scrambled up, rushing over to it. He pulled the door open and frowned in confusion.

Lysander O'Donohue stood in the hall, solemn as the grave. "Enoch. How are you?"

Enoch opened the door wider to allow him in, puzzled and alarmed. The task force never came to him. He went to them. In the past few days, they had not even allowed him that. If they were coming, then it meant something serious was amiss, and it took every ounce of his will not to panic.

"I'm well enough," he said, forcing a smile. "Is something the matter?"

"Nothing too serious." Lysander motioned to the table. "Can we sit?"

Enoch shrugged, thrusting his hands into his pockets as he crossed the floor. It was easier to hide them for a moment until they stopped shaking. "'Tis serious enough for you to come all the way to see me. I could have come to you."

The smallest of winces crossed Lysander's face. "I needed to come and see Sabine anyway, so I thought it would be easier than dragging you all the way into the city."

He wasn't lying, but Enoch wondered if mayhap that wasn't the whole truth too.

Lysander opened out his Leaf as Enoch sat. "Sabine mentioned that you're planning to leave the TRI."

"I was to ask her myself, but Janos offered to speak on my part." Enoch folded his arms on the table and wrapped his hands over his upper arms. "He thought it would distress me to speak of it."

"That bad?"

Enoch clenched his teeth together hard enough to make his cheeks ache. "I want to be somewhere else." He looked at Lysander, who was gazing at him with sympathy. "Janos has offered me shelter in his home."

"Sabine said," Lysander confirmed. "I think they're working out the logistics..." He must have seen the confusion in Enoch's face because he hesitated, then said, "There will be papers you need. Your identification documents and finances and so on. They'll need to make sure everything's in order so you can go straight into a normal life."

Enoch almost sagged with relief. "D'you think it'll take long?"

"Not really. The offer's been there since you arrived. I started putting it in place before I left, and they just need to ensure it's all up to date. You could be out of here by tomorrow."

Something was happening at least. "I'd wager that's not why you came to see me?"

"Good call." Lysander pushed aside some projections. "Something's come up, and we think you might be able to help—a person of interest who might have ties to the investigation."

Enoch made a face. "With the few times I have left the TRI to go to the city?"

"Perhaps." Lysander opened up a file and laid out three images on the table.

For a split second, Enoch forgot how to breathe.

Ada.

Not only that, but the first image was taken outside the inn where he had met her with Ben, and the last was...

"You had me followed?" He stared at the picture of himself at the canal, seated on the bench beside Ada, sharing his crisps. God above, if they were following him then, perhaps they'd followed him the previous day to the hotel. Perhaps they knew about Ben.

"Only this one time," Lysander said carefully. "We were concerned after you were approached by the man in the bar. We wanted to make sure you weren't at risk."

Enoch's mind was racing. They had spied on him. Ben had suspected it, but Enoch never had. Only the one time, Lysander said. Mayhap he spoke for true, but mayhap not. After all, they had called him out of the inn when the stranger approached. Mayhap they had sighted him in the inn and tried to warn him. Or mayhap they had eyes on him then already.

But now, they had pictures of Ada. Not only one either. They thought her an enemy, but why? A person of interest, Lysander said. Did they know of her link to Ben? Or did they perhaps think she had ties to the stranger?

Sweet Jesu, he was staring mute at the pictures, and Lysander was watching him, as if his silence was telling his secrets.

Better, then, to throw the hounds off the scent.

"You telt me I was to be allowed my private moments!" he said, low and angry. "I was promised that my times in the city would be mine alone! Yet I find I have a guard as if I am some prisoner in need of watching!"

"Enoch—"

"No!" He leapt to his feet, slapping his hand against the table. "No! I have little enough! I leave this place to have time of my own without eyes and cameras and watching! And now, I find you have set eyes on me wherever I am!"

"Only one time," Lysander repeated, his voice calm and even. He held up his hand. "I know, we should have warned you, but we needed to make sure you were safe."

"Safe." Enoch spat the word. "Safe as I am inside the fences and walls and under your eyes?"

"Enoch." Lysander sighed and bowed his head in contrition. "I know. I'm sorry we didn't tell you sooner."

"Is that why I have been forbidden from coming to the task force? You think I have some connection to this person?" Enoch pointed at her. "Who is she to you anyway? I sit with a woman and share some crisps, and you tell me she's my enemy?" He threw up his hands, disgusted. "Am I to have no friends?"

Lysander seemed remorseful, as well he should. "We shouldn't have done it without your consent, I know. We won't do it again; I can promise you that." He hesitated then pushed one of the images closer. "We do need to know about this woman, though."

Enoch shoved his chair out and stormed in a circle about the room. His blood drummed like thunder, and all it would take was one misspoken word and everything might fall apart. If they had followed him once, mayhap they had followed every time. Mayhap they had listened and already knew everything. Mayhap that was why they had not let him leave with Janos already.

Better to find what they already know and see where to go from there.

"Aye…" he said, returning to the table. "You said she's a…person of interest? D'you think she knows Master Ben?"

Lysander was silent for a moment. "Indirectly, perhaps." He tapped the second picture. "She seems to have some connection to the man from the bar, the one who met you."

Enoch tried not to let his relief show. A connection to the stranger was far safer than a link to Ben. "Aye?" He sank onto his seat. "What makes you say so?"

"The fact that she went straight to his building after he was at the bar," Lysander said. "She's been seen there on security feeds a few times."

Spying, Enoch thought. Seeking information that Ben could not.

"And she was the last person who had contact with Mack Robertson before he vanished. We think she helped arrange his extraction."

For a moment, Enoch could not understand him. "Mack? Vanished? Was he not arrested and to be kept in his house?"

Lysander looked grim. "Exactly. He had a medical appointment for adjustments to his bionic eye at a clinic. Somehow, he managed to slip the people who were assigned to keep watch on him."

Enoch sat back in his seat, shaken. No wonder Lysander had come to speak to Sabine himself. The TRI was Mack's master after all, and he had run…

"You think she helped him?"

"We can't be sure, but it seems like a possibility." Lysander looked across the table at him. "You met her."

Enoch chewed his lower lip. "At the canal. All the other seats were filled, so I sat by her. She seemed nice enough." He frowned. "I gave her my crisps."

"What did you talk about?"

Enoch's mind was abuzz. "The weather," he lied. "The ducks. My sausage bun. It— She dint ask about the TRI or anything." He paused. "Why d'you think she came by me? Did she think I might do as Mack did?"

"We don't know." Lysander said. "Her name checked out, but the address she provided was false, and we haven't been able to trace her based on the contact details she provided. We've found some records from her name, but it..." He sounded tired. "Let's just say there were some consistent inconsistencies. Jacob insists there's something off about it and about her."

"Off?" Enoch echoed.

Lysander rubbed the tip of his nose with his knuckle. "Falsified. They were...accurate to a point, but there were elements that didn't add up. We don't think she is who she says she is, and, if that's the case, we have no records for her. It's very unusual for someone to have no papers or records at all."

Something in the way he said it gave Enoch pause.

"You know me," he said.

"Yes." Lysander nodded slightly. "We do. That's what Jacob's worried about."

Enoch blinked dumbly at him. God above, Jacob saw far too clearly. "He thinks she came through a gate and all?"

"He's convinced himself, and, given that he was the man who brought time travel into the public eye, I'm inclined to trust his judgement and experience. She may be very discreet, but it's better to err on the side of caution."

"It would give you just cause for your fears." He scratched at his cheek, his sideburns whispering against his fingertips. "Do you think she'll come by me again?"

Lysander shook his head. "We think that she got what she came for with Mack." He closed the images. "You're sure you can't remember anything else she said? Anything useful?"

Enoch made a show of thinking hard. "Only that she preferred cheese crisps to mine."

It was hard to overlook the weary frustration that crossed Lysander's face. "Okay." He sighed. "It was worth asking you anyway, to cover all the bases." He closed up his Leaf. "It's probably best if you don't come to the task force for a few more days. It's busier than usual."

"Could I not help?"

"Not right now. The best you can do is enjoy your new life outside the TRI." He rose from the table, straightening his jacket. "We'll call when it'll be okay to come back in."

Enoch got up too. "I think it will be good to walk in the country again."

Lysander smiled, small and fond. "Definitely different from the compound." He headed for the door but paused. "If you're staying with Janos and Dieter, don't ever use Dieter's favourite cup. He gets territorial."

"A last piece of wise advice?"

"More of a warning," Lysander said with a rueful chuckle. "Take care, Enoch."

Enoch waited until the door was shut, then sank onto the chair, his legs quaking. God above, they had come far too close to ruin. If they had followed Ada, then everything would have been lost. Ben would have been caught.

Then there was the news of Mack. Since he had fled, he was like as not with their enemy. If he was with their enemy, it was only a matter of time before he used the gate. No small wonder the task force wanted to keep only the most skilled of officers to hand. If they were to find him, a man who scarce could manage his letters would be of no use to anyone.

The gate. Ben needed to know.

Enoch ran a shaking hand across his mouth, trying to gather his scattered thoughts. The sooner he could leave the TRI, the sooner he could return to Ben and tell him everything. Lysander had said it would be soon and...

And...

A terrible thought crept upon him.

Lysander had also promised he would not be watched, but the task force had broken that promise afore. If they watched him, they would follow where he led, and it would all be for nothing. *If* they watched him.

Jesu, would the risk be worth it? If they watched, he and Ben would be condemned to a life of misery without each other. If not, Enoch might have but a day or two with Ben before the gate opened and their lives were returned to another path.

"God's bones," he whispered, knocking his fist against the table.

After everything he had done for Ben's sake, to be asked for more...

What could he do? In truth, there was no choice. To risk all they had done for a few days of pleasure was the worst kind of foolishness. If he did it, if he led Ben's hunters to his door, he knew it would be the last they would see of each other, and Ben's father would be lost forever.

"Fuck." The word felt right in his mouth, bitter and angry. "Fuck!"

Was it too much to ask for a little joy before it was all stolen?

Or mayhap it was all a punishment for his deception to be denied those last few days. Ha. Of all the times for fate to play her hand, it had to be now.

And yet, Ben had to know: about the task force, about Mack fleeing, about the eyes that were watching for Ada.

Enoch stared blindly at the wall. There was too much to tell. The whore-pendant would not be enough with no more than times and places. Any messages sent on the TRI machines could be checked too.

No. The news had to be given in person. But how to do it, when there could be people watching his every move? If he had Ben's wits, he could have made some secret language with messages hidden in it. If he had Janos's skill with machines, he could have found a way to call out without being heard. If he had Sabine's authority, he could have gathered a throng of people large enough that he might slip away unnoticed.

God above, if he had any means to speak but his streams...

His eyes drifted to the piles of letters scattered about on the couch and the floor. His groupies. That was what Mack had called them. People fanatical and devoted to him. People who wanted to see him. He rose and went to the couch and picked up one of the letters. More than one had begged him to meet.

More than one. Dozens, even. One might even call it a throng.

Enoch slowly started to smile.

What manner of man was he, after all, if he disappointed his loyal admirers?

Chapter Twenty-Nine

"I'm not sure about this."

Ada straightened up, studying her handiwork. "You said the museum will have the most modern of machinery, yes?"

Ben's skin was pulled tight over the padding in his cheeks. "Yeah, but—"

"There is no 'but.'" Ada used a tissue to smear away a smudge of glue from the edge of his eyebrow. She lifted her Leaf and took a picture of his face. "If they have machines that can see through your false face, then you cannot use it. This is the simplest way to go unseen."

"I don't see how this is any better."

She chuckled, stepping away. "Look in the mirror, then. Tell me you would know yourself."

Ben scrambled up off the toilet and peered into the mirror. He couldn't help staring and cautiously touched his face. The padding had plumped out his cheeks, and she'd done some...thing with a box of makeup to make his nose appear longer and thinner. She'd even made his eyes bigger under new blond eyebrows.

"How—?" He spun to stare at her. "You're a witch, aren't you?"

Ada laughed. "I watched many videos about how to change one's face. Did you not see how I changed my own face when I visited our...friend's building?"

Now that he thought about it, Ben could remember different hairdos, different styles, subtle but never the same. He offered his reflection an inane grin. It fit with the cheery, round-faced man who stared back at him.

"You will need to pad yourself well," she added. "Many layers. A face so round would likely not have a body so thin."

"I'm still sure you're a witch," he said, following her to the main room of the safe house.

Unlike the old warehouses that had been his preferred hideouts, this particular building wasn't discreetly hidden away in the docklands. It was part of a long terrace of older residential buildings in the process of redevelopment and not far from Exchange Square and the main train station.

After being caught out in two semiderelict warehouses and far from civilisation, hiding out in a residential construction project in the city centre seemed like a sensible precaution. He'd paid off enough people to keep his end of the site untouched for at least a couple of months.

It also meant they had actual habitable rooms, instead of former offices and canteens. The lowest level—probably a coal cellar at some point in the past—housed all that was left of his equipment, including his last gate. Most of the windows were shuttered or papered over, and as far as anyone knew, it was sitting empty, awaiting renovation.

"A witch?" She sounded amused.

"You know far too much about everything."

"It may be so," she said enigmatically. She studied him again, tapping her finger against her chin. "Would you have me attend also?"

There were a thousand reasons for her not to go, especially the dozens of cameras that would be present. "It's going to be filmed. If Anton sees you in the footage, he might wonder what you're doing there as well as loitering at Mack's house. Better for you to keep a low profile."

She nodded reluctantly. "And yet you, the one they hunt for, will go?"

Ben pulled on shirt after shirt. "I don't have a choice."

It was half true. He had to go, but he couldn't lie. He wanted to go too.

Two nights before, his Leaf had pinged to notify him of an update in Enoch's streams. It had been surprising enough, especially since Enoch had lost his streaming partner. Then Ben had watched the stream and—like every other viewer—couldn't quite believe what he was seeing.

Enoch, ebullient and beaming, declared he was doing a final stream before he retired to a quiet life in the country, but it would be a live event where he would meet as many of his lovely supporters as could attend. And where else would a living historical artefact appear but his local museum? There would be a name signing—autograph session, Ben guessed—and photographs, and if people could dress in ways as befitted the lessons they had learned from the streams, Enoch would be delighted.

It wasn't for all of them, though. The last line of the stream made that clear.

"Come the morrow, I will see you devils in the halls of the museum!" He had beamed into the camera as if he was looking straight at Ben. "Come see me and dunt be late."

Ben had no idea how Enoch had persuaded the city's central museum to let him loose in their building, but somehow, they'd agreed to it and in less than forty-eight hours as well. Ben suspected the entrance fee would be worth its weight in gold. There were even rumours of people flocking in from all over the world, and the net was buzzing with discussion.

He was more worried about the fact that Enoch wanted him to meet in such a public place. Something had to be going on, and it had to be pretty bad if Enoch was desperate enough to go into a loud, busy, and inevitably crowded hall of people.

"Here." Ada held out two small metal nuts.

Ben took them, puzzled. "What are those for?"

"You said the man from the TRI can recognise you by your face and movement, yes? Put one of these in each of your shoes. It will be uncomfortable, but it will remind you to change your gait."

Honestly, how the hell did her brain work? "I feel like James Bond, and you're my Q." He sat on the couch that served as her bed, wedged the nuts into his shoes, and slipped his feet into them. When he straightened up, he grimaced. "That's going to be annoying as hell."

"Then they serve their purpose." She proffered the last piece of his costume. "Be careful."

The museum was only twenty minutes away, and the event wasn't due to start for another couple of hours, but the staff shift change was due much sooner. He clipped the freshly printed ID badge onto his shirt, glancing at the photograph on it. He looked appropriately bemused, which seemed to be a standard in civil service IDs. The museum always had a handful of temps running about, and no one would give an employee with the right identification a second glance.

There was already a queue outside the building when he arrived. Trailing banners were hanging on either side of the main doors, almost obscuring the Victorian frontage. It was kind of weird to see Enoch's face peering down at him, ten feet long and shivering in the breeze. They'd worked fast to get them done. Some opportunistic people were even selling T-shirts and postcards, despite the security team's best efforts to shoo them away.

He loitered at the far side of the building as if he was watching the crowd until another member of staff hurried by behind him and towards the staff entrance. She was shorter than him, so it only took a few steps for him to keep up with her. When she swiped her pass to open the door, she glanced at him and his ID and smiled, holding the door open for him.

"Seems like it's going to be a bit manic today, doesn't it?"

Ben closed the door behind them. "I got called in last minute. They said they needed some extra hands."

"Not surprised." The woman rooted in her pocket and pulled out a bundle of keys. "Do you know who you're looking for?"

"I was told to report up to the main hall by…" He made a show of opening up his Leaf and scanning through files. He'd made sure to check the people responsible for the event. "Someone called Chaudhry is in charge?"

"Ah! Mo. Yes." She waved a hand to one of the corridors. "Third door on your left will get you to the stairs. One flight up and through the blue door and you'll be in the main foyer. Someone will point you in the right direction from there."

The next hour became a careful game of making himself useful, while not running into Mo Chaudhry or anyone else who might spot that they had one too many members of staff. It wasn't difficult. The people in charge were rushing about, putting out last-minute fires, carrying out sound and lighting checks, and generally too preoccupied to notice the helpful blond who was unfolding tables on the sidelines.

He was lining up the chairs and straightening up boxes of photographs on the main table when the doors from the foyer opened, and he heard the muffled roar from the crowd outside. A prickle of excitement shot the length of his spine, and he turned in time to see Enoch walk into the room, flanked by a couple of museum staff. Several members of the security team peeled away and stood on either side of the door. No wonder, if the crowds outside were anything to go by.

Ben turned to the table and lined up the pictures that were already as straight as they could be as footsteps approached.

"—and you can see we have everything arranged."

They were only a few feet away.

"Aye." Enoch sounded as cheerful as ever. "I see you have pictures for the name writing there."

Ben shifted to face him. "You'll have cramp in your hand when you're done signing all of these."

The astonishment that skimmed across Enoch's face made all of Ada's torturous work on his face worthwhile.

Ben had to fight a grin as he held out one of the prints to Enoch. "If it's all right...?"

Enoch gawped at him, then at the picture. "Your pardon?"

"I don't really think it's appropriate," the staffer said sharply. "You're here to work not jump the queue."

Enoch waved a hand at once. "It's no bother. Best I test the pens afore we start, eh?" He flashed his sunniest smile at her. "I'll be well enough here with this lad. If you have aught you need to do, you'll find me here after."

The staffer glanced at her watch. "I need to check the schedule with Mr. Chaudhry." She glanced along the table. "I'll fetch a jug of water as well."

Enoch stared up at Ben as she walked away. "Jesu...look at you. I would never have known you, had you not spoken."

Ben laughed. "That's the point of a disguise." He proffered the photograph. "Cashing in on your fame, I see."

Enoch's fingers skimmed along Ben's as he took the photograph, but his expression turned serious. "Is there somewhere we can talk?" He bent over the table to sign the picture, keeping his voice lowered. "Somewhere with no eyes or ears?"

"Toilets are the best bet," Ben murmured. He glanced around, trying to remember the layout from his previous visits. There was a disabled bathroom not too far away. That would be a private room with a lock and no interruptions. "Hey!" He waved a hand to catch the attention of one of the other staff members. "I'm just going to show Mr. Baker where the bathroom is!"

They waved in acknowledgement, and he motioned for Enoch to come with him.

It felt strange to be walking along beside Enoch in a public place, surrounded by people, hidden by nothing but a few smudges of makeup, a wig, and a few layers of clothes. Enoch was so close by his side that their arms were brushing, and it was enough to make his hands tremble. They were so damn close to being free of it all, and they'd be able to touch without caring who saw them.

It was only lucky the toilet was tucked into a side corridor where no one would notice two men hurrying in, one after the other.

Ben pushed the door closed behind them and locked it. When he turned back to Enoch, the breath was driven from his lungs as Enoch grabbed him in a near-violent hug. He was quivering like a leaf.

Ben pulled back, pressing his palm to Enoch's cheek. "What is it? What's happened?"

"I have to stay," Enoch's voice cracked. "Christ above, I have to stay by them!"

Ben stared at him blankly. "What?"

"The task force!" Enoch said. "They put people to follow me! They seek Ada! If I leave, they may yet be watching. They would follow me to your door, and I cannot let it be!" He caught Ben's hand, squeezing it hard against his cheek. "I will not have them catch you, not now, not when we're all but done!"

The floor seemed to drop out from under them.

"I—I don't understand," Ben said slowly. "What do you mean they have eyes on Ada?"

Enoch took a steadying breath. "You were right. They must have eyes on the man we hunt." His eyes were wet and brimming over, but his face was taut with anger. "They saw her spying for you. They saw her by me. They saw her by Mack. They believe she's his master's agent."

"No." Ben's throat burned.

Enoch nodded against his palm. "Aye." His breath was hot against Ben's wrist. "They know she is not who she said. Jacob believes her to be a traveller. You *must* send her back! She's a danger to you!"

No. No, no, no, no, no. Everything was falling into pieces. No Enoch to go with him. Ada compromised. The task force getting closer and closer. He recoiled. The back of his leg hit the edge of the toilet, and he stumbled, almost falling.

"Ben!" Enoch caught his arms. "Listen, pet. Listen to me!" He pulled Ben closer to him, lowering his voice. "Mack has gone. The task force have lost him."

That brought Ben's racing thoughts to a crashing halt. "What? No. He was at home."

"Ada went to his home, aye?" Ben had a sinking feeling he knew where this was going. "The day after, he escaped the task force's attention. They think she had some part in it. They'll be hunting for her on the street cameras as they hunted you."

And since she hadn't known to hide herself, there was every chance they'd be able to follow some of her movements and find a pattern. "Shit..."

"Jacob telt me the day Mack escaped." Enoch was speaking quietly and urgently. "They want to find her. You must send her home or else have her lead them a dance. She must be away from you. As far as can be."

Right. Yes. That made sense.

"What about Mack?" he asked. "Do they know where he is?"

"I think that may be why they hunt for Ada—they have no trail for him." He hesitated. "You sent her to him after all. Do you know where he might be?"

Ben shook his head. "I hoped—we tried to get his girlfriend to help us when he wouldn't listen. We haven't heard anything from her. Don't know if she'll be able to do anything." He released a gust of air. If Orla came through, they might be able to stop everything from going wrong, but if not...

Christ, a life on the run had only seemed bearable with the promise of Enoch by his side. Now Enoch couldn't run, not without compromising both of them.

"Can she tell you where to find him?" Enoch cut across his thoughts again. "Orla. She wants him stopped as we do."

"I got Ada to give her a pendant like yours. Thought they'd watch out for a tracker, but not a necklace. If— I don't know if she'll use it, but if she does—"

"You'll be able to find them." Enoch breathed out slowly. "Good. 'Tis a good plan."

"It might not work." Ben wished he didn't sound so desolate. God, after everything he'd put Enoch through, the thought of it all being for nothing was unbearable. "She might not have a chance to use it."

"Don't think on it. You have done all you can. Now I will do the same." Enoch caught his shirt, pulled Ben down to his level, and kissed him hard. "Forgive me," he whispered against Ben's lips. "I would that I could go with you."

Ben swallowed around the lump in his throat. "I know."

Enoch stared at him, searching Ben's face as if he was memorising him. Ben didn't know which of them moved first, but they were kissing each other and pulling at each other's clothing and tangled themselves in the dozens of shirts he was wearing.

Skin met skin, and Ben groaned into Enoch's lips as rough nimble fingers squeezed his cock.

"We—"

"If you say we have no time, I'll twist it off," Enoch growled, grinding himself against Ben's thigh.

Ben laughed, hoarse and desperate. Enoch knew him too well. "Need to be quiet," he corrected. His breath hitched as Enoch slid his hand lower, fingers stroking Ben's balls.

"Not I." Enoch's mouth was hot against Ben's throat. "You, Master Ben. You can never keep silent."

Ben drew away to gaze at his lover. If it was to be the last time, it was the best way he could think of to say goodbye. He pushed Enoch's hand off his prick and went onto his knees in front of him. "Shut me up, then."

Emotions flooded Enoch's face, and he reached out—hand tremulous—to cup Ben's cheek. "Your face. I'd mess it."

Enoch wanted to, Ben could tell that much from the hunger in his expression, but Enoch was right. With the makeup and the padding and everything else Ada had done, the only way Ben could safely walk out of the museum was if he looked exactly the same as he had when he walked in.

If they were careful, if they took their time, and they were—

Someone knocked on the door, and Enoch started so sharply he almost pulled Ben's wig askew.

"Mr. Baker?" It was the staffer who had brought Enoch in. "Mr. Baker, are you all right?"

Enoch's head lolled, and Ben couldn't see his expression as he stared up at the ceiling. "Aye," he called through, his voice taut. "Aye, fine. Just a touch of the nerves."

"Oh! Oh, of course." She was silent for a moment before cautiously adding, "They're ready for you. Um. Just so you know."

"A moment and I'll come." Even without seeing Enoch's face, Ben could hear the frustration and sudden weariness in his voice. "A moment." He stepped away from Ben as he adjusted his clothing and tucked his cock in his trousers. His lips moved in a barely audible, "Shit."

Ben got to his feet, putting himself in order. "Sorry," he whispered, in case the woman was hanging about outside.

"Not your doing." He ran a hand over his face and turned to check himself in the mirror. "God's bones...I have to do it now, dunt I? I have to see them."

Ben stepped closer, wrapped his arms around Enoch's shoulders, and pulled him against Ben's chest. "You'll be fine." If his voice was betraying him, he ignored it and rubbed his cheek against Enoch's mussed up hair. "They love you. Just treat it like any other stream." He looked at their reflections in the mirror and forced a smile. "I'll watch it when I get home."

Enoch squeezed Ben's arm. "And Ada?"

Ben swallowed hard. "I'll figure something out." He kissed Enoch's ear and hugged him a little tighter. "I love you."

"Aye." Enoch's lips trembled. "I know." He drew Ben's arms down and turned, his eyes too bright and too serious. "Be careful." He opened his mouth as if he was going to say something else, then shut it, stepped around Ben, and unlocked the bathroom door. "Wait a moment," he said softly without turning. "She might yet linger."

Ben nodded, clenching and unclenching his hands. He pressed into the corner of the room, watching Enoch's reflection in the mirror as he walked out into the hall. The door swung shut behind him, and Ben was left alone.

Chapter Thirty

"I heard it all went well."

Enoch nodded, gazing through the window of the pod. He knew he should act joyful to come to a new home, but he was so damn tired. He watched the trees and fields rush by, streaks of green and brown and gold by the evening light.

"Exhausting?" His companion prompted.

Reluctantly, Enoch turned from the window. Janos sat opposite him, leaning comfortably in his seat, but there was a line between his brows that spoke of worry.

"It was...many people." Enoch turned over his right hand. His fingertips were smudged with ink. "I have never spoke to so many people in my life afore." He tried to smile. They had been kind and joyous and some even wore chickens upon their heads. "I—it—" Words failed him.

"Overwhelming?" Janos suggested with a crooked smile.

It was a good word for it. So much happiness and excitement and noise coming so hard upon grief and loss. There had been no time to pause nor think nor even to breathe. He looked out of the window again.

Janos said nothing more for the rest of the journey, and Enoch was grateful. His mind was pulled in a thousand directions at once, and if he had been asked any more pressing questions, he knew he would give way and shatter. It was all too much.

Would it be better to return to the TRI and hide in the familiar walls? To go somewhere new, even the house of a friend, seemed like it might be the final straw to break the donkey's back. Yet what reason could he give? Sabine had arranged everything with Janos to collect Enoch after the stream. It would seem strange if he were to beg to go back now, not after he had demanded to leave.

Question after question built up in his mind like bricks in a wall: Had Ben made his escape? Was Ada back where she belonged? Had Orla sent a message? Did they know where Mack was? If everything fell apart, would Ben ever be able to come close again?

He was lost in the muddle of his thoughts when Janos touched his knee, making him startle.

"We're here," Janos said, gazing at him with concern. "You are all right?"

"Yes." The lie took much effort. He followed Janos out of the pod, blinking in the warm evening sunlight.

Janos's home lay ahead of them, and for the first time in hours, Enoch truly smiled. Janos lived in a house Enoch might have chosen for himself. It was far older than many of the buildings in the city, like as not a farmhouse turned into a home with a garden spread out before it, and behind it, trees and fields. It even had a small brook running through the garden and a bridge made from aged wood.

"Something more of your age?" Janos suggested with a small smile.

Enoch nodded. "Better windows, I think. And less horse shit on the ground."

Janos patted him on the shoulder. "For you, I will bring horse shit, if you wish."

Enoch looked up at him. "You talk enough horse shit already."

Janos laughed, leading him along the path to the door.

The outside of the house seemed old, but inside the door, it proved as bright and modern as any building in the TRI compound. True enough, it had an old-fashioned fireplace with a hearthrug afore it and a broad chimney breast, but lights and machines gleamed all about and music played from the very walls. Through a doorway at the end of the room came the rattle of pans and dishes. The scent of heavy meaty food made his stomach curl and not in a pleasing way.

"Dieter!" Janos called out.

Dieter Schmidt, Janos's husband, peered through a doorway on the far side of the room. "Good timing! Food's just about ready." He came through the doorway, slinging a cloth over his shoulder. "Good to see you again, Enoch. Welcome to Hotel Nagy."

Enoch bowed his head in greeting. "Thank you for allowing me to stay."

Dieter waved a hand dismissively. "Fuck off. D'you know how many guests we've had here? Do you?" He sighed in frustration. "Sod all. I spent months getting the guest room fucking glorious and not a single fucker'll come and use it. It's about time."

Enoch could not help but gape at him and the amount of profanity.

Janos cleared his throat. "Dieter, not so much, maybe?"

Dieter coughed, as sheepish as a grown man could be. "Sorry. Old habits." He waved towards the table. "If you want to sit, I'll get you something to eat."

Enoch hesitated, and something in his face must have betrayed him.

"You are not hungry?" Janos murmured.

Jesu, how dreadful did he appear for Janos to notice it so quickly?

"Only tired," he lied. "Mayhap a little dry toast and some milk would be enough. I only— It has been a long day."

Janos and Dieter shared a glance that Enoch was too weary to understand.

"I'll get some toast on," Dieter said. "Jan, give him the tour, and I'll bring the food up when it's ready."

Janos put an arm lightly around Enoch's shoulder. He guided him through the house and pointed to the different rooms, should Enoch want to use them, then led him into a bedroom in the gabled roof of the house.

The room had a window that faced the sunset, a broad bedstead neatly made with white linens and a colourful knitted blanket, and a chest of drawers and a desk piled with Enoch's few possessions. It was far smaller than the rooms at the TRI, but it seemed much more like a home. Enoch sat on the end of the bed and ran his hand over the blanket.

"The bathroom is only in the hall if you need it," Janos said, standing in the doorway. "All of your things are here. If you need places for—" He cut himself off, shaking his head. "It is no hurry. You can rest tonight. Have some quiet and sleep. I think you must need it."

Enoch could scarcely look at him. It was too much, the kindness and concern when he most needed to show nothing. "Thank you." He plucked at the blanket. "Please beg Dieter's pardon for me. I did not mean to waste his food."

"It's not a problem." Dieter squeezed by Janos in the doorway. He had a plate stacked with toast in one hand and a mug in the other. He smiled. "We both know a thing or two about losing your appetite when you've had a tough day." He set the dishes on the desk beside the wall. "If you need anything, just yell. We'll be at the end of the hall or downstairs."

Enoch's words caught in his throat as he said, "Thank you." He glanced up to find Dieter watching him and had to turn away.

"Good night, Enoch," Janos said firmly. It was enough to make Dieter withdraw from the room, and then Janos closed the door behind both of them.

Enoch had no appetite, but he made himself rise and eat some of the toast. An empty stomach helped no man, and even a slice of toasted bread, thick with butter, was better than naught. He tried to ignore how much the toast quaked in his hand as he tried to ignore the tightness in his chest. It was difficult when a great hand seemed to squeeze him, crushing the breath and the strength out of him.

Ben was gone.

They would never see each other again.

It was as simple and as difficult as that.

If Ben succeeded, then he would never know. If Ben failed...

He dropped the half-eaten toast on the plate and pressed his mouth shut, his stomach twisting into knots again.

If Ben failed, mayhap they could find some means to flee. Enoch was no longer in the TRI's hands. It was one small step, but the task force would still be after Ben. For all Enoch knew, he might yet have them that followed him like his own shadow. Or mayhap Lysander spoke true and there was none set to watch him. How could he be sure?

He glanced to the door.

Janos was his friend. How better to keep eyes on someone than place them in the care of someone they trusted?

Enoch swore under his breath, angry at himself and at Lysander. Janos was his *friend*. It was a cruel world indeed if a man could no longer trust those he considered friends.

He returned to the bed, the mug of milk in his hand, and sat. He had his pendant, his whore's locket from Ben. Mayhap when Janos and Dieter left the house for work or some other matter, he could ask for their leave to have his...companion come by him? If Ben came with his face masked, surely it would—could—be enough?

But there was the danger of the task force watching and following and to risk all that for a bit of buggery and another chance to see...

He didn't know why he hurled the mug at the wall. He didn't know why he screamed like a stuck pig. It felt like he sat apart from himself, panting and staring as milk ran down the wall and footsteps thundered on the stairs.

"Enoch?" Janos knocked first, only once. "Will I come in?"

Enoch stared blindly at the broken pieces of the mug. A mess. There was a mess everywhere. Everything was blurring, and his eyes and throat were hurting. Stiff as an old man, he got to his knees to pick up the broken mug. His face was wet and hot, and he swore as broken china slipped across his fingers, blood in the milk upon the floor.

He was still there, folded over the broken cup and weeping like a child when Janos knelt by his side. He had no wit left, nothing to hold his mask in place. He dropped his head against Janos's chest and sobbed.

Chapter Thirty-One

"You're not listening to me!"

Ada didn't glance up from the pan she was stirring. "Oh, I heard you well enough. You would send me away from you. You believe I may be in danger." Her lips tightened into a thin line. "Do you think I am so foolish to allow myself to be followed?"

Ben threw up his hands in exasperation. "You think you understand the technology they have access to here! You don't! For all we know, they could be closing in on us any time now."

The wooden spoon clattered against the edge of the pan, and she turned to glare at him. "I know what it is to be threatened." Her voice was harder than usual, underneath it something Ben couldn't put his finger on. "I lived as a woman in a world made for men. I lived *alone*. I was not always old and unpleasing as I am now. I am well accustomed to eyes on me, people following where they should not. I *know* how to hide myself."

Ben found himself retreating from the fury in her eyes. "That's not the same—"

"To stay hidden? Oh, but it is!" She jabbed him in the chest with a bony finger. "Mark you, I know more of hiding than you ever could, boy. Perhaps the eyes are machines now. Perhaps there are fewer people walking abroad. It makes no difference if you have learned well to make yourself unseen."

Ben couldn't help thinking about the face she had constructed for him, the nuts that had left him with blisters on his feet, the dozens of changes she had made to herself with clothes and hair. Maybe she was right, and machines could be fooled and avoided, but if the task force knew about her, she couldn't be as good as she thought she was.

"They know about you," he said more quietly. "They have pictures of you."

Ada turned away from him and lifted the pan from the small gas flame she was using. "If they knew so much, then they would have found us already." She poured thick soup into a bowl and thrust it towards him. "Sit. Eat. Think."

Ben reluctantly obeyed, retreating into the room they shared. By the half-light from a streetlamp breaking through the paper over the windows, he sat on the couch and picked at the soup. He wasn't in the mood to eat, but it was easier than arguing. To his surprise, the soup wasn't bad, and by the time Ada joined him, he was drinking it straight from the bowl.

If that pleased her, she didn't say. She sat on the other end of the couch, sipping her own soup from a mug.

"You can't stay," he finally said, setting the bowl on his lap. "There's a hotel in a town up the coast. I'll— It's nice. Out of the way. It'll only be for a few days."

"Yet I cannot go. You will not have your...friend with you, and now, you would bid me leave? Who will help you then?"

Ben watched the last dribble of soup slip and slide across the bottom of the bowl. "It doesn't matter. You *can't* stay. You'd be in danger, and because of that, I'd be in danger. Enoch's given up his freedom to make sure we—I don't get caught. I'm not letting that be in vain."

"I can stay in hiding." She gazed along at him, and in the pale light, her lined skin even more creased with wrinkles of worry. "They need not see me abroad. You should not be alone. I swore I would stay with you until your task was done."

Ben sighed. "I don't know why. You don't even know me."

Ada moved a little closer, patting his wrist with her bony hand. "I know you have given me an adventure. I know you have brought me into this world and let me see what I would never have seen." She moved her hand to squeeze his. "I want to repay you for that. I want to help you to find that which you have lost."

Ben gazed blindly at their joined hands. What he'd lost. Time travel had taken his parents. Lies and deception from friends had forced him away from the place and people he'd considered home. His own crimes made it permanent.

All he had left was Enoch and this one last-ditch attempt to make things right.

Now, thanks to her, he didn't even have Enoch anymore.

"I don't want you to."

Ada flinched as if he'd struck her. "You would be alone."

He raised his eyes to hers. "I'm already alone. I've been alone for years." He pulled his hand from hers. "I don't want you here. I never wanted you here. If I have to drag you through the gate myself, then I'll do it."

She had no reason to act as wounded as she did. He got to his feet. So she wanted an adventure? So what? He'd never offered. She'd never asked. He carried the bowl through to the shabby kitchen, turned on the water, and ran it until it was hot enough to turn his skin pink.

When he heard her footsteps approaching the doorway, he glared at the water, scrubbing the already-clean bowl. Ada didn't say anything. She set her cup on the narrow strip of counter beside the sink and watched him for a few minutes, then turned and retreated into the other room.

Ben's breath escaped in a gust, and he blinked hard, scrubbing and scrubbing. It was stupid to get so upset. They'd known there was always going to be a risk. For God's sake, he'd always assumed he would be on his own at the end of the day. It was how things should have been, but Enoch had offered to come with him, and Ben...

He dropped the bowl into the sink, water sloshing over the lip of the basin. The metal rim of the sink dug into his palms, and he curled his fingers, his knuckles turning white.

It was *stupid*. He'd expected to be alone. He shouldn't have gotten his hopes up.

"Fuck," he whispered. He slammed one hand against the edge of the sink, hissing as pain shot up his arm. "Fuck!"

Kicking the cabinet didn't help. Nor did forcing the pot into the sink and scrubbing until his fingers ached and his hands were bright red from the heat.

By the time he returned to the other room, his anger and frustration had burned out. Yelling at an old woman who just wanted to help him wasn't going to do either of them any good. He hesitated in the doorway, the room much dimmer than the kitchen.

He glanced over to the mattress he slept on, and his breath hitched. The small lamp that he kept tucked out of the way beside the mattress, the one he needed to stave off the nightmares and remind him he wasn't in the dark, had been pulled out from its nook. It was switched on, casting a pale glow.

Ada had heard him cry out in the night before. She'd never asked about it, but she must have noticed the lamp that was always on through the night. Even after he'd treated her like shit, she'd switched it on for him because she knew the room would be dark when he came back. It—There wasn't any reason. She didn't need to do that.

He glanced across to the couch. She was already lying there, her back to the room. Maybe she was asleep. Maybe not. He ran a shivering hand over his face. It was warm and pink from the hot water, and suddenly wet again.

In the morning, they could talk like sensible people. He would make her a decent cup of coffee—she still couldn't understand the measurements—and he would explain and...and yes. Thank her. Thank her for noticing and for giving a damn.

As quietly as he could, he crept across the room to his mattress. Ada didn't even stir. Asleep then.

Ben curled up on the mattress, wrapped himself in his blanket, and turned his face towards the lamp. As he closed his eyes, he started considering all the ways he could try to gently explain to her it would be over soon anyway. She should leave, after all. It was safer than staying. Better than staying.

He didn't know what woke him.

It was getting lighter beyond the windows, and his lamp was on, but something...

His eyes fell on the empty couch, and he leaned sideways, squinting into the kitchen. If Ada was there, she was doing a good job of hiding. He pushed off his blankets and got to his feet, peering around the room. "Ada?"

She wasn't in the bathroom, all the lights off in every other room, and he fumbled for his torch as he ran barefoot down the stairs into the equally empty first storey. His heart thundered as he reached the lab where the tech was kept. The last gate stood cold and silent, definitely untouched.

"No..." Ben flashed his torch in every corner of the room. Stupid, stupid, stupid! It wasn't like she was hiding in a corner to jump out at him! If she wasn't in the flat itself and she wasn't anywhere in between she was gone. She had run.

He sprinted back up the stairs to the flat. If she was running to stay in the modern world, she was smart enough to take stuff with her. She wasn't an idiot. She knew about money and tech and everything else. She wouldn't have gone without supplies.

He stumbled into the main room, panting, and scoured the floor and shelves with his torch. His Leaf was there, but hers was gone. No surprise. Clothes too. Not all of them, though. One set, maybe two. He riffled through them, then frowned when the torchlight glinted off the edge of something on the floor, just under the couch. A box? He dropped to his knees and groped for it.

As soon as he picked it up, he recognised it. The box for the camo-patch.

"Shit..." He flipped it over in his hand, flicking the lid open with his thumb. It was empty. The camo-patch—the only way he could walk out in the world—was gone. She'd taken his disguise and run. She knew he needed it, and now, he was trapped like a rat in a cage.

The box fell from his shaking hand. He touched his Leaf, opening out a message box.

"Ada." He tried to keep his voice as even as possible. "Where are you?"

There was no reply.

He sank back on his heels.

Okay.

Okay.

Ada was gone. Ada, who he wanted to go, was gone. With his disguise. With a Leaf connected to him. Shit. Shit, shit, shit. He pressed his face into his hands, trying to gather his thoughts. She was gone and could lead them to him. Bad. She was gone. Good. But with the camo-patch. Very bad.

"Fuck," he whispered into his palms, rocking back and forth on his heels.

As the sun rose higher, brightening the room, he tore through her pile of possessions, searching for any clue where she might have gone. It wasn't until he finally stumbled into the kitchen that he found the scrap of a note lying on the counter.

Of course, he thought stupidly as he picked it up. Only place she could write it. No light but his nightlight in the rest of the flat.

It was only a few lines: *Ben. Forgive me. I will find the man whom you have been seeking. I will find his name for you. I promised I would aid you, and I shall. If you would have me leave thereafter, I will. Your friend.*

Ben stared at it, then curled his fingers, crumpling it into a ball. He stormed to the other room and snatched up his Leaf to send another message telling her so, to come back, that it was too late, and if they couldn't find him before, they wouldn't be able to now.

There was no reply.

The obvious thing would be to pinpoint her location then wait for her there in the pod without showing his face, but if she had the camo-patch, there was no guarantee he'd recognise her.

Still, he tried locating her through the link to her Leaf so he could at least work out where she was and how successful she might be. The connection was there, but somehow, he couldn't find any of the information he was looking for. It was as if she'd worked out how to switch off the location tracking.

It should have been easy enough to switch it on, but there was a password protection on it. Ben stared at the screen, frowning in puzzlement. He hadn't set that up, and Ada definitely didn't have the skills to do it.

He felt suddenly sick.

Someone else must have found her. The camo-patch wasn't enough. They must have caught her and locked the location so he couldn't find her and track her down as well. But which 'they'? The task force was after her, but they were bound by the law and wouldn't lock someone's Leaf like that, even if they were under arrest.

Their enemy, then?

Ben sat heavily on the floor, cold sweat breaking out across his skin. She was hunting the man who had started it all. He had no qualms about hurting and killing people, if Ben's father was anything to go by, and now, was it possible he had Ada? If she had her Leaf, he had to know. Maybe she was all right.

He stared at a knot in the wooden floor, trying to think. There had to be some way to ask to confirm who had her Leaf and whether she was safe, something only she knew. He chewed on his lower lip and hissed in pain as the skin broke and he tasted blood.

That brought him up short.

Blood on his lip. Like the first time they'd met, back in the woods.

His hands were quivering as he sent the message: *I've knocked my lip. What was that stuff you gave me to patch it up last time?*

No answer again. No surprise.

He knocked his fist against his thigh. God damn it. She should have gone home. She would have been safer then, and no one could have taken her prisoner or hurt her or anything like that. Why did she have to be so stubborn? Why couldn't she have just done what he asked? No one else needed to get hurt, especially not to help him.

His knuckles bit into his thigh, and he stared at the knot in the wood again.

No way to track her. No reply. No clues about her whereabouts apart from that building and the nameless man. No trail to follow because she liked to use her feet and not the pod network. No way to leave the safe house without an analogue disguise now that his digital one was gone. No time to go dark online to replace something that had taken him almost seven months to get a hold of in the first place.

If only he could have contacted the task force anonymously, let them know. Maybe their surveillance equipment would be good enough to pick her out, if Ben could give them a description of her clothing. But why would they believe him? Why would they care? As far as they knew, she was working for the man they were after. Even if he said she was with that stranger from the pub, they'd just shrug and say she'd gone back to her boss. Nothing they could do about that.

"Shit," he hissed though bloody lips, knuckling at his brow.

He almost leapt out of his skin when his Leaf chirped—a notification of a message. He groped for it and opened out the screens, but there was nothing incoming from Ada.

What then...?

Another message from another device he had set up himself for one reason and one reason alone. Ben's mouth went dry as dust. With numb hands, he opened the incoming message from Orla.

Chapter Thirty-Two

It was a fine day, the sky blue, the sun high, scarcely a cloud in the sky.

Enoch could not care less, body and soul wrung out like a cloth. He could not say how long he had wept the night afore, only certain that Janos had all but hauled him into the bed when he was spent, his head throbbing and his eyes aching. He was so sure he would not sleep and yet it seemed he was too exhausted to stay awake.

Once, he'd woken in the night, gasping. It took a moment to remember where he was. The room was dark but for a line of light coming from the hall through the half-open door which did little to drive off the nightmares. Damned gates and Ben's face and a hand just out of reach.

He sat, clutching at his chest, his heart racing as wild as a startled hare's, only for it to leap again at the sight of someone in the chair by the wall. Janos was there, asleep, chin to his chest and a blanket tucked over him. Watching over him, Enoch thought. Kindness or caution? How could he be sure?

When he woke in the morning, Janos was gone, but the blanket was there, folded neatly on the chair.

Janos had seen him in a poor state afore, but there was something different between suffering for the drink and weeping for a broken heart. Like as not, he'd told his husband. That was reason enough for Enoch to hide in the bathroom for as long as he could, standing in the shower until he was wrinkled as a dried plum.

Mercifully, Dieter was absent already when Enoch made his way down the stairs, though Janos was there. No work today, he said. Enoch wondered if he had chosen that or if he had been ordered to rest at the house so as to playact as warden.

Still, Janos seemed to sense that silence was welcome. They barely exchanged a word over breakfast, which Enoch only picked at before he retreated out to the garden behind the house.

Strange to be surrounded by nature again, no other buildings as far as the eye could see and no other people. No fences or high walls either.

They were quite a way from anywhere. The pod journey had been almost as far as the TRI from the heart of the city. Once, the silence might have been comforting, but now, it was too much.

With nothing to divert him, Enoch's thoughts were drawn back. It was almost akin to the call and response at evensong, one thought rising and another coming after. Ben, the TRI, the task force, the gates, the life he was to have that might yet be snatched away. One upon the other, they came. He walked the garden, trying to push them away, but some things were not made to be ignored.

More than once, his hand strayed to the pendant that hung against his chest. If he gave a place and time in the forest, mayhap they could steal a moment or two alone. But each time he thought on it, he knew the risk was too great. He could never be sure of not being watched, even by the eyes of a friend.

The sun rose higher, chasing the few clouds away.

Enoch was seated on the edge of the flagstone terrace when Janos came out to join him. He was humming as he came, no doubt to let Enoch know he was there, though he said nothing as he sat beside him. Enoch had his bare feet sunk in the grass, the end of his trews damped with morning dew. He had walked the length of the tamed garden a dozen times, circling about the beds of plants and even sitting for awhile on the swing that hung from a tree.

There was a clink of glass on stone, and Enoch finally glanced towards his friend.

Janos had not come empty-handed. He had two glasses and a tall, narrow bottle of golden liquid.

Enoch raised his eyebrows.

One side of Janos's mouth turned up. "Pálinka." He offered Enoch one of the glasses. "A drink from my country."

Enoch took the glass. "Your country?"

"Mm." Janos opened the bottle. "Many years ago, but I like to have a taste of it sometimes." He poured a measure for Enoch. "Dieter is an uncultured pig about alcohol. He will drink it like water to become pissed. Pálinka is better to share."

"And the lumps?" Enoch asked as he sniffed at the liquid.

Janos tilted the bottle to the light, illuminating the two dark objects at the bottom. "Plums, of course." He poured himself a glass and tapped it against Enoch's. "Egészségedre!"

"Eggy-she-gedra?" Enoch echoed, then took a careful sip. The drink was sharp and sweet. Warmth spread through him, his lips abuzz.

"Not so bad, yes?" Janos smiled out at the garden.

"Not so bad," Enoch agreed, taking another sip. It was a drink to enjoy, with fresh heat coming with every small mouthful.

Janos leaned back, pressing his false hand to the slabs behind them. His shirt drew tight on his large shoulders and arms, and he tilted his face to the sun. "This is my best kind of day. Warm and sun and good company."

Enoch smiled a little at that. "Two of three is good enough."

Janos cracked one eye open. "I am so terrible?"

Enoch gazed gloomily at the glass cradled between his hands. "I am—it is—I think I am poor company today."

Janos grunted, sitting up, and reached for the bottle. "Then we shall distract you from your sorrows." He added more pálinka to Enoch's glass and smiled. "Sabine told me I should take care of you."

"So you will have me fuddled?"

"Fuddled?"

Enoch tilted his glass. "In my cups."

Janos chuckled. "Fuddled... I like that." He topped up his own glass. "Maybe only a little? It will make things seem better, and we will not have the hangover in the morning."

Enoch made a doubtful sound but took another mouthful. If he paid heed to it, he could taste the sweetness of the plums. He let the drink sit on his tongue for a moment before swallowing. He felt it slide down his throat all the way to his empty belly.

The wind stirred, making the grass sway like waves and tossing the leaves on the trees. Birds sang and fluttered. It was pleasant enough to sit there, and Janos seemed to know silence was better than talking.

Enoch watched the shadows, cast by the fence and the trees, move across the grass as time slid by. His glass was empty, then filled again. A man could have been content with such things. And yet, his hand almost strayed to the chain at his neck.

A long while ago, he and Ben had lain together in the gardens behind Ben's old house. Afore all went wrong. Afore Enoch stepped into his shiny cage. It was a sin they would never have the chance again, 'specially on a day such as this.

The grass would be cool 'neath Ben's skin. The sun would chase away some little of his pallor. No machines would keep them apart; no gates would divert them. There would be nothing but the warmth and the sunlight and each other.

But Janos was by him and the task force might be watching and Ben was...

Ben was God only knew where, doing God only knew what.

Enoch sighed sadly and held out his empty glass once more.

"It does not help?" Janos murmured as he poured.

"'Tis only a brew, not magic." He tilted the glass, watching the drink swish this way and that. Clear as polished glass, it was. "D'you think it'll stop my thoughts if I drink enough?"

"I think it will stop anything if you drink enough." Janos sounded like he was a long way off, even though he was sitting right by Enoch. He cried out when Enoch set his glass down and took the bottle instead. "Be careful! It's stronger than it tastes."

Enoch made a face at him and drank another mouthful. The plums rolled over in the bottle, and he frowned, lowering it and poking his finger into the neck. "I want a plum."

"I don't think you will be able to pull them out with your fingers." Janos sounded mirthful.

Enoch turned the bottle to bring the plums to the neck and swore when the pálinka splashed on his trews. The damned plums were still stuck in the bottle.

"Let me," Janos said, taking the bottle from him. Like as not, he thought Enoch was going to spill it all. "Stay here. I'll be back in a moment."

Enoch pulled his feet up on the step and put his chin on his knee and stared at the grass. It was very green. There was a dandelion by the edge of the step and all. He leaned down carefully and pinched the stem 'til it broke.

Behind him, there were footsteps, and he held up the dandelion.

"I found it."

"A *pitypang*," Janos laughed. "They're good for tea."

Enoch blinked, peering up at him. "*Pitypang?*"

"That, in Hungarian." Janos had a bowl in his hand, and he smiled as he crouched down. "And this is your *szilva.*"

Enoch groped in the bowl. "My plum!" He caught one of the plums, wet and slippery as a fish betwixt his fingers. He held it, careful, for it was soft as...as soft as...as something soft, and he took little small bites from it.

Janos sat by him and put the bowl between them and looked at Enoch, grave as the priest on Sundays. "You are sad to leave the TRI? Or is it about him?"

Enoch chewed on the plum. Him. 'Course t'was about him, but t'was a secret also. Sworn to God and all that. "Like this place better'n the TRI." He waved about, dripping juice from the plum 'pon his breeches. "'Tis a fine place. Not so bright and shiny. Like a proper house, not a glass-walled box."

Janos glanced over his shoulder at his home. "I thought so too. Sometimes, it is good to have a place that is not so modern."

"Modern is..." Enoch scratched at his nose, thinking on all the buildings he had seen, all gleaming and cold and nothing snug and warm. "I dunt *not* like it—there's much good. I like to piss inside. Better that than outside. 'Specially when it turns cold."

Janos laughed. "Ah, yes. The bathrooms are very good. Hot water is a very good thing too."

Enoch had to agree. He had disliked them at first, strange and clean, but Ben always smelled fine, and it seemed to please him when Enoch smelled fine as well. By and by, they shared both tub and shower, sometimes for play, sometimes not. He scowled at the plum. Another thing that would be gone, if Ben did as he intended.

Janos knocked Enoch's elbow with his own, friendly. T'was the false one that Enoch had oft stared at but never touched. He changed his plum from one hand to the other, then prodded Janos's arm with a sticky fingertip.

"Does it hurt you?"

"Not much now." Janos turned his hand over, curling and uncurling his fingers. They were covered in a false skin, but when Enoch leaned close, he could hear the sound of tiny machines inside. "You have never asked before."

Enoch peered up at him with a sniff. "A man must mind his tongue, 'specially about bits another man has stuck on his self." He tapped Janos's arm. It sounded as solid as Enoch's own arm. "It looks the same as the other, near enough."

"That's the idea."

"Another good thing," Enoch declared as he ran his finger along the false skin. He took another small bite of his plum. "He telt me it was so."

"And you told the world in your streams."

Enoch sat up and put his plum in his other hand. "Mm. He liked them."

"He did."

Enoch put his head to the side. How did Janos know of Ben liking the streams? Strange. Best to be careful. He licked his fingers, all sticky and wet. "There will be no more of that," he said finally. Even if all went wrong, there was no reason any longer. Ben knew all he needed. Enoch was of no more use to him. He pushed the last piece of the plum into his mouth, biting down hard.

"Will you do something else like them? You seemed to enjoy them."

Enoch picked up his half-empty glass again. "I did them to make him laugh." He sighed, shaking his head that seemed uncommon heavy. "He will forget me by and by. And I will forget him and all."

Janos was quiet for a time. "I didn't know you cared so for him." There was something sad and serious in his voice. "No wonder you have been so upset."

Enoch's stomach was twisting into a knot. "What do you know of it?" he said, sharper than he wanted. Jesu, he was fuddled indeed. An empty belly and a sweet drink were an evil together.

Janos held up both his hands. "If the one I cared for used me and turned on me as Mack did to you—"

Enoch burst into a great peal of laughter. Christ above, they were speaking at cross purposes. "Mack? I dunt love Mack!" He staggered afoot on the grass. "Sweet Jesu, if t'were that easy…" The sun was hot on his head, and he spun, dizzied. "Jesu…no. Not Mack."

Janos looked as fuddled as Enoch felt. "Oh. Another friend, then?"

Enoch dipped his toes into a shadowed patch of grass, cool as water. "Another." He laughed again, but it turned sharp and bitter. "And he is gone an' all."

"The one who gave you that chain on your neck?"

Enoch frowned at Janos and clutched at his pendant. "'Tis mine." He wagged a finger. "You should not have seen it."

Janos gazed up at him. "You've been playing with it all day. I only wondered out of concern."

"Ha!" Enoch turned about, twisting the chain around his fingers. The pendant shone like a polished penny in the sun. "Aye, he gived it me." He pulled it 'gainst his neck until it hurt, and his throat and his eyes were hurting again. "And now he's gone, and soon everything else'll be gone an' all!"

"Everything else?"

Enoch pulled the chain hard and it snapped. "All of it," he whispered. "We'll forget, he said. We'll forget 'cause it will never happen, and if it will never happen, then we have nothing to remember." The little round shine in his hand was blurring, and his eyes burned. "I dunt want to forget."

A voice came from a long way off. "Forget who?"

It was only later, when they were out of the sun and the heat and there was food and water in him that Enoch remembered the oath and the name he was never to speak of like that. It was only when he saw Dieter come in and Janos speak to him in a language Enoch didn't know, only when he saw them eyeing him as if he was an enemy that he knew what he had said: Ben.

He scrambled from the table and ran towards the door to the garden. He got scarce a dozen paces onto the grass, reeling from the drink, before he was caught. Janos was bigger and faster and much stronger. Enoch screamed and swore, kicking and biting at any part of Janos that he could. Janos held him tighter, squeezing until Enoch could scarce catch a breath or fight.

"Why?" Janos's voice was harsh by his ear. "Why help him?" Enoch shook his head, pulling feebly against Janos's big arms. "He stole you from your own time! Why the fuck would you help him?"

Enoch twisted his neck to stare up at the man. "My life," he gasped out. "He gave me my life when I would have died." He laughed sharply. "How does a man repay that?"

Janos stared at him. By and by, his arms loosed enough for Enoch to breathe. "How indeed," Janos said quietly, gazing to his house. He gave out a low sigh. "The task force will need to know."

Of course. They needed to know of the traitor in their midst.

Enoch sagged in his grip. Ben was safe. That was all that mattered. Ben was safe.

He clung to that thought as they bore him to their pod. He groped for the chain at his neck, but it was gone. He stared blankly at them, and they spoke at him, but the words seemed a haze of sound. Ben was safe. Ben was safe, and they could not find him. That was enough.

It felt like some strange and terrible dream as they led him into the task force. Janos's hand was wrapped about his arm, tight as a vice. A sea of faces surrounded him and more voices over the top of him, his name, Janos speaking. Enoch folded over and was sick on the floor.

He was set in a chair and shivered as if chilled to the bone. It took a moment to know where he was, and then he saw the desk, the face across it. Lysander O'Donohue's office. Lysander was sitting across the way. Jacob Ofori was standing behind him, arms folded and glaring. Mariam Ashraf was at Lysander's side, her brown face turned paler, almost grey.

For a moment, they all said nothing, only gazing at him as if seeing him for the first time.

"Is it true? What Janos says?" Lysander folded his hands on the desk. They were clenched tight, the knuckles jutting sharp neath his skin. Enoch knew him well enough to know he was angry. "Were you working for Ben Sanders?"

Enoch wrapped his arms over his middle. "No."

"No? So Janos is lying?"

Enoch slid his tongue along his lips dry as dust. "Not...for. With." He took a quivering breath. "I—it was—I owed him a debt."

Lysander sank back in his seat. His cheek twitched, his mouth a thin line. "Where is he?"

Enoch shook his head.

"You don't know?" Jacob said. "Or you're not going to tell us." He leaned forward. "You'll only make things worse for yourself if you don't tell us everything now."

Enoch stared at the edge of Lysander's desk, dizzy and tired and angry with himself. "Gone," he said, low. "I telt him I was a danger to him." He forced himself to look up. "You dint believe him, not ever. Did you think he would forget his own father so easy?"

"We tried to find his father!" Mariam sounded as grieved as Enoch felt. "He knows we did."

Enoch gazed at her, the woman who was a mother to Ben. "Not enough, not for him." His voice cracked. "You knew that. He was desperate enough to walk through a gate alone."

Mariam paled, stricken, but Lysander did not.

"He's a criminal," he said sharply. "Lost father or not, he has committed more crimes than I can count. He's made you complicit and you'll be held accountable even if he isn't. It's time to stop protecting him, Enoch. You're in a hell of a lot of—"

The door swung open. "Boss!" Anton, one of the officers, leaned in.

"Can it wait?" Jacob snapped. "We're a little busy."

Anton glanced over his shoulder. "I don't think it can. It's *her*."

"Her?" Jacob echoed, then glanced to Lysander and Mariam before striding from the room.

Lysander rose but paused. "Don't go anywhere."

He followed Jacob out into the main room, leaving Enoch alone with Mariam.

"You knew. All the time, you knew." Her voice sounded fragile as spun glass.

Enoch lowered his eyes and stared at the grassy stains on his trews. "Aye." He caught a breath then said carefully, "He wanted to know you were well. That you were— He missed you."

Mariam's eyes were bright but there was anger in her expression too and grief. "Then he shouldn't have run off and lied to me," she snapped. "If he cared at all, he would have told me everything."

"He oped a gate," Enoch said unhappily. "If you knew—all the laws— you would have to have him arrested."

Mariam struck Lysander's chair. "I could have *helped*." Her voice was breaking apart. "He's my son, Enoch. Don't you think I would have protected him? Instead, he made things even worse, and now we're here!"

Enoch tugged at a loose thread on his shirt. "I dunt know," he confessed in a whisper. "I only know he was afraid, and I wanted to help him as he helped me."

She rounded the desk and crouched before him. "Tell me where he is."

He shook his head helplessly. "I dunt know. I was afeared of being watched. I told him to go."

She stared at him, searching his face. "Truly?"

He tugged at the thread until it snapped. She covered his hand with hers and bowed her head for a moment. That was how Jacob found them when he came back into the room.

"She wants to see you," he said.

Both of them looked up, bewildered.

"Who?" Enoch asked.

"Your...friend." Jacob's lips were drawn tight, his expression grim.

Enoch stared at him, befuddled. The drink, too little food, the sun. It was all too much. "My friend?" He could think of no one as he got unsteadily to his feet and walked to the other room. His heart dropped like a rock when he recognised the woman standing across the room. She was holding something in her hands, and he frowned in confusion. It was the power piece of one of Ben's gates.

"What are you doing here?" he asked stupidly. "Why have you brung that?"

"I needed to make sure everyone was paying attention." Ada smiled at him.

"Attention..." he echoed.

"I know where he's heading, and he'll need our help." Her eyes shifted to someone standing behind him. He heard Mariam draw a sharp breath. Surprised. No, more than that. Shocked.

Ada grinned. It changed her, yet something in her face stirred his memories. "Long time no see, Mariam."

Chapter Thirty-Three

The world was flashing by in streaks of light and shadow.

Ben twisted his bud over and over between his fingers, trying to keep himself calm. This was what he'd been working towards. This was where everything had been leading for months and years. This was no time to dissolve into panic.

The pod was zigzagging through the northern outskirts of the city, the fastest route to his destination, but it felt like the time on the clock hadn't changed for ages. He should have taken advantage of it—time stretching out like that—to figure out what he was going to do. For fuck's sake, he didn't even know if he was going to be in time, but if he was, if he could stop them...

Orla had only given him the coordinates.

Maybe it was done already. Until he got there, he couldn't be sure.

He flicked open a screen, drawing up some of the few pictures he had with Enoch. They were from those early days when Enoch still had no idea how a camera worked. He was skinnier then, wide-eyed. And they both almost seemed happy. Ben gazed at the picture of Enoch sprawled, asleep, on the bed they'd ended up sharing. Christ, it wasn't fair to come so far and be given a choice like this.

If it went his way. That was the problem.

If it was too late and everything fell apart, then Enoch would be left on his own out in the world. He was smart enough to get by. He would be okay. He'd figure something out. Maybe, if they were lucky, they'd even get to see each other again, even if there was a pane of glass between them.

And Ada...

It was all meant to be so simple: find the ones who did it, find the tech they stole from his dad's lab and finally pinpoint where and when he'd ended up and get him back, and that would be the end of it. Not...everything else.

The pod came to a stop.

Ben stared out, his heart pounding.

As far as he could tell, it seemed to be an industrial warehouse, dull grey and brick under the watery sunlight. A high fence circled it, decorated with the usual signs warning against trespassers, and a man in a uniform emerged from a booth by the gate, some kind of guard. Shit, shit, shit...

He climbed out of the pod, bracing his hand against the roof. Above him, cameras buzzed as they turned to focus on him, and he took a breath. Getting in was the key. He'd lied his way into situations before. Simple. Yeah. Just lie and smile and pray he didn't throw up.

"I'm sorry, sir." The guard approached. "This is private property. I'm going to have to ask you to leave."

Ben wished he could stop his heart racing. "I'm here to see your boss." Christ, his voice was cracking like a teenager's. "There are...services I believe he requires."

The guard, a tall, skinny man with sun-reddened cheeks and pale blue eyes, eyed him doubtfully. "I think you're mistaken. This is a fully staffed facility. We're not expecting any new contractors."

Ben's lips pulled into a tight smile. "Tell him Ben Sanders is here. He'll know what it's about."

"As I said, sir—"

Ben held up a hand and dropped it when he noticed how much it was wobbling. "Give him my name," he said quietly. "Believe me, this is a meeting he'll want to take."

The guard touched the bud in his ear, murmuring to his controller. He didn't seem impressed.

Ben pressed his palm to the side of the pod, the metal cool against his palm. His legs were threatening to give way under him, and he stared up into the cameras, praying that somewhere in the building, Mack was watching and could confirm Ben was who he said he was.

A moment later, the guard's frown deepened, but he touched a control panel on the gate. "Mr. Harper can spare a few minutes. Straight down the ramp, first right'll take you to the parking bay."

Ben got into his pod, trying to remember to breathe. His world felt like it was contracting to a pinpoint. Harper. He'd heard that name before. A long time ago, with the smell of Jacob's cologne and Mariam's perfume, when all the world seemed bigger. There were so many names he'd forgotten.

With effort, he managed to guide the pod to the assigned bay. There were a dozen pods there. Not a huge operation, then. Couldn't be, if Harper had kept it quiet for so long. Ben climbed out only twenty paces from the door and saw a silhouette, lit from behind, standing and waiting for him.

Sometimes, Ben had imagined how the encounter would play out. He wanted to think he would be calm and collected. He liked to think he could be suave, but any fantasies went out of the window as he got close enough to see the shining barrel of a gun in the man's hand. Ben stopped dead in his tracks.

"Quietly," the man said, his voice deep and firm. "Don't need to make a fuss."

Ben's mind crashed. He wanted to scream profanities. He wanted to run. He wanted to do anything that wasn't just standing there. Two more guards came out, took his arms, dragged him into the building. The man with the gun was in uniform as well. Not Harper. Wrong! Wrong, wrong, wrong!

The warehouse towered over him. Pipes and wires and cables and gantries. He stared around wildly, following the lines of the cables. All going to the same point. Something that needed a lot of power. Like his father's old labs. Old blueprints meant old-style tech meant old-style power sources. The gate. That was where they had the gate.

"No!" He threw himself forward against the guards' grip. He managed to jerk one arm loose and struck out with his free hand, catching the other guard across the head. It wasn't enough to break his hold, but a knee to the balls was, and Ben broke into a staggering run.

He barely got to the first flight of stairs when something hit him from behind. He fell forward and tumbled, rolling and skittering down the metal stairs. He landed hard on the concrete at the bottom, temple bouncing off the handrail, and his mouth filled up with blood, stars flashing behind his eyes.

There were hands on him again, dragging now. Corridor, stairs, a room, the floor, all blurred and strange and spotted with shadow.

Slowly, slowly, the light came back. Someone was kneeling by him. Sponge in hand. Cleaning the blood away.

"You shouldn't have come."

Ben peered at the face over him, indistinct and haloed by the lights behind it. Knew that voice. Different now. Mature. "Mack?"

The man sighed, nodding. "They sent you, didn't they?"

Ben struggled to push himself upright. The world swam, and he clutched at his head. "Sent me?"

"The TRI. The task force. Both of them." Mack's voice was flat.

Ben stared at him, vision drifting in and out of focus. Only a couple of years since they'd seen each other, but Mack looked much older. The round-faced giddy youth was gone, dark hollows circled his eyes as if he hadn't slept for days. He was even grey at the temples. "I don't—why would they send..." The memory of why he was there came crashing through the fog, and Ben caught his breath. "No. No, they didn't send me. I came to stop you."

Mack's lips compressed into a thin line, and he glanced over his shoulder. "I told you he wasn't here to help you. They're probably right behind him now."

Ben squinted at the far side of the room. Someone was standing out of the light, but he walked forward now. Older, thin, but the kind of thin that used to be fat. Like a glaring tortoise, wrinkled and grey-haired and angry. Harper. He had to be Harper.

"Then we go with what we have," he said. "Go and get ready."

Mack moved, but Ben grabbed his wrist.

"You can't." His heart was racing. "Mack, please! You can't go! It'll get you killed!"

Mack shook his hand off. "You people'll say anything, won't you?" He straightened up. "Did you put her up to it? That old woman? She was spouting some bullshit about it as well."

Ben rolled onto his knees and tried to rise, but the world wavered, his head throbbing. "It's true," he ground out. "All true. Jacob knew. Been trying to protect you from the word go." He tried to swallow around the lump in his throat. No rules about changing the future, were there? "He thinks you're the one who sees my dad and gets—"

"Mackenzie." Harper interrupted, his voice was hard as nails. "Enough of this."

Mack turned and hurried from the room. His footsteps boomed across the floor, and Ben winced, wrapping his hands over his temples.

"No, no, no..." He tried to rise, but a hand caught his shoulder, pushing him down. He stared up into the eyes of the man who had started all of it. So insignificant. Hardly a man to ruin so many lives. "Why? Why do you hate my dad so much?"

Harper's lips curled up disdainfully. "I never knew the man."

Ben stared at him. "I don't understand. Why do—you don't need—"

"I think I know what I need." Harper said. "I need to make sure your family's stupid little science experiment never happens."

Ben blinked at him stupidly, wondering how hard he'd hit his head. "You—that—what?" He winced, the thought like a sharp rock in his aching skull. "Time travel? You want...wait...you want to *stop* time travel?"

"It's done more than enough damage." Harper bent closer to him. "I'm going to kill it in its cradle, and we'll both have easier lives." He released Ben's shoulder and walked towards the door. "You'll be staying here, Mr. Sanders. I can't have you...interfering."

The door closed with a heavy clang, sealing him in. The room had no windows, and the floor and walls were bare. At least there was a light, a bare bulb in a frame on the ceiling. It was better than nothing as Ben stared after Harper.

Kill it in its cradle. Stop time travel.

Was it possible? If they went back far enough and took it away before it even got started, then it would unravel everything that came after. Ben's heart did a strange flip. His father would be around. Maybe his mother would be as well. And Enoch would never be condemned because a stupid, drunk time traveller would have left modern tech in the past. Everything would be okay for everyone.

Maybe it wouldn't be so bad to wait for his world to turn back to the way it could have been.

He sat against the wall, turning his head to press his aching temple against the cool brick. God, if he'd thought of that sooner. But every day in the TRI he'd heard all about how badly things could go, how things could get worse if you changed them.

The past was as unpredictable as the future. That was what they always said.

Ben gazed blindly at a crack running across the concrete floor. It split into two cracks and he traced a fingertip along the edge of it. Two futures from one past. Maybe it wouldn't be so bad.

The door of the room opened again.

"Ben Sanders?" A woman's voice this time.

He recognised the woman standing there, though he had only ever seen her in pictures—Mack's girlfriend, the one who'd helped Ben find his way to the warehouse. She wasn't much younger than Mack but looked as worn out as he did, her face pale and her hair pulled into a tiny ponytail. It was dark brown now, he noticed. Dyed. Probably to hide the colours she liked so much.

"Orla," he murmured, sitting up. "What are you doing here?"

Wariness flooded her face. "You know who I am?"

Ben dipped his chin. "I'm a friend of Enoch's."

Her eyes widened. "You're the friend he talked about? The one who would help?"

"The one who tried." He winced as his head throbbed. "You didn't need to come."

She came closer. "Mack asked me to bring you some painkillers and to check your head." She crouched in front of him. For someone running around a warehouse, her clothes were out of place and a little old-fashioned. There was something odd about that, but it felt like such an effort to bring his eyes from the outfit to her face. Orla leaned closer to dab the blood from his brow. "He said you're trying to stop them. Something about him getting hurt."

"Mm." Ben winced. "Does Mack know what the mission is?"

Orla's expression was strange, half in shadow, half in light. "It's nothing to worry about." The corner of her mouth turned up, but she wasn't smiling. "Just go to a house and borrow a computer hard drive or two. No big deal. We won't even see anyone, Mr. Harper said. In and out, and that's it."

Won't see anyone. No death. No blood. No body on the floor.

Not so bad. Was it?

Her words caught up with him.

We.

Ben caught her wrist as she patched his wounded head. "We? You're going with him?"

She didn't meet his eyes. "Someone has to keep him safe." She rocked back on her heels. "Mack's computer know-how could fill a teacup. They need to be sure they get the right thing, and I don't trust anyone else to watch his back like I will." That odd half-smile was on her face again. "Are you going to tell me I'm going to die too?"

Ben uncurled his fingers from her wrist. "I don't know."

"He said you wanted to stop us."

Ben lowered his head. "I don't know," he repeated in a whisper. He should. The rules his dad had written. The TRI. Everything he had learned in his childhood told him playing with the past was dangerous. And yet, he'd done it so many times.

Orla watched him for a long while as if waiting for him to say something and stop her. His silence seemed to be enough, and she straightened up. Her boots tapped on the concrete floor as she walked out of the room and closed the door behind her.

Ben lolled against the wall.

It felt...wrong to be sitting and doing nothing. After more than twenty years of shouting and fighting and doing everything to make his voice heard and find the answers, he was just sitting and waiting. For a gate to open. For his parents to be back. For them to open a gate to a time before...

A time before time travel...

A chill ran the length of his spine. Something...something about it was off.

A time before time travel. Dead in its cradle. That was what they were trying to do, wasn't it? Take the machines from his parents before they could be used. Steal the machines and none of it would ever happen. But that was wrong.

Someone did use a gate. Someone did take the machines. Someone *did* die. But not before time travel. That was a long time after. Long after his mother went through a gate and was lost. Long after the TRI was up and running.

Something was trying to get his attention beyond the fuzziness and the ache in his head.

Ben pressed his eyes shut, trying to work out what it was. Something was off. Something in the building was screaming out for his attention. Not the parking bay. Not the halls. Not the stairs or the walls.

He opened his eyes, horror crashing in on him.

The cables, he remembered. The cables were the old kind of power source used on the gates when he was a kid. If they were using the information that had been stolen the day his father disappeared, then they were using an old design for a gate. The old gates were always great for pinpointing a location. Every damn time, they would hit the spot, but time? They could be off. By a day, a week, a month...

By years.

"No..." Ben scrambled to his feet. If they didn't know that, if they didn't know to stabilise it to prevent the fluctuations in the temporal path, then the gate wouldn't work the right way. He ran to the door, hammering on it. It was an easy fix. He could fix it before they went, and everything went wrong. "Let me out! I need to help you! It won't work!"

They were going to be late, he realised, grabbing at the door handle and pulling at it until his arms burned in their sockets. They would do their jump and believe they were in the right time and walk straight into the day that had turned Ben's life upside down. They would go and they would die and nothing would change!

"Let me out!" He howled, pounding at the door with his fists. "Let me out! It's not going to work right! Let me fix it! Let me finish this!"

The door was solid, metal, unyielding. His vision swam, and there was blood on his hands.

"Please!" He screamed as loudly as he could. "For fuck's sake, they're going to die! PLEASE!"

Overhead, the light started to flicker.

Ben whipped around, staring up at it. A power surge. The gate had been activated.

"No!" He threw himself at the door, pounding. "NO! Mack! Don't!"

The light blazed brighter and brighter.

The door was sealed. The walls were impenetrable. As the bulb exploded and plunged Ben into the darkness again, he screamed.

Chapter Thirty-Four

The pod sped through the city, lights flaring on the roof. Once, Enoch might have found it exciting, but now his heart was in his mouth.

He had been in trouble with powerful people many a time. In the day, there were men who held his life in their hands. The threat of the gallows was a real one then, and yet Enoch knew he would prefer to be there, bound at the flogging post, than facing the cold anger of Lysander.

They were not alone in the pod, thank Jesu. Anton sat by Enoch, both of them facing Lysander who had not spoken a word since they got in. He was still as stone, his hands folded and his knuckles white as bone, like one of them statues of old Roman gods, only much more fearsome. Enoch dropped his gaze to the shiny silver bracelets circling his own wrists. Better not to look or be looked at.

Too much was happening and too fast.

Ada had spoken privately with Jacob, Mariam, Temple, and Lysander. She had brought them a piece of Ben's gate. For that they had given her their trust, and now, some half a dozen pods were racing through the city, wailing and flashing, to God only knew where.

They were following Ben's lead, it seemed. Ada had tied her computer to his and where he went, she could follow.

He'd heard Ada speak as the task force moved to action. He was being shackled, and she called out that he needed to be brought along. "Enoch might be the only one who can talk him down," she said, though she had not met his accusing stare. She knew how close they were, yet she gave that information freely to them who hunted him.

The betrayal should have sent him wild with outrage, but his own fury had been forgotten. Faced with Lysander's expression, he had shrunk away in silence. He scarce even dared to glance at the man or ask where they might be going.

"I'm curious." It was a good ten minutes afore Lysander broke the silence. "What did he promise you for your help?"

Enoch raised his eyes from his cuffs. "What?"

Lysander was still gazing at him. His face might have been cut from marble. Not a tick nor a twitch nor anything to show his feelings. "Every man has his price. What did Sanders promise you to make you betray the task force? The means to return to your own time? The coordinates to open the gate?"

Enoch shook his head, frowning in confusion. "He asked."

A silvering eyebrow arched. "He *asked*? As simple as that?"

Enoch twisted his left thumb against his right palm. "He changed his mind soon as he said it, but I knew he needed it to be done, so I done it."

"I find that unbelievable." Lysander tapped his thumbs together.

"'Tis the truth."

It was strange how much Lysander moved like a cat, tilting his head, his eyes half-closed. "You can understand why I might find that hard to believe, given the circumstances. Someone who has lied to my face and gone behind my back doing so out of the goodness of his heart, for no payment or reward?"

It was worse than a blow to hear the disdain and disappointment in Lysander's voice.

Worse yet for Lysander to believe he had done it for some kind of reward.

"It was ruining him," Enoch said quietly. "Ben. The nightmares of what had happened. The torment of it and knowing none would help him. How could I not spare him the pain and aid him where I could?"

Lysander's expression wavered with confusion. "You care about him."

Sweet Jesu, Enoch thought blankly. Could they not see that? Had they not noticed his fear when Ben vanished through the gate? Had they not wondered at his worry? He could only nod, wondering what else they had not seen.

"Why?"

It was a strange question to answer. Better ask a bird why it flew or a fish why it swam. "Because..." He hesitated and shook his head. "I dunt know. I only know I do." He shifted his wrists in his shackles. "At first, on account of him saving my life, I suppose." He shrugged. "Then, I came to know him."

"For a few weeks?" Anton snorted. Lysander speared him with a warning glare. "What? It's true. They knew each other what? Three weeks? Four?"

"He makes a valid point," Lysander said. "He may have saved your life, but he was lying every moment he was with you."

"Eh?" God's bones, it seemed like he had jumped ahead in a stream and missed something. Mayhap the drink in his blood was addling his head. "When?"

Lysander made a sharp gesture with one hand. "At the TRI," he said.

Enoch stared at him. "Oh." He shook his head. "Not then. Before that."

"Before—" There was a long silence. Lysander sagged back, staring. "My God..."

"Sir?" Anton glanced between them.

"'You can't accidentally stumble through a gate'..." Lysander breathed. "'Maybe he volunteered.' My God, that son of a bitch."

"What do you mean?" Anton asked, sounding as puzzled as Enoch.

"Ben told me exactly who and what you were," Lysander said, staring at Enoch. "Not even ten minutes after you arrived, he spelled it out for me, but I was too distracted to pay attention. A volunteer, someone who came through the gate deliberately." His face twisted in disbelief. "My *God*, you must have laughed."

Enoch recoiled. "No! No, we never!"

"Don't act the wounded innocent now," Lysander snapped. "You've played me—all of us—for fools for long enough."

"It int like that!" Enoch exclaimed, his face hot, and his head light. The drink and the emotion and all of it was too much. "It weren't about you! I done it all for him! I made him an oath to keep him safe until he could find his pa! Everything I done, it was all for him!"

"And why the hell would you care so much?" Lysander leaned forward, baring his teeth. His fury was enough to drive Enoch back in his seat. "And don't give me any bullshit about him saving your life. No man is that noble."

Enoch guessed Anton was likely staring at him as well, but it seemed he would burn to a cinder if he took his eyes away from Lysander's. "He's mine."

It made Lysander lean away, his eyebrows pulling together. "Yours?"

Enoch licked his bone-dry lips. "Mine. In law, if he'd have me. In body, if not."

"Oh my fucking God..." Anton breathed. "Holy Christ..."

It was strange to see Lysander lose the mastery of his face, dazed and bewildered as a lost child. "I—you're saying you and Ben..." He ran his fingertips over his furrowed brow and shook his head. "All this time? Since before you came through the gate?"

"Aye." Enoch stared at his hands. His nails had left marks in his palms. God above, he wanted to shout it from the rooftops now there was no need to hide it. His eyes burned, and he blinked hard. No need to hide, and yet it was the end of it all. They would never let him by Ben again.

"I—it—*how*?" Anton demanded. "I mean, before? How long before? How the fuck did we miss that?"

"I expect he used his gates." Lysander's voice was flat.

Enoch forced himself to meet Lysander's eyes again. "Sometimes, a man addled by grief and guilt will do a foolish thing when he's in his cups and despairing."

"Oh Christ..." Anton groaned.

"And found you?" Lysander prompted.

One side of Enoch's mouth drew up, though it was scarce a smile. "Someone had to pick him out of the ditch he had fallen into." He shrugged. "We drank a little more. We slept. He went on his way."

"And yet, here you are."

"Aye." Enoch hesitated. It could not be a betrayal to speak of it now. The truth had to be known. They knew Ben. They knew how he cared too much about all things. "He left something behind in my home. Not much, mind, but it seemed like some manner of witchcraft."

"Witchcraft?" Anton echoed, doubtful.

Enoch tapped the bud on his cuff. The screen lit up before him.

"And so," Lysander murmured, "he couldn't help but save you."

Enoch shrugged again. "I scarce remember. He would have given me a home in another town, safer than my own, in my own time." He almost laughed as he recalled Ben's indignant confusion. "I told him to go and bugger a donkey. I had no wish to go through another of those gates." He shivered. "'Tis a strange feeling to be taken apart and brought together again."

"But you were in the present, yeah?" Anton sounded even more bewildered. Enoch nodded. "But *they*—" He pointed at Lysander. "—thought you came from the past into the future through Ben's double gates? I mean, isn't that why you almost dropped dead? Because you crossed your times or some bollocks?"

"He wouldn't cross his own timeline," Lysander said slowly, and Enoch could see he was beginning to understand, "if he had been placed safely in the past. You arrived on the Wednesday. You didn't collapse until the Saturday. Where did he hide you? *When* did he hide you?"

Enoch chewed his lip, remembering Ben's urgent explanation. Science-magic or some such about his blood being wrong and needing it to be detoxed in old times. "A forest," he admitted. "A few weeks there to seem as I did of old."

Lysander seemed as if he had taken a blow to the head. "My God..."

"There's a thing." Anton studied Enoch. "I don't suppose you know anything about a bunch of envelopes that were posted in London the day after you arrived telling the world all about the mad new historical figure? I mean, if we're finding out you and Ben are behind everything, why not them as well?"

Enoch's face grew hot. "Ah."

"Oh for fuck's sake!" Lysander exclaimed.

"Sorry," Enoch said meekly.

"Sorry?" Lysander echoed. He pressed his forefingers to his lips, struggling to master himself. Finally, he took a breath. "Anything else you kept from us?"

Enoch shook his head.

"Danny's going to be over the moon about this." Both Enoch and Lysander glanced at Anton in confusion. "He's said from the word go that Ben was working with someone, didn't he? He was absolutely bloody-minded about it." Anton jerked his thumb at Enoch. "He wasn't wrong, was he?"

"Oh *great*." Lysander kneaded his temples. "This day just keeps on giving."

"I know it's worth nothing," Enoch said carefully, "but I *am* sorry."

"You're not the one who needs to be apologising," Lysander said darkly. "If that woman is right, then we'll have the right person in custody soon enough."

Enoch stared out the window to hide his expression, stomach knotting. So Ada was leading them all to Ben? With so many pods and the number of officers, it was impossible that Ben might be able to make his escape. For the first time, Enoch hoped Ben had done as he planned. Better freedom apart than both caged alone.

The rest of the journey was made in silence.

Enoch had no words left and could see no means by which he could save Ben if all else failed. He leaned against the window of the pod, staring blindly at the countryside beyond.

He was jarred to alertness when the pod came to a halt in the grounds of a vast warehouse that seemed to be built all of brick and iron. There were windows, but only above the level of the doors, as if they wished to keep out prying eyes.

A dull booming filled the air, and he looked askance at Anton and Lysander, who seemed as bewildered.

Lysander was out of the pod first, striding to join the other task force leaders. Ada stood with them, Mariam close by her.

Enoch climbed out more awkwardly, his shackled hands making matters difficult. He peered around and found the source of the sound—three officers with a metal log pounding against the door close to.

There was not much else about. A few pods, but no people besides those in uniforms. His heart fluttered suddenly. Ben's pod was there, parked neat between two others. There was no question. They had been betrayed.

"—think the power outage sealed everything," Jacob was speaking.

"It would make sense," Mariam agreed. "If they tried to use the gate without the necessary safeguards in place, the power surge would be enough to blow the power for every building in the complex."

Enoch swayed where he stood. So the gate had already been used, then? Ben had not been able to stop it. Why? He would have fought to the death to stop it. Enoch flinched at the very thought. Jesu, what if it had come to...

There was a moment of silence, the officers lowering their log to gather fresh strength.

Something caught his attention, a faint sound he could scarce make out.

The booming began anew.

"Wait!" He ran forward a step. "Stop a moment! I hear something!"

The officers glanced at Temple, who held up a hand, and silence fell once more.

Enoch closed his eyes, straining his ears.

"Someone's screaming." Anton said suddenly.

Enoch's breath shrivelled in his chest. "Ben!" He turned urgently to Mariam. "The power is gone, aye?"

"And the lights," she gasped. "He'll be in the dark."

"Shit!" Jacob jerked a hand and the booming began again, louder and harder.

"In the dark?" Lysander demanded. "What difference does that make?"

"Day his dad was lost," Jacob said, searching the front of the building. "Kid was locked in a safe room in the dark for hours. Lifetime of panic attacks and night terrors." He moved towards the building. "There are open windows farther up. Do we have a drone available?"

"Closest is at least two miles out," Temple said grimly. "This place is conveniently out of the way of everything including surveillance."

Enoch stared up at the front of the building. "I could fit." He pointed at the narrow window above the door. There was a crack in the glass. "If you can lift me up, I can break it and fit through."

Lysander, Jacob, and Temple drew close to one another, speaking in low voices, then Jacob motioned Enoch closer.

"You might be able to get the doors open manually from the inside, but they may be locked electronically," he said, unlocking the cuffs at Enoch's wrists. "We don't know the numbers they have in there, so keep your eyes open and don't try any heroics."

Enoch nodded, his heart racing. "I only want to get Ben out." He pulled his sleeves over his forearms. "D'you have anything I can use to break it?"

Temple held out her baton and torch. "You'll need these."

Enoch took them and ran with Anton and Jacob to the wall. Anton braced his hands against the wall, and Jacob cupped his palms to form a step. Enoch used it to vault onto Anton's shoulders. He and pounded at the window until the crack spread and fractured across the pane to fall inwards.

From the dark inside came the crash of glass hitting the floor. Enoch took a deep breath and shoved the baton inside his coat. His sleeves covered his hands enough to spare them the worst of the shards in the frame, and he gripped the edge of it, gathering his strength to hoist himself up.

"Enoch!" Lysander called. Enoch glanced over his shoulder. Lysander was pale as ash. "Be careful in there."

Enoch granted him a tight smile. "Aye, sir." He turned to the window and, pulling himself up, dropped into the dark.

Chapter Thirty-Five

The door wouldn't move.

Ben tasted metal. His trousers were wet again. Same as then. Same and cold and wet. Throat sore and raw. Chest too tight. Hard to breathe in the dark. Hands hurting too. Hot stickiness everywhere. Not even light at the bottom. No light anywhere.

Then, there was Jacob. Jacob and light and a badge.

Now, nothing.

Ben jerked his hand. Side of his fist against the door again. Rang like a gong.

Took time to gather his breath. Took all his breath to scream again.

He panted blood. Door was cold and hard against his forehead. Footsteps outside, clattering closer. Bolts sliding. Unlocked. Someone was unlocking it. Probably to shut him up. They'd hurt him before. Would do it again if he didn't do it first.

Ben backed up, one step then another, waiting, waiting, waiting. All the bolts undone. The creak of the handle, a narrow band of light cracked along the side of the frame. He threw himself at the door as hard as he could.

There was a grunt of pain. Something clattered. The light puttered away, but the door was open, and Ben staggered out of the dark, piss- and vomit-stinking room. Light. Light first. There was light, still bobbing about. A torch, rolling against the wall.

Ben ran towards it, almost tripping over its owner's arm. He hissed, kicking the grabby limb out of his way. The man was on the floor, groaning, but Ben didn't give a shit to see if he was okay. He had light. Light was a start. Everything else was in the dark, and he had a light.

The hall was long and full of dark doorways. No one else was there. Ben swung the torch, staring around. Strange place, so empty for somewhere so big. Maybe they had somewhere with light. Or there'd be more power in other parts. Power was important. He rubbed his head. He felt a lump and dry blood and hurt.

Power.

He needed to find the power. The power was the gate. The gate was the way to Dad.

His boots clanked on the floor and the noise made his head hurt even more. There were stairs ahead and dark red at the bottom. He stared at the red. Dry red. Like his head. He had fallen on stairs. These stairs? He swung the torch up. The light went up walls and high and higher all the way to the roof up there.

Cables. Power?

"Hey!"

Ben spun, torch up. Right in the face of a man. Man from the door. Man with the gun. Man with the screwed up eyes and arm up to shield them. Ben stared at him and at the gun, then swung the torch as hard as he could. Man on the floor. Another hit to keep him there.

Dark surrounded them again, and the torch wavered. The gun was warm from the man's fingers, heavy and strange in Ben's hand. He stepped over the man and swung the torch's beam to the roof again. Wrong. No cables. Wrong way. He picked out another corridor and started to walk.

Another voice in the dark. Another man, another gun.

Ben lifted his first. No shooting, he warned. Their weapon dropped and hands up. Don't want any attention. Just down the hall, down the hall, down the hall. Another small dark room for the other man to go into and to stay there. The door clanged shut. A lock on this one too. Ben slammed it in place.

Not many people here. Too big and too quiet and too dark. His light bobbed and flashed between rails and stairs. Small rooms turned big. Walls went up high, and breathing echoed. Maybe his own. Maybe not.

There was a noise ringing like a gong in the dark. Something banging somewhere far away. Metal on metal. Strange. Maybe his head. It hurt, and even the little bit of light was hurting it now. The beam was like a blade across the floor, and his feet clanked up more stairs.

Then there were cables down the wall. Big, thick ones all tied together. Like Dad's. Like the basement.

Ben stared at them and then followed them. He knew where they led: the gate. That was where he was meant to go. That was the plan. Get to the gate. Stop the gate. Maybe everything was dark, but he wasn't locked up now. Not in the safe room anymore. He could help. He could stop them.

Another door, another corridor, and a small stop to lean on a wall. The floor was moving under his feet. Even the gun and torch were getting all heavy. He was panting now, letting the light run along the cables. Not far. Couldn't be far. Not when he'd come such a long way already.

The banging stopped and there was nothing but his breathing. Sounded like a cave, deeper and louder, and he pushed off from the wall. It was getting harder to stand and to walk, and his head was sore. Took one step and another, on, following the white line of the cables. One step, two step, three step until his head hurt too much and he had to lean over.

Shouldn't have been able to be sick. Nothing for breakfast, but still sick and wet on his feet and the floor. New sound to the steps now, wet and whispering of his trousers.

In the distance there were voices. Far, far away behind, but closer in front. There was a door ahead, closed, and edged with light. The cables went that way, all the way to the inside of the building and down, down, down. Basement. Just like Dad.

The door swung into a room with lots of little torches and lots of big people. Machines everywhere and eyes staring at him. He stared back at them and saw the face of the one he had been searching for.

The gun was wobbly in his hand, but he pointed it at the man. Harper. That was his name.

"Don't open it," he whispered. His mouth tasted like sick and blood.

The man's face was pale, and his hands were up, but his eyes were bright. "Sorry, kid. You're too late."

Ben shook his head slowly. "No."

"Why do you think we're in the dark? It shorted out the power." The man moved closer, and Ben retreated. "It's over. Soon everything'll be undone."

Ben was watching through a bubble where nothing made sense. Christ, it was almost funny. Only almost. Only a little bit. "You're a fucking idiot," he said slowly. He took a gulping breath, trying to push away the dark. "You did this."

"Come on, kid..." The man was still coming closer, hands up. "You don't want to have that gun."

Ben looked at it and at him. "I do." He took an unsteady step forward, and the man backed up. "Stop you fucking up our lives anymore."

"You don't know what you're talking about." The man shook his head.

Someone moved at Ben's side, and he glared around. "The rest of you get the fuck out." Didn't know much about guns but knew enough to thumb the safety. In flashes of light and shadow, they rushed into the halls.

Only Harper was left, hands still up. "So you blame me, kid? What did I do to you?"

Ben bared his teeth. "This. All of this. Took his tech. Killed them both."

"I didn't—"

"You took my dad's shit," Ben snarled. "You don't have a fucking clue how it works. You used it and you fucked yourself. You fucked all of us. You *killed* them. Mack. Orla."

Harper's cheek was twitching. "I don't know what you're talking about."

"No," Ben agreed. "You really don't." He took another step closer. The pain was fading. The world narrowed to the gun in his hand and the man in front of it. "It was a woman who brought you the tech, wasn't it?" He laughed sharply. "I know a man died in the house, so it had to be a woman. Maybe about Orla's height. Same build." He hissed angrily. "And what do you know? Same fucking face."

Harper flinched as if he'd been slapped. "No. It—that wasn't her. It couldn't be her."

Ben dropped his torch to lean against the nearest workstation. "Oh, it was."

"No!" Harper turned, staring over his shoulder to a door. The cables went through it. The gate. The fucking broken useless faulty gate. "It worked," he said, his face twisted up in disbelief. "It *worked.* I saw them go through."

A thought crept up on Ben. It wasn't a pleasant one. "What happened to her?" Enoch liked her, he knew. Enoch thought she was sweet. Enoch would want to know.

Harper's face went paler. "I don't know."

Ben's stomach twisted up. "You're lying." He stared at the man who had used the tech. Stared at a man who had been in jail for a long, long time. Longer than just a robbery or anything to do with machines. Had to be more than that. Ben pressed his empty hand to his mouth. "You killed her..."

Harper didn't even try to deny it.

Ben couldn't be sure if he did it on purpose, but the gun recoiled on his hand. The echo of the shot and Harper's howl of pain echoed off the walls. The man fell to the ground, clutching his leg, blood rippling between his fingers.

"What happened to her?" he repeated, walking closer on legs so unsteady they could've belonged to someone else, as if he was standing just to the side of his own body, watching it all.

"Go to hell!" Harper snarled through clenched teeth.

Ben pointed the gun at his other leg. "You have two legs. Don't make me ask again."

Harper scrambled backwards across the floor. "She said she wanted me to get her back where she came from or she was going to run to the police! Tell them her whole crazy story! Blame me for something I didn't do! What the hell was I meant to do?"

Once, Ben knew he would have felt bad for shooting an old man in the leg. Now, staring at Harper, his blood on the floor and dripping between his fingers, Ben felt nothing but tired and hollowed out. Harper didn't care. He didn't care that people died. He'd even done it deliberately. He didn't care that he'd fucked over so many people and ruined so many lives.

Mack dead. Orla dead. They'd been there with him, alive, maybe minutes, maybe hours ago. They'd gone together. He'd chased his dream and ended up on a slab. She'd gone with Mack to protect him because she didn't trust Harper's people, and Harper had proved her fears were right.

Christ, what the hell was he meant to do? Was that a question any rational person would ask?

"Let her," Ben said quietly. "Let her live. Let her go." He shook his head in disgust. "What were you meant to do? Not be a murderous fucking psychopath!" He lifted the gun again. "I know my dad's alive, but I can't undo what you did to them." He shrugged. "At least I can stop you from doing it again to anyone else."

Harper scrabbled at the wall, trying to pull himself upright. "So you'll kill me?" He sounded panicked for the first time. "Just like that? Make yourself a... What was it? A murderous fucking psychopath?" His eyes darted towards the doorway, and he yelled, "This way! We're in here! He has a gun!"

Ben tilted his head. Footsteps on the stairs. He hadn't noticed them before. They were running and close and right outside, and all he had to do was pull the trigger and Harper wouldn't hurt anyone else again.

"Ben!"

He flinched at the voice, so close behind him. Wrong. She wasn't meant to be here. She was meant to go through the gate. She was meant to be safe and away and not here. No one was meant to be here or see him. "Go away."

Ada stepped into the room. The heels of shoes tapped closer. "Put the gun down, Ben. The police are in the building. They'll be here for him soon enough."

"He killed them," he whispered, staring at Harper along the shivering barrel of the gun. "He let them go through the gate. They're both dead now. He killed her."

"I know."

"You know…" Ben exhaled. "No, you don't. You don't understand what he's done." He used his other hand to steady the gun. It was wobbling too much. It was pathetic. There was no reason. No reason at all. "He's ruined so many lives."

"So you'd make yourself a murderer?" Ada laid her hand on his shoulder. "You're not a killer, Ben. I know what he did to you. I know what he did to our family, but you don't need his blood on your hands. It won't help."

Ben's vision was swimming, and his head felt light. "Don't," he whispered. God, why wouldn't she go away and leave and not look back. "Don't. He—it's—I want—he'll get away with it again. He'll hurt more people. I don't want him to hurt more people."

She laid her other hand on his arm gently. "And I don't want him to hurt you anymore either. I know your father would agree."

He didn't know if he laughed or sobbed. Everything was cold and hurting, and God, he just wanted to retreat to a corner and wrap his arms over his head and hide from everything. "You don't know what my father would want."

"That's where you're wrong, lamb," she murmured gently. "He and I talked long and hard about how we would raise our children."

Our children.

His brain had to be glitching. *Our children.* That was what she'd said. Our children. And before. Before, there was something else. *Our family.* Ours. Ours? Our children. Our family. Ours. We.

He tore his eyes from Harper to stare at her.

Ada smiled uncertainly at him, and he knew that expression. He saw it when he looked in the mirror.

"Mum?"

Chapter Thirty-Six

The world seemed uncommon loud and too bright after the darkness of the halls.

Enoch leaned against the wall beside the steps where he was sitting. He had found Ben. Or he had found the room and heard the screams and tried to open the door. He'd ended up on the floor, dazed, head ringing, and Ben—or some other madman—had stepped on him and run off with his torch.

Somehow, he had found his way to the front door in the darkness. The noise of the metal beating on metal had guided him to the broken window and cracks of light shining through. The screams had stopped, which was some small comfort, and he found himself drowning in daylight instead.

The yard of the building was thick with people, all asking him questions—who was there, where was Ben, had he found anyone, where ought they go? He described what little he could. There was not much to be seen, though he had hidden from the few men who had crossed his path. He had heard two speaking of another way out, away from those who would break through the front.

The crowd scattered. Some went around the side of the building with Jacob, others ran through the door with Temple. But three had lingered. Lysander, Mariam, and Ada.

Mariam had tended Enoch's wound, but Ada stood in the doorway, staring into the depths of the building. She only returned when she was called by Lysander, who stood by his pod, waiting.

When she came to Mariam's side, Enoch turned his darkest glare on her, not only for her betrayal of Ben, but for her lies to him and all.

"I know where he'll be." Her voice was low, and she had her eyes on Enoch but speaking for Mariam. She made a show of examining Enoch's broken head. "There are power lines. He'll be where the gate is. Lower level, best bet."

Mariam slanted a sideways glance at her. "What do you need?"

Ada wet her lip, her face ghastly pale. "A way in and out."

"What are you speaking about?" Enoch asked, too pained and weary to care for politeness.

Mariam leaned close and smoothed some liniment on his brow. "Trust me," she murmured, "and follow my lead." She turned her head and called over her shoulder. "Lysander!"

As Lysander approached, Ada retreated.

"Enoch said he was attacked in one of the side passages," Mariam said.

Enoch blinked at her, confused. "Aye." It was close enough to the truth, though having a door oped in his face was scarce an attack. "There were folk down that way, I think. I could hear voices."

"How many?" Lysander crouched to meet his eyes.

It felt ill to lie again to Lysander, so best to use the truth, such as it was. "I could not tell. It was dark, away from the windows, and none of them had torches."

"Do you remember which side?"

Enoch hesitated, closing his eyes. He recalled the clatter of his boots as he dropped from the narrow window and the way he had turned about. He held up his writing hand. "This way." He opened his eyes again. "I went this way."

"That's a good st—" A clang from the door made Lysander rise, spinning about.

Enoch stared, befuddled, at the door. It was closed again, and Ada was nowhere to be seen.

"Where is she?" Mariam exclaimed. For one so honest, she played the wide-eyed fool well.

"Shit!" Lysander ran towards the door, his hand moving for his bud. "Jacob, the woman's bolted. I think she's in the building. I'm going after her." He paused at the door, looking at Mariam. "Don't let him out of your sight."

Mariam nodded, gripping Enoch's shoulder.

As soon as the door closed behind Lysander, Mariam touched the bud at her wrist. "You have company. We'll keep the door clear."

Enoch stared at her. "What are you doing?"

Mariam stepped back from him and opened out a screen on her bud. She was near as pale as Ada, her lips trembling, and when she was done, she set aside the radio and pulled out her Leaf. "Wait."

The wind was up, and it was cold now. Enoch closed his eyes, his head aching. The brightness was too much, and Christ, he hadn't found Ben nor been of any use to man nor beast in the darkness. A hand on his shoulder brought him to his senses, and he forced his eyes open.

"Can you count to ten for me?" Mariam murmured.

Confused, Enoch counted up. "Why?"

"Because I need to know you can listen and understand what I'm saying," she said quietly. "Ben's pod is here. Can you control it?"

He stared at her, lost. Ben was within. He was without. What did it matter now? "Aye."

To his surprise, Mariam seemed pleased. "Good." She tilted his chin up and winced. "You'll live. It's messy, but it's not too deep. You don't need any stitches."

Enoch touched his head with a wince. His eyebrow was split across the middle and felt thick and hot to his fingertips.

"Don't touch it," Mariam said quickly. She glanced about, put a hand under his elbow, and helped him to his feet. "We need to be ready."

Enoch's spirit leapt. He remembered her words to him at the task force office, her anger and grief and confession—*I could have helped.*

"There are too many in there, both our people and theirs," he said, gently bobbing his aching head. "They will not be able to get out."

Mariam smiled grimly. "Oh, they're too stubborn to be caught now." She hurried him over to Ben's pod and touched the pad that allowed access.

Enoch hesitated before he touched the numbers Ben had taught him with the promise they would work for anything Ben had locked. It was easy enough to remember—the day and year they had first crossed paths. It would have no meaning for anyone but them. The pod door slid open, and Mariam leaned inside to touch the controls.

"You put yourself in danger," he said quietly. "The task force will not be pleased."

"I don't care about the task force." Mariam straightened from the controls. "I didn't listen to him. I didn't trust him. I put him on this path. I can't change the past, but at least I can help him to make his peace with it." She loosened her bracelet with her bud on it. "When you're clear, give this to him. He'll know why."

"You will not come with us?" Enoch glanced towards the building and its vast metal door. "How will you explain it? That you helped?"

She patted his shoulder. "You're going to escape, and I'm going to be left behind, bound and gagged."

"By who?" She raised her brows. "Me?"

"As soon as they're out." She undid her belt, a length of colourful braided cords, and held it out to him. "I've put a destination into the pod. It'll take about twenty minutes to get there."

"Where is it?"

"You don't need to know."

They both spun about when the door of the building creaked open. Mariam grasped his arm and pulled him a few paces away from the pod, no doubt fearful it might be Lysander or some other officer of the task force.

Two figures stepped into the light, and Enoch was running towards them afore he realised he could move.

Ben was leaning on Ada's shoulder. What parts of his face were visible through the blood were ashen. His brow was broken and one side of his face all bruised. The way he limped said there were other injuries too, and his clothes were sodden in vomit and piss. God above, he looked like he had been dragged from the lip of hell.

"I'm sorry," he whispered as soon as Enoch stepped under his other arm.

Enoch wrapped his arm about Ben's waist, gentling his touch when Ben flinched in pain. The weight of Ben's arm over his shoulder almost made him stagger. "No matter now."

"No." Ben's lips were cracked with blood. "Enoch, I have to t—"

"That can wait," Ada said urgently, guiding him forward. "Mariam?"

"The pod is ready." Mariam hurried towards them. She was staring at Ben as a woman dying of thirst would look at water. "Ben..."

"Aunt M..." Ben sounded as if he might weep. "I'm sorry."

She gently pushed Enoch to one side and took his place under Ben's arm. "I know." She glanced at Enoch. "Seal the door up. Block it. We'll get him in the pod."

Enoch ran up the steps to the door, pushed it closed, and searched about wildly for some means to lock it. It had a heavy curved handle that stuck outwards, and there were thick pipes running along the wall alongside it. Mercifully, there were broken spars of metal stacked close by. His fingers were scraped raw as he hoisted one up and wedged it between handles and pipes. Anyone who tried to pull the door inward would find it impossible.

"Good." Mariam was at his side. She held out her wrists. "Quickly."

"It must be tight," he warned as he lashed her wrists together. "Else they will know it was not done with intent."

She nodded. "Do it."

Enoch pulled the cords tight on her arms. He considered his hands, damp with Ben's blood, and pressed them to her veiled throat, leaving prints stained there.

"Good idea." From within the building, there were shouts and crashing steps. "Go! Quickly!"

Enoch pressed her wrists with his hands, staining them too, then turned and fled to the waiting pod. He glanced to the warehouse and saw Mariam throw herself down the four small steps and land in a heap at the bottom. She wrenched her scarf loose and lay still.

From within, someone was banging at the locked door.

"They're coming!" Enoch threw himself into the pod, halfway across Ada. The door hissed shut behind him, and the pod shuttled off, picking up speed as it raced towards the gates of the complex and out into the roads beyond.

"We should be clear in a moment," Ada said, kneeling on the seat to stare out behind them. "Mariam will buy us what time she can."

It was well, but as he righted himself, Enoch glanced to Ben.

He was not surprised to see his lover seated motionless and blank, his eyes fixed on nothing. It had come to naught. All of their scheming and plans had come to an end. They were together, which could only mean they had failed, and Ben's father was still lost to him.

Enoch clambered along the seat and touched his knee gently. "Ben."

Ben blinked slowly at him as if he could not understand what was being said. "They wouldn't listen," he whispered. "I told them what would happen, but they wouldn't listen."

"You did everything you might to stop them." Enoch wondered if those words could ever be enough.

Ben's face crumpled in grief. "Not enough. He wanted to go and—and—" He trailed off, shaking his head.

Enoch felt as if the words were shouted at him through a tunnel. "Mack..." His heart jumped and a sickening feeling swelled in his throat. "What of Orla? Where is she? Did you see her? Is she in there?"

Ben shook his head, tears cutting through the dried blood crusting his cheeks. "She went with him." He caught Enoch's hand in an iron grip, his fingers trembling. "She wanted to protect him. I told her—I *tried*, Enoch, I swear I tried."

Enoch frowned. "She—I dunt understand."

"She wanted to protect him." His voice cracked. "She wanted to save him. She—Harper—he killed her."

Enoch could scarce hear him. Orla. Sweet, good-heart Orla. Gone. Mack, he had feared and expected, but not Orla. Not with her smile and her softness and her kindness. "I know," he said as if the words would do either of them any good now. "You tried."

Ben's fingers tightened on his, and he wished he had words to comfort and assure, but they were gone.

"You did all you could," Ada murmured. "You can't take the blame for the choices that other people made." She slid off the seat to kneel before Ben, pressing her hands to his knees. "You know who was responsible for pushing them into this mess. He'll be dealt with."

Enoch stared blankly at her, wondering what she knew to be so certain. He turned to the window and the world flying by.

"Where do we go now?" he asked quietly. Not the TRI. Not the task force. God only knew where.

Ada sighed quietly, her features lined with weariness. "Somewhere safe."

Chapter Thirty-Seven

They weren't at the safe house. They weren't anywhere Ben recognised. Ada—no, not Ada, not anymore—got them in his pod and, as soon as they were in the city, switched to taxi pods until they arrived on a quiet street.

She had a key. Mariam had given it to her once he was in the pod.

The building was a house in the middle of a terrace. It wasn't until he got inside that he recognised where they were. There were pictures on the walls. Family photos. Mariam and three small children smiling. Faraz, Mariam's son, with his wife. The sprawling Ashraf clan. Even a shot with one white face in the throng.

On holiday. She'd told him that. He remembered a day in a garden that seemed like a lifetime ago.

Ben swayed where he stood, his hand tightly gripped in Enoch's.

Mariam had arranged it. She'd given Ada a key to her son's home, knowing it would be safe for them. She'd helped them get away from the task force. Mariam had *helped* them. Him, his lover, and his...

His head was aching, and he was lightheaded. The world had been turned upside down.

Jesus Christ, his mother. His mother was in front of them. The mother who had disappeared before he could even remember her. Stories and pictures were one thing. Now she was a living breathing person who shared his smile.

So many little things suddenly made sense: The fact that she lived so close to the stone circle where the gate first opened, the way she followed him through the gate without question and how willingly she helped him. And there was her skill with technology and blending into the modern world as if she was born in it because *of course she was*. God, he'd been so caught up in looking ahead, he hadn't seen who was standing right in front of him.

"Ben." Enoch squeezed his hand. "You should clean up. You're a right mess."

Ben couldn't help staring at her. Now that he knew what he knew, he could see it so clearly. He had pictures of her for God's sake. He had his dad's old photos, and he'd never noticed the same mole on her cheek and his own smile on her face and God, he was an idiot.

"I'll take him up to the bathroom," she said with a quick smile for Enoch. "There's ice in the freezer. You should put some on your brow. It'll reduce the swelling."

Ben had a feeling Enoch was staring. He didn't know. He couldn't know. Something had changed—everything had changed—but no one else had been there to see it. "She's right," Ben said. "Ice. I'll get cleaned up." He forced his fingers to unclasp from Enoch's. "I'll be back in a few minutes."

He wasn't surprised when Ada slipped her hand gently under his arm. He felt like shit and if he felt it, he probably looked worse. His clothes were stinking too. Piss, vomit, blood. She didn't seem to mind as she helped him up the stairs, though it seemed like a long way, and by the time they reached the top, he was leaning on her more than he wanted to.

"Mariam said her son and his family were away for a fortnight," Ada murmured. "They won't find us here."

Us.

Ben had to reach out and steady himself on the doorframe. "She knew you."

"It took her a minute, but she recognised me." Ada helped him into the bathroom and closed the lid of the toilet for him to sit. "She told the others, I think. I'm not sure they believed her."

He almost laughed. Not sure. That was a familiar feeling. "You're really her? My—you're my..." She nodded. "You didn't tell me."

Ada's face creased up in thousands of little lines. She started unbuttoning his blood-matted shirt for him. "I didn't know how," she said quietly. "I didn't know you. You were...you seemed so distressed. I didn't want to add to it."

He looked at her thin, wrinkled hands, helping him undress as if he was a child—her child—and his eyes stung. "You should have told me," he whispered, pressing his eyes shut. "I—I didn't know. I tried to send you away."

A warm hand pressed to his cheek, and he flinched in surprise. "I know." She tilted his face to hers, and she was smiling, and her eyes were as wet as his. "But where do you think you got your stubbornness from? It certainly wasn't your father."

He laughed unsteadily, holding her hand against his cheek. "I'm sorry. I made such a mess. I just—" His eyes were hurting and his throat, and his voice was breaking so much he couldn't get the words to stay together. "I'm sorry."

"Hey, hey," she scolded gently. "None of that." She stepped closer and wrapped him up in her arms. Ben shivered and clung to her, burying his face in her shoulder. She was warm and soft, and for a moment, he felt safe, and everything was quiet. "It's all right." She stroked his hair, brushing around the aching lump on his head. "I'm here now. We're both all right."

He half laughed, half sobbed. "All right. On the lam with two time travellers."

She rubbed the back of his neck comfortingly. "Technically." She waited until he lifted his head and smudged the tears from his cheeks. "We'll work something out, but first things first, you need to get out of these clothes and cleaned up. I'll get some fresh ones from the wardrobe. Mariam said you're about the same size as her boy."

Ben sat and knuckled at his eyes. "Yeah. Yeah, about." He tugged his shirt off and his T-shirt under it. They were both stiff in places, matted and filthy. It took more effort than he liked to get to his feet, his legs like jelly. "Thanks."

She smiled at him again. "It's nothing." She went over to the shower and turned on the water. "You'll be all right? I think your boyfriend might kill me if you collapse now."

Ben stared at her, owl-eyed. Jesus. Not only was his mum back, but she'd seen him with Enoch. She knew what was going on between them. "Um. Yeah. I'll be fine."

Ada reached up and patted his cheek. "In the shower," she said. "I'll leave the clothes by the door for you."

He stood under the hot stream of water for a long time, long after he gingerly washed his bloody hair and scrubbed himself all over. Maybe staying there was hiding, but it was—everything was too much to process. Mack and Orla were gone. Dad was gone too. The task force and the police had Harper. But Ben had his mother and Enoch and that...that was a lot.

He leaned against the tiled wall with his eyes squeezed shut.

Someone tapped on the door eventually.

"Ben?" Enoch opened the door a crack. "Is all well?"

Ben peered out through the steam that was filling the bathroom. "Yeah." He got out of the shower. "Yeah. Sorry." He grabbed one of the towels from the rail. "I—it's not been a great day."

Enoch closed the door behind him and reached for the towel. Ben let him take it and braced a hand on the wall to hold himself steady as Enoch gently towelled him, wincing in sympathy when he patted bruises and scrapes dry. "I'm sorry about your pa."

Ben shook his head. "They wouldn't listen." He reached out with his other hand and caught the back of Enoch's head, pulling him closer. "I'm glad you're here."

Enoch wrapped an arm around him. "Aye." He ran his hand the length of Ben's back. "Ada's cooking something down the stair. She dint think you'd et much today."

"No." Ben tugged at the dark curls at the base of Enoch's neck. "Forgot. Distracted."

"And given a bash." Enoch gently touched the lump on Ben's brow as he dried Ben's hair. "Your face is all black and blue."

Ben cradled Enoch's cheek. There was an impressive bruise and one of his eyebrows was split. "You're not much better."

Enoch made a face. "Aye, you daft sod. I thought you'd be happy to see me, and you flung the door in my face."

Ben blinked stupidly at him. "You what?"

"Who d'you think was come to let you out?" Enoch smiled crookedly. "I was the only one skinny enough to get through the window. I found you, and you knocked me on my crown, nabbed my torch, and buggered off."

It was all so ridiculous that Ben started laughing, and Enoch's smile widened to a grin, and they leaned into each other, rocking with mirth. They were both tired. Probably both concussed as well. And hadn't eaten. And were together after everything, when they thought they'd never see each other again. Sometimes a man just needed to laugh.

Enoch finally stepped back to finish drying him and leaned out the door to fetch the promised clothes. For someone in his early thirties, Faraz dressed like a conservative grandfather, and Ben could see Enoch snickering as he did up the buttons.

"You've worn worse," he pointed out.

Enoch patted his own belly. "Aye, but I am three hundred and more. You have no such reason." He glanced out of the doorway. "Will you be steady enough to go down the stairs?"

Ben nodded. "Bumped my head, not my legs."

Enoch swayed a hand. "To me, it looked like every part took a tumble."

He wasn't wrong about that. "Maybe a hand would be useful."

It took them a couple of minutes to descend the staircase, but before they went into the living room, Enoch pulled Ben to a halt. "Afore we go in, I have something for you." He pulled a bracelet out of his pocket. "Mariam said I was to give you this."

Ben stared at it, frowning. The shapes of the beads were familiar. "It's her Leaf." He glanced at Enoch. "Did she say why?"

"She said you'd know it."

Ben turned it over in his hand. For Mariam to give it, it had to be important, but why? He slipped it onto his wrist and followed Enoch through into the kitchen where Ada was stirring up a pan of soup. Empty cans stood in a row on the counter. Ada seemed lost in her thoughts, watching the wooden spoon cut through the soup.

"Ad—" Ben cut himself off even as she looked at him. It was one thing to have a mother in front of him, but he'd never really had someone to call that before. Mariam was always Aunt Mariam, but now, there was a mother, and he didn't even know what to call her.

She must have seen his confusion in his face. "You can use my name, if it's easier." There was something in her expression that made him feel strange and warm, and God, he'd forgotten what it was like to have someone look at him like that. "I know it's a lot to throw at you."

"What's amiss?" Enoch asked, frowning and confused. "Why do you speak like that? As one from hereabouts?"

Ben managed a brittle smile. "I think I should reintroduce you." He took a deeper breath, as if saying it would make it real, oh, he wanted it to be real. "Olivia, this is Enoch. My boyfriend. Enoch. This is Olivia. She's—she's my mother."

When she smiled, he couldn't help smiling in response.

"Bugger me..." Enoch breathed. "Are you for true?" He searched Ben's face. "But—but int she from the old times?" Ben saw the moment he realised. "Oh Christ's bones! She went through a gate and dint return!"

"Until now," Ada—Olivia agreed. She met Ben's eyes. "I found your initials on that tree at the circle. I put mine there too so you would know I was close."

Ben took a step closer to her, as piece after piece slid into place. "The ring around the letters."

"I thought if I waited, especially after I saw the letters..." She shook her head, gazing into the pot of soup. Her eyes were wet again. A tear rolled down her cheek. "I knew he was looking. Your father. I hoped— I knew he would work out how to make it stable."

A finger poked Ben from behind, and he glanced at Enoch who motioned urgently towards Olivia. He made an embracing gesture with both hands, but the best Ben could manage was to pat the woman on the shoulder.

"He didn't stop trying," he said. "Before we lost him, I mean."

"You told me." She laughed, her eyes bright and wet. "My God, look at the state of me." She hastily wiped her cheeks with both hands. "You'd think I'd be celebrating. Home and reunited with my boy. That's something, isn't it?"

Ben squeezed her shoulder. "I wish I'd got hold of the stuff Harper had. I thought—if I had it, maybe I could have found Dad. We could have looked..." He trailed off, staring into nothing. "Oh. Oh, I think—" He stepped away, fumbling with Mariam's bracelet. "Oh, she's got balls the size of Jupiter if she's doing what I think she's doing."

Neither of the others said anything, but the silence was more pointed than any question.

He flicked out a screen on the Leaf. "She's sent me a link to her machine at the task force! Her Leaf was synced to it! If I know Mariam, she'd make sure she could take her work home with her." He met Olivia's eyes. "She'll be the one to check the systems from the gate."

"And you'll see everything she sees?" Olivia guessed. "That woman is a cunning little genius."

"Only if I can log in," he warned her, but his heart was thundering. He'd managed to break Mariam's security clearances more than once before, and this time, she was handing him access. If she wanted him to see, she wouldn't have left him blind. He touched the screen, laughing aloud. "Well...that's not something I need to worry about."

Olivia leaned closer to study the screen. "A holiday photograph?"

"Sort of." He touched the login panel. "I wanted to go to Bletchley Park for my tenth birthday. She got us a private tour of the place." He tapped in six letters, not daring to breathe until the screen flared open into her account. "Not subtle, Aunt M."

"A secret message?" Enoch guessed.

Ben smiled at the screen. "Enigma." He spread the screen across the wall, searching for any sign of activity.

"They're probably busy trying to track us down," Olivia pointed out. "We should eat, while we have the chance."

Ben nodded. "Yeah. Yeah, we should." He sank to sit at the table.

Enoch squeezed in beside him, laying one hand on Ben's knee. "You may yet find him." He leaned closer. "You may yet have both your parents."

Ben pressed his knuckles against his mouth. "I know," he whispered, his voice breaking. He glanced over his shoulder at his mother as she poured soup into bowls. "I want him to know we found her. I want her to know he's home."

Enoch nuzzled his shoulder. "It'll be so. I'm sure of it."

Ben didn't dare to say he hoped so, but God, he did. No matter what came next, it wouldn't matter as long as his parents were back together.

Chapter Thirty-Eight

Evening was drawing in.

Enoch was trying to make himself of use in the kitchen. He could do naught on the machines to help them, but the bowls from their meal could be washed. It was something. Better than nothing, even if any fool could do it.

He watched the water pour from the tap, stirring up thick froths of bubbles, steam curling up about him.

It was easier to stay there, watching the water, than watch Ben gather his hopes again. They were meant to be done already. It was all meant to be done. God above, he wanted it all to stop. There was blood on the ground and bodies in the dirt. God's bones, he wanted it to be enough and to be done.

Some part of him wished to rejoice that Ben was yet with him, but grief and loss came too hard upon it. It was shameful to feel joy, knowing that his happiness had been bought at the cost of Mack and Orla's lives.

He closed his eyes, trying to think of nothing, but in vain. He remembered the sand, the laughter, Orla dabbing cream to the tip of his nose to keep him from burning. She went to protect Mack, Ben had said. She thought he would not be safe. Of course she did. She would risk her terrors to be by the side of one she loved.

"Enoch?"

Enoch jumped like a feart cat, his breath catching in his chest. "Jesu, Ben!" His voice was sharp as glass. "Dunt creep so!"

Ben stood in the doorway. He looked like death returned, pale and shadowed beneath his eyes. His brow furrowed. "Are you okay?"

Enoch turned back to the sink. His eyes were pricking, and he took a breath to steady himself. "Aye. Well enough." The tap was running, the water close to spilling over. He groped for it and twisted it off. "Best not to leave a mess, eh?"

"E…"

Enoch plunged his hands into the water, but the heat was too much. "Fut!" He fumbled for the tap once more, his skin turned an angry red.

"Here." Ben was by his side, turning on the tap and running the water cold. He caught both of Enoch's hands upon one of his, tilting them gently beneath the flow.

Enoch's breath caught, his eyes burning. His fingers wavered against Ben's. It was foolish and would help no one.

"It's okay to be upset." Ben slipped his other arm about Enoch's shoulders. "You don't need to pretend to be all right."

Enoch stared at his foolish trembling hands. The world was blurring afore his eyes, and heat streaked his cheeks. "I thought we could save him," he whispered. "Jesu, why dint he listen to me?"

"This isn't your fault. Don't you *dare* think it's your fault or mine or anyone else's." Ben's arm tightened about him. Ben's voice shook too. "He made his choice. Everyone warned him, and he still made the decision. It was a fucking stupid decision, but he made it himself. Whatever happened to him, it's his fault."

Enoch wanted to cry out Orla's name, but no sound came but a whimper. She had gone and was gone, and Christ, it was all wrong! All wrong! He pressed his hands to his face, trying to catch his breath, but the air was tearing from him and his chest and throat were burning.

"E..." Ben gathered him up, holding him tight. "I'm sorry. I'm sorry it happened. All of it. I know they were your friends."

Enoch buried his face in Ben's chest, his fingers hooking into Ben's back. "Not your doing," he rasped out.

Ben nodded against his head. "Too fucking right." He rubbed his hand the length of Enoch's back. "We've done some stupid shit in our time, but this was all him. Him and Harper. It's their fault she's gone too. Both of them."

"Fuckers," Enoch whispered. "Stupid fucking fuckers!"

Ben laughed damply against his ear. "You stay at Dieter's for one day..." He straightened up, cupping Enoch's jaw. His eyes were pink and wet. "We tried. We both did. We did everything we could to stop him. She was—she didn't—she tried as hard as we did."

"Aye." Enoch gulped a breath. "Not her doing either. Them. Only them." He rubbed at his nose with the back of his hand. "Z'bones, it has been a cruel day."

"Yeah." Ben curled his fingers into Enoch's hair. "At least we're together, eh?"

Enoch sniffed hard. "And your mam as well…"

"Yeah. My mother." Ben broke into a puzzled smile. "Didn't see that coming."

Enoch gave his waist a squeeze. "I'm pleased for that." He glanced to the door. "You should go and help her with your machines and that."

Ben hesitated. "You—are you going to be okay?"

Enoch couldn't lie. "By and by." He loosed his arm from Ben's waist. "Go. You have work to be done, and I must clean our mess."

Ben gave him another strange smile and returned to the other room. Enoch watched through the open door. He was content to step aside and allow them their time together. They had much to speak of, though neither of them seemed to have the words, and Enoch had no desire to be a wedge between them.

What must it be like to see someone long believed dead and gone. Or to be the one who had been lost only to be found by accident. Christ, his own mother had passed when he had scarce ten years. If she had walked into his life with so many years lost between them, what would she think of him? Like as not, she would have leathered him for the trouble he had caused in his life and then scolded him and embraced him in turn.

When the dishes were washed and the kitchen cleaned, he returned to the room, though neither Ben nor his mother seemed to notice. They were seated upon the couch, their eyes upon the screens afore them, so he tucked himself into a nook by the couch, close enough to reach for Ben if needed.

All the hours of mad rushing about and grief and fear and the little sleep he had the night afore crept upon him quietly. His chin sank to his chest, and his eyes grew heavy.

A rush of metal on metal made him open his eyes.

Olivia was drawing the curtains closed. It was dark outside. "In case the neighbours notice there's light in the house," she murmured when she saw he was watching her.

"Right enough." If Mariam was so sure no one would find them here, it seemed best to be sure there was no chance of discovery. He hesitated. "Is there anything I might do?"

Olivia glanced to Ben, who was in a world of his own making, his face lit by a dozen screens. "I think we just need to wait."

As he feared. He settled against the side of the couch as Olivia sat once more.

For all that they were doing naught, it seemed to Enoch that much was happening.

Ben was seated cross-legged on the floor, his mother upon the couch behind him, and they were both watching the screens that hung in the air before them. Neither of them moved, save for their eyes, as numbers and letters rolled out.

There was too much there for Enoch to follow himself. Without his reading aid, the best he could do was watch for a response from his companions. If anything of import was there, they would know it.

For minutes and hours, it seemed to go on.

He made himself useful, fetching them water and food from time to time before resuming his seat. With Ben in that mood, even if he spoke, Enoch knew there was little chance of an answer.

It was the depths of night when he heard Ben give a soft, sharp gasp.

"What is it?" he asked, breaking the strange silence that had stifled the room for hours.

Olivia had her hand upon Ben's shoulder. "She's cross-checking the data from the stolen drives with the information the TRI already held," she murmured. "If there are outstanding dates, we'll know where and when to look."

Enoch slid a little closer by Ben, covering Ben's hand with his own on Ben's upraised knee. God above, it was a nightmare to be seated on the brink of true loss and not to know when the blade might fall.

He felt more than saw the moment the truth was shown. Ben recoiled, his face twisting in grief and shock. Olivia made a small sound of distress, but Enoch's eyes were for Ben alone.

"What—?" he began.

Ben rolled away from him to his knees and scrambled to his feet. He swung about on his heel, anguish writ on his face. "Fuck!"

"The dates and coordinates are the same ones the TRI had. The same ones that Ben has always had," Olivia said quietly. She rose to approach her son. "Ben, there must be—"

He threw her hands off him, raising his palms, his body rigid. "Don't. *Don't.*"

Enoch stared at the screens. It made no sense. Ben was certain that his father was lost somewhere in time. Enoch was certain he was right. If the dates were the same in the stolen machines, they must have overlooked something. Time travel was difficult enough without the need to find one man in hundreds of years. Mayhap there was some sign that they had not noticed.

"—it's not the end of—"

"It is!" Ben's voice rose in pitch, drawing Enoch's attention from the screens. "I threw my whole fucking life away over a fantasy! The dates are all there! We went through them all! We checked the ones that matched with the letters!"

"Ben—"

"No!" Ben shrank from his mother. "No! This isn't—you don't—you can't..." He retreated, pressing his hands over his face.

Enoch scrambled up, heart thumping, and ran forward a step to grasp Olivia's arm. There were times when a child needed their mother, but there were also times when a man needed the one who knew and loved him best.

"Hold," he murmured to her, not ungently pushing her back.

He'd seen Ben work himself into a state oft enough to know Olivia's soothing tone would do nothing to calm him. Ben had much guilt, which turned inwards when things did not go as he wished or hoped.

Enoch approached him, caught Ben's wrists in an iron grip, and pulled his hands from his face. "Look to me." Ben was staring at nothing, and Enoch stepped in close to him, all but pressing against him, and growled, "Now, Master Ben. To me."

Ben shuddered as if waking and stared hopelessly at him. "He's gone," he whispered. "After everything, I couldn't save him."

"Your brain is addled," he said, firm and sure, his grip on Ben's wrists holding fast. "I think we're not yet done."

"But the dates—there's no more to try..."

Enoch snorted. "And that has stopped you afore? You have done what your father never could! You found your ma, despite all, and now you tell me you will give up? After all we have done?"

"But we've got nothing!" Ben protested, shaking his head. "How can we find someone with nowhere to start?"

"Nowhere to start?" Enoch jerked his head towards the screens. "Is that not somewhere?" He gave Ben's wrists a tug. "Think! You believe he lived, aye? Your ma, she knows these matters as well as you. D'you think she would allow you to continue this merry chase if you were wrong?"

Ben blinked stupidly at him and peered towards Olivia. Enoch did not dare to look to her, keeping his eyes fixed on Ben.

"If she is cruel enough to let you believe it possible," Enoch murmured, "I will thrash her myself, but I do not think it to be so." He released one wrist and brought his hand up to turn Ben's face to his. "You have all the places and times he might be. No more doubt or question. If he lives, he can be found at one of them."

"If."

"Fah!" Enoch struck him on the chest with his fist. "Do you not hear me? Mariam let us loose for she believes you! Your own mother believes it so! I have always believed you will be the one to find him! Do you tell me we are all fools?"

Ben's eyes were bright with emotion but a weak smile crossed his lips. "Well, you're with me, so I think that's a given..." He clasped his hand over Enoch's fist against his chest. "You really think we can find him?"

"You would have me repeat myself again?" Enoch rolled his eyes. "Z'bones! You are a demanding little bugger."

That earned a true smile, and Ben drew his other wrist free to wrap Enoch in his arms. "Thank you."

Enoch smiled against his chest. "For giving you yet more work?" He squeezed his arms at Ben's waist. "Now, have you done with your weeping and wailing and gnashing of teeth?"

Ben released a long breath. "Yeah. Yeah, I'm good." He stepped back and glanced over at Olivia. "Can you help me? We've—I've missed something. Maybe you'll see what we've overlooked?"

"Of course." Olivia's voice was warm. "We'll start from the beginning."

Chapter Thirty-Nine

Even with Ben's pounding head, stopping wasn't an option. A fresh pot of coffee sat on the table. Enoch slept, snoring on the couch, his arms wrapped around the cushion that was shoved under his head.

"All of these dates were his jumps?" Olivia asked, glancing up from the file she was reading, the light of the screen casting her in shades of blue. There were hundreds of dates, and she looked dazed, as if she was only just realising how much Ben's dad had been searching for her. "I wonder when he added the destination log."

Ben didn't need to ask why. "First logged jump was January 2037," he murmured. Only weeks after Olivia's gate shut and stranded her.

Olivia lowered her head, taking an unsteady breath. "I hoped..."

Ben leaned against the side of the table. "He wanted to find you and make sure you both got back safely," he said quietly. "I don't think he'd ever have stopped. Not if—" He shook his head. "I don't think he knew how to stop."

She made a small sound, pressed her knuckles to her lips.

Ben hesitated, then squeezed her shoulder, wishing he knew what he was meant to say or do. He'd never been good at the emotional stuff, especially not when someone was upset. Especially not when it was his long-lost mum come back from time travelling.

For a minute, they stayed like that, still as statues. Olivia took another deep breath, brushed her fingers along her cheeks and straightened up under his hand. "All right. I assume you've narrowed the window of possibility? Which dates shall we focus on?"

"These six." Ben tapped the main list, dismissing all irrelevant dates and leaving six highlighted in white. It covered a period from 1775 to 1819. Some had been visited several times. Some only once. "The TRI's historians said it was based on stuff they got from the original letter. Paper type, ink type, chemical breakdown."

She touched a date—1784. It opened up, showing several jumps. "That was where I was meant to be going."

Ben sank back on his chair, trying to imagine what it was like to not only time jump but to end up stranded in the wrong place with no idea if someone would ever find you. "Probably the first place he tried," he murmured.

"And somewhere he returned to several times." His mother tapped her knuckle against her lip. "Get rid of the dates that were only visited once. He clearly thought they didn't warrant further visits."

"But what if one of them is the place he ended up?"

Olivia shook her head. "If you were fleeing an attacker, would you have time to programme in new time coordinates?"

Ben recalled his own wild flight from the police. "It selected a destination for me when I was running for it. I'd rebooted the system and hadn't updated it all when they found me."

She waved a dismissive hand. "Those weren't selected for you. Those were the default temporal coordinates. That's why you ended up in the same place as me, exactly the same number of years after I did."

Ben felt like she'd yanked the rug out from under his feet. "What?"

Olivia looked puzzled. "You didn't know about them? When we wrote the original coding, we needed to make sure it wouldn't accidentally connect to some time in our own lifetime, so I programmed a temporal buffer—a period of time that the gate would automatically default to."

"The stone circle," he said. "To a fixed number of years ago?"

"Two hundred and thirty-four." She smiled sadly. "I thought he might work out that I'd ended up hitting the default. We hadn't reset that day, but sometimes the system glitched."

"But if he knew about the default—"

"If anything happened to the gate that day, it might have meant a complete rebuild. If he didn't have access to that particular section that I wrote, it was very easy to go wrong." She gave him a curious look. "But you managed to rewrite the coding correctly and found your way back to me."

Ben shrugged self-consciously. "There was a binary algorithm in some of the earlier gates. I thought I would try and incorporate the pattern into the work I was doing."

His mother's face creased in a smile. "You definitely take after me."

He couldn't help smiling in response and hastily forced his attention to the dates in front of them. "So if Dad had ended up at the default like I did..."

"He and I would have found each other by now," his mother confirmed. "Which means he didn't hit the default, which means he must have gone to one of these dates that he'd used before."

"So we get rid of the single-visit dates." He brushed three of the remaining five away. "It has to be one of these."

"And now, your evidence."

Ben opened up the scans of the letters he was so sure were from his father, somewhere in the past. There were four of them, in various states of decay, but he also had the transcriptions done by the TRI historians. He expanded the one that had always seemed the most useful. "When we went over this one, they were sure we had the right date. Lysander even got a team approved to go and do a sweep of the area."

Olivia leaned closer, peering at it. It was only a page long. "I hope to see you on the day we break ground at our new home," she read aloud. That was the line Ben had held onto for years, and that had come to nothing. She frowned, puzzled. "Our new home?"

"We—I thought it might be the day they broke ground at my—our house." Ben folded his arms on the tabletop, wrapping his hands over his elbows. "I mean, it makes sense. If he was in the past, the house would be new."

"And you know the day the building was begun?"

Ben prodded the glowing 1784. "Two years after that. The eighth of May."

Olivia's frown deepened. "And the team found no sign of him?"

"They got chased away from the building site and couldn't—" Ben stopped short at the expression on Olivia's face. She looked as if she had been slapped. "What?"

"Of course he wouldn't be at the building site," she said. "He never said he would be there."

"But it—the date..." Ben groaned. "Fuck me. That's just the date, isn't it? He never said he'd see us at the ground breaking, but we don't know where..." A lightning bolt had just struck his brain, and everything was suddenly illuminated. "I know where he'll be!"

Olivia broke into a smile. "The stone circle?"

"Where all time travellers go to meet," he agreed with a nod, scrambling up from his seat. "We need to get to the gate."

"Wait." Olivia rose more slowly.

"I've waited more than twenty years. I need—"

"Not to stumble at the finish line," his mother cut across him. "Think for a moment, Ben. We had to abandon your pod, because they would have tracked it. That means they know we will be resorting to public transport to get about. Do you imagine they won't have eyes on every transport link in the city? With their facial recognition, they'd be able to locate us in an instant."

Ben's heart sank. "Right."

He walked in a tight circle on the floor, trying to gather his thoughts. It was difficult, when all he could think of was the gate and the new coordinates and the fact that maybe, finally, his dad would be there waiting. But he had to focus. Think. Find a way to get to the gate before he got distracted. They all needed some kind of disguise, but everything they had used before was at the safe house.

It all came down to misdirection, again. Only this time, he couldn't send a lover from history in.

"We'll need to split up," he finally said. "They'll be searching for three of us."

"A good start," she agreed. "And if we can get lost in a crowd it'll make it more difficult for them. We could get a pod—"

Ben had already considered it. "I would be surprised if they didn't have access to the taxi pod security footage."

His mother winced. "It's a risk we can't take." She ran her hand over her face. "Public transport is probably the best bet, at the busiest times, but I'm only worried that we won't be able to find some decent disguises."

Ben could see her point. They were limited to the provisions in the house, which meant anything Faraz, his wife, and his three kids had lying around. He glanced over at one of the photos on the wall. "Nadiya, Faraz's wife wears a hijab. She's probably got some spare veils so at least one of us can go out covered from head to toe."

"I'll check the bathroom and see what else I can find. There must be some kind of makeup." She glanced over in the same direction, studying the photograph. "She looks like she'll have some of the basic essentials." She hesitated and glanced over at the couch. "Do you think Enoch would object to shaving?"

Ben blinked at the thought. Enoch was proud of his shaggy hair and thick sideburns. In fact, Ben couldn't remember a time when he'd ever seen Enoch without them. The mental picture of him smooth-shaven was jarring. "Would it help?"

"For what I have in mind?" There was something mischievous in his mother's expression. "I would say so."

Chapter Forty

Were it not for the danger surrounding them, Enoch might have believed Ben and his mother were making some manner of joke at his cost.

He stared at his face in the mirror, scarce able to see himself there. "I look foolish."

"You don't look anything like yourself," Olivia said as she brushed another lock of his hair up and pinned it in place with a shining clasp in the shape of a pink flower. "Which is exactly what we're aiming for."

Enoch rubbed at his smooth cheek with his fingertips, making a face. She had shaved him as smooth as a babe's arse then taken metal pincers and pulled out half of his eyebrows as well. His face seemed bare and strange and far thinner and paler than he liked.

"I'm sorry," Ben said quietly. He sat behind them both on the bed, and Enoch shifted his gaze to Ben's reflection. He was staring at his hands, pressed together between his knees. Thinking too hard, as ever.

"It'll grow again, by and by," Enoch said with a glance at his naked face. "Leastways, I'm not the only one dressed as a lass, eh?"

That made Ben glance at him and smile. "True." Ben rose from the bed and stepped closer to the dresser, the long skirts swishing about his ankles. "I've got to say I think you're pulling it off better than I am."

Enoch tilted his head to grin up at him. "Well, aye. We all know who is blessed with looks and who is blessed with wits."

Ben offered a hand, which Enoch took readily. "You're going to say you for both of them, aren't you?"

"Aye." Enoch widened his eyes, wondering how foolish the childish glitter on his lids made him appear. "I have my share of the wit, and I am not the one who will be walking abroad with a cloth tied over my face."

Ben pulled a face at him. "I don't know. I think we could find a bag to go on your head." He clutched Enoch's hand so tightly it almost hurt. "Don't go breaking any hearts while I'm gone."

Enoch drew Ben's hand to his lips and kissed his knuckles. "I," he said as gravely as he could, "look like I scarcely have a dozen years. I think I will be safe enough from any attentions."

"Mm." Ben uncurled a finger to stroke Enoch's cheek. It felt so strange, Ben's touch on skin untouched for so long. Enoch could not contain the shiver that ran through him. Ben noticed for he did it again, biting his own lip as he did.

"Ah," Enoch said, voice a little hoarser. "I see. Some are perverts like yourself."

"Oh, shut up." Ben leaned down and kissed him quickly, and Enoch half rose, pressing his free hand to the dresser to hold him steady.

A clatter on the dresser made him pull back. Ben was flushed to the tips of his ears, as if he had realised his mother was standing less than an arm's length from them, setting aside her tools. Enoch grinned, rose the rest of the way, and pulled Ben's mouth to his and kissed the breath from him.

"For luck," he said, wrapping his arms about Ben's waist and—out of sight—giving Ben's arse a good, firm squeeze.

Ben made a strangled sound and hastily stepped away. "I'll go and finish getting ready."

Enoch nodded gravely. "Aye. Best you do." He watched as Ben fled the room, and when he sat at the dresser, he saw the amusement in Olivia's reflection.

"You like teasing him, don't you?" She set to work on his hair again.

"I like doing many things with him," Enoch replied, watching her as she worked. She had never questioned what was between him and her son, nor placed any judgement. Mayhap she was pleased to see Ben in good spirits. And perhaps see him happier soon. He was quiet for a moment. "D'you truly think we will find his pa?"

She smoothed a last curl of hair into place and slid a pin in. "I do." She lowered her hands to rest on his shoulders. "But if the worst happens..."

He reached up to cover both her hands with his. "I will be there for him as long as he needs me."

Olivia smiled, but there was a sadness in it. No small wonder. She had returned to the child she had lost as a babe only to find him a man with his own life and his own lover, and with no notion what to do with a mother newly found. She opened her mouth as if to speak, but no sound came out. Enoch could guess what she wanted to say.

He turned about on the dresser stool. "Thank you for giving him this chance. We would not have it without you."

Her eyes grew bright, and she squeezed his fingers. After a moment, she sniffed hard and stepped back. "I think you're ready."

He rose and peered at himself in the long mirrors on the doors of the wardrobe. His face was different enough, but now, he seemed a girl about to become a woman. Olivia had found clothing belonging to the daughter of the house—a colourful blouse with a frilly skirt with rainbow tights hiding his hairy knees. The blouse was padded in two places, but only a little. His hair was a pile of curls atop his head, glittering with flowers. The light powder she had brushed onto his face gave him a pink-cheeked glow.

God's bones, it was like seeing a stranger who might have been his own sister.

"Good enough?"

"If they recognise me like this, I would eat my own foot," he said, dazed.

They went through the house to join Ben, but Enoch lingered behind, wincing and tugging at the tights. They were pulling up twixt his legs, and he had to fumble beneath the skirt to make them fit better.

"Maybe don't do that after you leave the house," Ben said as they came into the living room, where he was sitting on the arm of one of the two armchairs.

Enoch froze, hand on his cock, and stared at Ben who looked like nothing so much as a tent with eyes. And yet, he could tell when Ben smiled for his eyes creased up in the gap between the scarf over his head and the other over his face. Enoch couldn't help grinning at him.

"Enoch." Ben tilted his head. "Your hand."

Mercifully, Enoch yanked his hand free before Olivia turned about to see what he was doing. "I was making myself comfortable," he said. "I think it best that I can walk without my arse and other parts being cleaved in two."

Olivia and Ben both snorted with laughter.

"Classy young man you have there," Olivia said as she drew on the overcoat, the final part of her costume. She had coloured her hair with dye from the bathroom and added makeup to her face. That alone made her seem like a different person.

"And this is him on his best behaviour," Ben said. He was yet smiling, which was a relief. It would do none of them any good if his worries got the better of him. If his mood was good, it only needed to last a little longer. His eyes darted to the clock on the wall. "We'd better go before rush hour starts."

Enoch hesitated before speaking, but the truth was their plan had many risks and someone had to remind them of that. "What if something happens? If someone is caught? Do we all risk capture by waiting there? Or no? Can we let each another know?"

Olivia and Ben exchanged a glance.

"Radio silence is probably safer," she said. "We'll find each other when we get there."

"The gate has to be opened, whatever happens," Ben said. "Olivia, you know the temporal coordinates. If I don't make it, you can open it. If you don't make it, I can."

"We'll all make it, but if it'll help, fine." She seemed as grim as Enoch felt himself. "Shall we set a time to be there?"

"Let's aim for ten. That way, if any of us— We don't need to be there for long. Just long enough to get him home and get clear."

"And if any of us are caught?" Enoch said quietly. "What then? I dunt think the task force will be fooled into allowing us to escape again. We all need to know what has happened."

Olivia touched the pin on her shirt. "Set a message that can be sent with a touch, so even if they grab us, we can send a warning at once and abandon our buds so they can't track the connection. If we aren't caught but we get separated, we head for the stone circle."

The lines circling Ben's eyes deepened again. "Good idea." He opened a screen on his bud, his fingers darting over it. It was the work of a second, and he exhaled, the scarf over his mouth rippling. "Are we good to go?"

Enoch wished he had another reason to keep them there, but what could he say? That they were at risk of capture? That they would be discovered? That they were going to be torn apart for the rest of their lives? Jesu, that was the truth of all of their relationship.

Instead, he only stepped closer and took Ben's hand in his. He had no words left that could change or stop the future. Behind his veil, Ben's eyes grew brighter and wet. He turned his hand over in Enoch's and squeezed his fingers.

"I lo—"

Enoch pressed his other hand over Ben's mouth. "Don't say shit like that," he said as steadily as he could. He forced a smile. "We will see you soon enough."

They left the house separately. Ben slipped through the back gate and into the streets beyond, while Enoch and Olivia left by the front. They would lose themselves in crowds, Olivia murmured to him. It would soon be rush hour, and there would be plenty of people.

Enoch had no wit left to think about it, all his thoughts lingering on Ben. Olivia knew what she was about and she would lead them true, so he let her. After all, he was meant to be a child out with her mother. It would look best if he played the part. That he had no idea where they were only made it easier.

Their first move was to take a bus, packed to the edges with businesspeople on their way to work. It was close and full, and Jesu, he had forgotten how many people they would crush into one small space. He closed his eyes, trying not to think on it, but with so many bodies pressing in on all sides, it was difficult to even remember how to breathe.

Olivia must have seen the distress in his face for her hand covered his. "We can get off at the next stop."

He clung to her hand. "No," he whispered, keeping his voice as low as he could. "We need to go farther."

Only two stops later, she bundled him off the bus. It took him a few minutes more to realise he was still holding her hand to the point that her fingertips were crushed to white. He forced his hand open, trying to apologise, but his mouth was dust-dry, and he was shivering.

"Come with me," Olivia said, putting an arm over his shoulder, holding him as a mother would a child. He was closest to the wall, away from the middle of the crowded pavement as she led him on. She was shielding him from the rush of people.

They had no time to spare, but when she took him into a small coffee shop and bade him sit, his legs were quaking too much for him to refuse. He sank down, pressing his hands to the edge of the table.

"It's a lot to deal with." Olivia pulled a chair close beside him.

"It's foolish." His voice was so rough he scarce recognised it.

"It's human," Olivia said quietly. "Everyone has something that is too much for them." She rubbed his back comfortingly. "I'll get you a drink. We can wait until the rush starts to slow down."

He started to rise, but she pressed him back. "But Ben—"

"We have an hour to spare. Five minutes to catch your breath isn't a crime." She offered him a small smile. "I think he'd prefer to know you got there safe and well, don't you?"

Reluctantly Enoch nodded. "Right enough."

By the time she fetched a drink for him, his heart was slowing and his hands were no longer quaking. He held the glass, staring at the pink paint on his nails. It's human, she'd said. It was human, but Jesu, he had forgotten what that kind of fear felt like.

"Your pardon," he finally said quietly. "I thought it no longer troubled me."

Olivia shook her head. "You don't need to apologise. The only reason it doesn't bother me so much is because I remember what it's like. I prefer things to be quieter too."

It felt odd to know she was both part and not part of this modern world.

He sipped the cool, sugary drink. It was meant to taste like some kind of fruit, but was so sweet, he could not tell which. Olivia had a cup of tea, gazing into it, lost in thought. He watched her for a moment. "Was it strange?"

"Mm?" She raised her eyes from her tea.

"When you found yourself there? In the past?"

She nodded with a small sigh. "Yes. Very. Alone and isolated and no idea what time I was even in." She offered him a small smile. "But you must know what that felt like, coming here."

It was different, he thought. True, he had no notion where he was, but he had Ben by his side and a place he decided to call home. "Mayhap," he murmured. "I left a life behind, but it was not much of a life." He chewed his lip. "You had Ben. His father."

Pain crossed her face. "Yes. That was…hard. Knowing where they were. Knowing I couldn't get back to them myself."

Enoch stared into his drink. "I fear that," he confessed in a whisper. He forced himself to meet her eyes. "If he is caught. If we are. If we are pulled apart again with no means to see each another. I thought—" The words caught in his throat. "I thought I was ready to let him go, to save his father. We would have both forgotten all of it, so what did a little hurt matter?"

"But it still hurts." She reached over the table and took his hand. "It'll be all right, Enoch. We'll all be fine. I'm not going to let anything happen to my son, not after everything I've put him through. We'll get Tom and work from there."

He looked at her lined, aged hand on his. "Can you save him from a life on the run?" he asked quietly. "That has been his life for years. It's killing him piecemeal—the fear, the masks, the secrets. Even if all goes well, even if he saves his pa, he will have to run and run again." He raised his eyes to hers. "I dunt know how to save him from that."

Olivia's mouth drew into a thin line. "I'll think of something." She withdrew her hand and picked up her teacup. "Finish your drink. If we leave now, we'll be there well before he is."

Chapter Forty-One

Rain pattered against the glass of the safe house.

Ben turned the corner of the paper that covered the pane, peering out cautiously into the street below.

The safe house was only a few blocks away from some of the biggest and busiest streets in the city, which meant there were plenty of people coming and going, a fleet of umbrellas pressing up under the grey sky. Unfortunately, Enoch and his mother weren't among them yet. Or maybe they were, half-hidden by brollies or out of his line of sight.

Not for the first time, Ben missed his old hideouts. It had been much easier to keep eyes on the street there. That was the trouble with setting up his hiding place in the untouched section of a huge restoration project that belonged to some random stranger—only basic security cameras on the exterior of the building to watch for vandals, and most of them didn't even work.

Bribery could only take you so far, and it would have raised far too many questions if he'd demanded extra security cameras. That kind of thing made people wary, no matter how much money you offered them.

He crossed the floor, the boards creaking underfoot, to the back of the building. Like every house in the terrace, it had a small concrete courtyard—most of them piled with rubbish—framed with red-brick walls topped with glass on all sides. It served as a good hidden entrance, while the front of the building remained boarded up against trespassers.

The gate was closed and there was no sign of anyone there either.

Ben swore under his breath and checked his bud again.

It was almost ten.

They should have been here already.

He'd made it to the safe house in record time, hopping a couple of buses, the tram, and another stretch in a pod. The final leg had been on foot through the side streets, avoiding the worst of the CCTV cameras dotted about.

As an added precaution, he'd come in from the middle of the terrace, sticking close to the fence until he could get through one of the three access doors. He could just imagine the questions that would be raised if anyone had spotted someone dressed in a *niqab* ducking and diving across the stretch of building works, doing their best impression of a ninja.

From the access points, there were enough interconnecting doorways, broken walls, and hatches to linking basements for him to get from the middle to his end of the block without too much trouble and only a few bruises and scrapes from the masonry.

He'd been there for forty-five minutes already, and he'd come the long way.

There was no reason for them to be late.

He walked in a tight circle, trying to keep himself calm. They hadn't been caught. They'd prepared for that. If they'd been caught, he would know about it. No message meant they hadn't been caught, so traffic maybe?

He opened the traffic reports.

Nothing out of the ordinary there either.

Delayed then. If something was wrong, they would have found a way to let him know. So it couldn't be anything too serious. A missed pod, maybe, or getting lost in the labyrinth of streets. Something like that, probably. It made sense.

His bud chirped, making his heart skip a beat, and he checked it.

Ten o'clock.

He went across to the front window and peered out into the street again. If Enoch and Olivia were there, he couldn't spot them. Okay. They had agreed. The gate had to be opened, no matter what. He would do it, and no matter what happened, he would get out and find them at the stone circle after. Simple.

With the torch from his bud casting a beam ahead of him, he hurried down the concrete staircase into the lower level of the building. The last gate was waiting.

He stood in the doorway, letting the light play across the unfinished surface. Thick power cables, tied tightly together, coiled across the floor. It brought to mind his dad's lab, but also the chaos of the day before and Harper's sprawling facility and blood on the walls and bodies on the floor.

He forced himself to go in, stepping carefully over the trailing cables.

The last thing he wanted to do was use a wired gate. They were always much messier than a battery core and much more unstable. A badly built gate could make the power short out so easily. Harper's gate was proof of that.

Trouble was that the task force had taken every other option away.

He'd left the TRI with three battery cores, but they were all gone. The first one had been in Enoch's gate. The second one was lost when he fled through the gate all those months ago, and when the last warehouse was compromised, he hadn't had time to get to the gate and retrieve his last core.

He took an unsteady breath.

The gate had to be opened. They'd agreed on that, but God, he wished they were there with him to do it. He didn't want to do it alone again, not if he was wrong. And wrong or right, the gate worried him. Both his parents had gone through wired gates. Both of them had ended up lost. Okay, yes, he'd built every single safeguard to stop that happening, but what if it was his turn to be lost in time?

"Stop it." He reproached himself. "If worst comes to worst, you know what'll happen."

Even if the gate closed, even if he was tossed into some random spot in history, there were at least three different factions who would be more than willing to find him, if only to kick his arse for being an idiot and getting himself lost in time. Maybe four, if his mum succeeded where he failed and found his dad. Even if they didn't have a gate, there was Mariam who could put them in touch with the right people. Hell, if his dad walked into the TRI, they might just bow down and open a gate for him.

Ha. No.

Not bow down. Yell at, probably. Stare, definitely. Danny would probably shit himself.

And Enoch…

Christ, he could probably open a gate through lugh pure outrage. Ben could remember how badly Enoch had reacted the last time he thought he'd lost Ben. If it happened again, there wouldn't be a man that could stop him, now that all the secrets were out.

Of course, that wouldn't matter if Ben didn't get a move on and open the damned gate!

Instinct and habit made him check every single connection and safeguard that he'd built into the system. If it took a little longer than usual, who could judge him? It wasn't as if time travel hadn't screwed him over before. And privately, he couldn't help hoping that while he was doing the set-up, Enoch and his mother might actually show up.

By ten-thirty, they still weren't there, and there was nothing left to check.

Ben chewed on his lip as he expanded out the screen. It was crazy to be so nervous, he thought as he imported the temporal destination from his bud. Logical, but crazy too. The culmination of a decade of work and research and desperation, and now, to find out if he was right or wrong and if it had been worth it all after all...

He tapped the screen, approving time, date, and coordinates. All he had to do was open the gate and step through.

Footsteps on the stairs made him sag with relief. "I didn't think you were going to make it," he said, straightening up and turning.

The world froze around him, cold and sharp and terrible.

Lysander stood at the bottom of the stairs. "Hello, Ben."

Ben stared at him. No. Wrong. There was no way they could know about this place. No way he could have been seen or followed. He'd been careful. He'd checked and double-checked. "Ly." He swallowed hard around the lump in his throat. "Long time."

Lysander looked as inscrutable as usual, his pristine blue suit and perfectly coiffed appearance at odds with the bare brickworks and cracked masonry. There was more silver in his hair, made more noticeable by the severe way it was drawn away from his face, and more lines framing his eyes and mouth. His dark eyes darted beyond Ben, and his mouth tightened into a narrow line. "Another gate, huh?"

Ben's blood rushed in his ears. All he had to do was open the doorway and jump, but he was frozen to the spot. Ly. Of all people, it had to be fucking Ly. "How did you find me?" he asked, his voice rasping.

Lysander took a step closer, and Ben knew at once why Lysander was the one standing there and not Jacob or Mariam. Jacob was safe to Ben. He was fatherly and comforting and safe. Mariam was his second mother. Lysander was...less predictable and a hell of a lot more intimidating when he was angry.

"You need to find more trustworthy friends," he said coolly. "You taught us all that lesson."

Ben darted his tongue along his dry lips. "Enoch wouldn't."

"Your lady friend was less reliable."

Ben frowned, backing up another step. Olivia wanted to find Tom as much as Ben did. She would never have done anything to jeopardise that, not willingly. "No."

Lysander raised an eyebrow. "You seem very sure of that."

"I know that." Ben groped out for the controller.

Lysander crossed the floor in three steps and caught Ben's wrist in a steely grip. "I wouldn't try anything," he warned, his face so close Ben could count every eyelash, his eyes blazing.

Ben flinched as if struck. "Don't." His voice cracked. "Christ, Ly, please. Don't stop me."

Lysander's face twisted in disgust. "You expect me to stand here and let you break the law—laws we helped to write, for God's sake—again?" His fingers tightened on Ben's wrist. "My squad are waiting for us. You're done, Ben. It's over."

"But we found him! We know where he is!"

Lysander reared back, staring at him. "Sure," he said with a snort. "After all this time, you just happen to find him, right when I catch you?"

"It's true!" Ben wrapped his hand over Lysander's on his wrist, plucking helplessly at his fingers. "We figured it out! She knew where he would be waiting! I didn't know that, but *she* did!"

Lysander's brow creased. "She? Olivia? Why would she know that?"

Ben stared at him in confusion. "Didn't—I thought Mariam told you. She—that's my mum."

It felt like time had frozen. Lysander was still as stone. "Your mum," he said slowly. "No. Mariam introduced her as Olivia, not as..." His eyes widened. "Olivia Sanders..." He loosened his grip on Ben's wrist. "Your mother? She's your *mother*? The one who was lost in the past?"

Ben rubbed his wrist. "She knows where Dad'll be waiting. We have the place and the time and everything." He jerked his head towards the screen. "Please, Ly." His voice was so unsteady he could barely understand himself. "I know I fucked up and I lied to you and I'm so sorry, but I— He's my *dad*, and I thought—I had to believe if there was a chance..." He shook his head, blinking moisture from his eyes. "I'm sorry. I was a fucking selfish arse."

"You were," Lysander agreed quietly. "And now, you're expecting me to let you go? Apologies be damned?"

Ben's lips trembled. "I—I don't know. I—if you did—if you could…" He knuckled at his eye. "Christ knows I don't deserve it, but he's right there. He's waiting on the other side of that gate."

Lysander ran his hand over his mouth, his beard rasping against his fingertips. A narrow line deepened between his brows. "You're sure."

Was he? Technically, it was the last option. "This is the only place he could be. If he's not…" He shrugged. "If he's not, it's over. I've got nowhere else I can look."

Lysander's frown deepened. "If you go through, how can I be sure you'll come back? That this isn't another trick? It's not as if you haven't jumped out on us before."

Ben shrugged helplessly. "I'm tired, Ly. I—it's not what I wanted. Any of this. And with Mack—I don't want—too many people have died. I just—I want something to come out of all of this shit. If I can't find him, everything—everyone important to me is here." He unhooked his bud and held it out in tremulous fingers. "Please. Let me try."

Lysander took the bud carefully. "The minute you come back through that gate, I'll be waiting with my team. We can't let you walk again."

Ben gave a tired laugh. "I deserve that." He tried to smile, but it didn't reach his lips. "I'll come back. I promise, for what it's worth."

Lysander turned Ben's bud over in his palm and nodded. "One last try, and you come straight back."

Ben almost sagged on the spot. "*Thank you.*" He pressed his hands to his mouth and took a steadying breath before turning to the controls. "The gate'll stay open. It should be stable." He almost laughed, the relief like a rush in his veins. "I'll be as fast as I can."

"Ben."

"Yeah?" He turned, glancing over his shoulder.

Lysander was watching him, his expression sober. "I hope you're right."

Ben smiled unsteadily. "God, me too." He closed his eyes and hit the control, and the gate flared to life.

Chapter Forty-Two

"What do we do?" Enoch whispered.

Olivia held up her hand, motioning for him to be quiet.

They had arrived before ten o'clock, but so had others. Olivia noticed and walked them straight by the entrance to the safe house without stopping. "Task force agents," she murmured once they were out of earshot. Enoch had scarce even noticed them, his eyes fixed upon the pavement. He glanced back with a frown. They were in plain clothes and none had opened the door, which meant they were waiting.

Whether they were waiting for Enoch and Olivia or for Ben himself, Enoch wasn't sure.

"We'll use the long way," she said, taking his hand like a stern mother and hurrying him away up the street. They passed by a dozen gates, each the same as the one afore, before she glanced about and rushed him through.

The building was half-covered in metal rigging and scaffolds, but she ducked under it and led him to a door he would never have noticed himself. For someone so old, she was nimble as a goat as she darted deeper into the building. There were broken stairwells, cracked walls, and gaping holes between floorboards.

As they got closer to the end of the building—the safe house—Enoch heard voices ahead. They were rising from the cellar, and as he and Olivia drew closer, Enoch's breath caught. One of them was Ben. The other was Lysander.

"We must hel—"

Olivia crushed her hand over his mouth. "Hush," she breathed. "I need to hear." She started to move closer, stepping over the trailing wires that coiled from the sockets in the wall down the stairs into the basement.

Enoch forced himself to listen too.

"—my team. We can't let you walk again."

Ben would fight, he thought desperately. Ben would find some way out.

Enoch almost flinched when he heard the familiar tired laugh, and Ben said, "I deserve that." There was a small sigh. "I'll come back. I promise, for what it's worth."

No. Not after everything. No. It wasn't right to give up and to offer his hands for chains. He had to have a plan, some means of escape, some way he wouldn't be forced apart from Enoch again. But they were yet talking, and no one else was going to do anything, and Jesu, someone had to do something!

He ran forward towards the stairs, only for Olivia to grab him by the wrist.

"Wait!"

As if they had heard her below, there was a hum of power. At the familiar sound, the hair rose on the back of Enoch's neck a split second before light blazed up from the basement. The gate was open! Thank Christ, Ben had a way out after all!

Olivia released Enoch's wrist, and he stumbled.

"Do we stay here—what are you doing?" he asked.

She was standing close by the wall, counting down from ten, her eyes fixed on the doorway to the basement.

"Olivia?"

"We stay," she said and brought her foot down hard on the cables where they met the wall.

"No!" Enoch dived at her. "Don't! The gate!"

Even as he grabbed her and pulled her away, she struck again, and something cracked. Sparks leapt from the snapped cable, and the light from the cellar blinked out.

"No!" He threw her aside and ran to the top of the stairs. The gate was gone, closed up. He swung around, horrified. "You scheming hag! What have you done?!" She held up a hand, but he caught her by the throat, shaking her like a rag doll. "You broke the connection! That was his last gate! There's no way back! What in Christ's name were you thinking!?"

"Had to!"

Had to? He stared at her in horror even as she clawed at his hands.

"Enoch!"

Other hands were on him, pulling him off her, but he struggled, cursing.

"Enoch, stop!"

"De'il take you!" Enoch howled, stamping on the foot of the one holding him. He threw his head back, striking his captor in the face. "I'll have your guts, you lying witch!"

Olivia was leaning against the wall, hand to her throat. "What you asked me to do." Her voice was hoarse from his grip on her. "Trust me."

Enoch swore and kicked out again, but there were more people pouring in. In seconds, the room was full and stronger hands were on him, dragging him away. Big, dark hands. Strong and large enough to be Jacob's. He saw Lysander—blood all over his face—at Olivia's side, saw him take her arm, holding her up.

"Turncoat!" Enoch thrashed in Jacob's grasp. "Your own fucking son!"

"Enoch." Jacob's voice was a deep boom above him. "Enough."

Enoch tugged helplessly against Jacob's hands. "She done it! She shut the gate on him! He's gone! He int coming back!"

"Ly?" Jacob sounded uncertain.

Lysander's face was like stone, but he twitched his head in a nod. "Get him to the task force," he said. "We'll follow."

Enoch started to fight, but Jacob half led, half carried him out of the building. There were police pods and strips of blue-and-white ribbon strung across the street. One of the officers lifted the ribbon to let Enoch and Jacob pass under it.

Jacob didn't say a word until they were in a pod and it was moving. He sat opposite Enoch, his hands folded over his knees. "He went through the gate?"

Enoch had his legs pulled up to his chest, his arms tight about them to keep himself from lunging for the door and leaping out. "To fetch his pa." His chest hurt, and he was breathing too hard. "I'll beat her to messes for this."

"That might not be the best thing to say to a retired police officer," Jacob said quietly. "You don't think she planned this with Ben?"

Enoch stared at him in disbelief. It was true that he had slept while they worked the night afore, but Ben would never have allowed such a plan. He knew how much distress it had caused Enoch to see him disappeared into the past. He would never do such a thing again, not without warning Enoch and telling him how he would be found.

"I guess that's a no..." Jacob rubbed his eyes. "Shit."

"And her the only one that knows where he went," Enoch said bitterly. "She shut it behind him, and none other would know where to find him."

"She *knows*?"

"I believed them. That they'd found him." He swore again and dunted his chin on his knees. "Two-faced harpy."

The lines in Jacob's face were getting deeper by the moment. "You're sure she knows? And they were both convinced they would find Tom there?"

"What difference does it make?" Enoch snapped. "D'you think she'll turn over all her knowledge to you?"

"I don't know," Jacob admitted, "but if I have to think about it, I do like to have all the information." He touched the bud at his ear. "I think it's best Ly knows as well."

"For all the good it will do." Enoch sank into silence, glowering at Jacob's knees.

By rights, he knew he ought to have been afeard. The task force had him, and they knew of his lies. Like as not, he would be arrested and put in a cage for years to come. He should have been afeard, but all he could think of was the crackle of electricity and the gate going dark and Ben cast out in the past without warning.

He clenched his teeth together until his jaw ached.

He'd tried his utmost to save Mack from the past, but that had come to naught. On his account, Orla had been drawn in too, and Enoch had let it happen. All he had left was the chance to save Ben, and Olivia dint even allow him that! And she'd betrayed them and all! He'd asked that she save him from a life on the run. That dint mean tossing him into the past! That dint mean abandoning him there.

Even if he did find his pa, what manner of life could a man like Ben have in a time without electricity and machines? He lived and breathed them. To go without would be akin to lopping his legs off.

And why did Olivia bid them stay when they might have fled? As terrible as losing Ben was, what use could it be to let themselves be caged?

He was lost in bleak thoughts when the pod came to a halt outside the task force. Jacob motioned for Enoch to join him, and together, they walked up the familiar steps. The buzz of noise trailed into silence as the door swung shut behind them. There were some muffled laughs, and Enoch flashed a glare about the room.

There were fewer people than usual, but Enoch had no doubt that was because most of their force was at the safe house. They had a new time gate to keep safe after all. He turned his head at someone rising from their seat and flinched at the sight of Mariam. He couldn't bear to meet her eyes. After all she had done to aid their escape the day before, it had all been for naught.

He heard her catch a sharp breath. "It's true? About Ben?"

Jacob's hand fell on Enoch's shoulder. "It's true. Ly will be bringing Olivia in shortly." Jacob pressed his hand, steering Enoch forward. "You can wait in my office, all right?"

Enoch nodded. "I would speak with her when she comes," he said, low.

"You also said you wanted to—what was it? Beat her to messes?"

Enoch scowled. "One or t'other." He dropped into the chair in Jacob's office, then rose with an angry sound and pulled the damned tights off. They tore under his fingers, and he kicked off his shoes to rip the fabric off his feet. That was her damned disguise, and he jerked the pins from his hair. "Fuck!"

"Enoch." Jacob caught his shoulders, gentle for such a big fellow. "It's all right to be upset."

Enoch's fingers tangled in his hair. Tufts of hair were ripping out, but he needed the damned pins gone. He needed to feel himself, even if he looked like a fool. Not her daft little molly, all sparkly and bright. Not that. "Fuck!" His voice was cracking, and he hurled the pins at the desk and crammed his hands over his eyes. "Fuck!"

Jacob wrapped an arm about him and pulled him closer. "Come here, you poor sod."

Enoch pressed his fists against Jacob's ribs, but God's bones, he was tired and he was spent and it was all for naught. He let his head drop to Jacob's chest and pressed his eyes shut against the wetness building neath his lids. If he had to weep, no one else needed to know of it. Jacob sighed, rubbing the back of Enoch's neck, his hand warm and broad.

"I'm sorry it ended up this way," he said quietly. "Even if you are a lying little shitbag."

Enoch choked a pitiful half laugh, half sob. "Aye..."

For a long while, they stood there until Enoch at last drew away and rubbed both eyes with his fists.

"How about I find you something else to wear?" Jacob offered. "And something to clean up your face? You look like you fell into a basin of glitter."

Enoch nodded, wiping his nose on the back of his hand. "She thought to hide me."

Jacob smiled ruefully. "Well, if it helps, I would never have recognised you." He patted Enoch's shoulder. "Come on. We can use the changing room to clean up, and I'll find you something less...frilly to wear."

Jacob left him there with towels, soap, and the hot streaming shower, and Enoch felt no shame in hiding there as long as he could. By the time he returned to the main room, his fingers and toes were wrinkled as raisins, and he was wearing a T-shirt for a man thrice his size and exercise trousers borrowed from a female officer.

Leastways, his face was clean, and his eyes were clear, which meant he could see well enough as Lysander and Olivia came in.

Enoch winced, for Lysander's face was swollen and bruised. The man was known for his fine appearance, and if he was angry afore—

"Fuck me!" Danny exclaimed, scrambling up from his desk. "What happened?"

Lysander squinted in Enoch's direction. "Mr. Baker's head."

Danny stared between them and, to Enoch's surprise, smiled crookedly. "Well, at least I can say I've seen the bad-boy look."

Lysander even laughed quietly. Enoch curled his fingers into his T-shirt, uneasy. For a man who had been thwarted, Lysander seemed to be in very good spirits. Olivia must have made herself useful to him. She seemed as calm as he did, and when she met Enoch's eyes, she smiled.

Something was amiss.

He might have run at Olivia afore, but now, something was amiss. No one looked as they had moments earlier. They had lost the man they had been hunting, but no one in the task force seemed angry. Jacob's face was no longer so lined. Even Mariam looked relieved.

Enoch stared from face to face, uncertain.

Temple, the chief police officer of their operation, was speaking quietly with Jacob and Lysander. She seemed the only one who was displeased. "Are we sure this is the best solution?" she demanded. "You're asking a hell of a lot of me, O'Donohue."

"Given the alternative," Lysander replied, "I don't think we have much of a choice."

Temple pursed her lips. "I get Harper and his associates, understood? This..." She waved a hand, her upper lip curling. "Whatever the hell this is, it's out of my jurisdiction anyway. You know the time laws better than anyone. Who am I to get in the way?"

Enoch's stomach was curling, and he pressed both fists to his belly. "What's happening?" Jesu, he sounded feeble as a child. "I dunt understand."

Jacob came close to him and clapped a hand to his shoulder. "We're taking you back to the TRI," he said. "That's what's happening."

Chapter Forty-Three

Nothing said dignity like falling arse over tit into the grass.

Ben groaned, pushing himself up onto his knees and squinting against the sunlight. Blinding, after the darkness of the cellar, it took him a few seconds to get his bearings. The grass was longer—knee-deep, which explained why he'd tripped on entry—but yes! He'd landed in the middle of the stone circle.

He staggered to his feet, dusting himself off.

Right place. Now, to work out if it was the right time and return through the...

That was when he noticed the silence. Only birdsong and the whisper of wind in the trees, but no telltale crackling. His heart battered against his ribs as he turned. The gate should have been stable. He'd put safeguards in place. It was meant to stay open. He'd told Ly it would. He'd promised Ly it would.

Nothing there but the streak of black, smouldering grass where it had opened.

Ben stumbled back a step. No. No, no, no.

No gate meant no way back. They'd be waiting for him and he'd never get there, and they'd wait and wouldn't be able to find him, not with the task force taking his last gate. He clutched at his chest, his ribs feeling too tight, the air too thin to take in.

"Excuse me."

Through the white wall of panic, Ben heard the voice. He tried to gather himself and remember how to breathe and turned to face the speaker. What self-control he had left cracked like broken glass, and he was on his knees in the grass again.

Dad.

Dad walking towards him. Dad frowning and concerned. Dad crouching and grasping him by the shoulders. Dad looking almost the same, but like he'd stepped out of a costume drama. Almost, but not quite. A little greyer, a lot more lines, and a beard.

"—know it can be a bit of a shock," his father said warmly. "But you've made it. Take deep breaths. It helps."

Ben lifted a wondering hand to grasp at his arm. "It's you," he whispered, his vision blurring.

"I wasn't sure if the letters would reach anyone," Dad said, smiling, "but here you are. Glad to see the TRI is useful for something."

There should have been words, but Ben couldn't find any. All he could do was fall forward and hug his dad, breathing him in and burying his face in his shoulder. He couldn't stop the tears, not even if he tried, even as his dad patted him carefully on the back.

"Um. Are you all right?"

"Missed you." Every breath felt like a challenge.

Dad's hands were on his shoulders, pushing him back, and Dad was staring at him, confused.

"Do I know you?"

Ben's sobs turned into helpless laughter. Christ, he was doing what his mum had done to him. "It's me, Dad. It's—"

"Ben?" Dad's eyes went wide in shock. He caught Ben's face in his hands, staring at him. "My God...Ben..." He shook his head. "What—how long have I been gone?"

Ben pushed his arms aside and hugged him again, not wanting to lose a second of contact. "Too long," he whispered. "Far too fucking long."

His dad's arms were around him, tight as Ben's own. "Language," he chastised, his voice cracking, and Ben's tears came all over again, and fuck, they were crying all over each other and holding each other as if they'd never see each other again.

It took a long time for them to pull apart, and when they did, Ben swiped at his face with his sleeves. "I'm sorry. I didn't—I forgot about this place. I should have come here, but I didn't remember it until—" His eyes flew wide, and he grabbed his dad's arm again. "She's home! I found her! Oliv—my mum! I found her!"

His dad pressed his hand to his mouth, his eyes brightening again. "You found her?"

Ben nodded, unable to keep the smile off his face. "She was at the default. I found her by accident when I was running away from the police."

His dad half laughed in disbelief. "Running away from...my God. What on earth have I been missing?"

Ben self-consciously pushed his fingers through his hair. "Bit of a long story. TRI had to go public. Government-sanctioned now. It's a bit of a thing. Had some disagreements with them when they stopped searching for you, and...well...here I am." He laughed uncertainly. "Not that they'll ever know I was right."

His father was looking more and more confused. "Why not?"

Ben glanced over at the burned strip of grass. "The gate wasn't stable. Only one person knew where I was going, and she's on the run as well..."

His father's shoulders sagged. "Ah." He shook his head and slowly got to his feet. "I can't say I'm shocked. Time travel always has a knack of pulling the rug out from under you when you least expect it." He offered Ben his hand and pulled him to his feet. "Two out of three of us in the same time is something..."

Ben didn't let go of his hand. "I'm sorry, Dad. I should have paid more attention."

His dad yanked him forward and hugged him again. "None of that," he growled close to Ben's ear. Was he always so small? He'd always seemed so much bigger. "You found me. Yes, it took you a while, but no one else did it. You did."

"But we can't get back."

His dad leaned back to look him in the eye. "You said your mum is still there? In modern times? Where everyone knows about time travel?"

"Well, yeah..."

"And she knew exactly where you were coming?"

Ben nodded. "We both knew, in case one of us couldn't get to my gate."

"Your gate," his father echoed. "Which means there are other ones?"

"Only at the TRI," Ben said, shaking his head. "They wouldn't just let her use one of them."

His dad grinned. He'd lost one of his eyeteeth, but otherwise, that grin was the same as Ben remembered. "I wouldn't put anything past your mum. If she's lasted...how long would it be?"

"Thirty years. Give or take."

"My God." His dad shook his head, grief and wonder all over his face. "She's smart, your mum. She was always very good at thinking outside the box and getting what she wanted." He cuffed Ben's head gently. "If she knows where and when we are, she'll be back for us, you mark my words."

Ben looked uncertainly at the burned grass. God, he hoped his dad was right. "So we wait?"

His dad nodded. "I brought food with me, in case I had a long wait," he said, patting the satchel hanging by his hip. "We can have a picnic." He waded through the long grass and out of the confines of the stone circle to a very familiar tree. Ben stared up at it, and his dad chuckled. "You remember that, eh?"

Ben walked closer, squinting at the moss-edged letters. He could make out the *T* and the *B*, but something was missing. "There's no circle..."

"What's that?"

"Olivia—mum. She carved a circle around our initials, so we'd know she'd been there." He smiled crookedly. "Or she will. She'll be here in a few years." He shook his head. "Time travel is confusing."

"I can't disagree," his dad said as he sat at the foot of the tree in a patch of sunlight. He swung his satchel into his lap. "Hungry?"

Ben pressed a hand to his belly, suddenly ravenous. He'd eaten at breakfast, but that felt like ages ago. "A bit." He dropped to sit beside his dad, watching him snap open a pocketknife and cut into a small loaf of bread. "When—how long have you been here?"

His dad hummed thoughtfully as he carved chunks off a piece of smoked ham. "Two years, seven months, six days." He offered some of the meat and bread to Ben. "I tried dropping a few hints in letters for dates, but when no one showed up, I realised I'd have to be a bit more specific." He waved the knife towards the circle. "I hoped you'd remember. I know I made notes about it, but I couldn't remember if I put the coordinates or anything."

Ben built his bread and meat into a sandwich. "To be honest, I think everyone at the TRI was distracted with going public." He took a bite of the sandwich. "And they thought you'd been kidnapped as well..."

"Excuse me?"

Ben waved vaguely. "The break-in. When they couldn't find you and they didn't know about the basement. When the police found the gate, Mariam had a lot of questions to answer."

"Ah." His dad frowned. "What happened to those thieves? Did they catch them?"

Ben stopped chewing and forced himself to swallow. "You fought one of them."

His dad nodded slowly. "He seemed surprised when he saw me. He must've expected the house to be empty."

Mack, Ben thought, his stomach churning.

"We...stared at each other for a minute," his dad continued. "Daft, eh? I should have called for help. The police. Anything. I didn't. I couldn't."

Ben's throat tightened, mouth dry, and he put down his sandwich. "Did you hit him?"

His dad sighed, folding the knife away. "He ran at me. Grabbed me like he was losing his mind. He kept saying 'You're him! You're him, aren't you?' and..." He shuddered. "He started calling your name. I—thought you were safe, but I didn't know. I just needed to get him away before you came or he found you. There was a hammer on the bench..." A pained expression crossed his face. "The other one came in. Saw him on the floor. Saw me. Started screaming and came at me..."

"And you went for the gate."

"And I went for the gate," his dad said sadly. "Must have been desperate to think I could grab you through it. Thought I'd sealed myself in, but she managed to get the door open. Came after me."

"And the rest was history," Ben said quietly.

His dad was silent for a moment. "He didn't make it, did he?"

Ben shook his head, unable to meet his eyes.

His dad exhaled. "Yeah. I saw the blood, and he stopped moving, but—I didn't want to think about it."

"I told him not to go." Ben stared blankly at his crossed ankles. "Christ, I *told* him not to."

"I—what?"

Ben raised his eyes to his dad. "It's a long story."

His dad gazed over at the empty stone circle, then at him. "We have time."

It wasn't an easy tale to tell.

Even with all the logical reasons in the world, Ben knew he wouldn't come out looking like the good guy. Being branded an international fugitive and on the run for years wasn't something anyone would want to admit to their parent.

On top of that, there was the way he screwed over Enoch the first time they met, how he'd betrayed his friends and family at the TRI time and time again, and now, worst of all, the part he'd played in leading

Mack to his death. His dad only interrupted a couple of times to ask questions, but for the most part, he sat in silence and listened.

By the time Ben finally reached the past few days and the death and revelations that followed, the sun had slipped lower behind the trees, and it was turning cooler. His mouth was bone dry, and he stared at his hands, wrapped over his crossed ankles.

The wind rustled the leaves, and Ben scratched at a piece of dry grass clinging to his sock.

"Well..." His dad finally said quietly. "That's...a lot."

Ben chewed his lip.

A sun-darkened hand reached into his line of sight and covered Ben's hands. He looked up to find his dad's face close to his.

"I can see why you did it. It was bloody stupid, and I should give you a clip around the ear for it, but I understand." He seemed sadder, and that made Ben want to curl up in shame. "You got yourself in a lot of trouble just for me. You didn't need to do that."

"But...you're my dad." Ben turned one of his hands to grasp his dad's. He managed a strained laugh. "And you did it long before I did. You did it for mum." He paused and corrected himself, "Okay, maybe not the police and the international manhunt, but still..."

His dad sighed and threw his other arm round Ben's shoulders, dragging Ben up against his side. "Don't try that, you cheeky little sod."

Ben leaned into him, staring out into the stone circle.

"Dad," he ventured eventually.

"Mm?"

"I'm sorry."

His dad squeezed his shoulder, knocking his head against Ben's. "I know." He sounded like he was smiling when he spoke. "My fault for producing a little genius, I suppose. Couldn't be prouder, even if you do need a good hard kick in the pants."

"Yeah?"

"Yeah."

Ben almost managed a smile. He closed his eyes, letting his dad support him. It felt like he was breathing for the first time in decades. He'd done it. He'd done what he'd set out to do. Years of work and he was finally, finally done, and the weight was gone from his shoulders.

He must have fallen asleep because someone shook him to wakefulness.

He was halfway to his feet before he remembered where he was and when. He staggered, squinting about. His dad was struggling to his feet as well, hand up to shield his eyes. It was much darker, but not as dark as it should have been. A glow. Light from...the circle and a silhouette standing between it and them.

"Time to go, Ben," the silhouette said in a shockingly familiar voice. "*Qas?*"

Qasim El-Fahkri, one of the TRI's most respected retired agents, laughed. "Who else do you think they'd get with ten-minute's notice?"

But that didn't make any sense. Qasim was a trainer, and even if he had been an agent, there was no reason for him to be there. "Did the TRI sen—"

"Gate now," Qasim said, waving towards the glowing doorway. "Questions later. Hurry up. Riza'll kill me if I get stuck here again."

Ben caught his dad's arm. "We're going home."

His dad's face broke into a grin, and together, all three of them ran towards the gate.

Chapter Forty-Four

Enoch felt he was sitting in the thrall of some strange waking dream.

He had attended the opening of a gate once afore in the viewing room. Lysander had arranged for him to be there to see the strange science that had brought him from his own time. The room had been abuzz with activity and a dozen people each at a workstation. This time, there were but a handful of people and an equal number of empty seats.

The members of the task force outnumbered the TRI staff in the room: Lysander, Mariam, and Jacob. Janos and Danny manned two other machines. Enoch had never seen them all working together before, the two familiar places of his world crushed together in one room.

Their arrival at the TRI building had been stranger still. The corridors and halls were empty and silent, and they only briefly crossed paths with Sabine, who handed them a bundle of passes and vanished into one of the elevators. They had taken a second elevator, which swept them up to the viewing rooms.

"No one can or will know about this." Lysander had said it with such authority Enoch had not thought to question it.

Now, though, as he sat and waited, knees hugged anxiously to his chest, he wondered how they could think to keep it hidden. If they were right and found both Ben and his pa, how could they explain it? The return of the creator of time travel was something that would shock the world. If anyone doubted that, they only needed to look to Danny, who was beaming like a fool already.

People would find out about it. The truth would always come out, in one form or another.

"It's going to be all right."

Enoch glanced sidelong at the woman seated by him. Olivia was watching the screens with an expression of awe Enoch had oft seen on Ben's face. It was her invention too, he remembered, but she had only ever seen it in her husband and son's hands. To see it in this place where they had honed and polished it to perfection must seem a wonder.

"You knew they would do this?" He lowered his voice to a whisper. "Ope a gate to bring him home?"

She tore her gaze from the screens before them to gaze at him. "It was a calculated risk." Her voice was as quiet as his.

"Because they care about him?"

One side of her mouth crooked up. "In part." She pointed towards the gate. "After everything he did to try and find his father. The laws he broke. The crimes he committed. Can you imagine the danger it would pose to history to have someone with that mentality running about, trying to get home?"

Enoch gawped at her. "But he has his father. That was what he wanted."

Her wrinkled face creased in a smile. "I think you underestimate your importance."

He blinked foolishly at her. Surely not, he thought. Ben's father had always been his focus, no matter what. But Ben *had* changed the world for Enoch once, even before they knew each other well. With all that had come between them since...

Oh, he would do it again in a heartbeat.

She reached over and squeezed his hand. "I knew they couldn't leave him back there, whether for personal or professional reasons. Ergo, they would have to open a gate."

He frowned in confusion. "But why not leave his gate open?"

"And have them arrest him on sight when he came back? When he had so willingly promised to surrender himself?" She shook her head with a chuckle. "No, no. I couldn't have that. I had to make... arrangements."

"Arrange—"

"Holding steady." Janos looked up from his screen. "Three incoming."

Enoch leapt from the seat as if electrified, his heart racing.

Seconds later, three figures were outlined against the glow of the gate. The light winked out, and the electric hum fell silent.

"All accounted for." Qasim's voice rang over the speakers.

As Enoch's eyes adjusted to the dimmer light of the gate room, he caught his breath. Ben. Ben was there, holding the arm of another older man. The pair of them fell into each other's arms, slapping each other on the back. He could not be sure if they were weeping, for his own eyes were too wet to see.

"Welcome home, Tom," Mariam said, and her voice was as unsteady as Enoch knew his own would be. "Good to see you."

"Mariam?" Ben's father laughed. "Jesus, it's been a long time!"

Enoch glanced over his shoulder. Olivia was sitting in her seat, staring up at the screen, tears rolling down her cheeks despite her smile. "Your ma is here and all!" he called out.

"Olivia..." The way Ben's father breathed the name was like a prayer.

"I'll bring her over to the quarantine suite," Jacob said with a glance at Lysander. Even he looked pleased. "Enoch?"

Enoch hesitated. "You go," he said to Olivia. "See your family."

She rose and approached him to draw him into a brief embrace. "Thank you," she whispered by his ear, "for trusting me."

He could remember too well his fingers on her throat. Had Lysander not been there, he might have squeezed too hard. "T'was nothing," he croaked.

He returned to his seat, sinking into it as Jacob hurried Olivia out of the room. The gate room was empty a moment later. Only once all the machines were dark and the sound was gone did he let out the trembling breath he'd been holding.

"Tom Sanders..." Danny was the one to break the silence. "Tom motherfucking Sanders." He clapped his hands together with a shout of delight. "Jesus! We brought him home! The man who built this stuff! The brain behind all of this!"

Lysander had a hand on the happily weeping Mariam's shoulders, a broad smile on his face. "We did, but we can't take credit for all of it. We know who found him."

"Well, aye. Obviously, but still..."

"You are all right?"

Enoch jumped, startled. Janos had slipped over from the computers.

Enoch watched Danny and Lysander talking. He could scarce hear a word they were saying, his mind abuzz. Olivia had spoken of arrangements, but he had not had the chance to ask her what she meant. "He's back," he said quietly. "They all are."

Janos sat by him. "They are." He tilted his head. "And you are not happy?"

"For him? Yes." Enoch looked at his hands, twisting into knots in the long T-shirt he wore. "But what is to happen? He broke the law. I aided him." He shivered. "He was to be arrested, Olivia said."

Janos patted his shoulder. "This is not so simple. He has recovered two lost time travellers, though everyone thought it impossible. He has solved parts of an old police investigation and made sense of many things we did not understand for a long time."

"And that undoes his crimes?"

"That...changes how they will be looked at, I think." Janos smiled ruefully. "It would not be the first time that the...perspective has changed." He cuffed Enoch's shoulder again. "Come. I think you should be over in the quarantine block as well."

"He needs time with his family—"

"And you think that does not include you?" Janos raised his eyebrows. "He would have you there."

"With the threat of the noose over us?" Enoch exclaimed, then cursed under his breath when Lysander, Danny, and Mariam glanced over in bewilderment. He scrambled up from the chair, trying to gather himself. "Leave me be."

Mayhap it was cowardice, but he fled from the room and out into the cool, quiet halls.

The place was familiar after so many years, and if he could not run about loose in the grounds, there was one place he could go for air. The rooftop garden at the top of the building was as empty as the halls, and he ran out, the gravel crunching underfoot. The air was damp and warm, the sun breaking through the heavy clouds.

There were benches there, alongside the gravel paths and bushes and plants. He sank to sit on one of them and dragged furrows in the gravel with his shoes. Jesu, he should not have run. He had little left to fear, yet it loomed like a shadow over his every thought.

Footsteps crunched on the gravel moments later, and he glanced up. Lysander was walking towards him, his hands in his pockets. "I thought I might find you up here."

Enoch lowered his eyes to his knees, dragging his feet again. The furrow deepened beneath them.

Lysander sat by him, leaning back against the back of the bench. Finally he said, "The noose?"

Enoch shook his head. "I misspoke."

"Fear breeds honesty." Lysander sighed. "Enoch, do you really think so little of us?"

Enoch dragged his feet once more. "You have hunted him for so long. Now you can punish him as you wish." He took an unsteady breath. "Punish us."

Lysander was quiet for a time. "This is a strange place to work." Enoch eyed him, wary and puzzled. Lysander was gazing up at the sky, as if he could see across the world. "You're so sure something is impossible and that's an undisputable fact, and suddenly it isn't. It's impossible to write things in stone when that stone may be smashed to dust before your eyes."

"I—" Enoch blew out a breath. "I am very tired." He looked pleadingly at Lysander. "No more puzzles, I beg you."

Lysander gazed at him. "Ben said the same thing," he murmured, "not even eight hours ago. About being tired." He gazed back up at the sky. "We didn't believe him. About his dad. Not really."

Enoch nodded unhappily. "I know."

"We can't avoid the necessity of punishment." Lysander laced his fingers together in his lap. "You and I both know that. He's done too much to be allowed to walk free, despite proving us all wrong."

Enoch nodded again. It felt as if a blow was waiting to fall.

"However," Lysander continued, "it has been argued that placing him in a prison environment would be damaging to his already fragile emotional state." Enoch caught a breath, a prayer close upon his lips. "Given the cause of his activities has been recovered, he is unlikely to offend again, and given the circumstances surrounding his misdeeds, a plea for leniency has been put forward."

Enoch's heart was stuttering in his breast. "He will not be caged?"

Lysander's dark eyes met his. "With the leverage we have, he won't see the inside of a prison."

Enoch crushed his hands between his knees. "No prison?"

"That's not to say he'll go unpunished," Lysander continued, "but there are conditions that have been agreed upon which make a prison sentence impossible."

It felt as if all the air had left Enoch's breast. "Did—was this your idea?"

Lysander met his eyes. "I think you know who suggested it."

Enoch gave a weak laugh. "Jesu, his mother is a cunning witch..."

"Mm." Lysander actually laughed. "I do wonder what she would have done if we'd said we wouldn't go and get him back."

Enoch considered mother and son. "You would have come to regret it."

"I don't doubt that. She doesn't seem like the merciful sort."

"Best not to find out, I think."

Lysander chuckled. "Said the man who would have throttled her."

Enoch winced in remembrance. "I owe her a thousand pardons for that." He waved towards Lysander's face. "And you. I dint mean to bash your face so. I beg your pardon."

Lysander ran a finger across the dark bruising beneath his eyes. "I've had worse," he said with a small smile. "It'll heal." He pushed himself to his feet. "Now, do you want to go over to the quarantine bay? I think there's someone there who might want to see you."

Jesu, yes. To see Ben and to know he would not leave again...

Odd that he found himself rooted to the floor when he reached the door. After all, Ben had his family back. Some little worm of dread twisted inside him, the fear that maybe he would no longer be wanted or needed.

"Addle-pated fool," he chastised himself in a whisper and touched the control to open the door.

Father, mother, and son were seated together on a couch, leaning together in close congress, but all three looked towards the door as one.

Ben's father seemed bewildered, but Olivia smiled in welcome. "Enoch!"

Ben leapt to his feet and crossed the floor in half a dozen steps to pull Enoch into his arms. "You came!"

Enoch staggered as if the strings holding him upright were severed, and he clung to Ben, breathing in the scent of him, his fingers clutching at Ben's back. "No more gates?" he whispered.

Ben drew back, his face lit bright as candle flame. "No more fucking gates," he said and kissed him.

Enoch almost recoiled, startled. There were eyes in the room, none other than Ben's own parents, yet Ben had kissed him. He stared up at Ben and laughed in disbelief. No more gates or secrets or lies, only them. He reached up, uncaring of the eyes on them, and pulled Ben back down to kiss him again.

Chapter Forty-Five

There weren't any formal court proceedings, but despite the lack of judge or jury, there were several lawyers, high-ranking government officials and a hell of a lot of paperwork.

Of course, there had to be some show, which was why Ben was seated in a heavy wooden chair in a room with dark wood panelling and towering windows that let in bright slices of sunlight. A horseshoe of oak tables and grave faces surrounded him as—hour by hour—they went through the conditions of his surrender and sentence.

Ben didn't know how Lysander had managed, but somehow, he'd fixed things so Ben wasn't destined for a lengthy stay at His Majesty's pleasure. After everything he'd done and the mess he'd created, he'd expected it. He'd imagined it in the darkest hours of the night—a place where he'd be closed up on all sides with no way out.

Instead, he would live like a normal human being for the first time in years. Well, almost. Like a human under house arrest and with a limited range of motion within the grounds surrounding said house.

"And finally, we require your signature and print at the bottom." Victoria Cheung, the TRI's head of legal, circled the tables to approach him. She proffered a Leaf, the screen thick with text.

Ben looked up at her. "Which part is this for?"

She smiled thinly at him. "This document confirms that you forfeit all ownership of your research to the TRI, including all prototypes, developments, and any remaining equipment you have in your possession."

Even if it hadn't been one of the conditions of the deal, Ben knew he'd have signed it a thousand times over to be rid of it all. He scratched his name onto the contract and pressed his thumb to the glowing circle on the screen.

No more fucking gates.

He sank back in the seat with a sigh of relief.

There were some incidentals that needed to be reviewed—a stipend to cover the cost of living and bills and the like—but for the most part, it was all dealt with.

Everything he had inherited from his presumed dead and now very much alive parents had reverted to them after some complicated legal hoop jumping. Their house was officially theirs once more, and he'd been more than happy to surrender the majority of his financial assets to ensure they'd be provided for.

His remaining funds had been redistributed to cover the extensive costs of the task force and as a retainer for Enoch, who was currently on social probation given the part he had played in Ben's deception. According to the terms of the paperwork, he would have more freedom than Ben, but his actions would be monitored until he proved he would not be a liability.

More paperwork was discussed, more terms highlighted, and the sun gradually slid its way across the polished wooden floor.

It was well into the afternoon before Ben finally emerged into the dimmer halls, bleary-eyed and exhausted from so much intensive discussion, his custodian by his side. It had been a long time since he'd spent so much time with anyone, let alone talking and listening to so many people.

Footsteps on marble made him turn, a flush rising up his face at the sight of his parents approaching from the benches that lined the hallway. He'd tried to keep them as far from the whole mess as possible.

"You didn't need to come," he said self-consciously.

"We wanted to be here when you came out," his dad said.

"And I wanted to make sure everything went all right," Olivia added. "Not that I don't trust your friends, but—"

"She doesn't trust your friends," his father interrupted, earning a mock-reproachful look from his wife.

Ben glanced between them. They were standing close together, and his dad had one hand resting on his mum's back. She was leaning into him as well, although Ben didn't think either of them had noticed. Even if they were a generation apart, there was no mistaking the connection there.

"It went fine," he said with a quick smile. "Just very long and lots of talking. That's all." He glanced at his warden. "I'm guessing I'm going to my new home?"

The man nodded. "I'm to escort you there, and your monitoring anklet will be fitted on-site."

"We're coming too," Olivia said in a tone that brooked no refusal. "I want to see this prison they've arranged for him. There were conditions, and they need to be met."

Ben groaned. "You don't have to."

"You'll find it easier to let her sate her curiosity," his dad said with a smile belied by the sadder expression in his eyes. "I wouldn't mind seeing you settled as well. I mean, since you can't come home with us."

So, when Ben arrived at his new residence, both his parents and a slightly embarrassed warden were with him.

It definitely wasn't what he expected—a squat, one-storey cottage that had to be at least a couple of hundred years old. The roof had been replaced with some kind of false thatch, and from the style of the windows and the doors, it had undergone some serious renovation work in the not-too-distant past. There was even a small front garden with a hedge.

More than anything, it reminded him of Janos and Dieter's home, if only on a smaller scale. It definitely wasn't what he'd pictured when he heard the words house arrest.

Enoch, he thought as he gazed at it, was going to love it.

"Hm." His mother said behind him. "Not very big, is it?"

He glanced over his shoulder at her with a wry smile. "I remember where you lived. Compared to that, this is a palace."

Olivia chuckled and begrudgingly nodded. "True. And this one'll have facilities as well..."

"God, I missed toilet paper," his dad murmured as they walked up the short path to the front door. "You never consider it a luxury until you've wiped your arse with nettles."

"That's why you should always look before you squat," his mother said sagely. "Leaves first before any business."

Ben couldn't help laughing. "You're both as bad as each other."

They exchanged stupid, soft smiles that made his heart swell. Getting them back was good. Getting them back and seeing how happy they made each other was even better. Even his warden seemed to be caught up in the mood.

Ben came to a stop at the door. It was painted a rich shade of green with an old-fashioned brass knocker in the middle of it. "Will it be unlo—"

His question didn't need to be answered as the door swung inwards, and Enoch's beaming face greeted him. He blinked stupidly as his lover grabbed him by his belt and hauled him bodily into the house.

"Our new home!" Enoch declared excitedly, waving his free hand about. Doors opened off to the left and right of the hall with a bathroom directly in front of them. Dark beams crossing overhead complemented the cream-washed walls. "Four walls and a roof and all that comes in between!"

Ben laughed helplessly. "What are you even doing here?"

"I asked to be here afore you," Enoch said, wrapping his arm around Ben's waist. "I wanted to see it was all made right for your coming."

"You're as bad as her," Ben said, nodding back at his mother.

"A wise and clever woman." Enoch's face was a picture of virtue, as if he hadn't spotted Olivia and Ben's dad standing right behind them.

"I think it's more likely you came to steal your side of the bed first." Ben pulled him closer to hug him.

"And that," Enoch agreed cheerfully. "I think it will be a fine place."

"Yeah?"

Enoch beamed up at him. "When I have you here? Aye."

Ben stared at him and bent to bury his face in the unruly mess of Enoch's tangled dark hair. Enoch's arms tightened, and for a few minutes, Ben couldn't pull away, trying to wrap his head around the idea that this was real and he wouldn't have to abandon it or run or be chased. "A home," he whispered.

"Aye." Enoch gave him a last squeeze. "And Mariam has dinner on for you." He leaned sideways to peer at Ben's parents. "I think her feast will be enough for all."

Ben straightened up, startled. "Mariam?"

Since his not-quite-arrest, he hadn't seen her, although Enoch and his mother had both filled him in on the part Mariam had played in their escape.

She would have helped him if he'd gone to her. Enoch had told him that. Even though she was one of the task force, she'd wanted to help him. He remembered warnings and messages from anonymous allies, and he'd started to wonder maybe that was why she'd joined the task force as well.

Instead, he used the trust she'd placed in him to break the law, spurned her care, and abandoned the woman who'd been all but a mother to him.

"Um."

Enoch nudged him towards one of the doors. "Go and see if she needs help. I will show the house to your parents." He threw his arms wide. "I have no doubts you wish to see it all to be sure they have not locked him in a cage."

Olivia smiled crookedly. "I think he's got a good measure of me." She inclined her head towards the door. "Go and see Mariam. We'll be through in a minute."

Ben hesitated, then nodded. Sooner or later, he knew he'd have to see her. He pushed open the door, stepping into a living room.

There wasn't much in the way of furniture, only one armchair and a small cabinet, but there was plenty of space for more and a broad fireplace on the far wall. A couple of pictures hung on the whitewashed walls, and someone had put a bunch of flowers in a chipped mug on the window ledge.

"The couch should be delivered in the next couple of days."

Ben peered around the edge of the door to see Mariam standing in another doorway on the other side of the room. "Aunt M..."

"Hello, Ben."

He closed the door behind him and self-consciously hooked his thumbs into his pockets. Whether he was ten or thirty, she still had the ability to make him want to hide in a corner, ashamed of himself, when he ended up in trouble.

"You look well," he said tentatively.

It was true. In the three years since he'd spoken to her, she'd barely changed. Some of the lines in her face were a little deeper, it was true, but she looked much better than she had the last time he'd watched her from afar. She had her peacock hijab on, which was sort of a good sign, wasn't it? It was her special-occasion hijab, even if he didn't consider house arrest a special occasion.

She folded her arms. "Can't really say the same about you." She sighed. "You never did learn to take care of yourself, did you?"

He fidgeted and blurted out, "I'm sorry."

Her greying eyebrows rose. "Just like that?"

"Just like that." He rocked on the balls of his feet, staring at his toes. "I—I was an idiot when I was younger. It...escalated." He shook his head. "Should have thought. Should have explained. Told you everything. Asked for your help." He laughed uncertainly. "Got myself in a bit of trouble..."

"But you did ask." There was a tremor in her voice that made his head snap up. His heart twisted at the sight of tears in her eyes. "And I told you to stop." Her features crumpled. "No wonder you didn't want to ask again."

He took an abortive step towards her. "Don't."

She gave a brittle laugh and hastily brushed her eyes. "It's true, though. You needed someone to help you, and we all refused to listen."

He stared at her in dismay. "Bollocks! You helped. You gave me the search team! I'm the one that made a mess of everything! You did all you could for me! I'm just an idiot who doesn't know when to stop!"

"And who found both of your parents, even though the rest of us thought it was impossible."

Ben rubbed his forehead. "Look, can you stop thinking you're guilty for a minute so I can say sorry for actually being guilty?" They stared at each other across the living room and both laughed sadly. He lowered his hand and sighed. "When I...did whatever I did and brought back Enoch, I should've told you straight away. I just—it felt like a burning bridge. No way back from that."

"And they're always easier to burn after the first one." She walked towards him and offered her soft, plump hands. He took them, clasping her fingers as he had so many times before. "I kept an eye on you."

He twisted one of her rings with his thumb. "And sent warnings when they were getting too close?"

A flush of colour spread across her cheeks. "Ah."

He had to smile. "Busted."

"Only one," she clarified. "You managed well enough without any help."

"That warning to run?" he guessed, remembering the day he'd fled the café and left Enoch watching helplessly as the task force closed in.

She nodded, pressing a hand to his cheek. "I panicked, and then you went and dived through that gate, and I lost you after all."

He pressed his hand to hers. "I'm like a bad penny. I always turn up."

"On my own doorstep at that." She laughed, though there were tears in her eyes again. "Stupid boy," she said and pulled him into a hug. He almost crumpled to his knees there and then, hugging her as tightly as he could.

When she stepped away, moments later, she used the edge of her hijab to dry her cheeks. Ben knuckled at his eyes, sniffing hard.

"We should check on the dinner," she said. "Your parents. Are they here too?"

"Enoch's giving them the tour." He cocked his head. "You haven't seen Dad since he got back, have you?"

She shook her head. "I wanted to make sure we were all right first." She made a sound of surprise as he took her by the hand and led her towards the door into the hall.

"You need to shout at him," he said, "and tell him what an idiot he was for doing what he did. I'm not allowed to, because I did worse, but you can. I think mum'll let you as well."

She didn't even ask why. She didn't have to. She'd seen him at his screaming, panic-riddled worst in the weeks that followed his father's disappearance. She had been the one to clean up everything, not just the house and the will and the funeral, but the TRI as well.

As Ben opened the door, the four in the hall turned.

"Mariam!" His dad's expression brightened. "Good to see you!"

Ben stepped out of the blast radius as Mariam seemed to puff up with indignation.

"Hello, Tom." She stalked towards him. "We need to have a *talk*."

Ben urgently beckoned his mother, Enoch, and even the warden into the living room and hastily shut the door. "Trust me," he said to them, leaning against the door, "we don't want to be out there just now."

Olivia winced. "She'll leave him in one piece, won't she?"

Ben nodded. "She just needs to have...a word or two."

Through the thick panel of the door, there was the sound of a raised voice.

"So..." The warden sniffed the air. "Something smells good. Maybe we should go and check on it? In that other room? Which is away from the angry woman? I mean, we wouldn't want her to get angrier if it burns..."

"Wise," Enoch agreed, grabbing Ben by the hand. "Come. I'll show you where we will eat."

Ben glanced over his shoulder. Mariam was still ranting, but it was already starting to soften at the edges. "Yeah. Let's give them some privacy." He glanced at Olivia. "Are you coming, mum?" From the look on her face, he might have slapped her, which made him frown in confusion. "What?"

She smiled tentatively. "You've never called me mum before."

He blinked. "Oh." He smiled and offered her his other hand. "Well, you're going to have to get used to it."

As she squeezed his fingers, her smile widened. "I can do that."

Chapter Forty-Six

It had been raining in the night again.

Enoch had pulled on his sturdiest boots before risking the woods, but all the same, he came home thick to the ankle with mud. There was something comforting about the crack of wood underfoot and the smell of damp earth and fallen leaves. It brought back memories of another time and a place less clean and polished all the while. When it was warm, he sometimes even splashed about in the river.

Sometimes, Ben would walk with him on pleasant days, though it meant they had to be mindful of how far they went. Ben's freedom only extended as far as half a mile from their house and its small pair of gardens. The anklet he had to wear ensured that he could not press his luck. If they ventured too far, irate wardens would appear as if from thin air.

Enoch had greater freedom, though he rarely needed it. They had guests often enough, and if he ever felt the need to visit the city, he had people he could call on to accompany him to ensure his good behaviour.

One day, he thought he might even ask to go to the sea again, to remember the company and laughter he had found there. Not yet, though. Not with the funerals so recently passed and the memory so near.

As he pushed through the long grass at the edge of the woods and stepped out onto the lawn behind his home, he stopped short in surprise. A tall blond figure lounged in one of the chairs on the patio, face to the sun, his eyes closed.

Most of their guests came to see Ben, but Enoch could not help but smile at the sight of one of his own friends, especially with so few of them left. He hurried up the grass, his burden bouncing against his shoulder. Ben would not be best pleased about the blood on his shirt, but then Ben was a man of machines and tools. He disliked blood and gizzards and crusted dirt.

Janos turned his head, lazily opening his eyes as Enoch approached. He eyed the bundle slung over Enoch's shoulder, chuckling. "You know you can *buy* food, yes?"

Enoch made a face at him. "'Tis no easy thing to find a pigeon in the markets." He swung the two birds from his shoulder for Janos's inspection. He had downed the fat birds with a couple of stones from his sling. "They have grand birds from Africa, but not a pigeon to be seen."

"That is because pigeons taste like shit," Janos said gravely.

Enoch waved his words away. "You have yet to try my pigeon." He glanced towards the house. "Is Ben still at work?"

Janos nodded. "I said I would wait here for you. It is better not to be in his way when he works."

Enoch sat on the edge of the slabs of the patio. Even though Ben was no longer allowed to build machines or technology, and all of his work on computers was always watched, sometimes people would come from the TRI for guidance and advice. He knew gates better than anyone, and the TRI knew he could be of assistance. It pleased him to be useful, even if he would never again touch a temporal gate.

"He needs something to keep his mind busy," Enoch said as he unlaced the two pigeons, setting one beside him.

"Now that he no longer has to search for his father." Janos rose from the chair. "Give me the other. I can pluck it for you."

Enoch handed the second bird up to him and set to work plucking his. "I'm glad you have come. I thought you might be angry with me."

Janos snorted, rapidly stripping the bird of feathers as if he had done it a thousand times before. "You kept secrets to protect the person you love. People do foolish things for love." He flashed a grin at Enoch. "So, you are a fool."

Enoch laughed ruefully. "I am," he agreed.

"And now, you have your house and your man." Janos raised his eyebrows. "It goes well?"

Enoch hesitated. "I think it does. It is..." He frowned. "I dunt know. When I was a lad, this— I could not have dreamed this. To live with a man and none question it..." He shook his head with a quiet laugh. "It must sound so strange to you."

Lines of mirth creased about Janos's eyes and mouth. "Not so strange as you think." He nudged Enoch. "Now, you need to marry him, and you can have fat babies."

They stared at each other for a long moment, then both burst out laughing.

"Jesu! Why would you wish us upon any children? Have you no care for their well-being?"

Janos's shoulders shuddered with stifled amusement. "For the look on your face, it was worth it." He turned the pigeon over in his lap, sending a cloud of white feathers flying into the air. "I'm glad you are happy enough in this time. I know it is very different from where you came from."

Enoch set by his plucked bird and considered it. "There—sometimes, there are things I miss. Places. People." He smiled crookedly. "And then I remember a rope at my neck and know that at least I am alive to miss those places and people."

Janos turned over his false arm, curling and uncurling his fingers as if they pained him. "Being alive is always best. And having a handsome man to fuck is good also."

Enoch snorted. "Your husband is good to look at."

"You are saying the man you fuck is not handsome?" Janos's face a grave mask, feathers sticking from his grey-gold hair. "A sad world indeed when you must fuck an ugly man."

Enoch tossed a handful of darker feathers at him. "The man I fuck is handsome enough."

"Handsome enough," Janos echoed, nodding thoughtfully. "A passionate description." He ducked away from another handful of feathers, laughing. "Enough!" He held up his featherless bird. "What would you have me do?"

Enoch rose and took both birds. "Stay here. I will be back."

He returned a short while later, his bare feet patting on the flagstones. The birds were resting in the kitchen, and he had changed from his blood- and mud-stained clothes. He also carried a bottle of whisky in one hand and two glasses in the other.

"Not pálinka, I know," he said, dropping to sit by Janos, "but I thought we could share some."

Janos smiled. "I would be pleased to."

Enoch set the glasses between them and poured a measure each. "What should we drink to?"

Janos picked up his glass, tilting it. "To this strange world?"

"To this strange world," Enoch agreed, tapping their glasses together.

"And to the gates that allowed us to meet, no matter how much trouble they have caused."

Enoch grudgingly nodded. "To meeting strangers from different times."

Janos put his glass to his lip, then muttered, "And fucking them silly."

Enoch spluttered into his glass. "You are a cruel person," he grumbled, mopping at his shirt as Janos chuckled.

"I am a friend," Janos said. "This is what friends do."

"Hm." Enoch refilled his glass.

For a while, they sat there, sipping the whisky, the sun warm on their heads. Enoch sank his toes into the grass and watched the way the leaves moved in the breeze. If not for the house, they might have been at Janos's home on the day when all fell to pieces.

"I need to beg your pardon," Enoch murmured. "For all the lies. You deserve a better friend than that."

"And you deserve a friend who did not take you to the police at once," Janos said, offering him a small smile. "We are both at fault, I think." He slipped his hand into his pocket and brought out a small box. "They said I can return this to you."

Enoch frowned in bewilderment, setting down his glass. "What is it?"

Janos held it out to him, and he took it, opening it at once. On a bed of tissue lay the pendant Ben had given him so long ago. He stared blankly at it and picked it out of the box. The chain. He had broken the chain the day they'd caught him. He had thought it lost. Now, there was a new chain, and the pendant swung gently from his fingers.

"They used it to find him and his machines," Janos murmured. "Now, they have no need for it."

Enoch tapped it, sending it spinning. In truth, he had no need for it either. It served no purpose, but strange to say, he had missed its comforting weight on his chest and the way it felt when he turned it betwixt his fingers.

"My thanks," he said, slipping the chain over his head. The pendant settled over his heart, and he touched it with a fingertip. "It is only a trinket, but I feel happier knowing I have it back."

Janos smiled, refilled his glass, and handed it back to him. "Little things are important."

They were still sitting there, glasses half-drunk, when there was a yell from the kitchen.

Enoch glanced back over his shoulder. "I think Master Ben has discovered our dinner."

The door of the house swung wide, and Ben rushed out, his face flushed and his hair a tangle. By daylight, he was much fresher and stronger than he had been for years. "Enoch!" He hesitated at the sight of Janos. "All right, Janos?"

"Mm." Janos gazed earnestly up at him, but Enoch could spot the telltale twitch of a smile about his lips.

Enoch looked up at him, wide-eyed and innocent. "Yes, Master Ben?"

Ben swung back to face him, pointing towards the door. "D'you want to tell me why there's a dead bird on the counter wearing my sunglasses?"

Janos stifled a snort into the back of his fist.

"Because it was sunny?" Enoch said with a grin.

Ben made a face at him. "You're washing them for me! It's all...bald and dead and..." He waved a hand. "Never mind. Just wash them off! I don't want dead bird all over my sunglasses."

Janos clicked his tongue as Enoch got to his feet. "And you say I am a cruel and terrible person. I have never put my husband's sunglasses on a dead bird."

Enoch brushed Ben's arm in passing and murmured, "But he will soon. He only needed the idea."

Ben snickered despite his outrage. "Dieter's going to kill you."

Enoch only grinned.

Chapter Forty-Seven

The house was unnaturally quiet. Walls and floor and everything seemed the same, only it all seemed smaller. There were new photographs on the wall—no longer two young people cradling a baby and smiling. Three adults, all of them so much older.

The tiles of the hall were cold underfoot. Even his steps didn't make a sound.

Too quiet.

He saw the shape of a man in the front room. Walls were whiter than white, but the man stood in a puddle of red and slowly turned. Not a man. A boy. Younger. As young as he had been when he'd first come to the TRI. Blood and bone and staring.

Wrong.

Not right.

And beyond him, an open door and light pouring up, and he had to run. He knew he had to run because he would be too late, and they would be gone again, and even as he ran down the stairs, he saw their silhouettes against the gate. Too late. They were going to be—

"Ben!" Hands were on him, shaking him awake.

Ben jolted upright, gasping, so fast his head almost collided with Enoch's. It took a moment for the room to come into focus, the pale light of the nightlight glowing by the bedside. The clock next to it showed four thirty-six. "Shit!"

"I'm here. All's well." Enoch flung his limbs about Ben's, holding him closer, one thigh snaking across Ben's. Ben shuddered and sagged into his embrace, his heart haring wildly. "Again?"

Ben nodded. "As usual."

It was infuriating and depressing that even weeks after both his parents had come back into his life, the nightmares were showing no signs of abating. His brain was used to them after more than twenty years, he supposed. The fear of seeing them both torn away again was strong, even though all three of them had vowed to stay well clear of open temporal gates indefinitely.

"They'll be over by this afternoon." Enoch nuzzled his ear.

"This afternoon," Ben echoed, sinking back against the pillows. He flung his arm over his eyes and took deep breath. "Yeah. That's good."

His parents tried to visit as often as they could, but with two lives to rebuild after missing more than two decades, they had a lot to keep them busy. On top of that, the TRI was dealing with the shock of their founder reappearing. The media was having a field day with dozens of stations clamouring for an interview with the infamous lost time travellers.

By comparison, visiting their son under house arrest had to seem like a welcome break.

His mother had suggested staying with them, and God, he'd wished they could, but the house he had been allocated by the TRI was a modest one-bedroom affair with barely enough room to swing a cat. It was, he'd found out, the house that had been prepared for Enoch for his departure from the TRI, once he'd become used to the modern world. Despite the fact that it was going to be their prison, Enoch was delighted by it.

Ben had to admit it was growing on him as well.

It was the first place he'd really felt at home since the day that still haunted his nightmares. He didn't know if it was because everything else was behind him or because the house was so safe or because of Enoch, or if it was maybe all those things.

Even so, it hadn't kept the worst of his nightmares away.

Enoch sprawled half over him, his leg insinuating itself between Ben's. No matter how cold the night, Enoch always managed to be warm. "D'you think you might sleep again?" he murmured, dropping a kiss on the end of Ben's chin. "I can hold you down if need be." He wiggled his hips. "Or if you're roused already…"

Ben moved his arm enough to squint at him. It was daft how comforting it was to have him there, security blanket and lover in one affectionate gutter-minded package. "Are you ever not in the mood for that, you little slut?"

Enoch chuckled. "I went for years without. Can you fault me for glutting when I have you to myself?"

"Mm." He stroked the fingers of his other hand through Enoch's hair. "Bet the screaming nightmares are just such a turn-on."

Enoch rubbed his thigh lazily against Ben's cock. "A matter I can distract you from."

Ben curled his fingers into Enoch's hair, pulling Enoch's lips to his. "Please," he whispered.

Enoch splayed his fingers across Ben's chest. "I would have you breathe first," he murmured against Ben's lips. "Your heart feels like it may burst if I drive you too hard. Your parents would be angered if they come and find I have fucked the life from you."

Ben laughed unsteadily against his lips. "Yeah. That'd be awkward." He took a long breath, then another, trying to find some semblance of calm. "Fuck..."

Enoch stroked his side, as if he could be soothed like a wild horse. "Shall I tell you how I would have you?" he murmured, rocking his hips against Ben's thigh. "Or might that excite the breath from you too?"

Ben tugged his hair indignantly. "I'm not that useless."

Enoch lifted his head, his eyes wide and lips parted, and moved his hand to catch Ben's cock in a merciless grip that made Ben gasp in surprise. "Ah. I see." Enoch's expression was solemn, but the corner of his mouth twitched. "No breath to be stolen at all."

Ben reached down with his empty hand to cover Enoch's hand on his cock, holding it still. "Cheating bugger."

"Cheating?" Enoch gasped, offended.

"That's not *telling* me what you would do."

Enoch chuckled and loosened his grip. "Right true," he conceded, threading his fingers between Ben's. He lowered his head to nuzzle Ben's throat. "Your pardon. 'Tis early to think on words."

"Hm. But not to think of shagging?" Ben's breath hitched again as Enoch closed his teeth on Ben's windpipe, pressing just tightly enough to make his heart skip. He fisted his fingers into Enoch's hair with a hiss. "Enoch..."

Enoch laved his tongue over the bite. "You would look fetching in bonds," he murmured, nuzzling his way towards Ben's collarbone. "Long strands of smooth cord."

Ben licked suddenly dry lips. "Yeah?"

"Mm." Enoch ran his palm up the crease of Ben's hip, stroking his thumb through the mat of hair low on his belly. "Hands at your back, on your knees..." He breathed out a hot sigh against Ben's damp skin, sending a shiver through him. "At my mercy..."

He didn't need cords for that, and they both knew it, but the idea, the thought of it was making Ben's heart race again. "Wh-what would you do with me?"

Enoch's hand moved lower again, a fleeting touch, barely there. Ben shifted his hips, shifting one thigh to hold Enoch's closer to him. Enoch's lips turned in a smile against his collarbone, and the brush of Enoch's thickening sideburns tickled against Ben's bare chest as Enoch slid a little lower.

"Well?" he prompted.

Enoch caught Ben's nipple between his teeth and tugged enough to make Ben yelp, his hips jumping of their own accord. Enoch chuckled, wriggling even lower, leaving Ben's cock woefully neglected.

"Enoch!" Ben tugged on his hair. "Tell me!"

Enoch darted his tongue against Ben's navel but said nothing. He drew his cheek against Ben's belly, his jaw brushing against Ben's rising cock. His breath was warm, and he ran his hand along the outside of Ben's thigh, all but dragging Ben's limb up over his shoulder. When he pressed his mouth to the softer skin of Ben's inner thigh, Ben grabbed at the covers with his free hand, hissing between his teeth as Enoch drew hard on the skin, hard enough to leave a mark.

"Not telling!" he whined, blindly thrusting his hips in hope Enoch would take a hint. "Tell!"

Enoch stifled a laugh in Ben's thigh and turned his head to rub his cheek against Ben's cock. "Jesu, the second coming could be upon us before you learn patience!" He brought up his right hand to fondle Ben's cock, his left stroking Ben's thigh. When his mouth closed on Ben's cock, Ben knocked his head back against the pillows, tightening his fingers in Enoch's hair.

Enoch took his time, lazily lowering himself to take almost all of Ben's cock, dragging tongue and lips as his thumb and forefinger slowly circled Ben's cock in maddeningly slow strokes. It was enough to take Ben's every thought as he rocked his hips up, pressing Enoch's head closer, his heel pounding demandingly at Enoch's side.

"I thought," Enoch said suddenly, tightening his hand in a way that made Ben yelp in dismayed outrage, "I would see how long you could bear it."

Ben forced his head up from the pillow, staring wildly at him. Hands not moving. Mouth grinning and empty and not finishing the job. As if sensing his indignation, Enoch tightened the circle of finger and thumb.

"Don't you fucking dare!" Ben kicked at his back. "Don't you *dare!*"

"They have rings for cocks, y'see," Enoch continued, his grin growing even wider. "I thought I might try one on you and—"

If anyone asked him how he did it afterwards, Ben couldn't be sure, but somehow, he went from on his back with one leg over Enoch's shoulder to Enoch flat on his back on the bed, held beneath Ben's body. Enoch beamed up at him.

"That long, it seems," he said and gave Ben a firm slap on the arse. "It seems I'm at your mercy."

Ben caught his wrist, leaning over him and pinning his hands on either side of his head. "Yeah, you are." He rocked his hips against Enoch's belly, grinding against him. "Maybe I should see how long you can last."

Enoch pushed his hips up against Ben, his cock rubbing against Ben's arse. "Not any time at all," he said cheerfully, his eyes shining. "If you fancy, you need only sit back, and I'll see you well-tended."

It was rare enough for him to offer it that Ben blinked in surprise. "Yeah?"

Enoch nodded with a chuckle. "I'm but a helpless captive to your perversions." He punctuated it with an emphatic wriggle of his hips.

"You're an arsehole is what you are." Ben couldn't help smiling. He leaned over towards the bedside table and snatched the tube that had become a permanent feature. "You're spoiling me with this."

Enoch hissed between his teeth as Ben smeared lube onto his cock. "Aye. It's such a torment for me, this." He fixed his eyes on Ben's face as Ben slid back over him, both of them exhaling as Ben sank onto Enoch's cock. Enoch curled his fingers, clutching at the pillows on either side of his head. "Christ..."

Ben leaned over him again, catching Enoch's wrists and slowly rocking his hips, trying to find his rhythm. "Haven't done anything yet."

"You dunt see what I see," Enoch countered, breathing hard. "Need a hand?"

Ben laughed hoarsely. "Just a second." It wasn't as if he'd ever really been on top before, and Enoch grinning like it was his birthday was a ridiculous distraction. "I've never come from this angle before."

"I can see why," Enoch quipped, then dissolved into helpless laughter. He pulled one of his hands free and caught Ben by the hip. "Come. With me." He guided Ben to match the rock of his hips and gave him another firm slap on the arse. "Good lad."

"Shut up!" Ben laughed, grinding his cock against Enoch's belly. "I'm not a pony!"

Enoch's face was a picture of mischief. "But you're riding as if I am." He brought his hand round to catch Ben's cock, his hips moving harder and faster. Ben tried to match him, his breath coming faster as he thrust himself onto Enoch's cock. His heart drummed and Enoch's hand moved in urgent jerks on his cock, making his hips twitch even harder. Enoch's lips drew back from his teeth. "Christ..." he breathed.

Ben caught Enoch's hand around his cock, urging him on, breath dry on his tongue. Moving erratically. Urgently. Enoch was speaking too. His name. How fine he was. Fuck, how good he looked up there. It made Ben catch his breath and rock more wildly.

Meeting Enoch's eyes was all it took to throw him over the edge, with hand on cock and cock in arse and the rapt hunger on Enoch's face.

Enoch laughed in delight as cum spattered on his belly. "Not bad," he said, his voice a little hoarse, and groaned as Ben rocked again. Not fair, Ben thought, if only one of them ended up finishing. He met Enoch's eyes again and rocked slowly, over and over, until all Enoch had left were breathless profanities, and he pawed at Ben's thighs hard enough to bruise.

"You bugger," he finally breathed when he sagged under Ben. "You dirty, dirty bugger..."

Ben let his head rock back, taking deep breaths. "Takes one to know one." He swung himself off Enoch, sprawling onto his back on the bed. "Fuck..."

"Mm." Enoch groped out and patted him on the belly. "Think you might sleep a little more?"

Ben rolled onto his side, tipping himself half over Enoch. "Mm." He kissed him clumsily, then let his head slip to rest by Enoch's on the pillow. They were both sweaty and covered in cum, but he couldn't care less. He was warm and safe and loved and, Jesus Christ, so knackered. "Enoch?"

"Mm?"

"Y'can tie me up if you want."

Fingers stroked through his hair. "Aye?"

Ben nodded, tucking his face into Enoch's throat. "Mm. Only..." He paused, yawning widely. "Only later."

Enoch's ribs shivered with a stifled laugh. "Later," he agreed. He rubbed his jaw against Ben's brow. "Rest now."

"Mm." Ben closed his eyes, sleep already closing in. "We've got time."

Acknowledgements

I do have my fleet of usual suspects to thank for keeping me going and encouraging me to get this far. Beth, Ash, and Ru listened to an *awful* lot of babbling and self-doubt and everything else in between. Also Gus and Elizabetta, who took my words and polished them until they were shiny. To say nothing of Dreamspinner and NineStar who took a chance on my genre-blending adventures. It's been quite the ride, hasn't it?

About the Author

C.B. Lewis is small, Scottish, and writes pretty much anywhere, any time. She loves to travel and tends to bring home at least four new plot bunnies from every trip she goes on. She's very excited to conclude the Out of Time series.

Facebook: www.facebook.com/CB-Lewis-3692293759939573

Goodreads: www.goodreads.com/user/show/41277437-cblewis

Tumblr: www.tumblr.com/blog/cb-lewis

Website: www.cblewis.co.uk

Other books by this author

Out of Time Series
Time Taken
Time Turns

Also Available from NineStar Press

Connect with NineStar Press

Website: NineStarPress.com

Facebook: NineStarPress

Facebook Reader Group: NineStarNiche

Twitter: @ninestarpress

Tumblr: NineStarPress